hell's horizon

Also by Darren O'Shaughnessy in
Victor Gollancz/Millennium

ayuamarca
BOOK ONE OF THE CITY

hell's horizon

THE CITY: BOOK 2

Darren O'Shaughnessy

The right of Darren O'Shaughnessy to be identified
as the author of this work has
been asserted by him in accordance with the
Copyright, Designs and Patents Act 1988.

First published in Great Britain in 2000 by
Millennium
An imprint of Victor Gollancz
Orion House, 5 Upper St Martin's Lane, London WC2H 9EA

To receive information on the Millennium list, e-mail us at:
smy@orionbooks.co.uk

A CIP catalogue record for this book is available
from the British Library

ISBN 1 85798 918 X

Typeset by The Spartan Press Ltd,
Lymington, Hants

Printed in Great Britain by
Clays Ltd, St Ives plc

prologue

___

'two burning candles'

Lorna Jeery's head felt as though it was home to a hive of bees. Migraines were nothing new – she'd suffered with headaches most of her life – but lately they'd been intensifying. Her doctor sympathised but could offer no reasons for the severity of the attacks or proffer a cure. His sage-like advice had been to take an aspirin when the pain was at its peak, lie down in a dark room, breathe deeply and think positive thoughts.

Easy to say when you weren't tied to a demanding child. Al was a good kid and slept soundly by night, but that meant he was lively by day. Meditative breaks were not an option.

She'd asked Tom to stay home and help, but he'd laughed and told her to grow up. He put money on the table every week and saw to her material needs. His responsibilities were covered.

Al gurgled and shook his rattle at her. Lorna smiled, reached down to wipe drool from his chin, adjusted his cap to keep the sun out of his eyes, then carried on walking.

It was a beautiful spring day, the warmest of the year so far. She was looking forward to summer. She'd bought dozens of fancy costumes for Al and loved the idea of parading him around. They'd moved to a new neighbour-hood during the fall and she hadn't had time to make new friends yet. She'd been holed up with Al. It would be nice to get out of the house and introduce herself and Al to the locals.

'Myself and Al,' Lorna murmured, smiling. She was still getting used to the idea of motherhood. Things had progressed so quickly. She'd only known Tom a couple of

3

months when she fell pregnant. She'd worried about his reaction – Tom was a strange, moody man – but he'd been supportive and had volunteered to make an honest woman of her.

And here she was, Al nearly a whole year old, in a new home, a new role, a new life, and it all seemed to be happening to someone else.

Not that she regretted it. Sure, a few more years of freedom would have been nice, and there were times when she envied her friends and the fast lives they led. But she wouldn't give up Al (or Tom) for anything.

If only these damned migraines weren't tormenting her.

She sighed and pushed on for the drugstore. She had a pack and a half of aspirin back home, but wanted to stock up in case the good weather passed and she found herself housebound. Tom was away on business, and although she could call her mother if she wanted someone to babysit, she didn't like to impose. Her family disapproved of Tom Jeery – personal dislikes aside, he was black, and her parents were strong closet racists – and relations between them had been strained since she eloped to marry him without their consent.

At the drugstore she parked the pushchair to the left of the door and checked on Al. She could have pushed him inside, but the aisles were narrow and the attendants always frowned and served in icy silence when women came in with prams or pushchairs. She considered lifting him and carrying him in, but it was a lovely day and it seemed a shame to deny him the sun.

Lorna glanced cautiously up and down the street. She wouldn't leave her baby unattended if there was the slightest chance that he might be interfered with. But the paths were largely deserted. A couple of young kids were fooling about with a skateboard. An old lady was walking a shaggy poodle across the way. And a teenage,

4

ginger-haired girl in denim shorts and a loose T-shirt was ambling along towards the store, whistling an Elton John tune.

'You'll be safe enough,' Lorna told Al, taking her purse out of her handbag and checking to make sure she had change. 'Don't go nowhere, OK?' Al gurgled as if he understood. Lorna laughed, shoved her handbag down under Al's layers of blankets – sun or not, she wasn't going to risk him catching a cold – and headed into the store.

As soon as the door swung closed behind Lorna, the ginger-haired girl in the denim shorts and T-shirt rushed forward. She paused by the pushchair, checked to make sure no one was watching, grabbed the handle, pushed quickly past the store window, hurried to the end of the street, turned right and ran.

Al screamed as he was roughly bounced about and made plaintive 'Ah-ah' sounds, the closest he could get to 'Mama'. The girl ignored him and concentrated on her route. She'd been waiting months for a chance like this. She wasn't going to waste it. The priests would take an unfavourable view if she screwed up.

Several sharp turns later, she found herself in a shady alley, one of their pre-arranged meeting places. Hurrying to the fourth door on her left, she pounded on it five times with the palms of her hands. The response was immediate. The door flew open and a bald man dressed in white robes stepped partially out.

'You have the child?' he asked in the foreign language which the girl had spent the last several years learning to master.

She nodded. 'His mother's in a drugstore. It won't be long before she discovers he's missing.'

'We do not need much time,' the priest said, and stepped all the way out into the open. The girl could see his blind white eyes now, and a large mole on the left side of his

5

chin. All the white-robed priests were blind. She wasn't sure if they were born that way, or if their eyes were destroyed when they were children, or if they voluntarily surrendered their sight. There was much she didn't know about them, much they chose to conceal.

The girl undid the straps of the pushchair and helped the priest undress the baby. When Al was naked, the priest held him under one arm and strode out to the centre of the alley. The girl followed, but at a distance.

A small whitish stone was set in the middle of the road. The priest stepped onto it – the girl didn't know how the blind priests found their way around so surely – and raised the naked baby high above his head. Al struggled vainly and went on screaming for his mother.

The priest began to chant, words which even the girl's attuned ear could make no sense of. As he chanted, rain fell, a box of contained silver streaks, as though a rectangle had been cut out of the clouds.

As rain drenched the pair, the eyes of the blind priest glowed. His lips trembled, then stopped moving. Above him, the baby spluttered and tried to turn his face away from the downpour.

The girl watched the eyes of the priest become two pools of white fire. She had been told of the rain of the *villacs* but had never seen it before. According to the priests, this was the sun god's way of communicating with them. She hadn't previously believed in sun gods and heavenly hotlines, but now that she was faced with the rain she began to wonder.

Al had stopped fighting and no longer sought to turn away from the rain. He was staring up at the sky, eyes unblinking, as still and mute as the blind priest beneath him.

They stood like that for half a minute. Then the priest lowered the baby and fixed his blind gaze upon it. The girl, watching from outside the shower, noted that the baby's eyes were also glowing, but there was a yellowish-red tint to the light in Al's eyes.

The priest held Al in his left hand while pressing the fingers of his right to the baby's glowing eyes. Al didn't flinch at the touch, even though the fingers seemed to press against the corneas. After a few seconds, the priest let go. His fingers came away red, as though stained with blood, but the child did not act distressed.

The rain ceased, the lights faded in the eyes of boy and man, and after a few dazed seconds the *villac* shook his head and stepped off of the stone. Handing the baby back to the girl, he told her to dry him off and dress him.

'Did I bring the right one?' the girl asked, using a blanket from the pushchair to dry the baby, now filled with an eerie calm.

'Yes,' the priest sighed, rubbing the mole on his chin, which was wet from the rain.

'What will I do with him?' the girl enquired, slipping him back into his nappy, then reaching for his clothes.

'Leave him,' the priest instructed. 'Take the woman's handbag and anything else of value.'

'Did I do well?' the girl asked, desperate for a compliment.

'You did, Valerie.' The priest smiled and took his leave, exiting via the door through which he'd entered.

Valerie got Al dressed and back in his pushchair. He was starting to stir anxiously again. Valerie ran the blanket over his head of thick black hair, then took the handbag, blankets and some of the toys, and ran, the praise of the *villac* ringing in her ears.

Minutes later, an hysterical Lorna Jeery spotted the pram as she raced past the alley, came to a halt and stumbled slowly towards it, fearing the worst.

The feeling in her stomach when she came out of the

drugstore and discovered the pram was missing had been worse than any headache. She would have screamed, except her throat had constricted and choked her into silence.

After a terrifying eternity of seconds she'd hurried across the road and caught the old woman walking the dog. Had she seen anyone passing with a pushchair? No. She looked for the teenager but found no trace of her. The two children had also moved on but she found them further ahead and pressed them for information. They claimed ignorance at first, but then one said he'd seen a red-haired woman with a baby. When Lorna asked where she'd gone, he grinned and rubbed his fingers together. In a panic, she rooted through her purse, grabbed a handful of notes and thrust them into his hands. Unable to believe his luck, he'd not only told her which way the woman had gone, but took her back to show her.

Dreadful minutes followed, during which she ran up and down various streets, asking questions of everyone she saw, eyes peeled for anything that looked remotely like a pushchair. She'd been on the verge of abandoning the chase to call the police when she chanced upon the alley.

Lorna was sure Al had been abducted or killed. The silence as she drew nearer seemed proof of her horrible fears. Her conviction was so fierce that when she got close enough to the pushchair to peer in, she failed to notice Al and almost ran to phone the police. Then her eyes focused on the dark brown baby, she realized Al was present and alive, and relief flooded her system.

Tearing off the straps, she picked Al up and proceeded to sob over him, kissing his head and face, moaning thankfully. Al, not sure what to make of all the fuss, giggled and pulled her hair.

Once she'd calmed down, Lorna noted the missing handbag and blankets. The blankets didn't matter but the handbag was full of personal items and credit cards. She considered alerting the police but she knew from experience how futile that was. Simpler to contact her bank and cancel the cards direct, and write off everything else.

Grumbling to herself, she strapped Al back into his pushchair, swivelled around and started for home.

As she walked, the full force of her migraine returned, and she grimaced against the pain. She looked for her aspirin – she'd have swallowed them dry – but she'd dropped the paper bag they'd been in. She could have gone back to find them or buy more, but after her scare she wanted to get home as quickly as possible. She had a pack and a half to fall back on. She could come out again later for fresh supplies, or in the morning.

As she headed back, wincing from the headache, she glanced down at Al, and what she saw in his eyes caused her to slow, then come to a stop. It must have been a trick of the sun, but she could have sworn she'd seen flickers of reddish light in his eyes. While she stood, frowning, the effect multiplied, and it was as though his eyes had become two burning candles.

Staring wordlessly, she lost herself in the lights. Minutes passed unheeded, Lorna standing like a statue over the pram, Al gazing up at her with the solemn wisdom of one far older.

Finally the lights dimmed, the day resumed its shape, and Lorna pushed on, swiftly forgetting about the sparks in her son's eyes. She was almost home before realising that her headache had mysteriously passed. Later that week she bought several packets of aspirin to keep her going for the next few months. She needn't have bothered: from that day on, Lorna Jeery never suffered from migraines again. Their complete disappearance puzzled her, and she sometimes wondered if she should check with a doctor to make sure she was OK, but she didn't have time to brood over the nature of her blessing or go traipsing off to doctors. Her days were full. She had a growing boy to take care of. Her little Al . . .

part one

'she's my girlfriend'

In room 812 of the Skylight Hotel, a woman had been cut to pieces. Her motionless body lay face-down on the bed, its perforated spine seeping dark blood which trickled down her sides and gathered in the folds of the crumpled sheets beneath. A spider crept across her face at one stage, sensed death and scuttled away to safety.

Later a maid entered. Her name was Valerie Thomas. A heavy middle-aged woman, thick-limbed, gruff-mannered. She'd once been a pretty, ginger-haired snip of a girl, but had grown grey and hard-of-face with the passing years.

She spotted the body instantly. The light by the bed was on and it would have been hard to miss a naked woman with puckered stab wounds for a back. Any other maid would have shrieked, dropped her tools and bolted. Not Valerie. Death was nothing new to her.

Closing the door gently behind her, she moved closer to the body. A blood-stained knife lay on the floor. She was wearing plastic gloves but didn't touch it: best not to take chances. She stood over the corpse, gazing down appraisingly, admiring its figure.

Kneeling, she pressed two fingers against the victim's neck and checked for a pulse. Nothing. She was about to leave, when . . .

A vibration. Slight, but present. She prised one of the eyelids open. The pupil dilated in the light, and when she took her finger away the lid twitched and the mouth moved a couple of painful millimetres.

Valerie nodded sombrely and considered her options, before picking up the knife and scanning the wounds for a laceration large enough to work with. She found one near the heart. Leaning over, she prised the flesh apart with her fingers, inserted the tip of the blade and wriggled it around in gentle circles, holding the woman down with her other hand, until she felt the body shiver for the final time.

She checked the pulse, the eyes, the lips.

Dead.

Valerie grunted, dropped the knife, visited the bathroom and washed the blood off her gloves. When she was ready, she strolled to the door, opened it, mussed up her hair, adopted a terrified expression, took a deep breath, then let fly with a shrieking scream, bringing staff and tenants running.

1

Bill reeled in his line and changed flies. We'd been fishing since Friday – this was Sunday – and all we had to show for our efforts was an undernourished trout we'd have thrown back any other time.

'Reckon that'll improve our luck?' I asked.

'Probably not,' Bill sighed, tugging at the collar of his jacket. He wasn't enjoying himself. For me the lure of fishing was the break, the quiet, the time for reflection. Bill was a more demanding angler and grew impatient when things weren't going his way. 'I told you it was the wrong time of year,' he grunted.

'Quit griping,' I laughed. 'What would you be doing right now if we'd stayed? Reading or fiddling with your fireworks in the cellar. At least here we can relish the fresh air.'

'Long way to come for that,' Bill grumbled. 'Could have bought a few tanks of oxygen: same effect.'

'Couldn't buy the view,' I noted, nodding downstream at the trees and open fields. In the distance we could see the hump of the city's skyline. It looked even uglier from here than it did up close.

Bill's expression softened as he took in the countryside. 'Know what we should do?' he mused aloud. 'Build a shack up here and move out. Spend our days constructing flies and checking lines. Fish from dusk till dawn.'

'Sounds good to me, Huckleberry Finn. When are we setting out?'

Bill smiled and jiggled his line. 'We should do it.'

'I agree.'

'If we'd any sense, we'd jump at the chance.'

'I'm with you all the way.'

He sighed. 'But we won't, will we?'

'Nope.' He looked so miserable, I had to laugh. 'Bill, we're city slickers. We wouldn't last pissing time living wild.'

'Speak for yourself,' he snorted, though he knew I was right. Bill thrived on city life even more than I did. Take him away from the metropolitan buzz and he'd be a crab out of its shell. He belonged on the streets, badge pinned to his shirt, gun in its holder, bringing a touch of law to the vicious granite jungle.

But it was a nice idea, leaving the city and all that goes with it behind. Life would be much simpler in the hills, fishing the river, hunting, sleeping wild whenever we wanted. No duties or finances to worry about, no commitments, no ties. No conflict.

'How's the Cardinal these days?' Bill asked. The Cardinal ruled the city. He was – to borrow the language of the media – King of the Underworld. I worked for him. I was part of his armed forces, one of his Troops, a military bodyguard.

'You know I don't see much of him,' I muttered. I didn't like it when Bill talked shop: reminded me of the gulf between us, the rift I'd created by siding with the wrong side of the law.

'It's not too late to get out,' he said. 'There's plenty of good security jobs going. A man with your experience and contacts could make a – '

'Bill, don't.'

He cocked an eyebrow at me. 'Conscience pricking you, Al?'

'We've been through this before. I like what I do. I'm not gonna quit.'

'What if you're asked to kill a man one day?'

I sighed and stared into the cool night water, not answering.

'Maybe you've already been asked,' Bill noted after an uneasy few minutes of silence. 'Maybe you've complied.'

I maintained my silence.

'Have you, Al? Have you killed for that monster?'

I looked over at him. 'You really want to know?'

He chewed his lower lip, studied my face and shook his head. 'No. Guess I don't.'

I hated moments like these. We didn't discuss my duties with the Troops very often. It was easier not to. Bill was only bringing the subject up now because he was depressed by the scarcity of fish.

I checked my watch. 'We'll have to be on our way soon.'

'Yeah.' Bill didn't look happy. He reeled in his line and began dismantling his rod. Stood and gazed off at the city. 'Fog's up,' he said presently.

I glanced over his shoulder and saw banks of thick green fog billowing over the roofs of the city like a dome. The city was famous for its mysterious green fog, which blew up at random and made a mockery of meteorology.

'Great,' I groaned. 'Driving through that will add a couple of hours to our journey home.'

'Roads are fairly quiet this time of night,' Bill said. 'Shouldn't delay us too long. Want me to drive?'

'You drove out. My turn going back.'

'I know, but it's my car: don't want you wrapping it round a tree. I'll take the wheel if you'd prefer.'

I shook my head. 'It's OK. I don't mind.'

'In that case, I'll treat myself to another beer. Cheers.'

While Bill was cracking open a can, I began tidying everything away. It didn't take long. I asked if he wanted the trout but he said I could take it. I put it on ice and loaded it along with the gear.

I looked down upon the distant city again, which had now all but disappeared under the fog. A stranger to these parts might have missed it altogether: mistaken it for a shrouded lake.

'Looks like it's down to stay,' I noted.

'Yeah,' Bill agreed, rolling up a sleeping bag and sticking it in the back of the car. 'Could be a bad one.'

I'd no work that Monday – I'd booked the day off to make a long weekend of it – so I slept in late, a luxury I rarely enjoyed. I woke about ten and spent the next few hours propped up on the pillows, listening to the sounds of the street outside. It wasn't as busy as it would normally be: the fog kept a lot of people inside.

I turned on the bedside radio. A DJ was talking to a woman with piles. She was sick of the attached stigma. She wanted to build a society where people could discuss such matters openly, without fear of embarrassment. The DJ was on her side and invited listeners to ring in with their own – as he elegantly put it – 'piles files'.

I surfed the airwaves. Found a couple of politicians arguing about the fog. One – obviously in opposition – wanted to know why more wasn't being done to make life easier for the citizens during times of siege. He wanted extra strong street lights, special buses and trains to accommodate those afraid to drive, home delivery services for pensioners and single mothers, etc.

I didn't stick around for the retort. I'd heard it all before. You got these idiots on the radio every time the fog rolled in. If I kept on searching, I'd find a thin-voiced professor-of-whatever somewhere, explaining how the fog formed and how long we could expect it to last and what the authorities should be doing to prevent future upsets.

I switched off.

A stretch, a yawn, the bathroom. Drank some water, dug out a good book, switched on my reading lamp – necessary even if it hadn't been foggy: the dark rooms were one of the reasons this place was so cheap – and sat down for a couple of hours of glamorous molls and steel-eyed heroes.

Early afternoon, I rang Ellen.

'What's up?' she asked.

'Just checking to see if tonight's still on.' We'd made arrangements to go for dinner together. The Golden Moon: expensive, but Ellen was worth it.

'Of course it's still on. Why wouldn't it be?'

'You've been so busy lately, I thought you might want to cry off.'

'I *have* been busy,' she sighed, 'but I'm no slave. I can make it. Meet you there. Nine?'

'Nine,' I agreed, and she hung up.

I dialled Nic's number next. Nic had wanted to come on the fishing trip. Took off in a huff when I told her it was guys only. I wanted to make things up but there was no answer. I let it ring till the machine cut in, then severed the connection: I hate leaving messages.

I took the trout out of the fridge, stared at it and sighed. I'd meant to freeze it but there didn't seem much point: it would only serve to remind me how futile the trip had been. I decided to fry it and tuck in. It was so small, there was no danger of its spoiling my appetite.

As I was cutting off its head, I realised there was something in the fish's mouth. Prying its jaws apart, I discovered a round black ball. I dug it out, wiped it clean and held it up to the light. It was a startlingly black marble, with two golden worm-like squiggles down the sides. Puzzled – how had the trout taken the bait when its mouth was stuffed full with a marble? – I laid it on a shelf over the bread bin and got on with the cooking.

A few hours later, in my best casual clothes, I hailed a cab and went to meet Ellen, my recently decreed ex-wife.

The fog had started to clear, sooner than expected, so the cab made good time and I arrived early. I waited for Ellen in the lobby of the Golden Moon, which was a favourite restaurant of ours. The prices had gone up since our courting days, when we first discovered it, but little else had changed.

Ellen arrived promptly at nine looking her customary elegant best. She kissed my cheeks and gave me a hug. I could feel the jealous eyes of the men in the lobby on us. That was the great thing about dining with her in places like this: I might be black and shabby as a sheep in the run-up to shearing, but I still had the most beautiful woman in the city clinging to my arm.

'You could have worn a suit,' she said critically as we parted. It was an old complaint of hers.

'If I was seen in a suit, next thing I'd have to start shaving regularly, washing daily and changing my under-wear once a week.'

'Horror of horrors,' she smiled, straightening my tie. 'Did *I* buy you that shirt?'

'Probably.' It was a dark purple satin number, and of course she'd bought it: I despised the damn thing and wouldn't have worn it otherwise!

'Suits you,' she murmured. 'Will we head up?'

'Lead the way, Lady Guinevere.'

'After you, Sir Lancelot.'

A curt waiter directed us to our table. We ordered before sitting, disregarding the menu. In the old days there'd have been a carafe of wine to accompany the meal, but

Ellen knew I was struggling to stay off the alcohol, so we shared a bottle of mineral water instead.

'Any luck with the fishing?' she asked.

'Don't ask,' I groaned.

We discussed work – mostly Ellen's: she'd never enjoyed hearing about the Troops and what I'd been up to with them – and old friends and how our lives were developing.

It was my fault the marriage broke down. I got too involved with my work; spent endless nights out drinking with the boys; had a few flings; treated her like an accessory. She didn't need that shit. She was a beautiful, intelligent, career-minded woman who could have had her pick of men. She chose me when I was young and game for a laugh, prepared to listen to what she was saying and be there for her, when I had time and love and stability to offer. When I hit the bottle and acted like a prick, she dumped me, the way any sane woman would.

The food arrived and we tucked in. We'd always shared a healthy appetite, so neither of us said much till the plates had been cleared.

I glanced around the restaurant, noting once again how few of my own colour were present. I'm not especially dark-skinned – my father was black as coal but my mother was white – but in the Golden Moon I stood out like a drag queen.

'What's the special occasion?' Ellen asked, burping lightly.

'Just fancied a night out with the woman of my dreams.'

'Don't bullshit me, Jeery,' she snorted. 'I know how that mind of yours works: you don't do nothing without a reason.' The double negative was an old personal joke, harking back to the days when I used to chide her for her perfect diction. 'Last time you invited me out on a date was the day our divorce went through. Need money? Representation?' She worked for a law firm.

'You know I wouldn't come to you for that,' I said, upset that she would think such a thing.

'Jeery: I was joking,' she said, covering my big black hands with her small white ones. 'Don't go getting precious on me, Al.'

I smiled, turned my hands around and tickled her palms, the way she liked. 'Know what day it is?'

'Monday.'

Together we laughed drily: 'Ha ha.'

'Six months since the divorce was finalised,' I said.

She frowned and calculated. 'It was a Friday, wasn't it?'

'Yeah, but the date's the same.'

She shrugged. 'If you say so. That make this . . . what . . . a semi-anniversary?'

'I guess. I've tried not to dwell on it, but the date got stuck in my mind and I felt we should commemorate it.'

'You're a strange guy, Jeery,' Ellen commented.

'Only figured that out now?'

'This isn't a ploy to win your way back into my good books, is it?' she asked suspiciously.

'You mean get you drunk, harp on about the good old days, and hope it leads back to your place and a roll in the hay?' She nodded. 'Absolutely.' I raised my glass of mineral water and clinked it against hers. 'So drink up: a couple more of these and we'll be flying.'

'To flying,' she smirked, and returned the toast.

We lingered over dessert, reviewing the past and our divorce and how the six months had flown by. We'd been separated nearly two years by the time the papers were processed, so it wasn't as if we were raw from the rift. I'd straightened myself out and Ellen had forgiven me long before one of her colleagues drew the final legal line between us.

'Find yourself a woman yet?' Ellen asked as the meal drew to a close.

'No woman could replace you, m'lady,' I said, giving her the doe-eyed treatment. She tossed her napkin at me.

'Seriously.'

'Seriously?' I thought of Nic and smiled. 'Nothing meaningful. You?'

She sighed. 'The only men I seem to get chasing me these days are married middle-aged lawyers who think I'm easy because I'm a divorcee. It's becoming a struggle just to get laid.'

The waiter brought the bill and I settled up quickly, trying not to stare at the towering figure at the bottom. Ellen offered to go halves but I waved her money away. I hadn't treated her much the last few years of our marriage; I owed her at least a meal or two.

'Where are you off to now?' she asked.

'Back to the flat.'

'Ali still working downstairs?' I nodded. 'Tell him I'll be by one of these days for a bagel.' As newly-weds we'd lived in the apartment block that I'd returned to following the dissolution of our marriage. We'd shared some good times there, poor as we'd been.

'I'll pay for the cab,' Ellen said, as one pulled up in answer to her hail.

'That's OK,' I told her. 'I'm walking.'

'You sure? The fog's still pretty strong in places. You might get mown down.'

'I'll take my chances.' I kissed her cheeks. 'See you, Ellen.'

'Soon, Jeery,' she said, kissing me back. 'You don't need to wait for special occasions to ring, got it?'

'Got it.'

We smiled, then parted. I watched the cab disappear into the fog, then went for a reflective stroll.

Back home, I collected the black marble from the kitchen and took it to bed. I studied it for ages by the dim light of the street, running my fingers down along the streaks of gold. I fell asleep with it in the palm of my left hand, but when I woke in the morning it was gone, and although I searched all over for it, I couldn't find it anywhere. It had been abducted by the shades of the night.

2

Tuesday morning. Back to work.

I cycled to Shankar's for breakfast. One of the perks of working for the Cardinal: free meals at Shankar's. I wasn't a regular – most mornings I grabbed a bagel from Ali or a sandwich at work – but I liked to pop by a few times a week, to treat myself.

I parked out back. My bike was my only means of transport. I cycled everywhere, unless on a job with the Troops. I started using it when I got busted for drink-driving some years ago. Enjoyed it so much, I stuck with it even when I got my licence back.

Shankar's was a huge two-storey structure (the upper floor was made out of glass), barrenly decorated. Leonora Shankar – the proprietor and (according to certain rumours) mistress of the Cardinal – didn't go in for decorations.

I spotted a familiar flock of Troops gathered at a table near the door and slotted in. Jerry and Mike were the only ones from my shift but I knew the rest of them at least by name: only the most stubbornly private of men failed to make contacts in the Troops.

'Back from vacation,' Jerry noted, welcoming me with a raise of his mug. That led to enquiries as to where I'd been, and I spent a pleasant quarter of an hour describing my fishing venture.

'Wish I could get up there, fish or no,' a sad-eyed guy called Dan remarked. 'I've been working weekends since New Year's. Going up in the middle of the week ain't the same.'

'Switch shifts,' somebody told him.

'No point. The wife's on weekends too. Runs a restaurant with a coupla her sisters. If I took a weekend off without her, she'd think I was doing the dirty.'

'Women don't understand fishing,' Mike agreed. 'I'd go when I was younger. Every time I came back, I'd find my girlfriend going through my stuff, looking for evidence of a fling. Got sick of it in the end, had to give up the fishing.'

We all muttered our understanding and spent a few silent seconds reflecting on the ways of women. My coffee and toast arrived and I tucked in. I always started the day on a light stomach. Never did get the hang of heavy morning meals.

'Anything happen while I was away?' I asked.

'A couple of new boys started yesterday,' Jerry informed me. 'Been showing them the ropes. Brothers. Thick as planks.'

'And Tasso and Weld are at it again,' Mike added. Ford Tasso was the Cardinal's right-hand man. Used to be chief of the Troops. Frank Weld had replaced him a few years earlier but Tasso continued to think of the Troops as 'his men' and was constantly commandeering squadrons and criticising Frank's handling of them. I had sympathy for Frank but I liked Tasso and had to admit that life had been more interesting when he was head honcho. Frank was a better organiser but Tasso had been a more charismatic leader.

'What's it this time?' I enquired.

'Some broad was killed in the Skylight, Friday night,' Jerry told me. 'Nobody knows who did it. Wasn't authorised. The Cardinal's furious. He took it out on

Tasso and Tasso took it out on Frank. The two have been screaming at each other all weekend. Tasso's saying nobody would have got past the Troops when *he* was in charge; Frank's going on again about the security arrangements at the Skylight.'

Frank had been looking to upgrade security at the Skylight Hotel since he took over from Tasso. It was one of the Cardinal's key establishments, where many of his staff and clients stayed when in town, but unlike Party Central – which was pretty much impregnable – it was poorly guarded: no cameras and no ID requirements (except for those who didn't object to such measures). The Cardinal liked it that way, but Frank, who took the flak whenever anything went wrong, hated the set-up.

'Guess he'll be bitching at us all week,' I sighed.

'We've already had a day of it,' Jerry said. 'Yesterday'll go down as one of the biggest pain-in-the-ass Mondays in history. He was non-stop, morning till night. You were lucky you missed it.'

'Yeah,' Mike said, checking his watch and drinking up, 'but it'll be even worse if we're late in today. Slightest opportunity he gets, he'll be on our asses. Let's split.'

'But we've half an hour yet,' I protested.

'You think Frank'll give a shit?' Mike replied. 'I was ten minutes *early* yesterday and almost received my marching orders. Anyone coming in less than twenty minutes ahead of time today might as well not bother coming in at all.'

'Great to be back,' I sighed, finished my coffee and grabbed the last slice of toast. 'OK if I stick my bike in the back of the van and come with you guys?'

Jerry's got an inordinately soft spot for his van and normally vetoes any such requests. But he took pity on me this once, said I could, then helped me load it in, making sure I didn't scratch the paint.

*

Frank spotted us entering and made a big production of checking the clock in the downstairs rear locker room of Party Central. We were a good eighteen minutes ahead of schedule.

'Come in this late again,' he growled, 'and it'll be to pick up your personals. Get me?'

'Yes, sir, boss,' we replied smartly.

While Frank stormed out to berate latecomers as they arrived, we got into uniform. Dark blue trousers and jacket, light blue shirt (a similarly shaded jumper for cooler seasons). Green-blue beret. Black shin-length boots. No tie, thank God. I had three sets of uniforms which I kept spotlessly clean. Ford Tasso hadn't paid much attention to looks but Frank was big on presentation. Rightfully so, I guess. It was different in the old days, when the Troops were an illegal band of private cut-throats; the Cardinal had grown in stature since then and we were a publicly approved force now, with all the trappings of respectability. We even got the occasional tourist stopping by Party Central to check us out!

Jerry studied the shine of his boots, shook his head and worked up a mouthful of spit. Mine were OK so I headed up the flight of stairs to one of the building's many conference rooms, where my duties for the day would be posted.

The room was half-full of uniformed soldiers, some coming on duty like me, some going off, some on their break. I found my name on the bulletin board and scanned across to the right. Front door till lunch, yard patrol in the afternoon. That meant a rifle. I hated rifles. Never had much time for any weapon that required more than a single hand to operate.

I signed for the Kalashnikov – a throwback to Tasso's time: Frank was gradually introducing newer models but old-timers like me were slow to change – and a pretty young girl called Anra handed it over.

'Missed you yesterday,' she said. 'Out sick?'

'Holiday,' I explained.

'Anywhere exciting?'

'Up-river. Fishing.'

'*Fishing.*' Her contempt almost put me to shame. 'You on for some overtime this week?' she asked.

'Sure.'

'What suits you?'

'Tonight and tomorrow. I'll see after that.'

She made a note of it. Overtime was never a problem in the Troops. I'd been putting in a lot of extra hours the last year or so. Nothing better to do with my time. Besides, keeping busy made it easier to stay off the drink. When Ellen and I split, I hit the bottle hard. Almost got drummed out of the Troops. Sunk about as low as you can get without going under, before Bill pulled me out of the slump.

I spent the early part of the day out front of Party Central with nine other Troops and a couple of red-suited doormen. We were the first line of defence, which meant in the case of a serious assault on the premises, we'd be first to fall. We looked pretty lifeless to the hordes of people passing in and out, like we were only there for show, but we weren't. We were on constant alert, observing all who entered, guns perpetually cocked. We weren't after weapons – the metal detectors and X-ray machines would pinpoint those – but tell-tale facial expressions and tics. Our job was to spot cuckoos in the nest, people who didn't belong.

Each of us had spent years studying the art of body language and human psychology. It was par for the course. You didn't simply join the Troops and go on watch at Party Central. There was a six months' induction period, followed by a standard five years in various branches and posts. Then, if deemed worthy, you were introduced to the Party Central set-up: a couple of months patrolling the middle floors of the building, where you couldn't do any harm, then a gradual drift towards ground level; several months pounding the beat in the rear yard, eventually moving out to guard the fences, and finally – if you passed the tests with flying colours – the front of the building and the lobby, where only the best and most trusted were placed.

An unofficial extra requirement for front-line Troops was that they be familiar with the dark touch of death. None of the ten guards on front-door duty hadn't killed at least once in the name of the Cardinal.

I'd killed three times, all in the line of duty. The first had been a butcher, after a mere eleven months in the service. He hadn't been scheduled for execution. I'd gone round to his shop with a couple of more experienced Troops to squeeze protection money out of him. He was a stubborn, foolish old man. Lost his head. Let swing with a blade the size of a cow. My colleagues ducked to avoid the blows, no time to pull their pistols. That left me with a clear shot. I drew, took aim and – as he raised the knife high and roared like a bull – put four bullets through the centre of his forehead, neat as you please.

It was a month before they let me back into uniform. A month of psychiatric analysis. I didn't think such caution was necessary – as I kept telling them, I'd known what the job involved when I joined; I didn't enjoy killing but wasn't afraid of it either – but this was back when the Cardinal was fighting to have the Troops legalised: we were in the public eye, and a lot of people claimed we were no better than hired assassins. Tasso and his fellow administrators had to play the public cautiously. Hence the kid-glove treatment.

It was four years until I killed again, in a free-for-all shoot-em-up with Russian mafia muscling in on the

Cardinal's territory. A hundred of us against thirty Ivans. The fighting raged through an apartment block they'd annexed. I was part of the third phalanx of Troops sent in. Ran up against a teenager in a dark, smoky hallway. He had a sock filled with coins and stones. I had a dagger that could have slit a bear's chest open.

I started at Party Central a couple of weeks after that.

The third had been three years ago. A crooked cop. It was the first time I'd been specifically sent out to kill. I broke into his home while he was out. Gagged and tied up his wife and kid. Stood behind his bedroom door when I heard him entering downstairs. When he came in, I stepped up behind him and put the lips of my gun to the back of his head.

Boom.

I nearly quit the Troops after that. It wasn't the killing that got to me, but his status. He could just as easily have been a straight cop as a crooked one. Could have been *Bill*. You don't make choices when you're in the Troops: you go where told, shoot when ordered. I'd always known I might one day cross swords with Bill or some other acquaintance, but only seriously contemplated the possibility after my run-in with the cop.

I came agonisingly close to packing it in. Life would have been so different if I had. I might have patched things up with Ellen, for a start. I won't say the job's what came between us, but it didn't help. If I'd got out and found legitimate employment and spent more time working on my marriage than I did polishing my guns . . .

But past is past. No changing it. I dithered, drank, broke up with Ellen, drank some more. Bill finally weaned me off the bottle in his own inimitable way: dragged me out of my apartment one drunken night and stuck a gun barrel in my mouth. Told me his father drank himself to death. Said he wouldn't let it happen to me. He'd rather kill me

31

himself. Quicker that way. I'd stared into his eyes, found not even the ghost of a bluff, and went cold turkey the next day.

I had a long talk with Ford Tasso once I sobered up. Told him I was thinking of throwing in the towel. Spilled my moral doubts and fears. He listened silently. Doubtless he'd heard it all before. When I finished he shrugged his impossibly broad shoulders and sighed.

'What do you want me to say? Promise to keep you out of the way of any future killing? I can't. Death's what you've been trained for. To dish it out when obliged, to take it if required. Took a long time to make a Troop out of you, Algiers. If you want out, fine, you're out. But if you stay – and stay sober – you carry on the same as ever. No room for bleeding-heart liberals in the Troops.'

Tasso always served it to you straight.

I thought it over, looked into my soul, weighed up the options and decided I was better off here than anywhere else. At least I knew the score with the Troops. Though I prayed I'd never have to go face-to-face with Bill or any of my friends, if I did, at least I'd know it wasn't personal: if orders came down to kill Bill Casey, he was dead, regardless of anything I did or didn't choose to do. It mightn't have been the noblest of excuses – 'I did what I was told' – but it sufficed.

Spent lunch in an underground canteen watching sports on the TV. One of those world-sports programmes, cutting from surf trials to beach buggies to cliff-diving. It was on most days around this time and was the only kind of regular show on my itinerary: I didn't have a set at home and didn't keep up with soaps, the news, big games or any of that shit.

Frank turned up towards the end of my break. About

three-quarters of the people present sprang to their feet and started back to their posts, but he waved a hand at them and smiled ruefully. 'It's OK,' he groaned. 'I'm back to normal. No need to rush off.'

There were some cheers and everybody sat down again. That was the good thing about Frank: his moods passed quickly. He'd probably be up in arms again before the end of the week, but for the time being he was full of warmth and easy to approach.

'Have a good weekend, Al?' he asked, taking the seat beside me.

'So-so.'

'How's Bill?'

'Fine.'

Lots of people knew Bill. He ran a lucrative sideline in fireworks and had staged many private displays for friends and associates of the Cardinal. Bill was honest but realistic. If you were a cop in this city you could be straight but not antagonistic. It didn't pay to get on the wrong side of the Cardinal.

'Hear about the stairs?' Frank asked.

'What about them?'

'We're to keep off them, nights, till further notice.'

'How come?'

Frank shrugged. 'Orders from above. No patrols. No guards on the doors. Use the elevators whenever possible.' He wasn't happy about it. 'You use the stairs a lot, don't you?' he asked casually.

'If I'm going up, yeah. Keeps me in shape.'

He cleared his throat and glanced about to make sure no one was listening. 'You working overtime this week?'

'Three or four nights, most likely.'

'Mind taking the upper floors?'

I smiled. 'I'll go where told.'

'Good. And, y'know, I might send word a few times a

night that I want to see you down below, and, when you're coming – '

' – I'll take the stairs, right?'

'Right,' he grinned. 'Though if anyone asks,' he warned me, 'I never said a word. You're just taking the opportunity to grab a spot of exercise.' He stood, checked out the TV – two bare-chested giants were using their teeth and lengths of rope to haul trucks in a race against each other – and shook his head. 'Don't like leaving those stairs unguarded. There's shit going on here that has nothing to do with me, but if something goes wrong . . .'

Still shaking his head and muttering, he clapped me on the back and went about his rounds.

Cloak-and-dagger stuff like that was par for the course in Party Central. The Cardinal moved in mysterious ways and didn't always keep his underlings up to date on the action. You often saw men and women of power roaming the corridors of Party Central, pulling their hair out by the roots. The brave ones – like Tasso and Frank – took matters into their own hands and plotted behind the Cardinal's back, like putting a few of their men on the stairs if he'd ordered them off, or sending a couple of Troops along to cover a meet between himself and an associate when he'd given strict instructions not to. Which was fine if he didn't find out, but if he did . . .

I wasn't looking forward to taking the upper-floors watch – not much happened up there at night and mostly it was a boring case of checking locks and patrolling empty corridors – but it always paid to do a man like Frank Weld a favour: you never knew when you might need one in return.

I spent the afternoon in the massive rear yard of Party Central. This was my favourite spot. Business was brisk, as a result of which time – the foe of bodyguards worldwide –

34

flew by. Cars had to be checked and rechecked. The fence had to be probed hourly for weak points. Delivery teams, chauffeurs, executives: all were subjected to our scrutiny and tracked into the building if they looked in the least way suspicious. The yard could have been Party Central's Achilles' heel if not properly policed; as it was, you had a better chance of blasting your way through the front than you did of squeezing in by the back.

At the end of an uneventful shift I ducked out to grab a pizza. Shared it with a couple of guys in the canteen when I got back. Jerry was among them.

'Frank get on to you about the stairs?' he asked as we ate.

'Yeah. You too?'

'Me too.' Jerry pulled a face. 'I hate when he starts with the espionage shit. If the Cardinal says leave the stairs alone, we should leave 'em alone. For all we know, he plans running a team of cannibal ninja bastards up and down 'em all night long, and if we get in their way . . .'

Cannibal ninja bastards. I had to smile.

'You could have said no.'

'To Frank?' Jerry snorted. 'I also could have said "Here's my ass, Frank: ram my future and a stick of dynamite up there and blow me to fuck." It was different with Tasso: he didn't pout if you turned him down. But Frank . . .'

I nodded. Frank did tend to take things a little personally.

'Wanna go out later?' Jerry asked. 'I'm meeting a coupla guys in a club uptown.'

'No thanks.'

'You sure? It's a strip joint. Just had a new delivery of exotic foreign dolls according to the grapevine.'

Exotic foreign dolls and cannibal ninja bastards. Must have been fun to see the world through Jerry's eyes.

'I'll pass,' I told him. 'It's been a long day. I'm tired.'

'Don't say I didn't offer.'

Pizza finished, we took the elevator up, Jerry to the sixteenth, me a couple of storeys higher. Offices and personnel were few and far between this far up. Most petered out at the fourteenth. The Cardinal occupied the fifteenth. Beyond that sprawled the legendary floors of files: room after room packed with newspapers, reports, data compilations, populace surveys; birth and death certificates, volumes of city history, housing plans, income-tax returns. The myth ran that the Cardinal had a detailed dossier on every one of the city's millions. That couldn't be true, of course, but he probably had something on the majority of them.

I made the rounds of the mainly deserted rooms, breaking off two or three times an hour to meander down the stairs and back up again. I ran into other similarly deployed Troops a couple of times but we never acknowledged one another's presence.

I was on my way up from the third floor about half past nine when Frank came storming down, his face a black mass of furious lines.

'Jeery!' he snapped. 'What are you doing on these stairs? Haven't you heard they're off limits?'

I paused, wondering if he was joking or testing me.

'You want me off the stairs?' I asked cautiously.

'Of course I want you off the fucking – ' he started to roar, then caught himself and forced the bleakest of grins. 'Look, I know what I said earlier, but those orders are cancelled, OK?'

'OK.'

Frank studied my face, daring me to question him. When I didn't, he relaxed ever so slightly and drew a long disparaging breath. 'Know what the crazy bastard's doing now?' he hissed. 'Only ripping three-quarters of the guard out of the yard!'

'The yard?'

'Yeah! Told me it was part of an exercise.'

'What do you reckon he's up to?'

'Fucked if I know. Seems like he's clearing the way for an invasion. There's a gap out back that you could drive a fleet of tanks through. But what do *I* know? *I'm* just the head of this goddamned army. *I'm* a nobody.'

He fumed silently for a few seconds, then grimaced. 'Anyway, with all the other shit going on, we may as well forget about the stairs. Let the lunatic have his way. Finish your shift up top, then do whatever the hell you want the rest of the week.'

'Fair enough.'

'And pass the word on, would you?'

'You're the boss, Frank.'

'*Ha!*'

He stormed off down the stairs, muttering to himself like a madman. It was times like these I was glad I was nothing more than a foot soldier. Life must be hell at the top.

I saw the shift out, then took an elevator down to the basement and made straight for my locker. It had been a long night and I was looking forward to changing clothes and getting home. When I opened the door of my locker, something rolled out of the bottom and away down the floor. I thought it was a coin and I wasn't going to bother with it, but then I noticed the dark sheen of the rolling object and hurried after it. I stopped it with my foot – careful not to crush it – then picked it up and studied it with incredulous suspicion.

It was the small black marble I'd found in the trout's mouth and then lost. Only now the golden squiggles down its sides no longer reminded me of worms. They'd been broadened and touched up.

Now they looked like *snakes*.

37

3

The marble bugged the hell out of me and I slept fitfully. By morning I knew I must have had it on me all along, and was only imagining the change in the squiggles, but part of me wasn't convinced. I laid it on a wad of cotton wool on the mantelpiece in my living room and kept a close eye on it for the next day or two, but when nothing further happened I forgot about it and concentrated on work.

Wednesday was another busy but average day. I didn't get home till two in the morning. Spent the last four hours covering for a sick colleague on the fifteenth, one of seven Troops guarding the elevator doors. A further ten soldiers would usually be on each of the three stairway openings, and more patrolling the corridors, but due to the Cardinal's recent instructions the floor was largely deserted.

It could be difficult staying alert in such calm conditions. The still air, the peaceful corridors, the mostly inert elevator, the carpets tickling the soles of my feet. Party Central was layered with thick, expansive carpets from the first floor up. No shoes were allowed. Had to check them in downstairs, even if you were only running a quick errand. Most of those carpets were more comfortable than a mattress. The temptation to lie down and snooze was great.

But I was paid to ignore such temptations and I did. I focused on the doors of the elevator, anticipating a sneak attack, ready to draw and fire at the slightest sign of trouble, questions be damned.

I meant to ring Nic – still hadn't spoken to her since I got back – but didn't get a chance. It was too late when I got home so I simply undressed and crawled into bed again, same as the night before.

Thursday, the shit hit the fan.

I'd clocked on an hour before midday and was changing into my uniform in the basement when Vincent Carell stormed in, cursing like a sailor. Vincent was one of Ford Tasso's men. A gunsel is the only way to accurately describe him. Thin, face like a ferret, not blessed in the brains department, lived for his dick and his gun. I never knew why Tasso placed so much faith in him. Probably related. He certainly hadn't worked his way up the ranks the way the rest of us had.

A guy called Richey Harney was in the room with me, slipping off his boots. 'Richey!' Vincent barked. 'With me.'

Richey glanced up, his face pained. 'I was on my way home.'

'*Was*,' Vincent laughed sharply.

'But Frank said I could leave early. He – '

'I don't give a fuck what Frank said!'

'But it's my daughter's birthday,' Richey moaned. 'I missed her first communion last month. If I miss this, I'm out on my ass. It'll mean divorce.'

'Do I look like I give a fuck?' Vincent snapped.

Richey lowered his head and muttered something inaudible, then started lacing up his boots again. I took pity on him.

'Could you use me instead, Vincent? I just arrived: I'd be fresher than Richey.'

Vincent rolled his eyes, then nodded curtly. 'Sure. One asshole's the same as another. Clear it with whoever the fuck you have to, then meet me out back three minutes from now.'

'Thanks, man,' Richey said softly as Vincent left.

'No problem. You'd do the same for me, right?'

'Yeah.' Richey laughed rather sickly. 'Right.'

Vincent had calmed down by the time I reported for duty and was tapping on the dashboard of a glistening ambulance. 'I love these,' he said as I got in, then jammed his foot down and shot ahead. The Troops on the gate only just got it open in time to avoid a head-on collision. Their curses followed us out of Party Central.

'Where are we off to?' I asked, raising my voice to be heard over the blaring sirens which Vincent had activated.

'The Fridge,' Vincent replied, taking a corner like a Keystone Cop. He always drove like this when Tasso wasn't around.

'Dropping someone off?'

'Picking someone up.'

The Fridge was a huge, privately owned, illegal morgue, sometimes referred to by brave – but foolish and short-lived – reporters as the Elephant's Graveyard of the city. It was where the Cardinal's employees took undesirable corpses, bodies they didn't want washing up, victims they wished to keep on ice. Sometimes his own men were carted in, if they'd died in suspicious circumstances, requiring an autopsy. Apparently the best pathologists in the country plied their trade behind the cool, disguised walls of the Fridge.

'What's the deal?' I enquired. 'I've made a few deposits in the past but never a withdrawal. Doctor Frankenstein hasn't made a breakthrough, has he?' That was an old myth: that the Cardinal was sanctioning after-death experiments in an attempt to fashion a walking, talking cadaver, which he could occupy when it came time to leave his own mortal coil behind.

'Know what the Cardinal would do if he heard you say that?'

'What?'

'Laugh. Then rip your guts out and fashion a turban out of them.'

'I'll remember that. You gonna tell me what we're doing or not?'

Vincent swerved to avoid a necking couple who weren't paying attention to the road, pounded on the horn, gave them the finger, then looked at me and grinned. 'Wanna go back for another shot?' I shook my head. 'Spoilsport. You heard about the girl who got sliced at the Skylight Friday night?' he asked, slowing as we hit traffic.

I recalled my conversation with Jerry and Mike. 'Yeah. Find out who killed her yet?'

'No. Nobody knows anything about her. She checked in under a false name. May have been a hooker but wasn't a regular. We brought her out here to let the experts at her. They haven't got round to her yet: you know the sort of backlog there is at the Fridge. She wasn't supposed to be a priority but now she is: word's leaked and we've gotta take her back.'

'Back?'

'To the Skylight. A cop rang Tasso. Said someone had phoned in and told him what happened. We have till midnight to return and report her, or he sweeps in with his men. If she ain't there, he'll raise a stink, maybe go to the press.'

'So? Kill the cop, can the story. That's SOP, isn't it?'

'Yeah,' Vincent agreed. 'But it's simpler to let the cops have her now that they know about her.'

'Won't the state pathologist figure out how long she's been dead and cause a commotion?'

'The state pathologist drives a BMW,' Vincent said with a wink. 'He reports what we tell him.'

The Fridge looked innocuous from the outside. Set close to the docks, it was a huge dilapidated building, broken glass in the windows, a couple of lights shining to deter tramps, graffiti scrawled by design across the lower walls. We parked down a side alley and let ourselves in. A short stroll down a corridor, through a splintered door, and suddenly we were face to face with a vast whitewashed stone monstrosity.

The entire interior of the old building had been hollowed out and this enormous box had been constructed inside. Or else they'd built this first, then placed the frame of the older structure around it. I never did think to ask.

Vincent made his way to one of the entrances and tapped in the security code. The door hissed open and a cold blast of air swirled out to greet us. Vincent shivered. 'Should have brought my thermals,' he grumbled.

We entered.

This section of the Fridge contained nothing other than coffins. Cold, cubic, metal containers, they could have passed for standard storage lockers if I hadn't known better. They rose in ranks of five, rows of twenty to a block. I counted seven floors of the same on either side. And this was just the tip of the iceberg: turn in either direction at the end of this alley of cadavers and you'd find another no different. The Fridge was a maze of them. It would have made an ideal location for a horror-movie shoot. George A. Romero could have worked wonders with it.

Most of the nearby coffins were occupied, their doors tagged and hung with accompanying files. Alongside the usual statistics – gender, height, weight, address, next of kin – were attached details of how they died, when they were admitted and by whom, and what was to be done with the body. Very little of the information was censored since none but the Cardinal's own was ever admitted.

Vincent located an internal communicator and pressed a button.

'Dr Sines will be with you presently, Mr Carell,' a woman informed him before he had a chance to speak. 'Please remain where you are. Refreshments will be provided if requested.'

Vincent looked over at me and grinned. 'Hungry, Algiers?'

'I couldn't eat in here if I was starving.'

'Chicken-shit,' Vincent laughed, but ordered nothing either.

I climbed up a couple of flights and went walkabout while we were waiting, checking the roll-call of the dead, examining their testimonies. Men, women, children; cops, gangsters, priests; all were represented. Vincent joined me after a couple of impatient minutes and we padded along quietly, one after the other. It was supposed to be good luck to find the final resting place of one you knew. I didn't place much faith in Madam Luck but the Fridge had a way of making temporary converts out of even the most sceptical disbelievers.

'This is where we'll wind up, Algiers,' Vincent said quietly. 'A couple of coins over our eyes, jelly-like blood, blue skin and a slab for a bed.'

'Could be,' I agreed. 'What do they do with them all? Do they keep them, incinerate them, what?'

'A lot they keep. The Cardinal likes everything where he can put his finger on it, even the dead. Tasso's said it can't go on like it is, that they'll have to start clearing the older corpses out soon, but they haven't reached that point yet. Still plenty of room.'

'I'd rather burn than freeze in here,' I said.

'That's what hell's for, Algiers,' he laughed.

We moved up another flight and I finally stumbled upon a name I recognised.

'I remember this guy,' I said, nodding Vincent over. 'I was there when we took him out.'

'Theo Boratto,' Vincent mused, thinking back. 'Yeah, I was there too. That was the night we picked up Raimi.'

'Who?'

'Capac Raimi. The guy we let walk?'

That was right. I'd been part of the support platoon sent to eliminate Boratto and his cohorts, to pick off fleeing survivors should there be any. Tasso had lined us up beforehand and described a young man who would be with Boratto. He wasn't to be harmed. If necessary, we were to sacrifice our own lives before jeopardising his. No reason was given.

'He's working for the Cardinal now, isn't he?' I asked, recalling bits of gossip I'd picked up in Shankar's.

'Sure as shit is,' Vincent growled. 'The Cardinal's pet monkey.'

'Word has it he's being lined up for the big succession,' I said with a grin. The Cardinal had been panning for a successor for years. Tasso was his right-hand man but apparently had no interest in taking over when the big cheese bowed out. Every time someone new breezed into the upper ranks, word spread that he was a possible contender.

'Raimi? Succeed the Cardinal?' Vincent snorted. 'Not in a million years. Might end up heading *your* department – Frank's been getting on the wrong side of Tasso too often lately – but as far as – '

A tall man in a white uniform appeared beneath us and called up. 'Mr Carell?'

'Yeah?' Vincent replied, leaning over the bar.

'I'm Dr Sines. You're here to pick up Miss Skylight, aren't you?'

'Got it in one, Doc.'

We started down.

Sines didn't say much as he led the way through the arteries of the Fridge. Most of the people working here were somewhat aloof. None had ever bid me more than the time of day.

We emerged into a large, spotlessly white operating room. Stiff corpses hung from each wall by steel hooks, entrails trailing down their fronts. I'd been startled the first time I saw them. Thought they were real. It was only when I noticed the pathologist laughing and moved closer that I realised they were clever fakes. Lab humour.

Other doctors and assistants circled the room, ignoring us, most up to their elbows in blood and gore.

Our 'cargo' was lying face-down on a slab, naked, whitish-blue.

'I've taken her prints, measurements, photographs,' Dr Sines said. 'Had to work quickly to get them, but I did. Been examining her back while I was waiting. A clumsy piece of work. Amateurish.'

The back in question had been carved to pieces. Long slashes, deep gouges, thin red cuts and violent purple punctures. An uneven circle had been etched between her shoulder blades, several straight lines radiating from it at tangents.

'What's that?' I asked.

'Probably a sun symbol,' the doctor replied.

'I didn't notice that when I was bringing her in,' Vincent said.

'There was a lot more blood then. We've cleaned her up since. Amazing what comes out in the wash.' He smiled

45

briefly but Vincent and I remained stony-faced. 'How do you want her to go?'

'What do you mean?' Vincent asked.

'You want us to leave her like she is or should we bloody her up again, make it look like she's just been killed? She's to be returned to the scene of the crime as I understand things, yes?'

'Yeah.' Vincent scratched his nose uncertainly. 'Fuck it,' he decided, 'I got my suit bloody bringing her here: no point ruining it again dragging her back. We'll take her like she is.'

'Shouldn't we get a bag or something?' I asked, squeamish at the thought of having to lug her out to the ambulance and then up to the eighth floor of the Skylight by her bare, clammy arms and legs.

'Doc?'

'I think some form of wrapping would be appropriate.'

'Then step to it, man! We're working to a tight schedule.' Vincent winked at me as the doctor bristled and clicked his fingers at one of his assistants. 'Pays to keep them on their toes,' he whispered.

'You wouldn't find me pestering them,' I whispered back. 'Never know how they might take it out on you if you turn up here dead.'

Vincent shrugged. 'Like it matters a fuck. C'mon: let's get her onto her back, so we're ready to tip her in. You wanna take the left or right side?'

'I've no particular favourite.'

'Then I'll take the right: don't want to be the first to hear her heart if it starts beating again.' He laughed ghoulishly and grabbed her right arm as the assistant arrived with the bag. I took the left. It was cold. Stiff. Almost inhuman. 'Ready?' he asked. I nodded. 'A-one. A-two. A-three.'

We flipped her over onto her back. Vincent started

tugging her towards the edge of the slab and the bag. I pushed her along in tandem but then my gaze fell on her face and I froze.

'C'mon, Algiers,' Vincent huffed, still pulling. 'Don't leave me to do it all by my – '

He caught sight of my face and stopped.

'Christ, Algiers, you look whiter than the corpse. What's up?'

I shook my head numbly.

'Doc, what's wrong with him?'

'You want my professional opinion?'

'Yeah.'

'He seems to have suffered a bit of a shock.'

'No shit, Sherlock.' Vincent leant over and slapped my face. 'Algiers! Snap out of it. Focus on my lips.' I did as he said. 'What's. Wrong?' He spoke slowly, as if to a dim-witted child.

'The . . . girl,' I managed to sigh.

'Like you've never seen one before,' he chuckled. 'You going soft on me, Algiers? Growing leery of corpses in your old age?' He chuckled again, then stopped, eyes narrowing. 'Or maybe you know her?' he muttered.

I nodded wordlessly.

'Shit.' He licked his lips nervously. 'Who is she, Algiers?'

'Nuh-Nuh-Nuh-Nuh,' I stuttered.

'You wanna sit down? Doc, you got a chair?'

'I might be able to rustle one up,' came the dry reply.

'No. Don't need one,' I gasped. 'I'll be OK.'

'You're sure?'

'Yeah.'

'Good. So who is she?'

'She's . . . she's . . .'

'Here we go again. Take a deep breath, Algiers. Concentrate.'

I did as he recommended, looked him square in the eye and said it. 'Her name's Nic Hornyak.' A moment's silent beat and then I added the kicker: 'She's my girlfriend.'

4

First things first: we had to take Nic's body back to the Skylight. Vincent offered me an out but I said I'd see the job through: I'd been trained not to let personal feelings get in the way of work.

We said nothing as we crossed the city. What was there to say?

I averted my eyes as we bundled the corpse into the elevator at the Skylight. The general manager was waiting on the eighth floor with four Troops, who silently accepted our consignment. Vincent accompanied them to 812, making sure everything was suitably arranged. I stayed by the elevator, rubbing my hands up and down the sides of my thighs, wondering if this could be a dream. Maybe it was still Friday and I was up-river with Bill, dozing on the damp grassy banks.

'C'mon,' Vincent said, taking me by the elbow and guiding me into the elevator. 'I phoned Tasso. He's busy but said he'd ring Frank and have him meet us back at Party Central.'

I could tell Vincent was bursting with questions but he kept them to himself, respecting my stunned privacy. Frank was standing by the gate at Party Central. Told Vincent to park the ambulance and beat it. For once Vincent didn't argue.

We sat in a downstairs office and I told Frank about me and Nic Hornyak. He listened sympathetically, phrasing his questions as delicately as possible. When I was through, he took me for lunch to Shankar's. We ate quietly, heads down.

Upon our return to Party Central Frank asked me to repeat my story with a stenographer in attendance. I spent an hour and a half describing my brief relationship with Nicola, answering questions as thoroughly as I could.

The second interview concluded, Frank told me to take a break. I went for a long walk, sticking to the back-streets, oblivious to my surroundings, thinking about Nic.

When I got back, the Cardinal wanted to see me.

I hadn't seen as much of the Cardinal as a neutral observer might have supposed. He was a reclusive, rarely glimpsed creature. The more his empire had grown, the less he'd ventured from his base on the fifteenth floor of Party Central. He even dined and slept up there.

I thought about it while waiting to be admitted and could recall only eight or nine occasions on which I'd come within touching distance of the city's infamous crime lord. I'd shared a car with him once, on his way to the airport. He was heading for Rome to pay his last respects to a recently deceased pope, an old friend of his.

He hadn't said anything to me during the ride. I was up front, he was in the back with Ford Tasso, issuing last-minute orders. He had to be blindfolded before getting on the plane: it turned out he was terrified of flying. On the way back, Tasso told me and the two other Troops who'd been privy to the scene that if word of the Cardinal's fear leaked the three of us would be taken out and shot, no questions asked.

Another time, I ran into him coming out of a toilet on the ninth floor of Party Central. I held the door open and saluted as he tucked the hem of his shirt back inside his trousers. 'Thanks,' he said.

'Thanks.' The only word he'd exchanged with me prior to that night on the fifteenth floor.

Was I nervous? I was *petrified*. The one thing they don't teach you in the Troops is how to converse with the Cardinal. He was, at the very least, a legend, if not a god. How was I to address him? What would he ask me? How should I respond? I wasn't even sure I could tell him the time: my stomach was an anxious sack of sickness, my mind a sea of writhing worms. I was still reeling at the memory of finding Nic in the Fridge. Now *this*.

His personal secretary – Mags – tapped me on the shoulder. 'Mr Jeery,' she smiled. 'I've called you three times. He's ready. He's waiting.'

'Oh.' I wiped the sweat from my brow. 'Thanks.' I stood.

'Do you want a glass of water?' Mags asked.

My throat was dry but I shook my head. Last thing I wanted was my bladder acting up.

'Don't worry so much,' Mags said. 'He won't bite you.'

'Thank you.' I managed a weak smile. She squeezed my hand comfortingly, then led me to the door, knocked and gently shoved me in.

The first thing I noticed was the puppets. Dozens of them, hanging from the walls, draped across his huge desk, slumped over in corners. I'd heard about them of course – everybody knew about the Cardinal's penchant for puppets – but hadn't been anticipating the display. For a moment I thought I'd wandered into a toy store by accident. Then I spotted the Cardinal in a monstrous chair behind the desk and everything snapped back into place.

'Al!' He greeted me like an old friend. 'Take a seat. Make yourself at home. Get you anything? Coffee, a snack, a beer?'

'No. Thanks.' I was dazed by the pleasant reception. It

wasn't what I'd been expecting. I pulled up a plastic chair and sat opposite the Cardinal. Out of habit my fingers strayed to my beret and I began to straighten it. The Cardinal watched, amused.

'You can take it off if you want,' he said. 'Never did like those damned berets. Too similar to yarmulkas. They were Mr Tasso's idea.'

I smiled gratefully and removed it.

The Cardinal wasn't the handsomest of men. Nearly six and a half feet, though you couldn't tell when he was sitting down. Too thin for such a big man. A crooked nose. Cropped hair. An Adam's apple that looked like a golf ball stuck in the middle of his throat. Grey skin. A leering gap in his lower face for a mouth. His dress sense wasn't the keenest either: a baggy blue tracksuit and plimsolls. No jewellery. A cheap digital watch. If I dressed like that, I wouldn't make it past the rear gate of Party Central.

'Let's get down to business.' He came straight to the point. 'You were involved with Nicola Hornyak?' I nodded. A file nestled snugly on his lap. I'd love to have seen what was in it. 'Knew her long?'

'About a month.'

'You were intimate?'

'Yes.'

'But not . . .' His eyes flicked down to the notes. 'You told Mr Weld you weren't serious.'

'We'd been seeing a lot of each other. We were . . .' I coughed.

'Screwing?' the Cardinal suggested.

'Yes. We'd meet a few times a week for drinks, something to eat, head on home or to a hotel. But we weren't involved romantically.'

'Hmmm.' He studied his notes again. 'You say you went out drinking together. I thought you were teetotal.'

52

'I am. Nic ordered wine. I stuck to minerals.'

'What about drugs?'

'No.'

'Neither of you?'

'No.'

'Nicola Hornyak never did drugs?'

'Not with me.'

Again the 'hmm'. Then he changed tack. 'You've been with us quite a while, Al. A long, distinguished record. Respected by your superiors, admired by your colleagues. Brains. Talent. A hard worker. Haven't made much headway though, have you?'

I shrugged, smiling uncertainly. 'I get by.'

'But you don't move up.' He looked stern. 'A man of your ability and experience should have been promoted by now. I know you've been approached, both by Mr Tasso and Mr Weld, but each time they've offered you a leg-up you've turned them down.'

'I'm happy as I am.'

'Or afraid to advance?'

'That too,' I admitted. 'I've seen what happens to those who slip while scaling the corporate ladder. Cleaned up after a few of them. Never seemed worth it to me.'

'What if I handed you promotion on a plate? What if I said I was getting rid of Frank Weld and wanted you to take his place?'

I stared at him.

'I'm serious,' he said. 'Not about getting rid of Mr Weld – I have no intention of dismissing such a valued employee – but maybe moving him to some other branch of the organisation, where he won't be clashing with Mr Tasso all the time. I've been working on a short list of possible replacements. Would you care to be added to it?'

'I couldn't fill Frank's shoes,' I mumbled. 'I know nothing about management or leadership.'

'Mr Weld didn't either when he started. Few men do. Leaders aren't born: they grow.'

'I don't know what to say. I thought you wanted to talk about Nic. This is . . .' I searched in vain for the words.

'I've had my eye on you for some time,' the Cardinal said.

'On *me*?'

'Did you never wonder why Mr Tasso spent so much time on you when you joined the Troops? Why he took you under his wing?'

'I thought he liked me.'

The Cardinal laughed. 'Mr Tasso lacks the capacity to make emotional attachments. His time is mine. *I* was interested in you. I asked him to keep an eye on you.'

'Why?' I asked, dumbfounded.

'Because I knew your father.'

'Tom Jeery?'

He nodded. 'A fine man. Someone I was able to rely upon. I thought if the son turned out to be half as valuable as his father, he'd be a good man to have on the books.'

'I barely knew my father,' I said. 'He wasn't around much when I was growing up. Disappeared for good when I was seven or eight. I had no idea he was involved with you.'

'He asked me not to mention it. Didn't want his image tarnished.' The Cardinal turned over a sheet of paper. 'Did you kill Nicola Hornyak?' he asked, as though still discussing old friends and family.

'No!' I shouted, bewildered by his change of pace, momentarily losing my cool. 'I wasn't even here. I was out of town. On a – '

' – fishing trip. Yes. But that may have been a clever piece of subterfuge. A ruse. We have no way of knowing whether you actually went fishing or pretended you did. It's oddly convenient that your girlfriend's brutal murder coincides with your absence.'

'I was with a friend,' I growled. 'Bill Casey. He'll vouch for me. He was with me the entire time. We even shared the same tent.'

'I know.' The Cardinal smiled. 'I just wanted to see how you react when riled. You can learn a lot about a man by the way he acts when subjected to slanderous accusations.'

There was a knock on the door and Ford Tasso entered. 'Algiers,' he greeted me. 'Heard about the mess. How are you holding up?'

'Quite remarkably,' the Cardinal answered for me. 'He takes loss firmly on the chin. Barely fazed by it.'

'I'm fazed,' I said through gritted teeth. I didn't like what he was doing, the way he was treating me. I hadn't been especially close to Nic but I was hurting from what had happened. The Cardinal was acting like it was some big joke. That pissed me off.

'Look at the face on him,' the Cardinal chuckled. 'I bet he wishes he could throttle me.'

'Go easy on him,' Tasso said. 'Finding someone close in the Fridge like that would have knocked the wind out of the most seasoned of us. Frank told me he didn't even know she was missing.'

'You're back on speaking terms?'

'For the time being.' Tasso joined the Cardinal on the other side of the desk and glanced at the notes in his employer's lap. 'The cops don't know about Al,' he said. 'Want us to keep him under wraps?'

The Cardinal sniffed uninterestedly. 'Makes no difference whether they know or not.'

'How about you, Algiers? Want us to hush things up?'

'Bill knew I was seeing her,' I said.

'Bill?'

'Bill Casey,' the Cardinal explained. 'The two were away fishing together when the incident occurred.'

'And he knows about you two?' I nodded. 'Then we can't keep it to ourselves. Howard Kett's handling the case.' Kett was Bill's superior officer. Bill didn't have much time for him – Kett was a grade-A pain in the ass – but would feel compelled to bring to light information as important as this.

Tasso and the Cardinal discussed other business for a couple of minutes, while I sat there like a stuffed squirrel. I turned my thoughts inwards so I wasn't eavesdropping.

Their discussion at an end, Tasso departed. He offered his condolences one final time and slipped out.

'You weren't listening, were you?' the Cardinal challenged me as soon as his right-hand man was out of earshot.

'Pardon?'

'While I was chewing the cud with our friend Mr Tasso. I kept an eye on you. You deliberately tuned us out, didn't you?' I nodded warily. 'You shouldn't be so courteous, Al,' he chided me. 'Have you any idea what certain people would pay to be where you are, to have been present while I was in congress with my number one aide? These are the types of opportunities one should seize, not turn one's nose up at.'

'I'm not interested in seizing,' I responded. 'That's why I'd be no good as a replacement for Frank. I don't want to scheme and plot and knock people off if they get in my way. I'm a worker, not an organiser.'

'A pity. I had high hopes for you. Your father was a far more ambitious man.'

I shifted my chair a couple of inches closer to the desk. 'What did my father do for you, exactly?' I asked.

'Collected debts. Encouraged stubborn shopkeepers to see things my way. This was thirty, thirty-five years ago. We were still quite primitive then.'

'Do you know what happened to him?' I asked. 'Why he vanished?'

'Your mother never told you?'

I shook my head. 'She never spoke about my father. I think she was afraid of him. Whenever I asked, she said he was a bad man and I was to forget him. She died when I was teenager, before I could make more mature enquiries.'

'You never tried tracking him down?'

'Asked about him a few times, but nobody knew anything. Bill did some checking for me: came up blank. I always assumed he ran off with another woman.'

The Cardinal rose and slowly crossed the room to the huge window which afforded him a bird's-eye view of the city. He stood looking down upon it in silence. I stared at his vacated chair and waited for him to speak. I had a good idea what he was preparing himself to say.

'Tom Jeery was killed in the line of duty.' He glanced over his shoulder to check how I'd taken that; noted my neutral expression and continued. 'One of those stubborn shopkeepers I mentioned. Pulled a knife on him. Cut deeper than he intended. Severed an artery.'

'So he's dead.' I'd thought he must be, but had always held out hope that one day he'd walk back into my life, even if it was just so I could deck him for cutting out on me and my mother.

'Your mother knew,' the Cardinal said. 'I informed her personally, as I did in those days, before I started delegating. A hard, cold woman, if you'll allow me to say so. Kept her emotions to herself. Refused my offer of financial assistance. Wouldn't even let me pay for a decent burial.'

'Where *was* he buried?' I asked, head spinning.

'He wasn't.'

I frowned, eyes on the Cardinal's back. 'Then where . . . ?' I turned my head away and winced. 'The Fridge,' I groaned quietly.

'He was one of the first occupants. You could retrieve the body if you wish to lay it to rest. I have no objections. I only held on to it because your mother showed no interest.'

'After all these years . . . What would be the point?'

The Cardinal smiled. 'My thoughts exactly.' He beckoned me over to the window. 'See those cranes? Off to the right.' I pressed against the glass and searched the horizon until I found the cranes in question. 'That's where they're building the Manco Capac statue.'

'The what?'

'Manco Capac was an Incan god. After hundreds of years, somebody's decided to raise an effigy of him. It's going to be one of the most incredible monuments ever constructed. It will put this city on the architectural map. You must have heard about it: reporters have been discussing little else since it was commissioned.'

'I don't pay much attention to the news.'

'No matter. I only pointed it out to show what a *real* mark of respect for the dead is like. Sticking people in the ground or running them through a furnace: ha! I'd rather be jammed away in a dark corner of the Fridge or left outside to rot.

'Come,' he said. 'Back to the desk. This conversation is veering towards morbidity. Tom Jeery has been dead far too long to shed any tears over. Let's return to the corpse in question: Miss Hornyak. I don't like it when people use my facilities for their own ends. Her murderer made a fatal mistake when choosing the Skylight.'

He picked up the file he'd been studying earlier and lowered himself into his chair. I took my seat again and concentrated on what he was saying. I'd think about my father later, on my own time.

'Any idea who killed her?' he asked.

'No.'

'No enemies? Jealous ex-boyfriends? Business rivals?'

'She wasn't in business. She comes – came – from a wealthy family. Lived off inherited income. No enemies that I was aware of. Old boyfriends . . .' I shrugged. 'She was a beautiful woman. Rich. Exciting. I guess there's a cluster of them hanging around somewhere.'

'How did you meet? Miss Hornyak, as you said, was a woman of some means. Elegant. Much sought after. While you . . .' He hid his smile behind a hand. 'You're not what I would consider a catch.'

'We met at the AA.'

'She was an alcoholic?'

'Not really. She didn't talk much about it, but from what I picked up, her brother controlled the purse strings to the family fortune – her parents died when she was young; that was one of the things we had in common – and he felt she'd been drinking too much. He made her go. Threatened to cut her off if she didn't.'

'I see. So you got talking, one thing led to another, you realised you were two of a kind . . .'

'I wouldn't say that. Nic was in a different class. I knew nothing would come of our fling. We just fell into each other's lives for a while. It was a complication-free relationship.'

'Did you tell her what you did for a living before or after things started to develop?'

I thought back. 'Before, I guess.'

'You told her you were a Troop?'

'Yeah.'

'Maybe mentioned your familiarity with guns? Seeking to impress?'

59

'I suppose,' I chuckled.

'Hmmm.' There it was again. 'Ever consider the possibility that she was after more than sex or kicks?'

'I don't follow.'

He tossed a large photograph across the table. It was of Nic's carved back. There was a lot of blood, so it must have been taken in the Skylight or just after she'd been delivered to the Fridge. I didn't touch it.

'Not very pretty,' the Cardinal mused. 'You've noted the design in the centre?' I nodded. He fished something out of the file and threw it on top of the photograph. It was a golden brooch. I'd seen it on Nic a couple of times. At its centre was a mock-up of the sun.

'Recognise it?'

'Yes.'

'She was wearing it the night of her murder. I put it to you: it isn't coincidence. The two are related. Nicola Hornyak moved in dangerous circles. She became involved with men of violence. She was anticipating an attack of this nature. If so, is it not reasonable to assume that she would have sought protection? That she might have found a strong, physical boyfriend, adept in the ways of death? A soldier, maybe? Or a Troop?'

'She never mentioned any of this to me. We spent very little time together. It's possible . . .' But I wasn't convinced.

'I want to know who killed her,' the Cardinal said.

'I do too,' I breathed softly.

'Excellent!' he boomed, startling me. 'That's exactly what I hoped to hear. When can you start?'

'Start what?' I asked.

'The investigation. I want you to track down her killer. Find him, kill him, and bring me his bones to pick my teeth with.'

'But . . . I'm not a detective.'

'You are now,' he grinned, eyes twinkling, '*shamus.*'

I spent twenty minutes trying to convince him that I was the wrong man for the job.

'I know nothing about that line of work,' I insisted. 'I've been trained as a guard, to function as part of a unit. I know about lines of fire and body-searches and how to spot trouble and deal with it. I know shit about trailing people or planting bugs or research.'

'That's irrelevant,' the Cardinal said. 'I've had experts on the case since Saturday and they've uncovered nothing. You know the time-frame for catching a murderer in circumstances such as these, Mr Jeery?' He'd taken to addressing me formally, a mark of respect he usually reserved for his closest confidants. I should have been flattered but was too flustered to accept the compliment. 'Seventy-two hours. Three days to extrapolate from clues, interview witnesses and crack suspects. If you've turned nothing up by then, chances are you never will. That's what my experts tell me.'

'Then why set *me* on it? If the case is dead, what's the point?'

'A case never dies, Mr Jeery. People die. Empires die. Never mysteries. I want to find Nicola Hornyak's killer,' he reiterated. 'It's not a major thorn in my side – if your connection to her hadn't surfaced, I'd have relegated the issue to the back burner – but it irritates me. I dislike being the butt of somebody else's joke. The experts had their crack at it. Now it's time to do things my way.

'Do you know what Frank Weld did before starting work for me?' I was becoming accustomed to these sudden shifts.

'He was in the army, wasn't he?'

'No. That's a misleading rumour I circulated. He killed pigs.'

'Pigs?'

'I'm not bullshitting you. He worked in an abattoir. Killed pigs. Put a stun gun to their heads and fried their brains. Lost his job when he was found *interfering* with the carcasses.'

'Get the fuck out of here,' I laughed, imagining Frank on top of a dead pig, having his wicked way.

'All right,' the Cardinal smirked. 'I'm exaggerating. But only about the interfering. He did work in an abattoir and execute swine. Before that he worked in a fish factory. Before that he was a bouncer in a downtown night club. Before that he served nine years for killing a seventeen-year-old man in a brawl over a prostitute.'

'Is this on the level?' I asked, sobering up.

He nodded. 'Not the stuff generals are generally made of, wouldn't you say?'

'So how'd he end up head of the Troops?' It was the question he was expecting, the one he'd been angling for.

'You're aware of my nocturnal informants?'

'Sure.' The Cardinal had a personal herd of gossip-mongers. They came every night from various sectors of the city, men and women with secrets to impart. What they told him and what he did with that information, only he knew.

'Mr Weld was one of them. He came to tell me he'd caught his boss in the clutches of a young summer worker. A juicy piece of trivia I'd normally have filed away and left to simmer. But there was something about Mr Weld. Behind the shabby clothes, unkempt hair and blood-red eyes I could see a man of means struggling to emerge. So I took him into the fold, set my best groomers and trainers on him, and within months he was up and running. Came straight in at the top.

'I work on hunches, Mr Jeery. I place little faith in machines or systems or rules. I build on people. It's why

62

I've flourished while so many others have fallen by the wayside. The ability to see inside a man, to know what he's capable of, even if he doesn't know it himself: therein lies my secret.

'Do you know what power is, Mr Jeery? True power? It's the ability to manipulate other people and bend them to your own way of thinking. To do that, you must first understand them. *I* understand people. I understand *you*. You don't seek responsibility because you know what you could do with it. You're afraid of what you are and who you could be. You don't mind getting your hands dirty as long as you're not the one making the decisions, because you believe that leaves your soul clean of blemish.'

He paused a moment, allowing me time to challenge him. Shaking my head and lowering my gaze, I didn't.

'I've let you ride along anonymously so far,' he recommenced. 'I haven't pushed you or strewn obstacles in your path or pleaded with you to get off your lazy ass and disturb the status quo. I'm usually not so lenient but I figured it would be better to let you see sense in your own good time.

'You didn't, and events have conspired against you, so time's up. The days of blind obedience and moral carte blanche have come to an end. You have to show your true colours now. Put that brain of yours in gear. Contribute more than just footwork. If you can't or won't, I want nothing more to do with you. Take this case and prove yourself, Mr Jeery, or start looking for alternative employment.

'You have ten minutes to decide.'

Not wishing to appear a pushover, I spent nine of those minutes pretending to struggle with my options, but in truth there was never a choice: it was common knowledge that those the Cardinal does not bless, he curses. To defy him would have been suicide.

'All right,' I sighed despondently. 'Tell me what it is you want me to do.' Grinning, he leaned forward to explain, and the impression I had was of an eagle swooping in for the kill.

5

I'd switched my mobile off while in conference with the Cardinal. As I changed clothes in the basement, I turned it back on. It rang before I made the door. Bill.

'Al? I've got some – '

'I know,' I interrupted.

'You do?' He sounded relieved.

'Can I ring you later? I'm kind of – '

'Sure. Whenever you want. I'll be here.'

'Thanks.'

I cycled home with the Cardinal's file under one arm, coming to terms with all that had happened. Finding Nic . . . learning of my father's death . . . meeting the Cardinal . . . a forced career change.

He'd put my other duties on hold. I was an independent agent now. Free to operate as I pleased. Answerable to no one bar himself. I was to request assistance if I needed it. Frank, Tasso, the Troops, his lawyers: all would be made available should I ask.

But where to start?

I hurried up the stairs, let myself in, switched on the lights and opened the file. If I was lucky, the Cardinal's 'experts' would have made my beginning for me, and I could simply follow their directions, tidy up after them, make a few enquiries, chase a few red herrings, declare my investigation a failure and get back to where I belonged. If I worked quickly it might be over by the weekend.

It didn't take long to realise that wasn't on the cards.

The file was mind-boggling. Sheet after sheet of facts: where Nic went to school, her grades, her sources of income; friends, associates, names of those who'd made deliveries to her home; a seemingly complete list of shops she'd favoured with her custom, clubs she'd frequented, vacations she'd enjoyed.

After an hour of running blindly through the rows of statistics, I threw the file away, stripped and had a shower. Turned it up hot, then down cold. Came out shivering and sparkling all over. Dried myself, wrapped a towel round my middle and returned to the discarded papers.

A few minutes later, I closed the file and laid it aside. The only way to approach something like this was with a purpose. What did I want from this file? What did I *need*?

Drawing up a sheet of paper, I jotted down a few thoughts.

The names of those closest to her would be essential. I knew she had a brother but what about other relatives? Maybe someone stood to gain financially from her death.

Old boyfriends. Could be a jealous ex-lover among them.

Her sun brooch and the carving on her back. I'd have to check on those. Find out where she got the brooch. Go through the list of organisations she was a member of: perhaps one of them boasted a sun symbol as its insignia.

What else . . . ?

The night in question. Last Friday. I'd have to know where she'd been and who she'd been with and who'd seen her and what she'd been doing. That would be the best place to start: I might pick up a name or two there that would make my other enquiries less complicated.

Laying down my pen, I turned aside from Nic for a while

to ponder the death of my father, Tom Jeery. It had been a shock and I wasn't sure what I should be feeling. Even though I hadn't known Nic very well, I knew more about her than I did about my father. He'd been a vague figure in my life, hardly ever home when I was a child, turning up out of the blue every so often, disturbing my mother, disrupting our daily routine. I had very few clear memories of him. A couple of trips to the cinema. An afternoon spent together in a park. Playing soccer on the road behind my house.

I'd always thought he was a salesman. I'd never felt close to him, never felt we had anything in common. And now . . .

Now I'd learned that we were both in the pay of the same master, that years before I'd made any move to join the ranks of the Cardinal he'd been there, testing the waters, preparing the way. I felt somehow cheated, as though he'd stolen my horse from under me. Many of my childhood friends had turned to criminal avenues, but I was the only one from the old neighbourhood to serve with the Troops. I'd thought I was something hot when Ford Tasso singled me out for special treatment. Now I knew he'd only done it because of my father. That bugged me.

I'd have to think on it some more. Make further enquiries, find out what sort of a man he'd been, what kind of impact I should allow his death to have on me. But not now. I'd deal with Nic first and get the Cardinal off my back. Playing detective was going to take up a lot of my time. I couldn't afford distractions.

I passed a couple more hours scouring the file, digging out names and relevant details. There was more to Nic Hornyak than I'd ever imagined. I'd never pegged her for a virgin, but according to these reports she'd been with everything on two legs in the city. If I had to search among

67

the ranks of ex-lovers for her killer, it would be a long, arduous task.

I'd had enough for one night, so laid the file aside and prepared for bed. I'd go over it more thoroughly in the morning. Hopefully the sleep would clear my head and I'd be able to think directly.

It was while I was brushing my teeth that it hit me.

Laying the toothpaste aside, I wiped around my mouth and returned to the file. Picking it up, I leafed through, counting pages. Forty-three, all told, excluding photographs, of which there were plenty.

I checked some of the entries. Many of the sheets were photocopies with dates on the top going back to Tuesday, Monday, Sunday. Interviews had been conducted with friends and relations. A lot of sweat and man-hours had gone into this. The investigation appeared to have been launched early Saturday morning, which was when the first of the photocopies had been made.

But Vincent hadn't known the corpse's identity! Nor had Dr Sines. The official line was: nobody did. She'd died a Jane Doe and had lain in the Fridge, unidentified, until I turned up.

So how the hell had this dossier been compiled?

Frank wanted to see me the next morning, so I made Party Central my first port of call. He was in his office, catching up on a frightening tower of paperwork. He signed his name to stray pieces of paper while we talked.

'Heard about your promotion,' he grunted. 'Congratulations.'

'Thanks.'

'The Cardinal's told me I'm to be at your beck and call.'

'Yeah?' I grinned. 'Like a personal assistant?'

'Sort of.'

'I've got some errands I need running.'

'Fuck you.'

I laughed and handed him a stack of papers.

'Any idea what it's all about?' I asked. 'Why he picked on me and what he expects?'

'Didn't he tell you?'

'He did and he didn't. Said I should be setting my sights higher. Told me I was wasting my time where I was. I get the impression this is a test of some sort but I haven't a clue what I'll win if I pass.' I considered mentioning the Cardinal's offer to move me into Frank's chair but thought better of it.

'The Cardinal's a queer fish.' Frank smiled. 'As if you need to be told. Sometimes he seems to do shit just for the fun of it. And maybe he does. Many think so. Me, I beg to differ. I don't think he spits without considering the merits of every available angle. I don't know what he has in mind for you but I'm sure there's more to it than meets the eye.'

'How should I proceed?' I asked.

'Why ask me? I'm not a detective.'

'But you've had dealings with them. You know more about it than me. Do I need cameras, tape recorders, bugs? Approaching people: do I pretend I'm a real detective, or try worming information out of them? What about the cops? And how do I recognise a clue from a lump of dog-shit?'

Frank laughed and pointed at the space above the door behind my head. I turned and looked up. A sign hung there. 'When in doubt, decide!'

'Ford Tasso said that to me the day I started. When life got me down, I had one of the girls print it up. I look at it twenty times a day, more if I have to.'

'If I wanted dry old proverbs I'd have bought a fortune cookie.'

Frank shrugged. 'You asked for my advice: there it is. There's a thousand ways you could investigate. Sitting around thinking won't get you anywhere. Nor will following the beaten path: the Cardinal doesn't want that. When I started, I made some lousy judgement calls, but they were *my* decisions. The Cardinal respected that and left me to work things out. You've gotta do the same. Make your choice and go out on a limb. Worst you can do is fail.'

'I was looking for advice of a more practical nature,' I grumbled.

'Then look elsewhere,' Frank told me, and that was the end of our discussion.

I met Bill next, in a bar close to Party Central. We ordered sandwiches and sat in a quiet corner, away from the crowd, discussing Nic and what had happened.

'How are you bearing up?' he asked.

'Pretty well, considering.'

'I damn near fainted when Kett told me. We were joking about her Friday, on the way up, remember?'

'You said, if the fish didn't bite, we should phone, invite her up and tell her to bring a friend.'

'I'm sorry, Al.'

'Don't be. You didn't know her. I barely knew her myself.' I took a bite out of the sandwich – the bread was stale – and chewed mechanically. 'Who told Kett about her?'

'He won't say. All I know is, he got a call at home, Thursday morning. Somebody told him there'd been a murder at the Skylight and the body had been removed. Gave him the room number, time, a description of the victim.'

'Her name too?'

'Yes.'

'Any idea who the caller might have been?'

'If it had been any other hotel, I'd have said a maid or bellboy. But employees are screened vigorously at the

Skylight. They're loyal. My guess is it was another guest, somebody with a conscience.'

'Not many of those at the Skylight,' I chuckled.

'Or it could have been the killer.'

'You reckon?'

Bill nodded. 'The symbol gouged into her back: he didn't do that for fun. When someone goes to that much trouble he's looking to be noticed. He might have wanted the case dragged through the media, so he could gloat. Or maybe he's planning to strike again and wants to be recognised when he does.'

'A serial killer?'

'Possibly. But from what I've gathered it was a clumsy kill. Slow and messy. So we've either got a beginner on our hands or somebody who wants us to *think* he's a beginner.'

Dr Sines had said much the same thing about the wounds.

'Any clues?' I asked. 'Any leads?'

'Not by the time *we* arrived, but the better part of a week had passed before we were called onto the scene. Whoever brought her back might as well have dropped her off at the station. Would have saved time and made no difference to our investigations whatsoever.'

I hadn't told Bill that I'd collected Nic's body from the Fridge. Didn't intend to. Those were the kinds of details you learnt early on in the Troops to withhold from friends. Nor did I plan to tell him about my meeting with the Cardinal.

'What are your chances of catching him?' I asked.

'Slim to none,' Bill answered immediately. 'If we'd been informed as soon as she was discovered . . .' He sighed. 'The pathologist will do his best, but I don't think he'll discover anything. We've questioned the staff: nothing. There's a few still to go but we won't get anything out of them. Unless he strikes again or Kett receives another phone call: *nada*.'

I nodded slowly. I'd figured as much.

'What about a private investigation? Any point?'

'You could hire someone if you like,' Bill said. 'Be costly. Don't think it would achieve anything. But it couldn't do any harm.'

'What if *I* was to investigate?'

He frowned. 'Personally?' I nodded. 'Don't be crazy, Al. What do you know about detective work? It's not as easy as it looks in the movies.'

'I know. But I'm serious, Bill. How would I go about it?'

He studied me silently for all of a minute.

'You're not asking for my opinion, are you, Al? You're committed to this, no matter what I say. Right?'

'Right.'

'Jesus.' He pushed the remains of his sandwich away. 'How far are you into this already?'

'I've got some names. Background information.'

'Any angles?'

'I was hoping you'd provide me with them. Old enemies, a family feud: something like that.'

He smiled wryly. 'I told you: it's not like it is in the movies. Motives and deaths of this nature rarely go together. Nic checked in under a fairly transparent pseudonym: Jane Dowe. Why do people normally give false names in hotels?'

'Because they're there to fuck?'

'Crude but precise. Chances are she picked a guy up, took him back to the Skylight, he went psycho, end of story. No way of connecting them, no way of tracing him.'

'Did anybody see them together?'

'The receptionist remembers Nic but insists there was no one with her in the lobby. 814 was an out-of-town businessman: we've tried tracking him down, but no joy. The old couple in 816 went to bed early and slept the whole night through.'

'If I go ahead and investigate,' I said slowly, 'where would be the best place to start?'

He sighed and rubbed the back of his neck. He looked old and tired in the dim light. Bill had been talking about taking early retirement for a couple of years: looking at him now, I began to think maybe he *should* pack it in, before the job made a premature end of him.

'You might glean something from the staff at the Skylight,' he admitted reluctantly. 'As you'd expect, they weren't overly anxious to talk to us. Given your inside connections, there's a chance they'd be more open, assuming they know anything. But leave it for a couple of days,' he warned. 'You don't want to run into Kett. Let us complete our investigations and move on before you go poking your nose in.'

The previous detectives had already interviewed the staff and come up blank but I'd have a crack myself, as Bill suggested, when the dust died down.

'What about friends and family?' I asked. 'Anybody suspicious?'

'None that we know of, though we've only been on the case twenty-four hours and those are the kinds of details you don't unearth immediately. Her closest friend was a girl called Priscilla Perdue. Know her?' I nodded. The name was in the file and Nic had spoken of her a few times. 'And there's her brother. We couldn't get anything out of him. He didn't bat an eyelid when we called him in to tell him about the death and ask him to identify the body.'

'That's peculiar, isn't it?'

'Not really. People react to death in all kinds of ways. Very few weep openly in front of the police.

'Apart from those two, I can't advise you. I might know

73

more in a day or two but right now we're struggling to get inside her head: Nic kept her personal life to herself. In fact, if you haven't any objections. I'd like to hear what *you* have to say about her . . .'

I ran Bill through my time with Nic. We ordered another round of drinks (two orange juices). Towards the end of our talk he returned to the topic of detective work and honoured me with some much-needed advice.

I shouldn't bother with bugs or tapes: such technology was for the professionals. He told me to be honest when interviewing people, tell them who I was and why I was interested in Nicola. 'That way they'll have sympathy for you and may be more inclined to talk. Pretend to be a real detective, they'll see through you and close up shop.'

He stressed the importance of keeping things simple. 'Don't weave webs of intrigue. Murder's not a complicated business. If you start building up networks of suspects and theories, you'll chase your tail into madness. Take people at their word. Turn a blind eye to notions of conspiracy. Always look to narrow your options. Never believe the worst of someone. Jump to no conclusions, especially dire ones.'

I listened intently, filing his words away.

We parted with a handshake and a smile. If Bill had grave misgivings about my getting involved he kept them to himself. Told me to call if I needed help or ran into a blank wall. I promised to let him know if I discovered anything.

I cycled back to Party Central and flicked through the file one more time. The moment had come to make my first decision and take my first step. I might have waited a few days before interviewing those close to Nic – news of her death was less than a day old and they'd still be in mourning – but, keeping Frank's motto in mind ('When in doubt, decide!'), I made the deicision to take the bull by the horns.

Leaving the building, I grabbed my bike, tucked my pen and notebook away in a jacket pocket, and set off for the twisting maze of city streets beyond the confines of the gate. As I cycled into the wind, a cliché whistled through my thoughts, and I grinned: Al Jeery was on the case!

part two

'i'm your man'

6

I called on her brother first. Nic had never told me much about him, apart from his name, Nick, which was confusingly similar to her own. Nicholas and Nicola, but both had used the abbreviations since childhood, prompted by their father, who had a peculiar sense of humour.

I'd asked why they let the arrangement stand now that he was dead. It was because neither wanted to change. She liked Nic and he liked Nick. Besides, they didn't see a lot of each other, so it wasn't that big an issue.

I'd learnt more about him from the file. He was twenty-nine, three years older than Nic. He inherited the bulk of the estate when their parents died and was to have been Nic's economic guardian until she turned thirty, whereupon she could have drawn from her share of the funds as she pleased. He'd no head for business but wasn't profligate either: he hadn't frittered the family fortune away and there was still a sizeable amount left in the kitty.

The two weren't close, but no divide of any import had been noted between them: they just didn't have much in common. Or, to put it another way, they had *too much* in common: as well as sharing names, they also shared a taste in men. Nick Hornyak was, as the file succinctly phrased it, 'bent as a eunuch'. He came out as a teenager and never looked back.

Nick lived in the family mansion, in the suburbs. A grand architectural monstrosity, oozing old money. It had been Nic's home too, though she hardly spent more than a few months there in the last several years of her life.

The butler wasn't impressed when he answered the door and saw my bike leaning against one of the pillars. 'Deliveries to the rear,' he said snootily, and I had to jam my foot in the door to buy the time necessary to explain who I was and why I was there.

Master Nick, he informed me, was not at home and was not expected back any time soon. He didn't answer when I asked where I could find the absent master, so I invented a tale and said I had some personal belongings of Nic's I wanted to pass on. He deliberated for a couple of grudging seconds, then told me I'd probably find Nick at a club called the Red Throat.

I'd meant to ask him about Nic – household staff are supposed to know all the secrets of their lords and ladies – but his cool manner had thrown me. I'd felt like a fish out of water to begin with: the last thing I'd needed was being taken down a peg by the grandson of Clifton Webb.

The Red Throat used to be called the Nag's Ass. It had been a real dive until a decade or so ago. I'd come here a couple of times during my early tenure with the Troops, hunting lowlifes. The neighbourhood had improved since then and the Nag's Ass had come up in the world. The name wasn't the only change: it had undergone complete renovation, an extra floor had been added, the front had been adorned with blushing red bricks, and stained-glass windows of various designs dotted the walls. I wouldn't have recognised the place if I'd been passing.

Bouncers guarded the door, even though it was early in the day and there was no obvious call for them. They stared neutrally at me as I passed, eyes sloppily searching my body for revealing bulges. I could have sneaked a bazooka past these bozos. They wouldn't have lasted pissing-time in the Troops.

The red walls inside were draped with pink banners and sensuous photos of James Dean, Keanu Reeves, Leonardo Di Caprio and hordes of more recent pin-up boys. Low, throbbing music spilled from the many speakers. A 'wet jockstrap' video played on the TV sets.

I wandered over to the bar and waited patiently while the barkeep – female in appearance, though I had my doubts – polished glasses. I was casing the joint (I had the detective lingo down pat!) when the barman – his voice ruined the disguise – cut in.

'Hi there,' he greeted me. 'New in town?'

'What makes you ask that?'

'Don't recall seeing you around before.'

'You've got a memory for faces?'

'No. We're packed wall-to-wall most nights and I don't even notice the regulars in the crush. But days are quieter. The usual crowd. You get to know them.' He went on polishing.

'Do you know a guy called Nick Hornyak?' I asked.

'Maybe.' He grew wary. The hand polishing the glass slowed. He was getting ready to call a bouncer.

'A friend of mine told me to look him up,' I lied, upping my voice an octave. 'Said he might show me round the city and set me up with a place to stay.'

The barman smiled and resumed polishing, doubts vanishing with the smudges on the glass. 'He's over shooting pool.' He nodded towards one of the tables in an alcove to the left. 'Alone. Practising. Likes to work on his technique.' Eyes twinkling, he took my order – lemon juice – and put one of the spotless glasses to use.

I walked over slowly, studying Nic's brother. Looked younger than his years, tall, handsome, expensive silk shirt, a gold Saint Christopher medallion dangling from his neck, long hair gelled back. He'd have to watch that hair: dangerously thin. By the time he was thirty-five he'd be sticking chunks back on with glue. I knew about hair. Used to date a hairdresser.

He strolled around to my side of the table as I approached and I saw he was wearing a miniskirt. He flicked me the eye, grinned, bent to make his shot. I traced the seam of his blue tights up his long, shapely legs. From this angle he would have excited any male who didn't know better. He even had the female roll of the hips pegged down.

He sunk the black, turned, leaned against the table and smiled. 'Got a fag?' I shook my head. 'Want one?' It may have been the quickest come-on in history.

'I like your dress,' I replied drily.

'Silly, isn't it?' he simpered, lighting a cigarette. 'I only wear it for comfort, when I'm hanging around. I would have made more of an effort if I'd been expecting company.'

'My name's Al Jeery, Mr Hornyak,' I said, trying not to let the shaded eyes and lips unnerve me. 'You may have heard of me?'

'Should I have?'

'I was a friend of your sister's.'

'Oh.' His guard came up instantly. 'She had a lot of friends. They've been coming round in droves to share their condolences. You'd be amazed how many are reporters.'

'I'm not a reporter, Mr Hornyak. I'd been seeing Nic for about a month before she died. We were close.'

'Lots of people were *close* to Nicola. How do I know you're telling the truth? I had one esteemed member of the press pretending to be a long-lost cousin last night.'

'I met her at the AA. We were – '

'The AA? What was Nic doing there, for God's sake?'

82

I frowned. 'You didn't know she was attending?'

'My sister and I rarely discussed matters other than those of a rivetingly sexual nature. I never pried into her personal affairs and she didn't pry into mine.'

'But she told me she was there at *your* command. That you threatened to cancel her allowance if she didn't sort herself out.'

'I made no financial demands of Nicola. She took what she liked. I never said boo.' I was confused: he noted it and smiled. 'Nicola was a complicated woman, Al. I knew her twenty-six years and she still had the capacity to startle me. A month would have been barely enough time to scratch the surface. Don't let it worry you: she often spun lies and fairy tales.' His eyelids shot up with the 'fairy'.

'Why are you here?' he asked.

'I'm curious. I want to know why she was killed and who did it. The police are writing her off as a statistic. I think she deserves better. I think she deserves the truth.'

'A crusader,' he whistled. 'Are you a detective, Al?'

'Not by profession. But I've got time. Resources are available to me. And I'm interested. I'd like to talk with you about her and ask some questions. You don't mind?'

He thought it over. Then, shrugging: 'It's a slow afternoon. I was getting bored, knocking balls about.' A big grin. 'How can I help?'

'OK,' I began, smiling nervously and opening my notebook, hoping I looked like I knew what I was doing. 'Let's begin with the basics. Did you see Nic the day of her death?'

'No.'

'When did you last see her?'

He scratched his chin. 'About two weeks before the murder. We ran into each other in a club. We exchanged

83

some words about the atmosphere, the fashion, the music. Parted after a couple of minutes and went our separate ways.'

'You didn't see her again?'

'No.'

'Did you talk with her on the phone?'

'No. Nor on the Internet. And I didn't fax her a letter. And I didn't send smoke signals. As I said, we weren't close. We'd team up occasionally for a night on the town, but that would only be three, maybe four times a year.' He stubbed out his barely smoked cigarette, turned and shot pool again. 'I don't have much time for women, and Nic didn't have much time for my kind of man.'

'Who was she with when you last saw her?'

'Some black guy with a bald head. I didn't recognize him. He was sitting by himself at a table, looking stand-offish.'

'Notice anything about him? Any distinguishing features?'

'I think he was tall. Thin. Black as sin.' Nick smiled. 'That was quite poetic, wasn't it?'

'You should publish. Anything else?'

'I really didn't get a good look. It was night, a dark, smoky club full of people. I wasn't interested.'

I made a note of the bald, thin, black man and moved on.

'Did anyone have the knives out for Nic?'

'If they did, I'd have told the police and they'd have questioned the guilty party.'

'People don't always tell the cops everything. Sometimes they have things they'd rather not say. I've no love for the police.'

'But Al,' he laughed, '*I* like them. We get lots of officers here. I've always found them most obliging.'

'You really don't know anything about her death?'

84

'Once again: we didn't see much of each other. There's nothing I can tell you that I didn't . . .' He paused.

'Yes?' I prompted him.

'She was wearing a brooch when she was killed.'

'With a symbol of the sun on it. Yes?'

'The police asked me if I knew about it. I didn't. But a few of her friends who rang me since the news broke – *real* friends – told me it had been a present from some mystic guy she used to see.'

Her file had mentioned her interest in the occult. I flipped my notebook over and quickly scanned down some of the peripheral names I'd scribbled in the back. 'It wasn't Rudi Ziegler, was it?'

'The very one. Nic was into dark magic, contacting the dead, fortune-telling, crackpot stuff like that. Maybe Ziegler chopped her up to appease some dark god of his.'

'You've been watching too many horror films,' I said. 'He gave her the brooch? That's for definite?'

'According to those in the know. I was going to contact the police about it. Do you think I should?'

'I doubt if it'll matter. They'll find out from the same sources as you.' I made a big ring around Ziegler's name and stared at it thoughtfully, then circled it again. 'Did you know this Rudi Ziegler?'

'Heavens, no! I wouldn't be seen dead in the company of witch doctors. Spirits of the dead indeed! I see quite enough stiff ones as it is, without looking for them in glass balls and Ouija boards.'

'You know nothing about him?'

'Only what I've heard from Nic and a few of my less sophisticated friends who frequent those sorts of places. As far as I can make out, he's a hole-in-the-wall Houdini, mirrors and hidden speakers and sudden flashes of light.'

'Anything else you can tell me?'

85

He thought for a minute. 'Nothing springs to mind.'

'You don't seem too cut-up about her death,' I commented.

He sniffed. 'What can I do? She's dead. *C'est la vie.* I'm not into grief trips. It's a hard world out there. Nic knew that. There have been nights when *I've* had my head kicked in, when lovers have turned mean. It's an occupational hazard. But what's the alternative? Marry, settle down and have kids?' He laughed shortly. 'I don't think so.'

'What if it wasn't a random murder? She may have been targeted. What if you're next on the list? A distant relative looking to get his hands on the Hornyak money. Someone your father destroyed in business years ago. A disgruntled employee.'

'It wasn't.' He potted the black once more, lit another cigarette, racked the balls up and went on with his game. He was certainly persevering. 'Nic got unlucky. She picked the wrong person and paid the price. Tough, but not unpredictable.'

'You're the soul of compassion,' I said bitterly.

'Screw compassion. I'm used to death. I've watched friends go with the big A. Seen guys stabbed to death outside clubs like this, purely because of where they stick their dicks. Death's everywhere. You live with it or go nuts. And I say nuts are for the monkeys.

'Besides, there isn't much about Nic that I miss. I wouldn't have wished death on her, but it could have happened to nicer people, you know what I mean?'

'Not really.'

He fixed his gaze on me. 'Nic was my sister and I loved her. But she was no angel. You only knew her a month: trust me, you got the best of her.'

'That's not a very nice thing to say.'

'That bald guy in the club I was telling you about: that

was two weeks ago. Were you still *close* with Nicola then, Al?'

I stiffened, preparing a retort, then realised he wasn't insulting me, merely opening my eyes to the truth. I relaxed and nodded slowly.

'You weren't the first she did the dirty on. You don't even make the first few dozen. If you think she was a virginal damsel and it's your duty as knight errant to wreak vengeance, you're a fool. My advice: let it lie. She wasn't worth such devotion.'

The depth of his honesty unsettled me and I realised, as I had when studying her file, how little I'd known about her.

'I'll leave you to your pool now, Nick,' I said.

'So soon? Stay awhile, Al. Go a few frames with me. You never know where it might lead. I've a wardrobe full of Nic's old clothes at home and I can still fit into most of them.'

'Tempting,' I grinned, 'but no thanks.'

'Rotter,' he pouted, then winked. ''Bye, Al.'

''Bye, Nick.'

'Call again some day. Catch me in something *hot*.'

I smiled, shook my head and left.

I felt reasonably good as I cycled back to Party Central. I'd made a start, and while I hadn't cracked the case wide open, I hadn't collapsed at the first hurdle either. I was rather pleased with the way the questioning had gone. I'd handled myself professionally. *And* I'd stumbled onto a possible clue in the process: Rudi Ziegler.

Maybe I was cut out for this detective business after all . . .

I jotted down a few thoughts following my meeting with Nick. Apart from the Ziegler connection, there was the AA discrepancy to ponder. Why should Nic have lied to me? Most probably she just didn't want to admit she had a problem. A lot of people at AA meetings started out 'without a problem' and were only there 'at the insistence of' (fill in the blank).

I made a note of it all the same – I'd need a new notebook soon if this kept up – then put it to one side and rang Priscilla Perdue. No answer at home, so I tried the beauty salon where she was an assistant manager. I had to brave the suspicious questions of two cautious secretaries but finally I was put through.

'Priscilla here. Sorry about the delay: journalists have been on my tail all day. How may I help?' She had a cute, squeaky voice.

'My name's Al Jeery, Miss Perdue. I was a friend of Nic Hornyak's. I was – '

'Al Jeery,' she interrupted, and I heard her tapping the back of her teeth with her tongue. 'I know that name. You were Nic's little brown soldier.'

I cleared my throat. 'Excuse me?'

Her laughter pealed out of my handset. 'I'm sorry. Please don't be offended. That's how Nic described you. She said she was dating a big, brown, bulky soldier, with toffee-coloured skin, thick stubble for hair and the physique of an action doll. I was dead jealous.'

I didn't know what to think about that, so I cleared my throat again and said: 'Miss Perdue, I'd like to discuss Nic with you. I'm running a private investigation into her – '

'Do you mind if we do this some other time?' she interrupted. 'I'm not in the best frame of mind and I'd rather talk about Nic outside of working hours. Doesn't do to cry in front of the customers.'

I closed my pad and thrust it to one side.

'Of course,' I said. 'I'll ring after the funeral and – '

'Oh, you needn't wait that long. I've been surrounded by well-wishers since news of the murder broke, but they're all old friends and they've nothing new to say. Are you free tonight?'

'Sure.'

'You have my address?' I had. 'Pick me up, ten o'clock?'

'I don't have a car,' I told her.

'That's all right. I have.'

I spent the intervening hours reading about Priscilla, preparing for our meeting. She hailed from a modestly well-off family. Twenty-seven. Married for a couple of years when she was nineteen. Husband owned a chain of clothes boutiques. Shot dead during a hold-up. She got involved with his attorney, who ran off with most of her money, never to be seen again. No serious relationships since then, but many short-term flings.

The photos were few and poor, the most recent from the days of her marriage. I reported the lack of up-to-date material when handing the file back to the secretary on the seventeenth floor, whence it had come. That was SOP when you encountered sub-standard data charts. My comments would be passed on and, within days, a team of operatives would be scanning newspapers and records, gathering photographs, business transcripts, gossip titbits, etc., updating and fleshing out her profile.

I went home, to change. I hadn't asked where we'd be going so I didn't know whether to dress formally or not. From my reading, I knew Priscilla to be supremely flexible: she was as likely to pop up in a quayside hooker's den as she was to appear at a mayoral function. I played it safe and dressed casual but smart; tucked a tie into my pocket in case it was required.

She lived in an apartment block which, though nothing special, put my poor complex to shame. Couldn't be doing too badly if she was able to maintain payments on a pad in a place like this.

I was about to buzz for her when she appeared, clad in

blue, car keys in her left hand. She was on the short side but otherwise as close to perfect as I'd seen in a long while. A body that could have been sculpted, open blue sparkling eyes, round red lips, delicate cheekbones, and a long head of blond hair which would have been any stylist's delight.

'Mr Jeery, I presume,' she said, quickly eyeing me up.

'Miss Perdue.'

'Call me Priscilla. And I'll call you Al.' She jangled the keys and smiled. 'Race you to the car.' And off she set, sprinting past me, a strong stride. I had no option but to follow.

She was slightly out of breath when we reached her car, a fifteen-year-old Ford. I wasn't.

'You're in good shape,' she complimented me.

'For my age,' I modestly agreed.

We sat in. She noticed my critical eye roving the interior of the shoddy car.

'It's a car like this or a cheaper apartment,' she explained.

'I thought you managed the salon.' Flattering her.

'Assistant manager. I do most of the work but my boss claims most of the profits. I make enough to keep me in style if I spend wisely. Unfortunately I've never had a head for money. It comes, it goes, and hardly any ever seems to be left over at the close of the weekend.'

She drove carefully, eyes glued to the road, not talking.

When she pulled up and I saw where we were – the Kool Kats Klub – I stiffened automatically and a lot of the joy seeped out of the evening. Priscilla noted this and frowned. 'What's wrong?'

I subjected her to as level a gaze as I could muster. 'Nice choice of venue,' I said sarcastically.

'The Kool Kat?' she laughed. 'I come here all the time. What do you have against . . .' She slapped her forehead and groaned. 'How much dumber can I get? I'm sorry, Al. I didn't think. We'll leave.'

'No.' I forced a smile. She was testing me; she knew exactly what she was doing when she picked this place. 'We'll stay.'

The Kool Kats Klub was better known as the Ku Klux Klub, the name it had originally opened under, until the clamouring of irate citizens forced the change. It was a breeding ground for the racist rich, a blessed social lounge free of us inferior blacks. I'd been inside once with the Troops to apprehend a practising paedophile. The sympathy of the clientele, as I dragged the white son of a bitch out past his brethren, was firmly on the abuser's side, even though they knew him for what he was.

It hadn't changed much. All the walls painted white, as though to drive their elitist point home. White customers, white staff, even a couple of pure white cats which roamed the halls imperiously.

The receptionist's nostrils flared when he spotted my brown face bobbing into the lobby, and when he smiled it looked as though he was passing a kidney stone. 'May I help you, *sir?*' he asked icily, hands fidgeting nervously at the buttons of his waistcoat.

'I'm collecting for disabled Negro war veterans,' I said, just for his reaction. If his jaw had been detachable it would have dropped to the floor, sprouted legs and scuttled away in shock.

'Ignore him, Martin,' Priscilla said, taking my arm and giggling. 'Mr Jeery is my guest for the night. I trust he will be treated with respect.'

The receptionist focused on Priscilla and smiled shakily. 'Miss Perdue. Of course. With respect. Any guest of yours is a guest of ours.' His eyes flared beadily over me again. 'Would you care to be seated anywhere in particular?'

'My usual table, Martin.'

'Your usual . . .' He coughed, nodded sharply and led us in.

Priscilla's usual table was situated in the centre of the dining hall, which meant I was in plain sight of everyone present.

'Miss Perdue,' our host said once he'd seated us. He faced me and blanched. '*Sir*,' he added with a curt nod and hurried away.

'Thanks, Martin.' I tossed the smallest coin I could find after him. The clink as it hit the marble floor was the loudest sound in the restaurant.

Faces darkened as I was studied by the incredulous diners (though mine remained the darkest in the house). Young angry women whispered to their partners, who shook their heads, sneered, then deliberately turned their backs on me. A couple of young boys shouted, 'Look at the nigger!' and were quickly shushed by their mothers, who then quietly applauded them.

Priscilla acted as though nothing was wrong and I went along with her, smiling vacuously, idly examining the decor, pretending to be one of the gang, perfectly at home, unaware of the atmosphere.

'We seem to be creating something of a scandal,' Priscilla whispered as we were handed wine menus by a silently outraged waiter.

'That's what we came for, wasn't it?'

'Why, Al,' she gasped, widening her eyes innocently. 'Whatever do you mean?'

'You wanted to see what would happen when you threw Nic's little brown soldier to the lions.'

'Al! I never – '

'Save it,' I said pleasantly. 'We both know the game and we both know the score. Now let's forget this shit and talk about Nic.'

'You may leave if you wish,' she said, eyes downcast.

'And miss the best meal of my life? I wouldn't dream of it. I'm gonna order everything on the menu and you're gonna pick up the bill. Right, Miss Perdue? *Priscilla*.'

'Touché,' she said, angling her head to the left and nodding. 'So, tell me what it is you want. Let's get the business out of the way and then we can eat.'

I asked about her friendship with Nic, how long they'd known each other, what sort of a life Nic had led, the men she'd known, if she'd been in any trouble lately.

They'd been best friends for years. Nic had led a full life. She'd lived fast and partied hard. There had been lots of men, more than Priscilla had been able to keep up with. No trouble: everyone liked Nic. She was popular all over.

'Is it possible one of her male friends grew jealous?' I asked.

'Maybe. She did sometimes string the poor dears along. I told her she shouldn't, but Nic found it hard to let go of her men. She was peculiar that way. But none of the boyfriends I knew would ever have done something like that.'

'Could you give me a few names?'

'I'd rather not,' she said plainly. 'I'm a respecter of confidences. I told the police – I had to – but now my lips are sealed.' She leaned forward curiously. 'I detect a trace of professional interest in your questions, Al. I thought you simply wanted to know more about Nic, because you were curious. But that isn't it, is it?'

'I want to know who killed her.'

'We all *want* to know. But *you* plan to find out, right?' I made no reply but she read the answer in my face. 'So you're a detective on top of being a soldier. A man of many talents.'

'I'm no detective. I just want to make a few enquiries, help the cops if I can. They're overworked and underpaid. An open case like Nic's is likely to slip between the cracks.

If I can uncover a suspect or some clues, I can pass them on to those in the know and maybe something will come of it.'

'Why not hire someone who knows what he's doing?'

A good question. I couldn't tell Priscilla it was to appease the Cardinal, so I rubbed my fingers together and said: 'Moolah.'

'God, I know about that. So you've taken the task upon yourself. You're either very brave or very stupid.'

'A little bit of both, I think. How about it, Priscilla? Will you give me a list of Nic's old boyfriends now?'

She shook her head. 'Sorry. I'm even less inclined to reveal their identities now that I know what you're up to. I don't like the idea of an amateur sleuth running around after my friends, bothering them. No offence intended.'

'None taken.' Our drinks arrived, wine for Priscilla, a non-alcoholic cocktail for me. Mine had probably been spat in by every waiter in the building – twice by good old Martin – but I drank it anyway and made a show of enjoying it.

'How about a guy called Rudi Ziegler?' I asked, wiping around my lips with a napkin that sported a large KKK crest in the lower right corner. 'Know him?'

Priscilla hesitated, then, since I knew the name anyway, nodded. 'A fortune-teller. Nic thought he was marvellous. She pleaded with me to accompany her to his seances or tarot readings or whatever it is he does.'

'You never went?'

'I don't believe in such nonsense.'

'Nic did?'

'Absolutely. If it wasn't Ziegler, it was Madam Ouspen-kaya or Mister Merlin. Remember when *Time* ran that article about this city's supernatural underbelly, and how we have a higher proportion of mystics and crackpots than anybody else?'

'Sure.' Even though I was unattuned to the media, I hadn't been able to escape the Great *Time* Debates. For six months it was all anyone in the city talked about.

'They ran a list of names – hundreds, maybe thousands – and Nic ran through them for me one day. She knew practically seven out of every ten.'

'But Ziegler was special?' I asked hopefully.

She shrugged. 'Ziegler was flavour of the month. She'd been hung up on others before him; there would have been others after.'

Priscilla was playing with her wineglass. Most of her fingers were adorned with rings, two or three to a finger. One on her left hand had a flat round top, out of which jutted a diagram of the sun.

'Do you know anything about a brooch of Nic's?' I asked, eyes on the ring. 'There was a picture of the sun on it. She was wearing – '

' – it when she died,' Priscilla finished. 'Yes. I heard. It was a present from Ziegler. I told Nick – her brother – about it when he rang. And the police.'

'Think it means anything?'

'No. It was a worthless trinket. Apparently Ziegler hands out lots of similarly designed jewellery to his clients.' She raised the hand with the sun ring and flashed it at me. 'Nic got this from him too. She gave it to me because I said I liked it. I only started wearing it this morning. It reminds me of her.'

She lapsed into silence and twisted the ring a few times with the fingers of her other hand.

'Generosity was always one of Nic's failings.' Her voice was close to breaking. 'She was forever giving people personal belongings which they admired. This ring's a cheap bauble but she'd have given it to me even if it had been worth a king's ransom.'

Another indignant waiter arrived to take our order. I'd

meant to pick the most expensive dishes on the menu, but Priscilla's sudden slide into sentiment had softened me. There was a cold edge to Priscilla Perdue – bringing me to the KKK had been a calculated act of provocation – but I had a feeling that at heart she was warmer than she acted, or maybe even knew. So I ordered a plain fish dish which wouldn't leave her penniless.

We chatted about Nic some more. Priscilla had last seen her four days before the murder. Nic had been acting strangely all week. She'd seemed out of sorts, distant, so Priscilla had left her alone.

'You think she sensed what was coming?' I asked.

'Possibly. Or it may just have been one of her moods. She was a great one for moods. Often fell into lengthy periods of sullen silence and went off to be by herself.'

'I know you don't want to discuss her boyfriends,' I said, 'but there's one I was hoping to check on. A tall, bald black man. Do you know if she was seeing anyone like that?'

'You mean the guy with the snakes?'

'Snakes?'

'I saw them together a couple of times. She never introduced us. Only laughed when I asked his name and said he was her snake-boy.'

'What's the deal with the snakes? Did he own one?'

'He had two. Carried them with him everywhere.' She laughed as my face registered confusion. 'Not real snakes, dummy,' she explained. 'Tattoos. On his cheeks.'

I froze, stared down at the table and collected my thoughts.

'Are you all right?' Priscilla asked. 'You look ill.'

I counted to ten inside my head and when I spoke it was with only the vaguest hint of a stutter. 'Nic was seeing a tall, bald black man with snakes tattooed on his face?'

'Yes.'

'Down his cheeks, one on either side, multicoloured?'

96

'Yes.' She smiled uncertainly. 'You know him?'

'I know of him.'

I placed my napkin on the table and stood. 'I have to leave now.'

'*Leave?*' She stood up as I stepped away from the table. 'What's going on, Al? Did I say something wrong?'

'No. I just have to go now.'

'But the meal is on its way.'

'I've lost my appetite.'

'But . . . *Al!*'

I was gone before she could say any more.

Outside, I walked fast, head down, away from the Ku Klux Klub and its exclusive band of patrons, ignoring the hisses, catcalls and slow handclaps which accompanied my departure. I walked until my lungs pained me, then paused, doubled over, took several deep breaths, and walked some more.

Finally I stopped by a deserted bus shelter and perched upon one of the folding plastic chairs.

Black. Tall. Bald. Snakes tattooed on his cheeks. Only one man in the city answered to such a description: Paucar Wami. The city's longest-serving, deadliest and most feared serial killer. Some said he was the devil himself.

One thing was for sure: if Paucar Wami was involved, there wasn't a hog's hope in hell that I was going to be. I didn't care what the Cardinal threatened to do: I would make an appointment, tell him what had transpired, then sign off. I'd rather face the wrath of the Cardinal than the prospect of a showdown with the hero of the damned, Paucar Wami. Any day.

7

By the time I arrived home I was dying for a drink. Nights are the worst time for a reformed alcoholic, especially one living alone. The long hours of dark loneliness and need; the nocturnal thirst; memories of past, brighter, livelier nights, when the bottle was your ally and the world was your friend.

I usually combated the craving with food. I'd tuck into a burger or a Chinese or fried chicken, read some trashy novel and do my best to tune out the real world and its many liquid pitfalls. Tonight it was extra important to divert my thoughts, and quickly, before fear and hunger combined to push me over the edge of sobriety.

Pulling up to the kerb outside my apartment, I hurried into the bagel shop downstairs. A guy called Ali runs it. That's not his real name but it's what everyone calls him. He's a nice sort, chirpy, always ready with a smile, on first-name terms with most of his customers.

'Hello, my friend,' he greeted me.

'Hi, Ali,' I smiled back, anxious to place my order but not wishing to appear rude.

'Dining at home tonight?' he asked.

'Why not? It's cheap and the company's good.'

He laughed. 'You will not get fat this way, my friend. You have need of a wife. A woman would fatten you up.'

'Then she'd nag me about my love handles. I'd have to exercise to work the weight off. And then I'd be thin again.'

'There is wisdom in your words,' he chuckled, turning to the bagels. 'Salmon and cream-cheese?'

'Four times over,' I said, stomach rumbling, glad he'd dispensed with the small talk.

'Four?' he asked, blinking.

'You said I needed fattening up.'

Ali stuck the wrapped bagels into the microwave and adjusted the setting. I'd often asked how an Indian like him ended up running a joint like this. He always tapped his nose secretively and responded with a cryptic, 'Allah moves in mysterious ways.'

'How is our friend the Cardinal today?' he asked as he handed over the bagels. According to Ali, the Cardinal used to call into a shop he ran further uptown many years ago. I used to tell him I never saw the Cardinal but he didn't believe me, so I'd taken to acting as if the two of us were the best of buddies.

'He's fine. Asked after you the other day.'

'Did he?'

'Yeah. Said you should call by some night, chat about old times.'

'I may just do that,' he said, grinning from ear to ear.

I shook the bag of bagels at him. 'I'm off before these get cold. See you, Ali.'

'Soon, my friend.'

I unwrapped one of the bagels and chewed on it as I made my way up the stairs. I'd finished it by the time I let myself in and the other three didn't last much longer. Licking my lips, I realised I needed more food, so I hurried back downstairs to the nearby 7–11 and loaded up on chocolate and snacks. I spent a few hours nibbling and trying to concentrate on a biography of Ian Fleming, the guy who invented James Bond. But it was hard. Thoughts of Paucar Wami crowded all else out. And whenever I managed momentarily to forget about him, my eyes would flick to the dark marble with the gold squiggles over the mantelpiece and the worry flooded back in. The marble and Wami couldn't be connected, but it now seemed to serve as some kind of omen or warning, and looking at it filled me with unease.

Priscilla rang, close to midnight, a welcome distraction. She apologised for taking me to the Kool Kats Klub and spoiling my meal. I told her my hasty departure had nothing to do with her. She asked if it was on account of the bald black man she'd mentioned. I said I didn't want to discuss that.

She suggested another rendezvous, this time at a place of my choosing. I said maybe. She urged me to think about it: she really wanted to see me again. Also, if I was serious about investigating Nic's murder, she'd like to help any way she could, short of giving me the names of her old boyfriends. I said I'd keep her offer in mind, we discussed Nic some more, then she hung up.

I returned to the Fleming biography but couldn't focus. My mind kept fixing on the image of Paucar Wami with Nic. I'd never met the notorious killer but was able to picture him, tall, dark, sinister, arms wrapped around Nic in room 812 of the Skylight, fingers working at her back, lips sucking the life from her pain-contorted mouth.

I put the book to one side, undressed and readied myself for bed. But sleep was harder to slip into than the biography and I spent most of the night twisting and turning, chasing Morpheus in vain. On the few occasions I dozed off, I slept fitfully and dreamt of long, undulating snakes with forked, sinister, flicking tongues.

I was up at six, ate a slow breakfast, then cycled to Party

Central to book an audience with the Cardinal. I was told he wouldn't be available until late evening, unless it was an emergency. I said I'd wait, let the secretary take my name and arrange a time, then headed down to a cafeteria to brood on Nic and Paucar Wami.

I'd calmed down since the night before. Though my fear of Wami persisted, I knew that I couldn't simply march into the Cardinal's office and tell him I was through. The Cardinal had a quick temper and was easily riled. I'd have to be diplomatic. I'd tell him about Wami and state my reluctance to continue; hopefully he'd show mercy and let me off the hook.

If he didn't? I'd worry about that when and if I had to.

In the meantime I decided to set up an interview with Rudi Ziegler if he'd agree to meet me. I hadn't intended contacting him so soon – it was rather early in the investigation to be interviewing potential suspects; I'd wanted to test myself on more of Nic's friends and relatives – but this way I could face the Cardinal with the proof that I hadn't been sitting around taking it easy.

I requested Ziegler's file, expecting a slim volume like Nic's, only for a thick ledger to arrive. I took it to a private reading room and pored over it. It was mostly lists of his clients and the details – where known – of what he'd been up to with them and how much he was milking them for. I skipped the bulk of it and focused on his background info.

Rudi Ziegler was his real name. Fifty-one years old. His father was of Eastern European stock but Rudi had lived his whole life here. A confirmed bachelor. No close family. No clashes with the law. Declared about ninety thousand annually but drew in the region of one-fifty to two hundred. Had a good reputation but wasn't above ripping off wealthy old dames with more money than sense. Went abroad every year for a month's holiday in the sun. Didn't own much in the way of property apart from a couple of moderate villas on the continent. No business interests outside of his own.

He specialised in Incan guides. From what I could gather by the notes in the margins, every medium has a spirit guide who helps put the medium in contact with the dear departed. Usually it's an Indian or a little girl, but Ziegler preferred Incas. And – this caught my attention – the Incas used to worship the sun.

I scribbled down: 'Incas – sun worshippers – Nic's brooch – Priscilla's ring – carving on Nic's back – *connection???*'

I was hoping there'd be some dirt on him – clients who had mysteriously vanished; other contacts of his who'd met with nasty ends – but if there was, I couldn't find any. If the Cardinal didn't yank me off the case I'd return to this file later, but the day was wearing on and I wanted to be back in plenty of time for my big meeting. I returned the file, then rang Ziegler: an answering machine. I hung up at the end of his invitation to leave a message and pondered my next move. I could wait, hang around and ring again, or I could head over and try catching him at home.

I was in no mood for waiting, so I tucked Ziegler's address away in a pocket, fetched my bike and went searching.

He lived above a butcher's shop in an unfashionable part of the city. I parked out front and chained my back wheel tight to a lamp-post. The lower hall door was open, so I entered. The smell of blood tracked me up the stairs like a persistent dog. I found his door, checked my pad to make sure I had the right number, and knocked.

A sleepish Ziegler answered. He was overweight, flesh hanging off him like warm wax, a face – quivering grey lips, red spider webs for eyes, purple vein-shot cheeks – that was being destroyed by drink: vodka, judging by the half-empty bottle in his hand. Dressed in a shabby robe and moth-eaten slippers. Hard to believe this wreck of a man drew a couple of hundred grand a year.

'May I help you?' he asked in an oddly lyrical voice. I took another look at him, surprised the throat had survived the ravages of drink when all else hadn't.

'Rudi Ziegler?'

'That is I. Come in, please.' I followed him in and he shut the door. He moved gracefully, belying his haggard face and body. 'Do you drink?' he asked, offering me a swig. I shook my head. 'Wise man. Demons dwell within.'

He blew his nose into a large satin handkerchief and studied me through bloodshot eyes. 'You're here about Nicola, aren't you?'

I twitched. 'How did you know?'

'I have my ways,' he said, lowering his face so that it darkened and split into a wizardish smile. 'She came to me in a vision last night and said I could expect a stranger to call and ask intrusive questions. She told me not to cooperate.' I stared, mouth agape, until his laughter took the spine-tingling sting out of the moment.

'A joke,' he sighed. 'The dead don't talk to me, despite what my business card says. I've just had so many people over here this last week or so, first detectives, then the police, that I've grown accustomed to their inquisitive appearance. Besides, none of my customers turn up uninvited.'

'What detectives were these?' I asked curiously.

'They didn't leave names. Nor did they tell me what they wanted. It was only when I heard about her death that I figured it out.'

They must have been the Cardinal's men, the ones who put the file on Nic together.

'May I ask some questions, Mr Ziegler?'

'By all means. Follow, dear boy, follow.' He led the way through to a large room which served as his chamber of work. The walls were covered with billowing curtains and the scent of incense hung heavily in the air. A large table occupied the centre of the room. Clothes and bric-a-brac were scattered untidily everywhere I looked. A huge sun medallion was pinned to the ceiling.

When we were seated I told him who I was, explained how I wasn't an official detective, just a concerned friend. He said it didn't matter, he'd talk to me anyway.

I started by asking about his profession. 'Is this where you work?'

'It is.' He cast an eye over the room. 'Though it's usually not in such a state. Nicola's death has left its mark.' He shook the bottle of vodka. 'You wouldn't normally see this out so early either.'

'Can you tell me more about what you do? Do you tell fortunes, locate missing people, speak with the dead?'

'I'm a dabbler.' He stood and tidied some magazines away. 'I provide whatever it is my clients wish. If they want their fortune read, I put the crystal ball or tarot to use. If they want to speak to the dead, I oblige: I'm quite good at throwing my voice and disguising it. If they want to *see* the dead, I do that too. Mirrors and smoke. Projected images.'

'How about dark magic?'

'I don't believe in magic. I trade in tricks, shadows, illusions. Nothing else.'

'But if your client believes, and wants to see demons and devils: what then?'

'I turn them away. Illusions stretch so far but no farther. I'm good, Mr Jeery, a professional. But I have my limits.'

'You don't dabble in the dark arts at all?'

'Never. I use Ouija boards and cards, yes, but never in the right way, never – '

'The *right* way?' I was on him in a flash.

'The correct way. The actual – '

'You just said you didn't believe in any of that.'

'I don't, but – '

'Then surely *any* way's the *right* way.' I was being deliberately confrontational: I had a feeling Ziegler would babble on indefinitely unless pinned down, and I wanted him dealing straight with me before we moved on to talk about Nic.

He dabbed at his forehead with his handkerchief and downed another shot of vodka. '*I* don't believe,' he said softly, 'but there are people who do. One encounters things in my line which cannot be explained, apparitions which cannot be accounted for. Are they demons? Souls of the dead made visible? I don't know. I only play games with the forces of the arcane. Games are all I'm interested in.'

'Was Nicola Hornyak only interested in games?' I asked.

'No. At first she was happy with what I had to offer: my usual bag of voices, Incan spirits, clouds of fog and changes in temperature. But she wanted to take it further.'

'How far?'

'She wanted . . .' He laughed. 'She wanted a lover. A spirit lover. She wanted to screw a demon.'

'Christ.' I sat back in the chair. That didn't sound like the Nic I'd known, but Ziegler didn't appear to be lying.

'I fobbed her off for a time with vague promises – I claimed to be privy to certain ancient rites – but eventually, when pressed, had to say that I was afraid of opening up dark portals which were best left closed. That sort of garbage.'

'Why not tell her the truth?'

'And put myself out of business? I never tell my clients they're barking up banana trees. You don't get rich that way.'

I mused on his words, then asked what happened next.

'She moved on. Most of her type do.'

'To another mystic?'

'I'm not really sure. She came a few more times, but not as regularly as before.'

'When did you last see her?'

'About a month before her death. Maybe three weeks. I'm not certain. I don't have a secretary and don't keep notes: I respect the privacy of my clients.'

'Why did she come?'

'To show off. To show me her demon lover.'

I frowned. 'What are you talking about?'

'She came with a menacing-looking black man. According to her, he was her lover-from-beyond. She wouldn't tell me how she'd contacted him, but said he was everything she had ever wanted, and more.' He giggled into a fist. 'Silly little woman. I'd love to know what he did to convince her of his credentials.'

'What did he look like?' I asked, though I already knew.

'Very dark-skinned. Tall. Bald. Tattoos of snakes on both cheeks. Looked like a civilised witch doctor.'

'Did he speak while he was here?'

'No. He remained in the background. She was only here a few minutes. Popped in to show him off, as I said, then she was on her merry little way. Off to make whoopee with Beelzebub.'

That tied it up for me. Nic had run into Paucar Wami while playing games, he'd toyed with her until she ceased to amuse him, then made an end of her. But I decided to press ahead with a few more questions: if, as I hoped, this interview marked the end of my career as a private detective, I wanted to go out on a high note.

'You know Nic was wearing a brooch when she was found?'

'One of mine. Yes. And a symbol of the sun had been carved into her back.'

I nodded up at the sun symbol attached to the ceiling. 'You use Incan spirit guides, don't you?'

'During seances, yes. They add a touch of exoticism.'

'Could Nic's death tie in with that? Might the killer have been one of your other clients, somebody you'd – '

'I doubt it,' he interrupted. 'The Incas were as brutal as any other conquering nation, but they weren't savages. Besides, they worshipped the sun. If Nic was intended as a sacrifice to the Incan gods – which is what you seem to be suggesting – she'd have been murdered during the day, for the sun god to see. And why murder her at the Skylight? You've heard of the Manco Capac statue?'

I was about to say I hadn't when I recalled the Cardinal making mention of it. 'Yes.'

'That would be the perfect location for a sacrifice, if one was so inclined. If Nic had been killed there, I'd say pursue the angle. As things stand, a much likelier explanation is that her killer noticed the brooch and copied its design, to throw a red herring into the works.'

That made sense, though I didn't admit it out loud.

'Did she ever bring anybody else here or come with anyone?'

'No. I prefer to meet clients on a one-to-one basis. They tend to get boisterous if they come in pairs or groups.'

'Who introduced her to you?'

He hesitated. 'One of her friends. I forget her name. She attended a few sessions. Quit not long after persuading Nicola to come. Hasn't been back since. I've never had a good memory for names.'

On impulse, I produced one of the photos of Priscilla which I'd taken from her file, the best of a bad lot. 'This her?'

He masked his look of recognition quickly – barely more than a slight lift of his eyebrows – but I'd been trained to notice the most minor of bodily tics. 'I'm not sure,' he said steadily. 'That might have been her. The face looks familiar but I couldn't say for sure.'

He was lying. Priscilla had lied too: she told me she'd never been here, never met him.

I pocketed the photo and stood. 'Well, thanks for seeing me, Mr Ziegler.' He rose, smiling. 'You don't have any names you could pass on, do you? Other mystics she'd have been likely to visit?'

He lifted his hands helplessly. 'I could give you a dozen. A hundred. But I'm not part of a network: I rarely make referrals. I have no idea who she may or may not have seen. You can try ringing round but I doubt you'll get very far: we're generally a reluctant shower when it comes to divulging clients' identities. Only a two-bit operator would reveal a client's name, and Nicola was not the sort to get involved with merchants like that. She was a cautious lady. Light-hearted but not light-headed.'

'Well, thanks again.' I shook his hand.

'Glad to be of assistance,' he said. 'She was a genteel lady, very polite. She did not deserve to meet with such a horrible end.'

'If I need to contact you again?' I asked.

'Any time. Mornings are best: it's when I'm at my quietest. But if it's urgent, any time.'

'Great. Be seeing you.'

'Take care, Mr Jeery,' he said, and closed the door.

I hurried down the stairs, the smell of blood rising from the shop below to greet me, sticking in my nostrils, to my clothes, my hair. I'd need a shower when I got home: wouldn't do to visit the Cardinal stinking like a gutted pig.

The mystic knew Priscilla. And she knew him. I could understand Ziegler's covering up – client confidentiality – but why would Priscilla have lied about something so trivial? Oh, hell: I'd done enough figuring. Let the experts piece it together from here. I just wanted out of this mess and to be back on patrol at Party Central.

*

I waited two hours to see the Cardinal, at the end of which I was told he would be unavailable for the remainder of the night. Cancellations weren't rare with the Cardinal: his time was at a premium. Members of government and foreign dignitaries had been stood up many times before me, so I didn't take it personally. I rescheduled for three o'clock Sunday afternoon, gave the secretary my regards and took the elevator down to the basement, where I changed out of my uniform again.

I took it easy cycling home. A light breeze was blowing at my back most of the way and I coasted along, pedalling only when absolutely necessary. As I pulled up outside my apartment block a light went on in a car parked several metres further up. I glanced over – my training always followed me home: 'switching off' was one of the first things drummed out of you when you joined the Troops – and saw Howard Kett hunched over behind the wheel, eyeing me coldly. The light went off and I knew that meant he wanted to see me. Pronto.

Leaving my bike, I went to see what Kett was after. I let myself in the passenger door. We sat in darkness for all of a minute, saying nothing, Kett staring directly ahead. Kett was an old-fashioned cop. Big heart, big hands, big thick head of Irish descent. Did a lot of community work in his spare time. Solid gold if you were a law-abiding citizen; one of hell's demons if you weren't. He had a special loathing for the Cardinal and those who served him.

'You're an arrogant son of a bitch,' he finally growled.

'You came all this way to tell me that, Howie?' He hated the nickname. 'You should have used the phone.'

'I came by this morning but you were gone. Been sitting here the best part of an hour.'

'Again: the phone.'

'You were banging that Hornyak kid, weren't you?' No beating about the bush. The insolence would have startled me if it had been anybody else. With Kett, I expected it.

'I wouldn't have put it that way, but yes,' I said as evenly as I could. 'What about it?'

'Why didn't you come forward when you heard what happened?'

'No point. I didn't know her very well. I was out of town when she was killed. Nothing to tell. I figured, if you wanted to question me, you'd come. And *voilà*: here you are.'

'Did Casey know you were seeing her?'

'No,' I lied bluntly.

'Bullshit,' Kett snarled. 'I always said his friendship with you would be the downfall of him. If I ever find out he knew you were involved with her and deliberately suppressed it, he's finished. I'll drum him out myself.'

'Bill's my friend, not my confessor.' I leant back in the seat and flicked on the overhead light. Kett immediately quenched it. So he didn't want to be seen with me: that meant he wasn't here on official police business. My interest was tweaked.

'What's up, Howie? Planning to ride roughshod over me? Figuring on beating a confession out of my poor black hide?'

'Like you wouldn't have a team of the Cardinal's lawyers on me in ten seconds flat if I did.' He leaned over and prodded me in the chest. 'But I'll tell you this, Jeery: if you bother Nicholas Hornyak again, I'll do more than slap you about and break a couple of bones. Get me?'

'What's Nick Hornyak got to do with anything?' I asked quietly.

'I know you were pestering him.'

'How?'

'I have my sources,' he said smugly.

'All I did was ask him some questions. He didn't – '

'You don't have the right to ask him shit!' Kett roared, then lowered his voice for fear of attracting attention. 'What do you think you're up to, sticking your nose in where it's not wanted? You were humping the broad: so what? So was every leprous son of a whore with a one-inch excuse for a dick. Don't interfere, Jeery. This isn't your affair.'

'Whose is it? Yours?' I laughed. 'You haven't a hope in hell of finding her killer and you know it.'

'That ain't here and that ain't there. *I'm* paid to check on dumb bitches like this who go and get themselves fucked over; *you* aren't. I don't want you sniffing around, OK?'

'You can't stop me.'

'No?'

I smiled in the darkness. 'No.'

Kett faced away from me and cursed quietly. 'OK,' he muttered once he'd calmed down. 'Let's talk about this reasonably. We don't have to be at each other's throat all the time.' I'd never seen Kett trying to soft-talk one of my kind before: it was an eye-opening experience. 'You were right when you said we probably won't find her killer, and if you want to waste your time chasing him, I won't try blocking you – though I could if I wanted,' he insisted, reverting to true form. 'But I'm prepared to leave you be,' he vowed, slipping back into his sweetness-and-pie routine, 'if you play ball and don't go meddling where you shouldn't.'

'I'm listening, Howie.'

'Nick Hornyak didn't kill her.'

'I never said he did.'

'So why question him?'

'That's a dumb question for a cop to ask,' I chided him.

'OK,' he bristled. 'You wanted to learn more about her,

where she came from, what sort of a life she led. You wanted to rub him up for clues and contacts. Fair enough. But that's where it ends. I don't want you going near him again.'

'Why? Has he something to hide?'

'No. But he likes his privacy.'

'Don't we all?'

'Sure, but Hornyak's got the money to *protect* it. He has friends in high places, friends who know people like me, friends who don't like it when he runs to them with tales of being manhandled by some punk ex-humper of his sister.'

'I didn't manhandle him. I asked him some questions. He answered politely. We got on well. We parted on good terms. I don't see what the problem is.'

'I don't care what you *see* or what you *think*,' Kett sneered. 'I've warned you nicely, Jeery: stay away from Nick Hornyak. Next time – if you ignore me – it mightn't be a cop that's sent, understand? And it might be more than a simple verbal warning.'

'You threatening me, Howie?'

He laughed. 'Now who's asking the dumb questions?'

'These "friends" of Nick's,' I said slowly. 'Don't suppose you'd care to pass their names on to me, would you? So I could drop them a line and let them know – '

'Out,' he snapped, reaching over and opening the door. Taking the hint, I swung my legs out and stepped onto the pavement. 'And this conversation never happened,' he hissed. I smiled at him in answer and slammed the door in his face.

Upstairs, I dug out my notebook and jotted down a brief transcription of my encounter with Kett. When I was done, I read over what I'd written, scratched behind my ears with the tip of my pen and wondered what it added up to. I'd said nothing to Nick to warrant such treatment. I thought my meeting with the male half of the Hornyak clan had gone splendidly. I'd sensed no antipathy from Nick, no reason to suspect him of any involvement with the murder. Not until this.

It didn't make sense. Sending Kett after me had only served to raise my suspicions. I found it hard to believe the sharp little man I'd found playing pool in the Red Throat could make such a clumsy move, implicating himself when there was no need. He might be playing with me – using the ever-serious Kett to wind me up – but so soon after his sister's death? Callous as he'd appeared, I didn't think he was heartless. So either I'd misread him completely and he was a nervous, easily panicked, bumbling moron with a guilty conscience, or . . .

What? He was a patsy? One of those 'friends' Howie mentioned might have heard I'd been round to see Nick; he might have checked up on me, unearthed my connection with the Cardinal, and grown worried that I might stumble across his name in the course of my investigations; not wanting to show his hand, he sent Kett over to throw me off the scent by tricking me into focusing on Nick. It was too elaborate a scheme – there were quicker, surer ways for people with that sort of power to deal with irritating flies like me – but how else to explain it?

I thought that one over. There *was* another possibility: that the 'friends' were a myth and Kett was covering his *own* ass. First the anonymous phone call tipping him off to Nic's whereabouts; now this. I never had Kett pegged for a genius but how dumb *was* he? Dumb enough to believe I wouldn't see through such an unsubtle ploy, if that's what it was? Dumb enough to think I'd jump when he barked and steer clear of Nick on his say-so?

If he *was* that dumb, the question became: what was it he didn't want me to find out? That *he* was the killer? I couldn't believe it – Howard Kett was no murderer, whatever his faults – but thinking about it kept me awake long after midnight.

8

I was passing a peaceful Sunday morning in bed, enjoying the silence, when someone knocked on the door. I groaned, shrugged off the covers, pulled on a pair of shorts and a shirt, and went to see who it was. I discovered a skinny mulatto kid on the landing, leaning on a skateboard almost as big as himself.

'Help you, son?' I said as pleasantly as I could.

'Al Jeery?'

'Yeah.'

'Fabio asked me to fetch you. Says he needs those hands of yours.'

'Oh.' It had been a couple of years since Fabio last called upon me but I knew instantly what he wanted. I said, 'Give me a few minutes to change,' and slipped back inside.

I asked him where we were going when I was dressed but he wouldn't tell me: insisted on leading the way. Hopped on his board, waited for me to mount my bike, then set off, cutting a fair pace through the quiet Sunday streets. I had to be sharp to keep up, especially when he turned corners in a screech of dust and vanished halfway down dark alleys while I was struggling to brake and correct my course.

It was a muggy day and I soon began to wish I'd stuck

with the shorts, but it was too late to turn back. I'd just have to sweat and bear it.

My guide led me deep into the south of the city, its literal heart of darkness, where my caramel skin was as light a shade as you were likely to find. It was familiar territory – I'd grown up here – but I hadn't been back much since marrying Ellen and moving out. Only ever dropped in on business or when summoned by Fabio.

The skateboard whizz stopped outside a six-storey block of sorry-ass apartments, most of which were occupied by squatters or those sub-existing just above the poverty line.

'He's in 4B,' the kid sniffed.

'Thanks.' I started up.

'Hey! He said you'd tip.'

I eyed the grifter humorously. I knew he wouldn't have skated all the way over and back unless he'd been paid in advance. But I've a soft spot for cocky little runts, having been one myself. I tossed a handful of coins which he caught mid-air. Leapt back on his board and disappeared. Didn't occur to him to thank me.

I climbed the creaking stairs to the fourth and found Fabio sat in a chair outside 4B, sipping a cola, waiting patiently. Fabio was the city's oldest pimp, a hundred and three if the rumours were to be believed. He'd been a big shot once, before the Cardinal came to power, but these days eked out a meagre living off of a handful of ageing ladies of the night. He called them his retirement posse.

'Morning, Algeria,' he greeted me in his slow old drawl.

'Fabio.' I took his wrinkly, age-spotted hand and shook it gently. He'd been good to me when I was growing up. Running errands for him had kept me in pocket money and he'd watched out for me when my mother died.

'How're the hands?' he asked, turning them over to examine my palms.

'Haven't used them a lot lately. Not since you last called me out. The drink put paid to that.'

'You're off it now though, ain't you?'

'Yeah.'

Fabio stroked the smooth palms. 'Reckon you can still work the magic?' he asked softly.

'I'll try,' I said, 'but I can't promise anything.'

'That'll do for me.' He stood and pushed through the open door. A large black woman was on the floor of the tiny but tidy living room inside, playing with a boy no more than five or six years old. She looked up at me and smiled.

'Algeria, this is Florence,' Fabio introduced us. 'Flo, this is Al Jeery, the deadbeat I was telling you about.'

'I'm pleased to meet you, Mr Jeery.' She had a warm voice.

'Same here, ma'am,' I replied, then cocked an eyebrow at Fabio. 'Her or the kid?' I whispered.

'The kid,' he whispered back. 'Father's doing fifteen: killed a white electrician in a brawl. Used to be pretty free with his belt when he was around. Maybe even worse, but we ain't sure about that. Kid's been having nightmares. Flo's tried explaining that he don't have nothing to fear, that the bastard's locked up and won't be coming back, but it ain't helped. He's a bright kid but he's falling to pieces. Barely sleeps, tired all day, gets into fights. She's had to take him out of school: too unruly.'

'He should see a psychiatrist,' I said. 'Sounds like he's got real problems. You know I don't stick my oar in when it's shit like this.'

'Look about you, Algeria,' Fabio hissed. 'This look like the Skylight? Flo's one of my girls, but she's barely working now: spends all her time stuck in here, fussing over the kid.'

'You're not helping her out of the goodness of your heart, then.'

He snorted. 'As if! Course I've a stake in this. If Flo don't earn, I don't earn. But that don't change the facts: this kid and his ma need help, Algeria, and it's you or it's nothing. Freeze them out and it'll go bad for both of them.'

Fabio knew I was a sucker for a lost cause. This wasn't the first time he'd tugged at my heartstrings to manipulate me, but I never could bring myself to hate him for it.

'I'll give it a go,' I sighed, removing my jacket. 'But if he resists, or it doesn't work first time, I won't push, OK?'

'It'll work,' Fabio assured me, and nodded at Flo to stand.

'What's your son's name?' I asked.

'Drake.' She was nervous. 'You won't hurt him, will you?'

I smiled at her. 'No. Fabio's explained what I do?'

'Kind of.'

'There's no risk involved. It works or it doesn't. The worst that can happen to Drake is that he goes on like he is. Do you have a pack of cards?' She handed them over. She'd been holding on to them since before I came and they were warm from the heat of her sweaty hands.

I knelt down on the floor and waited for the kid to look up and catch my eye. When he did I put on my brightest smile. 'Hi, Drake. My name's Al. I'm a friend of your mother's.'

He studied me suspiciously. 'Are you gonna take me away?' He had a thin, reedy voice.

'Why do you think that, Drake?'

'My dad said if I wasn't good, a man would come and take me away.'

'But you've been good, haven't you?'

'I been kicked out of school,' he said, half ashamed, half proud.

'That's nothing. I got kicked out of three or four schools when I was a kid.' It was the truth. 'Never did me any harm. Does a lad good to have a break from all that teaching.'

'What were you kicked out for?' Drake asked.

'Can't say. Not in front of a lady.' I winked at Flo. 'Want to see a card trick, Drake?'

He perked up. 'Is it a good one?'

'Best around.'

'My friend Spike does loads of tricks. He's taught me a few.'

'I bet he's never shown you one like this.' I started shuffling slowly. 'Keep your eyes on the cards.' I shuffled for the better part of a minute, then slapped four cards down on the floor. 'Pick one but don't tell me.' He ran his eyes over the cards. 'Picked?' He nodded. I gathered up the cards and shuffled again. 'Watch the deck,' I told him. 'Don't look away even for a second. Trick won't work if you do.'

I increased the speed of the shuffle, speaking softly while my hands occupied his eyes, telling him to keep watching. I flipped the entire deck over, so he could see the faces of the cards, and moved up another couple of notches, now telling him to watch the colours, to focus on the numbers, to concentrate.

After a couple of minutes I laid another four cards down. 'Is one of them the card you picked?' He gazed down at the cards in silence, as though he wasn't sure, then slowly shook his head. I picked them up and shuffled again. This time I didn't have to tell him to watch the cards: his eyes followed of their own accord.

Three or four minutes later, I laid the cards aside and waved a hand in front of Drake's wide-open eyes: no reaction. I smiled tightly at Fabio and Flo. 'It's working. Have a pillow ready for when I'm through.'

I placed the index and middle fingers of both hands on either side of Drake's head and softly massaged his temples, creating tiny smooth circles. I crossed my legs and sat directly opposite the boy, hunched over so our eyes were level.

'Look into my eyes, Drake,' I whispered. 'Focus on my pupils.' He did as I commanded. 'Do you see cards in them? Colours?' He nodded. 'I want you to concentrate on the colours and count up to fifty inside your head. Can you count to fifty, Drake?' He shook his head no. 'Then count to ten, five times. Can you do that?' A nod. 'Good boy. When you're done, close your eyes and sleep. But carry on listening to what I'm saying, OK?' Again, a nod. 'Start counting.'

I continued rubbing his temples while our gazes were locked. I tried not to blink. I spoke as he counted, commenting on the colours, the blood-red hearts, the night-black clubs, the sparkling diamonds, the plain spades. When he closed his eyes, I took a deep breath, let my lids shut and pressed my forehead to his.

'Breathe slowly, Drake,' I said. 'Take a breath, hold it for five seconds, let it out, then breathe in again.' I breathed the same way and within minutes we were coordinated, lungs working in harmony, as though connected. My fingers never stopped at his temples, neither slowing nor quickening.

'I want you to think about your nightmares, Drake. Who appears in them?' I felt his frown and his head shook slightly. 'It's all right. You can tell me. Nobody can hurt you while I'm here. Who appears in your dreams?'

'Dad,' he said quietly.

'Think about Dad. Focus on him and the way he looks when you sleep at night, the things he does. Are you doing it, Drake?'

'Yes.' He was frightened but he trusted me.

'Now I'm gonna help you push the nightmares away. You feel my head against yours?' A nod. 'Imagine there's a tunnel between our heads, linking us. It's wide, as wide as it needs to be. You see it, Drake?'

'Black,' he whispered.

'Yes, it's black. But you needn't be afraid. It's only a tunnel. There's red in it too, if you look closely. Can you see the red?'

A pause, then: 'Yes. Red. Like the cards.'

'Exactly. Just like the cards. That's all it is, Drake: a tunnel of cards. Are you afraid of it?'

'No.' Positive this time.

'Good. Now take those nightmares, Drake, all the pictures of your dad, and push them down the tunnel. It's easy. They'll slide down like ice cream through a cone on a really hot day. Are you pushing?'

'Yes.'

'Don't push hard, but push steadily. Push until they're gone from your head, every last one of them, until they've come out the other end of the tunnel, onto *my* side.'

'They're bad dreams. I don't want to give them to you.'

'It's OK, Drake,' I said, touched by his concern. 'They can't hurt me. I know how to deal with them.'

A long silence followed. I could feel Drake straining, pushing as told, his tiny muscles quivering as he thrust with all the potential of his young body. I pictured his bad thoughts spilling into my mind and mentally thrust them to the rear of my brain as they gushed in, where the weight of my will squashed them, rendering them harmless.

Eventually he went limp and started to fall away from me. I held him in place with my fingers and said: 'Don't move, Drake, not yet. We aren't finished.'

'I'm tired,' he moaned.

'Me too. But it won't be much longer.' When he was

121

straight, I returned to my gentle circular motions. 'Are all the nightmares gone?'

'All gone,' he whispered.

'Good. Now I want you to close off the tunnel. Just pull at a few of the cards and the whole lot will come tumbling down. Are you pulling, Drake?'

'Yes.'

'Are the cards collapsing?'

'No, they're . . . Yes!' He got excited. 'Now they are. Falling all over the place. Cards everywhere.'

'Is the tunnel gone?'

'Almost. It's going . . . it's . . . There. Gone.'

I slowly peeled my head away from the boy's. I left my fingers where they were and kept my eyes shut. 'When I remove my hands, Drake, I want you to lie down and rest. You've done a lot of good work today. You'll be tired. Don't fight sleep when it comes: you've nothing to be scared of any more. The nightmares are gone, you got rid of them, they won't ever come back. OK?'

'Are you sure?' he asked.

'I'm sure. You pushed them down the tunnel, then you tore it apart. There's no way back for them. Understand?'

A pause, then: 'No way back.'

'Gone for good?'

He nodded. 'Gone for good.'

'Count to ten now, Drake, and when you get to the end, I'll let go and you can sleep. Do you want to sleep?'

'Yes. Sleepy.'

'Start counting.'

When he reached ten he toppled away from me. I caught him by the shoulders before he could connect with the floor and hurt himself. I opened my eyes and called for the pillow. Fabio laid it on the floor and I leant the boy down, positioning his head so it rested on the soft material, then tucking his arms in and straightening his legs.

'There,' I said, sitting upright, exhausted. 'He should be all right now. He might be a little confused when he wakes. Treat him carefully for a day or two, give him plenty to eat, keep him inside. If he seems OK after that, let him out to play, then try him at school.'

'Will the dreams come back?' Flo asked, standing over the sleeping boy, a look of uncertain hope etched into her features.

'I doubt it. If they do, send for me and I'll try again. But he should be fine.' I know I told Fabio I'd only give it one shot, but that was before meeting the boy: it's never easy to be clinical once you become personally involved.

'You want something to eat or drink, Algeria?' Fabio asked.

'A glass of water, please, then some fresh air.'

'Coming right up.'

Flo coughed and looked sheepish. 'I can't pay you right now, but in a month or two – '

I raised a quieting hand. 'Send me a card next Christmas, tell me how he's doing, and we'll call it quits.'

'Thank you, Mr Jeery,' she sobbed, taking my hands and squeezing hard. 'Thank you.'

'Thank *you*, ma'am,' I replied, 'for trusting me.'

Fabio handed me the water, I gulped at it, then he led me downstairs, out into the open, to recover.

I'd been 'curing' people since I was a kid, guided by Fabio, who'd been the first to take note of my calming influence. He'd spotted me befriending wild cats and dogs. I used to slide up to them, ignoring their growls or raised hackles, talking softly, extending my hands, and within minutes they'd be flopping over onto their backs, offering me their stomachs to rub, letting me play with their ears and feed them scraps.

Fabio initially tested me on a scattering of people plagued with migraines. He found that by talking to and touching them I was able to bring substantial measures of relief to their lives: headaches flew in front of me. After that it was troubled elderly friends of his, old men and women who sat around, mumbling to themselves, tormented by visions of the past. We'd sit with them, I'd hold their hands and talk, and they seemed lighter of spirit when we departed. One old dear said she'd had her first full night of sleep in twenty years after one of my visits.

Over the years Fabio helped me develop my healing skills, basing my techniques on those of others. We tried various methods before settling on the cards, which suited me best. Fabio hoped to make a killing out of me, bringing me along slowly, keeping it low-key so I didn't attract the attention of sharper operators. Then he planned to launch me on a wealthier class of clientele and make them pay through the nose.

Things didn't work out that way. My mother was proud of my healing abilities but believed it would be immoral to profit from them. She blocked Fabio's efforts to make a cash cow of me, coming down hard when she caught him pulling a sly one behind her back, terminating contact between the two of us, sometimes for months at a stretch.

He tried convincing me to go on the road with him when she died but I wasn't in the best of moods and for a couple of years I wanted nothing to do with sick people. I turned my back on my powers, on the ill, on Fabio. He remained a good friend – maybe because he liked me; maybe because he thought I'd come good in the end – but by the time I got my life back on track I was part of the Troops, prone to spending less time in the old neighbourhood, and the lure of the healing profession had passed me by.

Resigning himself to my lack of interest, Fabio settled on asking for occasional favours, only calling on me when he was in a fix. Nobody other than Fabio and those I helped knew of my powers: I never advertised or broached the subject. I didn't want hordes of miracle-worshippers camping out on my doorstep, making my life a misery.

I'd no idea where the power stemmed from. I didn't believe in God, I hadn't made a study of the phenomenon, it wasn't something I sought or cherished. It was just part of me, a talent I'd been born with. Maybe it was the city: as *Time* had attested, these streets were paved with supernatural wonders. Perhaps some of the wonder had rubbed off on me, as it had on others.

I'd almost forgotten about the power these last few years. Like I said to Fabio, the drink had screwed up my head. I could hardly help others when I was in dire need of aid myself. And since sobering up I'd had more pressing matters on my mind: divorce, staying sober, work, building a new life.

I thought about it while sitting in the wreck of a burnt-out car with Fabio at the foot of the block. In silence I brooded upon the old questions: How do I do it? Can any harm come of it? Is it spiritual, physical, psychological? Did I really help Drake or had I just driven the demons deep for a while?

Fabio sighed eventually and patted me on the back. 'You ain't lost your touch, Algeria. You were smooth back there. Way quicker than you were last time I called you out.'

I grunted, recalling the hours I'd spent on his last 'customer', another of his street maidens, a young woman who'd been in and out of mental hospitals her entire life. I was still drinking at the time. I seemed to help her, but a few months later she plunged to her death in the river.

'Thinking about Cassie?' he asked, reading it in my eyes. 'That wasn't your fault. She was messed up bad. If anybody was in the wrong, it was me, for letting you at her in the state you were in.'

'Think I could have saved her if she'd been here today?'

He shrugged. 'Who knows? A kid like Drake hasn't had time to let the pain sink deep. Different when a sufferer's older and the trouble ain't so easily identifiable. You tried. That's the most any of us can do.'

I stared up through the fire-eroded roof, letting the sun warm some energy back into me.

'Feel good?' Fabio asked.

'Yeah. Tired, but good.'

'You should do it more often.'

I smiled. 'Hire a tent? Pin a bible to my forehead? Go out into the world and cure the masses? Earn a fortune?'

'That ain't what I'm talking about. You got a real honest-to-God talent, Algeria. It's a sin to waste it, working for the Cardinal, staining your hands with blood when you could be using them to heal. It ain't right and you know it.'

'I couldn't do this full time, Fabio. It's nice to come over here every so often, do a good deed and go back feeling like the man who broke the bank at Monte Carlo, but the Troops are my living. I fit in there. It's where I belong.'

'A man of healing don't belong nowhere but among those who need him,' Fabio sniffed righteously. 'You should be helping people live, not killing them.'

'I don't kill many,' I replied lowly.

'Makes no difference. You got a calling. You're special. I'm no holier-than-thou missionary: I've killed in my time, yes I have, and I ain't proud of it, but I'd do it again. But you . . .' He shook his head and gazed out the side window. 'I'm wasting my breath, ain't I?'

'What you say is right,' I admitted, 'but this is the path I've chosen. This is where I landed, where I am.'

'OK. I'll shut up about it.' He turned and studied me seriously. 'How's life otherwise? Get over the shock of finding your woman in the Fridge yet?'

I shook my head, bemused. 'How'd you know about that?'

'I pick things up.' He wasn't boasting. Fabio was as close to the heartbeat of this city as anyone I knew. I decided, since he'd mentioned it, to ask a few questions. There was no telling what I might pick up from an old gossipmonger like Fabio.

'Any idea who killed her?'

'Word is it was a crazy, maybe from out of town. A john she picked up somewhere and – '

'A *john*? She was on the game?'

'You didn't know?'

'No.' Saying it weakly. Stunned.

'Well, she wasn't a regular. And she kept it quiet. Nobody would have known, except sometimes she'd ball a guy in an alley or take him back to her apartment or a fancy hotel, and he'd talk, bragging the way you do when you're young.'

'Nic was a *hooker*?'

'An amateur. That could be another angle: she might have tricked where she shouldn't, or rubbed a pimp up the wrong way. But word of that would've spread by now. My money's on the john.'

This was news to me. Nicola being on the game changed everything. I'd been looking for old boyfriends when it seemed I should have been scouring the streets for *clients*. According to the file none of her known ex-beaus were the killing kind, and Priscilla had told me she suspected none of them, but a *john* . . .

'Did you know any of her clients?' I asked.

'A couple, but they're both in the clear: I did a bit of checking. As for the rest, I haven't a clue. I never heard of her going with the same john twice. You can ask about if you like but I doubt you'll unearth anything. Your best bet is to have a chat with a bitch called Priscilla Perdue. They used to – '

He stopped when he saw my face falling.

'Know her?'

'I had a drink with her last night.'

'How come?'

'I didn't know Nic very well. I've been trying to put together a clearer picture of her. It seems important, now that she's gone.'

'Uh-huh.' If he guessed I was lying, he kept his suspicions under wraps. 'That Perdue's a nasty piece of work, ain't she?'

'She seemed sweet enough.' I hastened to her defence. Then I remembered the Ku Klux Klub. 'A little rough round the edges maybe.'

'She ain't got no edges,' Fabio chuckled. 'She's sharp all over, like a porcupine.'

'She said nothing to me about Nic being a hooker. Is she one too?'

Fabio shrugged. 'She takes money sometimes, but I think it's the fucking she's more interested in. She's a strange bitch. Used to dress spooky a few years back, all in black, holes in the skirts around her rose bush, so everyone could see. Walked about with her tail in the air, like those posh-ass cats in the Pepe Le Pew cartoons.'

'She and Nic hung out?'

'Not a lot, but they scored together a few times, which was odd: Nic normally worked alone. That's why I reckon you should check her out if you're as serious about this as you seem.'

'Think she had anything to do with the murder?'

He thought about it at length before answering. 'It wouldn't *surprise* me, but it's not something I'd assume. She's spooky, like I said, but as far as I know she's never been into anything other than good old-fashioned sleaze.'

'But you think I should quiz her about Nic?'

'If you're looking for names of clients. She mightn't have them – I don't know how close the two were – but if she don't, nobody I can think of has.'

We chatted a bit more about the two girls – he had no further revelations to make – then about life in general. He asked how I was getting on at Party Central and – since he didn't seem to know I'd been reassigned – I said everything was fine. I started to ask after old friends but then noticed the time and said I had to run: I'd a meeting with the Cardinal to prepare for (though I kept that, like my reasons for asking about Nic, to myself).

Fabio told me not to be such a stranger, to call again soon for a proper chat. I said I would but we both knew it was an idle promise. I asked him to keep me appraised of Drake's progress and to let me know if the nightmares returned. We parted with a handshake and a few words of farewell, then I was on my way to Party Central for my showdown with the Cardinal.

The Cardinal was seated by the window when I entered, playing with a puppet, looking pensive. When he spotted my reflection in the glass he turned and brightened.

'Mr Jeery!' he boomed. 'If you've cracked the case already, I'll be indescribably impressed.'

'Afraid not,' I grinned ruefully. 'I've made inroads but that's not why I'm here. There's a problem . . .'

I told him about my meetings with Nick, Ziegler and Priscilla, the descriptions of Nic's companion which each had presented me with, and my belief that this man was

Paucar Wami. He listened silently, his face a mask of uncertain lines.

'You've been busy,' he grunted when I finished, carefully laying aside the puppet.

'I thought I should tell you about him before I went any further.'

'You did right.' He began biting the nails of his right hand. 'Tell me what else you're discovered about her.'

I went through the past three days as fully as possible. I told him about Nic's secret life as a lady of the night, and her connection with Priscilla Perdue; about Ziegler, his sun symbols and pretending not to know Priscilla. He took it in, saying nothing, letting me tell it my own way.

'You think she may have been a sacrificial lamb to the god of the sun?' he asked at the end.

'I wouldn't rule it out, but it was probably just camouflage: she told Ziegler that Wami was her demon lover; he knew that and may have carved the sun symbol into her back to switch the finger of guilt to the medium.'

'You believe Ziegler's innocent?'

'I thought he might be involved when Priscilla lied to me about knowing him – it suggested some sinister link between the trio – but now that I know about Nic and Priscilla's sexual escapades I'm not so sure. Priscilla may have had ulterior motives for keeping quiet about him.'

'Such as?'

'He might have known about her and Nic. She could have been trying to steer me away from the true extent of her dealings with Nic, not her involvement with Ziegler.'

'So prostitution is your strongest angle: you think she was killed by a customer?'

'If it wasn't Wami, my vote goes to the anonymous john.'

He nodded slowly, then said: 'It *wasn't* Wami.'

'Oh?' I didn't dare say more.

'You're forgetting the way she was killed: the messy slashes. The experts say it was the work of an amateur.'

'That could have been a red herring,' I suggested. 'He mightn't have wanted to be linked to the death. It may have been intended to throw us off the scent.'

The Cardinal smiled. 'You know nothing about Paucar Wami. He has killed under many guises in his time, but never pretended to be anything other than a cold-hearted professional. He takes pride in his work and fears no one. He would never purposefully spoil the beauty of a kill.'

'You think killing's beautiful?' I kept a neutral tone.

'I can take or leave it, as needs dictate. But to Wami it's an art form. He has made death his life's study. It's all that interests him. Murdering in this fashion would be entirely out of character.'

I shifted on my feet – he hadn't asked me to sit – and cleared my throat. 'Sir, you're correct when you say I don't know anything about Paucar Wami. But I know he's a killer. And I know he – or somebody fitting his description – was seen with Nic in the weeks prior to her death. In the absence of any other concrete suspect, I think it would be lunacy to – '

'Are you calling me a lunatic, Mr Jeery?' the Cardinal asked. He didn't seem insulted, merely curious.

'No, sir,' I checked. 'Of course not. But I think we should explore this. If he's out of town, we can cross him off our list. But if he's here and he *was* the one she was seen with . . .'

The Cardinal was silent a while. When he spoke, it was over his fingernails, and only barely audible. 'Wami *is* here. He took out a punk called Johnny Grace a couple of days ago.'

I rolled forward onto the balls of my toes as though to breathe in the fumes of proof. 'That's for certain?'

'Yes.'

I wanted to shout, 'There! You see!' but didn't. Instead I held my tongue and let the Cardinal draw the conclusions himself. After several minutes of silent brooding, he spoke.

'If Wami is the killer – and, regardless of the evidence, I still harbour strenuous doubts – we must tread carefully. He's not a man to cross. I'd like to know his reasons for killing Nicola Hornyak, and why he chose the Skylight, but I won't push for an explanation. Knowing it was him would be answer enough.'

I phrased my next question as cautiously as possible. 'Do you need *me* to unmask him? I know you've had dealings with Wami in the past. Couldn't you get in contact and . . . ?'

The Cardinal's face darkened. 'Are you telling me how to run my investigation?' he snapped.

'No, sir, I was just – '

'Just nothing!' he roared. 'If I wanted to ring Wami I'd ring him. I don't need a flunkey like you telling me – ' He cut himself short. I stood quivering before him, fearing for my future. After a few seconds of seething silence, he grinned wickedly. 'Stop shaking. I'm not going to eat you.'

'Could I have that in writing, sir?'

His grin spread. 'I like you, Jeery. We'll get along fine if you don't tell me what to do. I've never been much of a one for taking orders, even if they're in the form of polite suggestions.

'I *could* contact Paucar Wami and put the question to him myself.' He paused. 'But I won't. That would be cheating.'

'Cheating who, sir, if you don't mind my asking?'

'Thee and me, Mr Jeery. I promised you a chance to make a name for yourself. It wouldn't be fair to deny you after you've made such an impressive start.'

'I wouldn't mind,' I hastily interjected.

He laughed throatily. 'Besides, I'd also be cheating

myself out of a ripping good show. It's skewed drama of this nature which renews my faith in life, Mr Jeery. I'm a man of low tolerance. Ordinary diversions bore me: alcohol, drugs, books, gambling, women: all are wasted on me.

'Do you know what keeps me going, Mr Jeery? People out of their depth. I thrive on it.'

'Some call that sadism.' A potentially perilous answer but he took it in his stride.

'I? A sadist?' He dismissed the notion with a curt snort. 'Sadists enjoy watching people suffer. I prefer to see people triumph, or at least put up a good fight as they go down. The thought of a confrontation between you and Paucar Wami fascinates me. How will you react if faced with him? What will you say? If he threatens your life, will you run or stand up to him?'

'No doubt about it,' I said. 'I'll run.'

'I don't think so,' the Cardinal smiled. 'That's why I chose you for this investigation. Not because I knew about Wami's possible involvement but because I sensed situations of this nature might develop, situations which would exhaust a normal man but which one of your resolve and resources might endeavour to surmount.'

'What resolve and resources? I don't have any!'

'You sell yourself short,' he contradicted me.

He could be an infuriating son of a bitch when he wanted. How can you argue with a man who's full of praise for you?

'What happens now?' I asked. 'I go after Wami, he kills me, you look for a new source of entertainment?'

'Possibly,' the Cardinal nodded. 'Though it needn't pan out that way. I still think we should grant Wami the benefit of the doubt. If you approach him diplomatically, you might emerge from the encounter unscathed. Plus, if he is the killer, I won't demand his head, just proof. If you can pin him to the scene of the crime without confronting or antagonising him, all the better.'

'If I made a formal request to be transferred – '

' – I would turn it down.'

I put on a brave front. 'And if I quit?'

'Resign from the Troops?' The Cardinal stroked his nose thoughtfully. 'That would be disappointing,' he murmured.

'Would you punish me?'

'No. You wouldn't be worth it. I'd wonder how I'd misjudged a man so badly, then dismiss you from my thoughts and leave you to eke out your worthless, shameful excuse of a life.'

'Who gave you the right to pass moral judgement?' I snapped.

'Nobody gave it,' he replied coolly. 'I took it.' When I looked away, disgusted, he slid into his sympathetic mode. 'What you must understand, Mr Jeery, is that I am just a spectator. I set the ball rolling, true, but that's where my input ends. It's not *me* you stand to fail: it's *yourself.* Think back over these last few days: hasn't it felt good to be out on your own, making decisions, following your instinct, homing in on the truth?'

I nodded slowly. 'I've enjoyed it more than I thought.'

'Because this is what you were meant for,' he said. 'Not so much the investigating, rather the use of your mind. You are one of those rare beings with the power to create your own destiny. I'm trying to free you. That's not my main motive – the game appeals to me the most – but that's what's in it for you. All I get out of this is amusement; you can gain *freedom.*'

'You're the original Good Samaritan, aren't you?' I grumbled.

'More the genie of the lamp,' he answered earnestly. 'I can make dreams come true – but at a price.'

'What's *my* price?' I asked.

He shrugged. 'That's the thing: you never know until you wish.'

'If I stick with it,' I spoke my thoughts aloud, 'what will be the next step?'

'Locate Wami. Reconstruct his movements on the night of the murder. Explore his relationship with Miss Hornyak. If you can arrange a personal audience it will be easy to ascertain whether he is guilty or not: Paucar Wami does not lie.'

'Never?'

'About killing, no.'

'A killer with a code of ethics. Cute.'

'It's ego, not ethics. He can afford honesty since he lacks fear. He speaks the truth because it can't hurt him: those who would seek to use his words against him are easily eliminated.'

'If he killed Nic, and tells me about it, will he kill me too?'

'If he thinks you'll become a nuisance, yes.'

The Cardinal's honesty was refreshing but unsettling. I decided to meet it with some of my own. 'How much cooperation can I expect if I go after him? You've been protecting Paucar Wami for decades, keeping his name out of the media, quashing reports, quelling gossip. Are there files on him?'

'None that are accessible. We have an understanding: I keep tabs on him but keep them to myself; in return, he doesn't kill me.'

'Wami couldn't get to *you*, could he?' I asked.

'Paucar Wami can get to anyone he likes,' the Cardinal answered evenly. 'Only the dead are beyond his reach. Any man who thinks differently is a fool, and Mama Dorak raised no fools.' That was his real name, Ferdinand Dorak, though it was rarely used.

I hesitated, not wishing to capitulate without the

semblance of a struggle. I asked more questions about Wami, which he blatantly deflected. He even refused to give me a full description, revealing no more than I already knew: that Wami was tall, dark, bald and tattooed. I requested photographs, fingerprints, contact names, past addresses: all denied.

Eventually he checked the time and said I'd have to leave: he had two more scheduled meetings; business couldn't grind to a halt on my account. He needed a decision: was I on the case or not?

I should have backed out. I could sense the stakes mounting and had a feeling I was getting in over my head. Wami wouldn't be as easy to find or talk to as Nick, Ziegler or Priscilla. This was my chance to cut my losses and run. Tuck my tail between my legs and slink out like a skunk.

And I would have, pride be damned, if not for the Cardinal's slyly raised eyebrows. He *expected* me to back out. Provoked by that look, determined not to gratify the smug son of a bitch, I stuck out my hand, took the Cardinal's, looked him square in the eye and stated as pompously as possible: 'Mr Dorak, I'm your man.'

9

I reported to Party Central first thing Monday morning
and spent hours locked away in the vaults of the upper
floors, trying to make sense of the phenomenon which
went by the name of Paucar Wami.

He was one of the city's most vivid yet oddly muted
legends. I'd heard rumours of his monstrous deeds while
growing up and, for a long time, that's what I thought he
was: a fairy-tale monster. I didn't believe such a clinically
precise assassin could exist outside of fiction. I wrote him off
as a bogeyman and it wasn't until I joined the Troops that I
realised he was more than a series of fabricated stories.

Yet even to the Troops he was a mythical shadow, rarely
seen, never openly acknowledged or discussed. New
recruits learned – unofficially, by word of mouth – never
to mess with Wami. If you spotted him lurking around
Party Central, you let him pass. If you encountered him
while on duty, you turned a blind eye. He was to be treated
like the invisible man.

Yet it was only when I went looking for him in the files
that I began to understand how low-profile he actually
was. He'd been around since the tail-end of the seventies,
murdering dozens, sometimes hundreds a year. The
records should have been bulging with mentions of his
name. But . . .

There was no trace of him. His name was absent from all the newspapers and police reports that I had access to. No birth certificate. No school or college statistics. He'd never paid taxes. Wasn't listed on medical forms. Owned no property, at least not under his own name. No cars or guns registered to him.

In the course of my investigation I noticed entries which had been tampered with. It wasn't the first time I'd encountered such criminal reappraisal. The Cardinal liked to write the history of the city his way, regardless of the facts. If that meant altering headlines and articles in the newspaper archives – to remove the name of a patsy from print, for example, to make it look like he never existed – so be it. If fresh video footage had to be shot to replace visually recorded events, his technicians – many were first-class graduates of the film industry – shot it.

There must be a huge mother of a file on Wami somewhere, but locating it proved impossible. As far as the accessible data went, Wami was a ghost. After several frustrating hours I accepted this crazy fact, abandoned the computers and dusty old files, and went looking for the truth on the streets.

I had a widespread network of informal contacts, and though many knew nothing of the killer or refused to talk if they did, I found plenty of people willing to swap Wami tales with me, usually in return for a round of drinks. The difficulty was separating the truth from invention. The thing about Wami was, he'd pulled off so many incredible stunts, it was possible to believe anything about him. Normally, if someone spun a yarn about a lone assassin wiping out a twelve-strong Triad faction with his bare fists, I'd dismiss it. But I knew the Triad story was true because I'd been on mopping-up duty that night.

Some of the tales were obviously false: those which

claimed he could move at superhuman speeds, lift cars above his head and scale glassy walls like a spider, breathe fire and disappear into clouds of smoke, not bleed when cut. But most, far-fetched as they might seem, were plausible; if not true, then based on a kernel of truth.

For all the larger-than-life accounts, I was no wiser at the end of the evening than I'd been at the start. I'd learned much about his methods, targets and noms de plumes – he was known by many names, some of which I jotted down to check on later – but nothing about the *man*, where he came from or what motivated him or how one tracked him down. He had no cronies. There was no known procedure for hiring him. Nobody had a photo of him or an address or a phone number. He seemed to be without relatives and friends and a past.

I put out a few feelers, asking to be notified if he was spotted or if anybody unearthed pertinent facts about his whereabouts, movements or history. I made fancy promises – mostly of the financial variety, though in some instances I pledged drugs, women or weapons in exchange for information – which I hoped I'd be able to honour if I had to: the Cardinal had told me to feel free when it came to dipping in his coffers, but would he feel so benevolent if I splashed his money about like it was going out of fashion?

Having taken the first steps towards locating the famed killer, I decided I'd had enough of Paucar Wami for one day. It was time to explore other angles. Time to talk to the staff at the Skylight.

The manager was out when I arrived but the assistant manager recognised my name from a circular which had been doing the rounds over the weekend. He placed himself at my disposal and said I'd been cleared to speak to whomever I wished. If anyone refused to cooperate, I was to refer them to him and he'd sort things out.

I spent the afternoon casing the hotel, talking to all the staff I could find. I learnt nothing. They hadn't seen anyone suspicious lurking in the corridors of the eighth floor, and only a lone receptionist remembered seeing Nic the night of her death. Even the Troops who guarded the doors and fire escapes were no help. I hadn't expected them to be: the brief was different for Troops assigned to the Skylight. At Party Central we were expected to note faces and question the presence of all who entered. Here, the Troops were under orders to concentrate on visual body-searches, only to take an interest in someone if they spotted a hidden weapon. The Skylight was not a fortress. Guests were supposed to feel at ease.

One person objected to my questioning: the maid who'd discovered Nic's body: Valerie Thomas. She was a big woman, plain ugly, with a disdainful streak the width of a river. She was doing her chores when I caught up with her and refused to pause. I had to chase her about from room to room while we talked.

'She was dead when you found her?' I asked.

'She wasn't doing no dancing,' she snorted.

'I mean *completely* dead? The coroners put the time of death very close to when the body was found. It's possible she might have been alive when you entered. Did you check?'

'You know what I did,' she said. 'I saw the body, I got a shock, I screamed. I didn't go anywhere near it.'

She didn't strike me as the screaming kind.

'You're sure? Some people might feel compelled to check for a pulse, or just hang around and stare. If you *did* look at her or touch her, it's nothing to be ashamed of.'

'I opened the door,' she said. 'I saw the body. I screamed. I didn't go near it.'

She could have sung her testimony: there was a rehearsed quality about it.

'You saw nothing else? On the floor or bed?'

'Just the knife.'

'Nothing else?'

'No.'

'No jewellery, money, anything like that?'

She stopped and stared at me. 'If I'd seen anything else, it'd be in there.' She nodded towards my notebook, which I was lugging about like a security blanket.

'Unless you took it,' I said quietly.

Her eyes narrowed. 'What are you implying?' she hissed. 'Are you accusing me of theft? I don't have to take that shit.'

'I didn't mean any offence,' I hastily assured her. 'It's just, if I saw something on the floor, a diamond necklace or a roll of money, and it was lying there, easy pickings, nobody about, I'd – '

'I *saw* nothing,' she snapped. 'I *picked up* nothing. I'm clean. Ask the boss. I haven't stolen a thing, ever. Even if a guest has checked out and left it behind. I hand in lost property. You ask. I'm clean. I saw and took *nothing*. You accuse me of theft again, I'll throw this bucket of water in your face.'

'Ma'am, I'm sorry. But there's a dead girl involved and – '

'I know who's involved. I found her.'

I took a deep breath and ate humble pie. 'Good day, Mrs Thomas,' I said, offering my hand, which she ignored. 'Thanks for your time.'

'Piss off,' she replied curtly. So I did.

I called into 812 in the course of my rounds. The room where Nic had been butchered. It was no different to any of the other rooms but it felt colder, emptier. I circled the neatly made bed, imagining Nic tied to it – her hands and legs had been bound – gagged, struggling, screaming silently as her life was cut out of her. It had been slow, painful, clumsy. It must have been awful.

Could I have saved her if I'd been in town? Had she favoured me with her company in return for protection, as the Cardinal had suggested? Perhaps she'd been ringing my mobile while I was motoring out of the city with Bill, getting no answer because I'd left it behind. Maybe, in her panic, she forgot I was away for the weekend and spent her last tortured hours wondering where I was and why I wasn't riding to her rescue.

Then again, maybe I was the furthest thing from her mind. Perhaps there had been no deeper motive: she may have just picked me up for sex. Either way, I'd probably never know. She was gone, and all her reasons and answers with her.

I mentioned Valerie Thomas's gruffness to the manager, Terry Archer, who turned up towards the end of my enquiries, and asked if there was anything suspicious about her demeanour. He shook his head.

'She's been like that since the day she started. Even speaks to *me* that way. But she's a good worker so I leave her be. I'll take a rude workhorse over a polite layabout any day.'

'Might she have taken something from the room?'

'It would be completely out of character if she did.' We were in Terry's office. He leant back in a thick leather chair and yawned. 'Beg pardon. This murder's played havoc with my schedule. I spent the weekend shacked up here, dealing with irate policemen, trying to keep the peace between them and the Troops.'

I smiled. We were forever in conflict of one kind or another with the cops. It irked them to play second fiddle to a band of renegade mercenaries. They loved any excuse to barge in and read the riot act.

'Find out anything?' Terry asked.

'No. I thought somebody might have recognised her, but . . .'

'Hundreds of customers pass through the Skylight every day,' he sympathised, 'and those are only the official guests. More use the restaurant, bars and function rooms. If somebody doesn't want to be noticed, they usually aren't.'

'What did the police make of it?'

'At first they reckoned she'd tagged along with a one-night stand. Then they discovered she was a sometimes prostitute – you knew that?' – I nodded – 'and decided it was a customer she'd either brought back or met in the hotel.' He didn't seem too gone on the theory.

'You don't agree?'

'The Skylight has its share of night-walkers, same as hotels the world over. But it's a closed shop. Unwanted competition is harshly dealt with by those who've staked their patch. Even a part-time, amateur prostitute knows better than to bring a trick back here.'

'Maybe that's what happened; one of the regulars took umbrage and . . .' He was shaking his head before I could finish.

'I wouldn't put some of them above it, but they wouldn't do it here. You don't kill on the Cardinal's turf. They'd have taken her elsewhere.'

'Perhaps she *was* a regular,' I suggested. 'Maybe this wasn't the first time she'd used the Skylight. Have you any way of checking?'

Terry reached into a drawer, produced a slim purple file and tossed it across. I opened it to discover a long list of names, both male and female.

'The regulars?' I guessed.

'Every hooker's name goes in there,' Terry said. 'Even those who only use our rooms once in a blue moon.'

'They let you tag them?' I asked, scanning the names.

'It works to their advantage. Those on the list aren't troubled by security. Tidy room discounts. The first to be called when a guest requests company.'

'What if one of them – '

I stopped. The file contained close to twenty sheets, not just names, but phone numbers, contacts, sexual specialities, background details, medical histories, even photographs. Near the bottom of the sixth sheet was a name which jumped out at me.

Priscilla Perdue.

Terry leant over the table, craning his neck to read the name. 'Priscilla Perdue,' he muttered, thinking hard. 'A blonde. Very upmarket. Has a thing for women. Yes?'

'A thing for women?' I repeated.

'I believe so. It doesn't say here but I think it's mostly those of the fairer sex she swings for.'

'Does she use the Skylight often?'

'Once or twice a month perhaps. You usually know when she's about: unlike many of our professionals, she's loud. Blazes in, customer in tow, acting like a movie queen. In fact,' he frowned, 'we're not sure if she's on the game or not – word is she doesn't charge – but we put her on the list all the same. Better safe than sorry.'

'Do you have a photo of her?'

'No, but I can get one if you'd like.'

'Please.'

I read the brief profile while Terry faxed for a photo. There was nothing there I didn't already know: height, weight, measurements, place of work. Even the photo, when it came, was familiar: one of the poorer shots from the file in Party Central.

'Mind if I quiz some of your staff again?' I asked.

'Quiz away,' Terry said. 'Tip me off if you learn anything: I love being in the know.'

An hour later, I left the Skylight in a daze, stunned by what I'd uncovered. I didn't tell Terry. It was best to keep something like this quiet, at least until I'd had time to mull it over by myself.

Plenty of the staff recognised Priscilla from the photo but it was the response of three in particular – a receptionist, a barman and a waitress in the ground-floor bar – which set my head spinning. All had ID'd her and then, in answer to my second question, 'When did you last see her?', replied:

'The Friday before last. She checked in by herself. Quieter than usual. Less flamboyant. But it was definitely her.'

'Last Friday week. Ordered a pina colada. Took it to a table in a corner. Nobody with her that I saw.'

'Friday, I think. Not this one: a week further back. I collected her glass after she'd left. She barely touched it. She was on her own most of the time, but I think I recall seeing somebody drop by her table for a minute or so, not long before she left.'

The Friday before last. The night of death.

Priscilla had been in the Skylight when Nic was killed.

10

Nic's funeral was the next day. I'd been in two minds about whether or not I should go but on the morning I decided I couldn't miss it. I wasn't much of a funeral connoisseur – hadn't been to any since my mother's – but this was different: it was business.

There was a police cordon outside the crematorium to keep back the press and spectators, and only her closest relatives and friends were being admitted. My name wasn't on the official list and the cop on duty refused to admit me or pass on my name to any of the mourners inside for verification.

A quick call to Bill fixed that. I put him on to the cop, the two exchanged quiet words, the cop nodded a few times, smiled, lifted the barrier and waved me through, handing back the mobile as I passed.

'If anybody objects,' he told me, 'you'll have to leave.'

'OK.'

'Don't create a scene. If I have to go in and drag you out, it'll look bad, both for me *and* Bill Casey.'

'I understand,' I said, slipping him a crisp token of my appreciation.

The small funeral parlour was nine-tenths empty. It was almost time for the ceremony yet I counted no more than fourteen heads, most of them unfamiliar. Nick was up front, expressionless, dressed as soberly as a judge. Priscilla Perdue was beside him, weeping into a handkerchief, sporadically clutching the hands of a woman I didn't recognise to her left, pressing them to her cheeks or lips, smiling bravely.

Rudi Ziegler was seated near the rear of the room. He was weeping loudly, hands on knees, letting the tears course down his face unchecked. Nearly everybody was sobbing, except me and Nick. I didn't cry because it would have been hypocritical: I hadn't known her that well and her death had left me feeling more aggrieved than grief-stricken. What was Nick's excuse?

Nic rested in a rainbow-hued coffin, moulded out of some kind of plastic. It lay parallel to the altar, which – as far as I knew – was unusual: I thought it was standard practice for the dead to be facing head-on. The top quarter of the coffin was transparent, so we could see Nic's head and shoulders. She was a beautiful corpse, reposed and serene as only the dead can be. Her face had been left unmarked by her assailant and I couldn't stare at it for long without getting a lump in my cynical old throat.

I got a shock when the priest emerged: it was Elvis Presley! Quiff and sideburns, wiggling hips, flares, loud suit, the lot. Most of the mourners split into brief smiles when they saw him striding to the head of the coffin. Obviously this was an in-joke I wasn't privy to.

He gave a nice speech. Said Nic hadn't been especially religious, but hadn't been a stranger to church either. She had been a young, beautiful, life-loving creature, who'd struck him as a deep, honest, thoughtful being, with far more to her character than the frivolous front she liked to adopt.

He said this was how Nic had wanted to go, with lots of colour and a touch of merry madness. If she was looking on now, he hoped she was enjoying the show. 'This one's for you, Nic,' he mumbled in his best Elvis impersonation, then launched into 'Heartbreak Hotel', a cruel choice, in my opinion, given the circumstances of her death.

As he gyrated his way to a conclusion two of his assistants – both dressed as seventies glam rockers – emerged from the sides and loaded the coffin onto a conveyor belt. Elvis stood to attention and crooned, 'Glory, glory, hallelujah,' slipping off into the shadows as he sang. Somebody threw an unseen lever and the coffin glided backwards; Nic's final journey.

Rudi Ziegler howled aloud at that point, stumbled to his feet and brushed past me, lurching for the exit, sobbing pitifully like an old drama queen.

A few of the mourners glanced over their shoulders to see what the commotion was. Priscilla was one of the curious. She spotted me and tilted her head quizzically, then smiled weakly and mouthed the words, 'See you after?' I nodded. The coffin began to disappear through the curtains and she diverted her gaze, took Nick's hands and squeezed hard. He still hadn't shed any tears, though he looked shakier than before.

I ducked out before the finale. I'd seen enough. I knew what would happen behind the curtains – the body would be taken from the coffin, incinerated, the bones fed into a machine to be ground into ash – but what would they do with the coffin? Respray and use it again? Give it to Nick to take home? I could have asked one of Elvis's assistants, who had come out ahead of the mourners and was now scattering large scented flowers along the hall floor, but I wasn't that desperate to know.

The mourners began to file out, turning left as they came, following the path of flowers. I stood to the right of the door, military stance, hands crossed in front of my abdomen, head bowed as a mark of respect. Most of the small band ignored me but one old man paused and half-turned. I started to raise a hand and smile, then saw his blank white eyes and realised he was blind. I lowered the hand and coughed politely instead of smiling. His head twitched, then he nodded, as if to acknowledge my presence. Faced away, listened for the footsteps of the others, and strolled sedately along after them.

Nick and Priscilla came last. I was about to step forward to offer my condolences but she spotted me and shook her head: stand back. She led Nick along the corridor – he was walking mechanically, the only sign that he'd been affected by the service – handed him over to one of his friends, then backtracked.

'Thank you for coming,' she said, shaking my hand. 'Nic would have liked that.' Her eyes were red from tears. She was clad in a dark dress which would have sexily accentuated her curves any other time but now seemed to drag on her bones like a dirty cloth sack.

'I wasn't sure I'd be welcome,' I muttered.

'Of course you're welcome.' She dabbed at her eyes with her handkerchief. 'I just didn't want Nick to see you: he's been bottling his emotions in and I think he's looking for an excuse to let fly. He might have gone for you, since there's no one else for him to attack.'

'What was with the Elvis routine?' I asked.

Priscilla smiled in spite of her grief. 'Nic loved Elvis. This was what she would have wanted. She hated pomp.'

'Who chose the song?'

She winced. 'I did. It was Nic's favourite. I only realised how inappropriate it was when he started singing: it just hadn't occurred to me till then. I could have sunk through the floor. Do you think anyone was miffed?'

'They seemed to take it in their stride.'

She glanced up the corridor. Nick had disappeared from sight. 'I'd better head after him. He's arranged a wake back at the family home. Invited a load of friends, most of whom hardly knew Nic. It'll develop into an orgy if there's nobody sensible at hand to control things. Want to come?' I shook my head. 'You can if you like. Nick will have calmed down after a couple of stiff drinks.'

'Thanks but I'd feel out of place. I prefer saying my farewells in private.'

'If you're sure . . .' She started away.

'Could we get together soon?' I asked. 'Dinner? A drink? There are some questions I'd like to ask.'

'Of course. Not tonight, though. How about tomorrow?'

'Great.' I hesitated. 'You weren't thinking of taking me to the Kool Kats Klub again, were you?'

She had the good grace to blush. 'I apologised for that already. How about Cafran's? Know it?'

'I can find it. Seven?'

'Seven's fine.'

She brushed my cheeks with her lips and departed.

I stood there a few minutes, letting her coast out of sight, then slowly followed. Outside the mourners were getting into their cars. I looked around for the blind man, wondering who he was leaving with, but couldn't locate him. A journalist moved in to take a photo of me but the cop who'd barred my way earlier stepped in front of him, had a few words in his ear and sent him packing.

'Didn't think you'd want your picture in the papers,' he said.

'You were right. Thanks.'

'Don't mention it. It's my neck too: I'd have had to explain to my superiors what you were doing here.' His eyebrows lifted. Looking over my shoulder I saw Elvis emerging, peeling off his sideburns. 'One of the mourners?' the cop asked.

'No. That's the priest.' He checked to see if I was pulling his leg. Giggled when he realised I was serious.

'Wish I could have been there. Did he sing?'

'Like a bird.' I asked to see the list of mourners. Quickly jotted down the names for future reference. Frowned and re-counted. 'There's only thirteen here.'

'That's right.'

'But there were fourteen at the service.'

'Including you, yes.'

'I mean without me.' I thought about the blind man and asked if the cop had noticed him.

'No. And I checked everyone through.'

'Could he have entered any other way?'

'I can check with the guys on the other doors if you want. Most likely he was from another party and got lost, or else he's a professional mourner.'

'A professional?'

'There's always a few hanging around. They drift from funeral to funeral, looking for handouts. Want me to look into it?'

'Don't bother. It's not important.' I tucked my notebook away, thanked him for his help, took one last glance at the palace of the dead, shivered as I spotted a stream of smoke rising in the still air overhead, then turned my back on the crematorium and hurried away.

I'd meant to chase Wami's ghost again after the funeral but couldn't rid myself of the image of Nic writhing inside the oven – or whatever it is they use to burn the bodies – flames creeping over her flesh, consuming her whole. I wouldn't be able to keep my mind on my work, so I put it to one side for the day and headed for the Fridge to pay a belated call on another member of the unto-infinity club.

A girl called Velouria noted my request, checked my credentials, then tapped the name into a computer: Tom Jeery. It came up blank. 'When was he left here?' she asked.

'I don't know the exact date. Early to mid-eighties.'

'Then he probably wouldn't be on file.' She keyed out of the screen and rose. 'We can't transfer names across without permission: the system's too easy to hack into. We only started putting them on disc in the late nineties, checking whether we should or not as each new inhabitant was brought in. Never bothered backdating: too much hassle trying to track down relatives or connected personnel.'

'You're saying you can't find him?'

'Of course we can,' she sniffed, 'unless he was entered as a John Doe. But it'll take a while: without a precise date I'll have to go through a load of entry books. Do you want to leave it with me and come back?'

'I'll wait,' I told her, and settled into one of the uncomfortable plastic reception chairs.

I wasn't sure what I hoped to gain by the visit. I'd hardly ever dropped by my mother's grave, and I'd loved *her*. Maybe I hoped to unleash a flood of memories when faced with his tomb: though my father hadn't spent much time around the house when I was growing up, I was sure I must be harbouring more memories of him than the meagre few I was currently aware of.

Several doctors and assistants passed by as I was waiting, barely glancing at me. So I was surprised when one stopped and addressed me warmly.

'Lost another girlfriend?'

I didn't recognise the grinning doctor when I looked up, but had him placed within the few seconds it took to rise and take his hand. 'Dr Sines.'

'Bit of a shock last time you were here,' he chuckled. 'Recover yet?'

'Just about. They cremated her today.'

'Oh?' He didn't seem overly interested. 'They normally hold on to the body for longer in cases such as these. She must have had relatives with connections.'

An impatient colleague of the doctor, who'd been marching with him, had stopped further along and now asked Sines if he was coming. Snappy, as though he had no intention of standing around waiting for him if he wasn't.

'In a minute,' Sines snapped back. 'So,' he said to me, 'find out where she was murdered?'

'Excuse me?'

'Nicola Hornyak. You're handling the investigation, aren't you?' I nodded wordlessly. 'So have you located the scene of the crime or are you still searching?'

'I don't understand. Nic was killed at the Skylight. Wasn't she?'

He laughed humourlessly. 'You haven't been keeping up to date, Jeery. From the subcutaneous particles we discovered – the dirt in her cuts – she couldn't have been killed in the Skylight. She *died* there, but the wounds were inflicted earlier, possibly on a building site, judging by the amount of sand and industrial dust.'

I stared, boggle-eyed, as if he was growing a third head. 'Why the hell wasn't I informed?' I roared.

'Don't ask me. I passed our findings on, first thing Saturday morning. The state coroner reached the same conclusion, I hear, although he's been . . . ahem . . . *persuaded* not to go public with the data.'

'Who did you tell?' I asked, wishing I could throttle him.

'It was FMEO.'

'What?'

'For My Eyes Only. *My* being the Cardinal.'

'You told the Cardinal?'

'Yes.'

'Everything?'

'All that I've just told you. He mentioned your name and said he'd pass it along. Thanked me for my promptness. Asked me to keep it under my hat. Which I have.' He frowned. 'Until now. I assumed you knew. He said he was going to . . . You won't tell him I let it slip, will you?' Looking worried.

I shook my head slowly. 'Not if you'll keep me informed of any subsequent developments. Let me give you my number.' I scribbled it down on a piece of paper. Sines tucked it away without glancing at it.

'There's nothing else to tell,' he said. 'I faxed my full report to the Cardinal, but basically it was a long-winded version of what I've told you. The assault took place somewhere other than the hotel. Her assailant may have thought she was dead when he took her there: she can't have been too lively when she was dropped off. She died a few hours later, around the time her body was discovered.'

'And you think she may have been killed on a building site?'

'It's a strong possibility. Of course, it may have been in a garage or somebody's back-yard: the materials would have been present if the occupant was building a wall or putting on an extension or simply had them lying around from before.'

Velouria arrived back, smiling, holding a file to her chest. 'When you're ready, Mr Jeery,' she said.

'I have to go,' I told Sines.

'You're not the only one.'

'You'll ring me if anything new crops up?'

'It won't, but yes, if it does, I will.'

'Thanks.' I clapped him on the back. 'If you don't, I'll drop you in the shit with the Cardinal.'

'Charming.' He smiled icily, and went about his business.

'Ready?' Velouria asked.

'In a minute.' The news had knocked me soaring out of bounds. Nic hadn't been killed in the Skylight. What bearing did that have on the case? For starters, it seemed to rule out the single killer theory: the Troops guarding the hotel weren't the most alert in the organisation but they wouldn't fail to spot somebody dragging in a corpse, not unless someone else was distracting their attention at the time. Perhaps one of *them* had been in league with the killer: I'd have to check them out. And what of Priscilla? I knew she'd been in the lobby and restaurant the night of the murder, which had seemed to implicate her. But if Nic had been killed elsewhere . . .

I'd have to spend more time on this. I wasn't thinking clearly at the moment, so I pushed it to the back of my mind and left it there. I'd return to it later, in my apartment, after a good meal and a long shower, and try figuring things out.

I followed Velouria through the maze of coffin-lined corridors. My brain kept throwing Sines's words back at me but I came down hard on it, refusing to be drawn into the marsh of possibilities. I was here to pay my respects to my father. Nic could wait. There was more to life than the investigation.

The geology of the maze shifted subtly the further we progressed. The style of the containers changed: they were larger, rounded at the edges, some trellised; the stairways were made of metal, not the hard white plastic I was used to; there were fewer coffins per row – one or two even stood by themselves; flower-basket frames hung from hooks on the doors (though bouquets were scarce). Velouria noticed my interest and explained: this was the older section of the Fridge; the original designers had tried to inject a modicum of warmth, unaware of its true purpose. The current administrative team was planning to renovate in the near future – they could fit twenty per cent more bodies in once the coffins were streamlined to match the general design – but that would be a monster of a job, which nobody was looking forward to.

Velouria stopped at the second coffin of a row of six. They were stacked two-high here. My father's was the lower bunk. I stared at his name, embossed on a thin strip of metal. No file was attached. I enquired about this.

Velouria checked her notes. 'It wasn't intentionally omitted. The information on these older inmates is often sketchier than on more recent arrivals. Most were simply dumped, a name was left, sometimes a few brief details, sometimes not. We've probably got a file on him some-where. I can look it up for you if you want.'

'No. Thanks all the same.' I read the name again and cleared my throat. 'I'd like to be alone, if that's OK.'

'Sure. Want me to wait nearby or can you find your own way out?'

'I've a good sense of direction. You can leave.'

'All right. If you get lost – and, trust me, it's easier than you'd think – buzz for help and we'll send someone to find you.'

She left and I was alone. With my father.

I ran my fingers over the name and shivered as I thought ahead and realised that this could be me one day, locked away in one of these cramped cubicles, never visited, never disturbed. If I had children – not that I had any current plans along those lines – would they wind up standing here like I was, tracing my name with their fingers, wondering what their old man had been like? It was a depressing notion.

I stood around, waiting for memories to flood back, but they didn't. I resurrected my old snapshots of him but found nothing new. Maybe if I saw the body . . .

I didn't act on the thought straightaway. He'd been here a long time. The refrigeration process couldn't always be relied upon. The body might have decayed. I could find myself face to face with one of those rotting-flesh zombies that movie-makers are so fond of. The picture I had of Tom

Jeery was of a tall, strong and healthy man: did I want to risk replacing that with an image of a time-eaten corpse, sunken cheeks, exposed bones and a fetid stench?

Following lengthy quiet deliberation, I decided to peek. Though it hadn't been easy to look at Nic's face in the crematorium, I was glad I'd seen it: I had a final image of her to cling to, which drew a delineating line between the live and dead Nic. It did one good to look upon the faces of the dead.

I considered checking with Velouria before proceeding, but he was *my* father: if anyone had the right to open the coffin, it was me. I studied the door. Some of the newer models came equipped with computerised locks but this was a plain old spin-lock, no keys or codes required. I spun the wheel slowly. There was a crackle when the door opened, old ice shattering, then I felt the slab sliding forward a few centimetres of its own accord, before shuddering to a halt.

I wiped around my brow, took firm hold of the door, swung it back, grabbed the slab and tugged. It resisted, then came free and slid out smoothly, a wave of white icy gas rising from it, causing me to cough and avert my eyes. When I'd recovered, I leant into the misty fog, waving my hands, dispersing it. As it cleared, the slab came into focus and I held my breath, searching for my father's face.

The mist lifted. Only thin, wispy tendrils remained. And when they cleared . . .

Nothing. The coffin was empty.

I remained rooted to the spot for what seemed an age, wondering if my eyes were playing tricks, or if the body had slipped to the floor, or remained jammed inside. I bent over and peered in: there was nothing further back. Examined the floor: nothing. I checked the sides of the container for holes: solid as could be.

As I was withdrawing, a small object caught my eye and

I realised the slab wasn't entirely barren. A piece of paper occupied the space where my father should have been, neatly folded in half and resting on its edges. I picked it up and stepped away from the coffin, mind going in a thousand different directions all at once. I checked one more time for a corpse – as if I could have missed it! – then unfolded the paper with trembling fingers and read the three short, mystifying words printed in black across it: OUT TO LUNCH.

part three

'a severed human head'

Part Three

11

I spent the next few hours raising unholy hell. I summoned Velouria and her immediate superiors, along with one of the managing directors who happened to be present at the time. I ranted and raved. Made dire threats. Took out my gun at one stage and waved it over my head like an Indian shaking a tomahawk. Eventually they sent along my good buddy Dr Sines to calm me down. He tried leading me away to a quiet, secluded ante-room but I stood my ground: I had crazy thoughts of the body being replaced while I was absent.

'Bodies go missing all the time,' he sighed, sliding out a cigarette, offering me one – which I refused – and lighting up. The posse of doctors and nurses who'd gathered to watch the sparks fly was dispersing as he spoke. 'It's no big deal.'

'No big . . . ? He was my father!' I roared.

'A father – ' Sines noted, flicking through the file ' – you never visited or checked on until today.'

'I didn't know he was here,' I growled.

Sines couldn't have looked less sympathetic. 'If his own son wasn't interested in his whereabouts, you can't be too surprised that we weren't either.'

'You're paid to take an interest!'

'No,' he corrected me. 'We're paid to check bodies in and

stack them away. If we're told to care for a body and see that nothing happens to it, we do. Otherwise it's fair game.'

'Fair game for *who?*'

Sines asked if he could push in the slab and close the door of my father's tomb. I took one final look, put the note back and said he could. He made sure nobody was close enough to hear what he was going to say next. Satisfied we were alone, he continued in a lower tone.

'Any number of people could have made off with it. Your own lot for starters: the Troops. They come here every so often and cart a corpse or two away.'

'What for?'

'You'd have a better idea of that than me. Maybe they return them to their families, or sell off the body parts to the highest bidder. For all I know they could be feeding tribes of impoverished cannibals in the Amazon. They're your people, Jeery, not mine. You figure them out.

'Then there are certain doctors – and this is something I never admitted – who second occasional bodies for experimentation. You're aware of the Fridge Frankenstein myths?' I nodded. 'They're not as far from the truth as you might think. Good bodies are hard to come by on the outside. Not here. If one of my colleagues needs a cadaver – for its kidneys, eyes, brain or whatever – he takes one. No forms to fill in and no questions asked, unless the body in question has been tagged for sanctuary, and those are rarely interfered with.'

'That's sick,' I muttered.

'Really? And if one of them cures cancer as a result of his experiments?' He smiled. 'But let's not get into an argument about medical ethics. Besides, I think the presence of the note precludes professional involvement: pathologists are not noted for an advanced sense of humour. My guess is it's one of our less mature underlings.'

'The nurses?'

'Nurses, porters, watchmen, maintenance men, canteen staff: take your pick.'

'What would they want with the body?'

'Use your imagination,' he chuckled. 'Somebody wants to be the talk of a Hallowe'en party, or wants to scare the wits out of his dear old grandmother, or wants to cut a head off and use it as a bowling ball. The possibilities are endless.'

'How do we narrow them down?' I asked.

'We don't. Your father's body's been here a long, long time: it could have been taken a week after his arrival or yesterday. An investigation can be instigated if you insist, but I'd advise against it: the odds of revealing the culprit are slim at best, and nobody likes a trouble maker.'

I'd calmed down – Sines had a soothing influence – and, thinking it over, I knew he was right. Raising a stink would be counterproductive. The staff at the Fridge would object to my interference, which would mean calling in the Troops, who hated coming out on matters like this. Plus, it would eat into my time and distract me from the *real* mystery: Nic.

'I'll leave it,' I decided, 'but not indefinitely: that's my *father* your boys have fucked about with, Sines. How would you feel if it was your old man?'

'Peeved,' he smirked. 'Listen, I'll do some asking around on the quiet. Pretend I'm fishing for anecdotes. Might learn more that way: a practical joker won't confess to an official investigator, but may be incapable of keeping his lips zipped if he thinks he's bragging to a fellow clown.'

'Thanks, Sines.' I hadn't expected the offer. I was touched.

'But on one condition,' he added.

'Name it.'

He pulled a pained expression and shook his ID badge at me. 'Would you please call me *Dr* Sines?'

As I was making notes of my meeting with Sines back home I remembered something Rudi Ziegler had said. Flipping back a few pages I found my minutes of that encounter and located the relevant section. When I'd asked Ziegler if he thought the carving on Nic's back had anything to do with the Incan brooch she was wearing, he said he doubted it; the Incans were sun-worshippers and she was killed at night, and besides, why kill her at the Skylight? If it had been Incans, a more suitable venue would have been the site of the Manco Capac statue.

Flipping forward, I jotted down the words in capitals: MANCO CAPAC STATUE – INVESTIGATE and circled them heavily with my pen. It was too late to go there now – they'd be closing down for the day, if they hadn't already – but first thing tomorrow . . .

I felt too agitated to stay indoors. If I sat around brooding, my thoughts would return to the bare slab, the hiss of gas and my father's absent corpse. I needed to be active.

I took to the streets and asked after Paucar Wami again. Word of my interest in him had spread and many knew why: they'd heard about Nic and my connection to her. The rumour doing the rounds was that I'd loved her and had sworn a blood-oath over her dead body to get even with her killer. I didn't bother denying it.

I learned nothing new, though there was a lot more talk about Wami tonight: there had been a few sightings of the killer and these, coupled with the questions I'd been asking, had convinced many people of his guilt. A number of informants claimed to have seen Wami kill her, and a few poor souls swore blind they'd helped him, but when pushed, none could produce the slightest shred of actual evidence.

I rolled home late, legs stiff from the cycling, notebook full of names, half-leads and theories. Several people had mentioned Fabio – he allegedly knew more about Wami than most – but I didn't want to go calling around so soon after our last meeting, making it look like I was asking for a favour in return for my curative turn. I'd give it a couple of days and only try the centenarian pimp if all else failed.

I delayed going to bed, cleaning up round the apartment and tiring myself out, so I'd fall asleep quickly and not lie awake, tossing and turning and thinking about my father.

It didn't work. Tired as I was, sleep proved elusive, coming in fits and spurts, and when I did manage to drop off for a few minutes, my dreams were filled with images of empty coffins, laughing skeletons with heads the size of beach balls, and screaming, dislocated ghosts.

The building site was abuzz with activity. Men popped in and out of Portakabins like ants out of an anthill. Foremen with megaphones coordinated their troops with tinny bellows. Overhead cranes shifted huge weights from one end of the site to the other. Most attention focused on the centre of the industrial wasteland, where scaffolding surrounded a huge pair of concrete legs.

I wandered around the site without being questioned, observing the goings-on with interest. Judging by the size of the legs, the completed statue would be monstrous. I wondered who was financing its construction. I checked some vans and cabins for names, but there were several companies involved, all of whom had probably been subcontracted. I tried bending a few ears, but the labourers were reluctant to be drawn into conversation – they were behind schedule, I learned, and would miss out on bonuses if they weren't finished on time – and I didn't want to press too hard for fear of raising their curiosity.

The spearheader must have been incredibly influential, whoever he was. This was a busy part of the city. Construction was interfering with traffic, and I'm sure the dust and noise weren't welcomed by those in the neighbouring office buildings. You'd need friends in high places to nudge something like this along. I wondered if one of those *friends* was also a friend of Nick Hornyak's, maybe the one who sicced Kett on me.

I was meandering about, looking for evidence of wrong-doings – a ludicrous task, given the cluttered size of the site – and exchanging pleasantries with the natives when I spotted a familiar figure near the scaffolding, talking to a foreman. I waited until he was alone, then snuck up behind him and murmured in his ear: 'Are you following me, Mr Ziegler?'

Ziegler spun on his heels, blinking anxiously. He was dressed in a heavy plastic coat, industrial green overalls and rubber boots, and was wearing a pair of goggles to protect his eyes from the dust. When he saw me he relaxed and raised the goggles.

'Al Jeery,' he smiled, fanning his face with his pudgy hands. 'You gave me a start.' He frowned. 'Why ask if I'm following you?'

'You were at the funeral yesterday; so was I. Now you're here; and so am I. Coincidence?'

'You were at the funeral? I didn't see you.' He exhaled heavily through his nostrils. 'Then again, I didn't notice much, apart from Nicola. I thought it was barbaric of them to install that see-through upper lid. Her brother's idea, I heard.

'As for being here, I've been coming three or four days a week for the last fortnight. I petitioned for a statue to be erected in memory of our Incan forebears some years ago,

166

but it came to nothing. Now this.' He beamed like a child at Christmas.

'That's Manco Capac?' I asked. 'The sun god?'

'The *son* of a sun god,' Ziegler corrected me. 'Manco Capac was the founding father of the Incan empire. His followers believed he was a direct descendant of the sun deity.'

'That so?' I acted studious. 'When and where did this guy live, exactly?'

'About 1200 AD, along the western coast of South America.'

'Mind telling me what we're doing building a monument to him here, today?'

'This city has strong Incan roots. Didn't you know?' From my blank expression he gathered I didn't. 'This used to be an Indian village in earlier times,' he explained. 'A small winter-time settlement. In the sixteenth century – as the Spanish were hacking seven shades of excrement out of the South Americans – a band of Incas arrived, settled and made it home.'

'How'd they get here?' I asked curiously.

Ziegler shrugged. 'That's the big mystery. Nobody knows. There's never been any other evidence of Incan influence this far off their beaten track. It's puzzled archaeologists for decades. When the signs were first unearthed, most thought it was a practical joke, that old Incan artefacts had been buried by pranksters. Further investigation proved that wasn't so. Incas *were* here. Not only that: they made this city what it is, laying the foundations upon which the modern version has been built.'

'That mean we're a bunch of Incan offspring?' I asked.

'Our bloodlines are intriguingly mixed,' Ziegler said, readjusting his goggles as a dust cloud swept over us. 'Many tribes have found their way here over the centuries.

But those whose roots stretch back more than a couple of generations are almost surely linked – however tenuously – to the Incans.'

'And one's decided to pay tribute at long last.' I smiled. 'Who said the modern generation had no respect for its elders?'

Ziegler smiled with me. 'Actually, I'm not sure who the mystery benefactor is. But I'd imagine it's somebody with an informed opinion of his heritage. And yes, it *is* nice to see. As someone who's spent his life dabbling with things Incan, for me it's a tremendously exciting development. It's not just a statue they're building, but a museum. They'll be shipping in ornaments, manufacturing replicas, hosting wild Inca-style parties to advertise their presence.'

'That won't do your business any harm,' I noted.

'True – and don't think I'm not making plans to carve out my own thick slice of the cash calf – but that's not why I'm here. The financial aspects pale in the face of the staggering aesthetic majesty of the project.'

Ziegler stared lovingly up at the statue. I didn't like to break into his reverie, so I studied it with him, watching as the cranes added to the lower sections of the legs, thickening them – I guessed – to support the massive upper body.

'This guy, Manco Capac,' I said. 'How do they know what he looks like? I mean, 1200 AD: that's quite a while ago.'

'It is indeed,' Ziegler agreed. 'But even primitive cavemen had artists to capture their visages for posterity's sake. I'm not sure which source the designers have gone with for the statue, but there are several possible portraits to choose from. The finished result may not be entirely accurate, but it's the symbolism which counts.'

Symbolism. Symbols . . .

'Didn't you tell me those Incas had a thing for human sacrifice?' I asked, trying to sound casual.

Ziegler nodded. 'Almost every society has a history of offering those of its own to the gods. The Incas were no different, although they were more subtle about it than most.'

'How can you have a subtle sacrifice?' I laughed.

His face misted over. 'They were artists. They would pick the most desirable of their virgins – male and female – and deck them out in fine robes, adorn them with flowers, feed them exotic fruits and parade them around like gods. Then they'd slip them drugs to dull their senses, haul them high up a mountain and leave them in an exposed holy place to freeze. There wasn't much pain, just a gentle drifting-off to death and a glorious union with the gods.' He sighed happily. 'It must have been beautiful.'

I decided not to comment on that.

'Was that how they killed all their victims? They never varied the routine? Never used, say . . . *knives?*'

He cocked a mischievous eyebrow. 'The Incas weren't averse to variety. They reserved the glorious sacrifices for special occasions. I'm sure there were plenty of other, smaller, messier sacrifices. But not with knives: the Incas were not metallurgists.'

I took that on board. 'They must have had cutting implements of one kind or another,' I said.

'Of course. Jagged rocks, crystals, sharpened bones.'

'So they had knives of a sort.'

Ziegler smiled thinly and agreed: 'Of a sort.'

'Remember what you said about Nic and the carving on her back?'

'Refresh my memory.'

'You said, if it had been Inca-related, they wouldn't have killed her in the Skylight: they'd have done it out here.'

'I put that to you as a proposition, not a theory.'

'Whatever. You still stand by it?'

He looked puzzled. 'I still think this would be as good a place as any for a sacrifice to the sun to be made, yes, but she wasn't killed here. She was killed at the hotel.'

I said nothing, but coughed discreetly and glanced away.

Ziegler faced me and lifted the goggles in spite of the dust. 'Are you implying she *wasn't*?'

I hesitated, pondering whether to play my ace or not, then opted against it: better not to broadcast. If I got lucky (as TV detectives got lucky every week), the criminal would fall into my lap and let slip that he knew Nic hadn't been killed in the Skylight.

'Of course she was killed at the hotel,' I said. 'But maybe she'd been here beforehand. Did you ever discuss this place with her?'

'I mentioned it to her the last time we met, I think, but only in passing. She'd moved on from Incas and the sun by then.'

A truck approached and we had to get out of its way. Ziegler led me clear, treading confidently, clearly at home. As we moved I spotted a tall man in robes standing not far from us. He seemed to be gazing up at the statue but he couldn't have been, because when he turned, I saw that his eyes were white. They stared blindly in my direction, as the eyes of the man in the funeral parlour had. At first I thought they might be one and the same, but that was ridiculous: a man without the use of his eyes was hardly likely to be trailing me about the city.

'How big's this thing going to be anyway?' I asked, keeping an eye on the man in the robes, idly wondering what someone so ill dressed for the occasion was doing on a building site.

'About nine hundred feet,' Ziegler replied.

I stopped in my tracks and stared at him. 'Nine *hundred*? Christ, that's huge! That's about, what . . . three hundred metres?'

'More or less.'

'Why the hell are they building it so big?' I asked.

'It will be hollow inside,' Ziegler told me. 'The museum artefacts will be housed in the body, for view on the way up. It's also been designed to receive the fullest effects of the sun: the head's going to be packed with mirrors, which will turn it into a giant sphere of sunlight. You'll be able to climb to the top when it's finished and bask in a room so bright it'll be like sitting inside the sun.'

'Sounds dangerous. Light that bright could – ' I looked around for the man in the robes, but he'd absconded ' – blind you.'

'It's going to be months before initial construction is complete,' Ziegler went on. 'Possibly a few years before it opens its doors to the public. Hopefully, if I stick around and get noticed, they'll let me in early. Still, it's going to be a long, miserable wait.'

'Can you answer a question for me?' I asked out of the blue.

'I'll try.'

I pointed at the crane. 'How do they set those things upright?'

Ziegler shook his head. 'I haven't the foggiest.'

'Puzzles the shit out of me whenever I think of it.'

'Why don't you check with somebody who knows?'

'I should. Each time it pops into my head, I mean to, then I go and forget about it again.'

We didn't say much for several minutes. Just stood and stared at the towering cranes, immersed in our thoughts. Ziegler was probably dreaming about those Incas of his. *I* was thinking about the symbol carved into Nic's back, and how chummy the mystic had been with the foreman, wondering where he got his uniform from, and how I would set about learning more of his business and interest in the Incas.

Finally he stirred. 'I must be leaving,' he said. 'I'm seeing a client in an hour. By the time I get home, wash and change, it'll be – '

He stopped and stared off into the distance. It took me a few seconds to spot what he was so intent on, then I saw it: a fall of rain that looked like a vertical slide to the heavens.

Ziegler hurried towards it and I moved quickly to keep up. 'What is it?' I asked as we ran.

'The rain of the gods,' he gasped, face flushed with excitement. 'Have you never seen it?'

'No.'

'It is not common. This is only my third sighting.'

We stopped short of the extraordinary rainfall, which was hitting the ground about a hundred metres beyond the statue. The area was fenced off and no guards or workmen were nearby. Ziegler wrung his hands so much as he stared, it's a wonder he didn't squeeze them to pulp.

'Incredible,' he sighed. 'I've never been this close.'

'It's odd,' I agreed. The rain fell in a perfect rectangle, maybe two metres wide by half a metre deep. The surrounding area – the entire yard! – was bone dry. I'd never seen anything like it.

'The *villacs* believed this was the voice of the god of the sun,' Ziegler informed me. 'This was how they communicated with him.'

'*Villacs?*' I enquired.

'Ancient Incan priests.'

'Oh.'

While we were studying the shower, the blind man I'd noticed earlier emerged around the far side. He was closer to the rain than we were and his white robes were specked with wet spots. I was able to examine him in greater detail. He had short white hair. Looked pretty old. A distasteful mole sprouted from the left side of his chin. His head bobbed forwards and backwards, lightly, and he seemed oblivious to our presence.

I turned to ask Ziegler more about these *villacs* he'd mentioned – like were there any in operation today, and where could I reach them – when the blind man darted towards me, grabbed me by the left arm and spun me into the rectangle of rain. I opened my mouth to roar at him, but before I could utter a syllable the world disintegrated into shards of light and I had to cover my eyes with my hands or risk being blinded like my assailant.

When I removed my fingers after a couple of wary seconds, I was no longer in the yard. I wasn't even in the city. I was standing on a rock at the edge of a soaring cliff, gazing down on a fertile valley.

'It's beautiful, isn't it?' someone asked. Turning, I spotted the blind man from the yard.

'Yes,' I answered peacefully, returning to the view. Part of me knew this wasn't right, this couldn't be happening, but the majority of my mind had fallen prey to the mesmerising lucidity of the vision (which I knew it had to be).

'We must leave soon,' the blind man said, and I nodded in reply. 'We can never return.'

'No,' I agreed. 'Never.'

'But we will build anew. And this time we will build for ever.'

'For ever,' I echoed.

'See the rivers?' He pointed to three tributaries which trickled down from the mountains, met in the valley and formed one large snake of a river. 'You know what they are?' I shook my head. 'The rivers of blood,' he said and I could see he spoke the literal truth: they were rosy red.

'The blood of flesh,' he said, pointing to the river furthest left. 'The blood of dreams made flesh.' This time he pointed to the river to the far right.

'And the blood of flesh of dreams,' I said, nodding at the middle line of red.

'Yes,' he beamed. 'Excellent. And the place where they meet: do you know what that is called?' I thought in silence for a moment, but came up blank. 'It is the future,' he said. 'And it is ours.'

The blind man moved behind me and placed his fingers on my shoulders. I made no move to stop him as he gently pushed me forward. Nor did I scream or feel the slightest sense of fear as I fell. Instead, I spread my arms, raised my chin, and flew. I glided like a natural born aviator over the middle river of blood, close enough to touch it if I wished. When I reached the spot where it joined with the other two, I hovered in the air and stared down into the churning pool of blood at the intersection.

There were faces in the red pool, none of which I recognised. Old and young, male and female, black and white. They eddied lazily round the pool, like dead flies caught between conflicting currents. After a while, I realised there was a face beneath the others, a giant face which filled the base of the pool. At first I thought it was my own worn face I was gazing at, but then the blood lightened a shade and I noticed murky snakes writhing down the spectre's cheeks. I couldn't make out the finer details of its features but knew it must be Paucar Wami. The thought failed to frighten me. Nothing in this world of fantastic visions could scare me.

While I watched, the vision of Paucar Wami opened its eyes – dark green slits – and smiled. Its lips mouthed the word 'Come', and I dived into the pool in response. As soon as I parted the surface of the bloody waters, a red gauze dropped over my eyes. The red swiftly turned to black, and then I was slipping out of the vision, out of the pool, back into the real world and . . .

. . . rain.

I opened my eyes and gazed upwards as the rain cascaded down. Then arms were yanking at me and I let myself be guided out. I was expecting the blind man who'd propelled me into the shower, but it was the less mysterious Rudi Ziegler who had hold of me.

'You're drenched through,' he tutted, tugging at the sleeves of my jacket, as though that alone could dry me.

'What happened?' I asked numbly. I took a step forward, lost control of my legs and slumped to the ground.

'Some nut thrust you into the rain,' Ziegler said, crouching beside me. 'I've spent the last minute trying to drag you out. You seemed oblivious to me.'

'My mind was . . . elsewhere.' Then, as my senses returned, I glanced around suspiciously. 'Where is he?' I asked. 'Where'd the blind man go?'

'Heaven knows,' Ziegler sighed. 'He rushed off while I was trying to extract you from the rain.'

'A pity,' I muttered, and stood. Ziegler helped me.

'Will you be all right?' he asked as I wobbled uncertainly.

'I'll be fine,' I said, taking a couple of nervous half-steps. I felt more confident after that. My strength was returning. 'Fine,' I repeated, and smiled to show I meant it.

'The rain's stopping,' Ziegler said. Glancing up, I saw the last few drops fall. There were no clouds overhead. I wondered where the rain had come from.

'If you're sure you'll be all right, I really must be going,' Ziegler said. 'My client won't wait and – '

'That's fine,' I interrupted. 'Go.'

'You're sure you're . . . ?'

'A 1,' I vowed.

Ziegler didn't look convinced, but he nodded and started to leave. 'Are you coming?' he asked.

'In a while,' I said. 'I want to rest a bit first. Dry off in the sun.'

'I can send someone to check on you.'

'That won't be necessary.'

He paused. I flashed an assured grin. He smiled in return, bid me farewell, and left. Once he was gone, I sat again, stared at the spot where the fallen rain was seeping into the ground, and pondered at length the meaning of my vision, in particular the face I'd half-glimpsed at the bottom of the pool of blood.

I changed into dry clothes back home. I couldn't get the vision out of my mind. I'd never experienced anything like that. Although I'd known it was a vision, even while immersed in it, it had been overpowering. What had brought it on? The blind man? The rain? My own imagination?

Since the questions were unanswerable, I put them to one side and went in search of Paucar Wami again. After the vision it seemed more important than ever to find the fabled killer.

It was a vain search. Rumours among those who knew of him were rife – he'd been seen in the north of the city; he'd murdered a priest in Swiss Square; he was holed up on the fifteenth floor of Party Central with the Cardinal – but apart from the Johnny Grace reports, none could be verified. Nobody knew where he was or what he was here for or how long he intended to stay.

Hard as it was to shake the vision, I let my thoughts turn towards Rudi Ziegler in the evening. If he was Nic's killer I'd eat my beret, but I couldn't shake the feeling that he was tied in with it somehow. Perhaps one of his other customers was an Inca freak too, or maybe he knew a fellow mystic who Nic had been involved with. I needed to find out how he dealt with clients who wanted to go a stage further, and who he referred them to.

I could have sicced one of the Cardinal's goons on him – it would be nice to exercise my new-found powers and watch others dance to my tune – but the Cardinal hadn't told me the truth about Nic and where she was killed. I couldn't rely on him or those who answered to him. I'd have to use my own person, someone I could trust implicitly. My options were narrow: I didn't want to involve Bill; that left Ellen.

She was suspicious when I called and asked her to meet me at Cafran's for supper. She wanted to know what I was after. I wouldn't say. That fuelled her curiosity, so she agreed to meet me at nine, which gave me two hours to talk matters over with Priscilla and get her out of the way.

I dropped a progress report off at Party Central – the Cardinal hadn't asked for regular updates but I figured it was best to keep him informed – exchanged hellos with colleagues I hadn't seen much of lately, then headed home for another change of clothes.

As before, I didn't know how to dress for my date with Miss Perdue, but decided to play it safe: smartest suit in my wardrobe, shoes polished until I could see the cracks in the ceiling in them, cuff links, a snazzy tie. I even ran a comb through my hair – it doesn't take much combing – and flossed my teeth. I wouldn't be shown up by her, no matter where she took me.

I arrived a quarter of an hour early and wished I hadn't, as it meant fifteen extra minutes of looking like a fool. Cafran's was a nice little place, but it wasn't a suit-and-tie job. Most of its clientele were older than me, dressed casually, regulars who fitted in like the rubber plants. I could feel them staring at me, wondering if I was a low-key gangster here to carry out a hit. I stuck out like a sore thumb: King Kong's.

Priscilla was twenty minutes late but didn't apologise. She was dressed in the skimpiest of material: a green length of rope around her torso – barely enough to cover her breasts – and a skirt so short it was little more than a glorified belt.

'My, my,' she smiled, 'look at Mr Penguin.'

'One more word and I'm out of here,' I replied gruffly. 'I feel like a coffin-bearer at a circus.'

Her smile dropped. 'Not the most timely of similes,' she pouted, then shrugged and stroked my cheek with a fingernail. 'But I'll forgive you.' She pressed close into me and adopted a gruff, cockney accent. 'Gizzus a kiss, guvnor.'

'Look, you're late,' I said, half-tempted to plant one on her just to see how she'd take it. 'Let's get to our table.'

'The night's young, Al.'

'But I'm not. I've business after this. I'm in a hurry.'

'All right.' She laughed pleasantly and took my arm. 'Come.'

We sat by the front window, at the head of the restaurant, where everybody could gawp at me. I settled into my chair, trying not to twitch in the stifling suit, and picked up the menu.

'I thought this would be somewhere posh,' I confessed. 'You should have told me it was . . .' I stopped talking and listened to the music dripping from the speakers. 'Is that "Yellow Submarine"?' I asked incredulously. 'I haven't heard that one in years.'

'They play all those old corny songs here,' she said. 'That's why I like it. It's a fun place to eat.'

'Great,' I groaned. 'Makes my suit all the damn dumber.'

'Cheer up,' she giggled. 'At least you're distinctive. And don't bother with the menu: since you're in such a hurry, we'll do without the meal. A quick drink and I'm gone.' A short waiter in red braces – with an I LOVE CAFRAN'S badge pinned to his breast – approached. 'A pina colada,' Priscilla said promptly. 'Al?'

'Mineral water, please.' He nodded dutifully and departed to fetch the drinks. We talked about the funeral and the mourners. Priscilla hadn't noticed the blind man but knew most of the others and filled me in on their backgrounds and relationships with Nicola. I'd only meant to dwell on the preliminaries for a couple of minutes but one anecdote led to another and soon the time was flying by. When I found myself reminiscing about my nights of passion with Nic, I halted mid-sentence, glanced at my watch, realised eight o'clock – and two more drinks – had come and gone, and knuckled down to business.

I steepled my hands, cleared my throat and crab-talked up to the big questions as delicately as I could. 'You remember you told me you wanted to help find out who killed Nic?' She nodded. 'You know I've been making some investigations?' She nodded again. 'Well, there's a few . . . That is, if you don't mind, I'd like to . . .'

She laughed when she saw the difficulty I was in. 'Go ahead, spit it out. I'm a big girl. I can take it.'

'It gets pretty personal,' I warned her.

She tipped her glass at me and lowered her lids. 'Here's to getting personal.'

'All right.' I stared down at the table, even though I should have been watching her face to gauge whether she was answering truthfully or not. 'You lied to me about not knowing Rudi Ziegler.'

A brief pause, then: 'Yes. I'm a regular client. I go a couple of times a month. I don't believe in that sort of nonsense but it amuses me. I let him play with his mirrors and summon fake spirits. I gasp and clap my hands and shake in my chair, like on a ghost train, then pay up and trot along home. He's a fabulous entertainer.'

'Have you seen him since Nic's death, apart from at the funeral?'

'Yes. I introduced Nic to him. If he was involved in her death, I would have felt at least partly to blame. I asked if he knew anything about her murder. He told me he didn't. I believed him.'

'Why did you lie to me about him?'

'I don't know.' She tossed her hair. 'Maybe I didn't want to seem like a silly little girl who throws her money away on cheap spooks.'

'Maybe there were other reasons.'

'Maybe,' she admitted coolly.

I waited for her to break the silence. I didn't want to push her any more than I had to. Finally she sighed and took a drink.

'OK. There were things I didn't want you finding out. *Seeeecrets.*' She made a big production of the word. 'I thought, if you knew about Rudi and me, you might sniff around and worm them out of him.'

'Why mention him at all if that was the case?'

'Because I figured you'd know about him anyway and it might look suspicious if I played it dumb.'

'These secrets,' I said, watching my fingers curl into involuntary fists. 'Was one of them about you and Nic? About what you did in your spare time?'

A long silence. Then: 'Don't play it coy, Al. My daddy used to say a man's got to open the can before spilling the beans. What exactly are you asking?'

I blurted it out. 'Were you and Nic hookers?'

From my lead-up she was expecting it and reacted calmly. 'Yes.' A beat. 'We were.' Another beat. 'I introduced her to *that* as well.' A slow, measured drink. 'Some friend, huh?'

'Tell me about it,' I said, adding a 'please' to the end.

She finished her drink and crooked a finger at the waiter. I left my glass where it was. She didn't say anything until the pina colada arrived. I glanced up when she started to speak and saw that now she was the one staring at the table.

'It wasn't about money. Not for Nic anyway: she was loaded. I did it for the cash occasionally, when strapped, but most of the time it was for fun. Picking rich guys up and taking them to slums; latching on to a bare-in-the-ass-of-his-pants bum and treating him to a night at the Skylight or some other similarly impressive establishment. Doing things we could never ask our boyfriends to do.'

'How long had this been going on?'

'I'd been doing it since my late teens, on and off. Nic only started a year or so ago.'

'Was she doing it while dating me?' I asked, thinking of the few times I'd made love to her without a condom, worrying about my health on top of everything else.

'Not often – the game had lost a lot of its appeal – but yes. The night of her murder . . .' She stalled.

'Go on,' I prompted her.

She shook her head and gasped: 'I can't.'

'You must.' When a long silence followed, a silence she showed no sign of breaking, I prodded her back into life with: 'I know you were at the Skylight.'

Her head shot up. She'd been on the verge of tears but the shock froze them at the corners of her eyes. '*How?*'

'I told you: I've been investigating.' A smug grin almost made it to my lips but I thrust it back just in time.

Priscilla slowly twisted her glass, first to the left, then right, eyes on the drops of condensation as they slid down towards the base. She didn't look up until she was finished unburdening herself.

'Nic had set up a trick. We were meant to do him

together. We did that quite a lot: she liked three-way action. I arrived in advance of the appointment and booked the room. 812. Signed as Jane Dowe. Didn't need to – they know me at the Skylight – just force of habit. Headed for the bar. On the way I ran into an old customer. I don't have regulars, but this was a Chinese businessman who I'd been with several times before. We got chatting, he asked me up to his room, I said I had a prior engagement, he laughed and told me to name my price.'

'What's this guy's name?'

'None of your business,' she responded sharply. 'Besides, he was only here for a couple of days. He's back in China now.'

'Hard to check on,' I commented.

'If I'd known what was going to happen,' she said bitterly, 'I'd have arranged for a more convenient alibi.'

'Let's get back to the Skylight,' I said quietly, not wanting to lose her to her emotions. 'He told you to name your price. Then?'

'I named it. We haggled – the Chinese love to haggle – and arrived at a mutually acceptable sum. He had some business to attend to. Gave me the card to his room, told me to let myself in and slip into something sexy. I struck for the bar first and ordered a drink. Nic turned up on time. I explained the change in plans.'

'How did she react?'

'Nonchalant. She didn't mind. Business is business.'

'She didn't seem scared or apprehensive?'

'No.'

'You don't think she had any idea of what was coming?'

'Hardly.'

'What happened next?'

'She went her way, I went mine.'

'That was it?'

'Just about. I gave her the card to 812 before she left.'

'She went straight up?'

'I presume so. I didn't leave with her: I'd slipped my shoes off while waiting, so I stayed a few seconds to put them back on.'

'Did she tell you the name of her john?'

I could see Priscilla's withering smile reflected in the panels of the glass. 'We'd hardly be sitting here talking about it if she had. I wouldn't have let shame stop me revealing the name of her killer if I knew it.'

'You didn't see him? He wasn't in the lobby?'

'Nic had gone up by the time I came out.'

'She didn't say anything about him? His nationality, job, whether he was rich or poor, what he looked like?'

'Nothing.' Her fingers stopped twirling the glass and she gripped it firmly. 'My Chinaman was in poor form that night. I finished early – about half eleven – and started for home. I was on the sixth floor. As I got into the elevator, I thought about calling up to the eighth and joining Nic for the latter rounds. I almost did.'

'What stopped you?'

She sighed. 'I couldn't be bothered. Went home and got a good night's sleep instead, rare for a Friday. I rang Nic the next day to ask how things had gone. Didn't think anything of it when she didn't answer. A couple of friends enquired about her over the next few days – they were wondering where she'd got to – but I never connected her absence with that night in the Skylight, not until . . .'

She broke off and took several long, deep breaths. The tears had forced their way back into the frame and were rolling down her cheeks in time with the watery pearls on her glass.

'She was still alive at half eleven,' she moaned. 'If I'd gone up, or if I'd gone with her earlier, when I was meant to . . .'

'You might have been killed too,' I said, touching her hands with mine, briefly, wishing to be supportive without seeming forward.

'Or I might have saved her,' she sobbed. 'She was all alone. The first time she pulled a trick, she begged me to go with her: she was afraid. I told her not to be silly and sent her off with him, laughing. She came back that time, but not this. I should have been there. I . . .'

Again she broke off, and this time I knew there'd be no recovery. Our interview was at a close. I covered her hands with mine – I felt confident enough to make contact this time: she was crying too hard to miscontrue the gesture – and made soft, cooing noises, gently guiding her out of the doldrums and back to normal conversation.

She smiled weakly when the worst of the grief had passed. 'Thank you,' she said.

'For what: reducing you to tears? I'm a clumsy oaf. I should have kept my mouth shut.'

'No.' She took one of her hands from mine and wiped the tears from her face, then tenderly laid her palm against my left cheek. It was cool from the glass. 'It was good that you confronted me. I needed to confess. It was tearing me apart. If you hadn't dragged it out of me, it might have set in and festered. This way it's out in the open. I can cry about it now and maybe start to forgive myself.'

'There's nothing to forgive,' I assured her, to which she pulled a maybe/maybe not face, then reclaimed her other hand and set about restoring her looks, wiping away the worst of the tears, applying light layers of make-up while I sat there, twiddling my thumbs, wishing I was holding her hands again.

Snapping her compact shut, she rose. I was getting up to walk her to her cab when she laid a hand on my forearm and smiled. 'It's OK. Finish your drink. I'll pick up the tab on my way.'

'Don't be silly,' I said, but she squeezed lightly and stopped me.

'Please, Al. I'd like to be alone. I'll give you a call soon, when I feel up to it.'

'OK,' I said. 'But let me pay. I arranged this meeting: it's only fair that – '

'I won't stay and argue.' She grinned, made a fast turn and scurried away, only to find her path blocked by another woman. They collided, clutched at each other to prevent a fall, then laughed and separated. 'I'm sorry,' Priscilla said, 'I wasn't looking.'

'Not at all,' the other woman replied. 'You had the right of way. I should have . . . Oh, so there you are.' This last part was addressed to me. 'What the hell are you doing in a suit?'

'You know each other?' Priscilla asked, politely standing aside so that Ellen – early, for once in her life – had a clear view of me.

'Yes.' I rose awkwardly, as though caught in a clandestine embrace – for a brief second I forgot we were divorced and I was free to see whoever I pleased – and welcomed my second guest of the night. 'Priscilla, I'd like you to meet Ellen Fraser. Ellen, Priscilla Perdue.'

'Doubling up on dates, Al?' Ellen mocked me, shaking hands with Priscilla. 'You're getting cheap in your old age.'

'Please,' Priscilla said quickly. 'Don't get the wrong idea. We weren't here on a date. It was a merely a – '

Ellen laughed and raised her hands. 'No need to apologise. I'm not dating the sap either.'

'Oh?' Priscilla blinked and looked at me questioningly.

'Ellen and I used to be married,' I muttered.

'*Oh.*' She opened her mouth to say something, thought better of it and made the sign for buttoning her lips. 'None of my business. I'll leave you two alone.'

'You don't have to leave on my account,' Ellen said.

'I was leaving anyway,' Priscilla told her, winked at me, said goodbye and exited.

Ellen watched Priscilla march away in her skimpy top and skirt, a sly smile hovering at the edges of her mouth. 'New girl?' she asked casually.

'A friend of a friend,' I answered truthfully.

'Really?' She turned the full force of her gaze on me. 'So that's what friends of a friend are wearing these times.'

'Skip it,' I mumbled gruffly. 'Let's order.'

'Yes, boss,' she said, hiding behind a menu to cover her smirk.

She asked what the occasion was while we were waiting for the meal to arrive. Ellen always came straight to the point.

'You heard about the girl who was murdered in the Skylight last Thursday?' The official public date of her death.

'Sure. The papers have been making a meal of it. They love going after the Cardinal. It's not often they get the chance.'

'I knew her,' I said.

Ellen frowned. 'Socially?'

'We were lovers.' I'd meant to present a condensed version of the facts – keeping the Cardinal and the extent of my involvement out of it – but I'd never been good at keeping secrets from Ellen and soon the whole story was tumbling out, warts and all. I told her about my fling with Nic, how I'd found her, when she'd been killed, what I'd learned of her since then, my meetings with the Cardinal, Priscilla, Ziegler and the rest. The only cards I played close to my chest were Paucar Wami, the vision I'd had, and my father: knowing about Wami might scare her off when I asked her for help; I would have been embarrassed talking about the vision; and Tom Jeery was my concern alone.

The tale took us through dinner and dessert, on to our post-meal drinks (two mineral waters). She listened quietly, displaying no emotions other than an occasional raised eyebrow, and kept her questions to a minimum.

When I finished she shook her head, sipped at her drink and said, 'Wow.' I held my tongue, knowing there'd be more once she'd thought on it some. 'The Cardinal. After all these years. Is he as impressive face to face as they say?'

'Yes and no. He's larger than life, more imposing than anyone I've met, but there's something small-time about him, like he's this tough kid in the biggest sandbox in the city.'

'You used to say you'd run for the hills if the Cardinal took a personal interest in you,' she reminded me.

'I almost did. If not for Nic . . .'

'How close *were* you two?'

'Not very. I hadn't guessed how duplicitous she was. I knew she'd been around but I'd no idea she was a . . .' I didn't like to say it, so I didn't. 'There was very little romance.'

'So why get involved now she's dead?' A blunt but fair query.

'Maybe because, deep down, I hoped it would lead to love. Maybe because, whatever else, she was a friend and I don't like the idea of this happening to a friend. Maybe because . . .' I stalled.

' . . . you like the idea of cracking the case and being king for an hour?' Ellen suggested, seeing inside my mind as she'd always been able to.

'Would it be so bad if I did? I've kept my head down most of my life and coasted along. Maybe this is my chance to shine. You used to say I was meant for better things, didn't you?'

'Absolutely. I deplored the way you accepted your lot and settled for the life you'd wandered into. It helped drive me away from you. Ambition's good, Al. Getting out of Party Central and standing on your own two feet could be the best thing that's happened to you in a long, long time. But there's a difference between standing alone and standing up to your neck in shit.'

'Meaning you think I should ditch the case?' I loved the way she'd put it so plainly.

'Not necessarily. If this is what you want, go for it. But it's a messy business. I had dealings with detectives a few years ago when Preston's' – the insurance company she worked for – 'decided to branch out and stuck me with the paperwork. What those guys go through isn't pretty: hours spent following people around, bugging phones, invading privacy in ways I don't like to think about. Detectives destroy relationships, people, lives. I'm not sure you're cut out for it.'

'But this is different. It's personal. I won't hurt anybody.'

'Detectives can't make a pledge like that. You might have to.'

I stared down at the table. 'You think I should cry off?'

Ellen sighed. 'That's not my call. I'm not your wife any more, Al: what you do is none of my business. All I'm saying is: think before you act. Don't rush in half-hearted. Do it right and *know* what you're doing, or don't do it at all.'

Ellen's advice made sense, but it was too late to distract me: I'd sailed through my initial period of uncertainty, when I could have been swayed, and now the thought of leaving things up in the air, unresolved, wasn't on the agenda.

Ellen watched intently as I pretended to mull her words over, saw what was in my mind and tutted impatiently.

'You might let me know when I'm wasting my breath. You haven't the slightest intention of quitting, have you?'

'Not really,' I chuckled apologetically.

'So why drag me out and bare your soul if not for my sage-like advice?'

I smiled sheepishly and said, 'For your help,' then drew her back to Rudi Ziegler and explained my hunch, how I felt the murderer might be connected to him, how I needed to learn more about the mystic and didn't feel I could trust the Cardinal's people.

Ellen said nothing until I'd finished, then fixed me with one of her iciest stares and snapped, 'You're insane.'

'Is that a no?' I quipped.

'This guy could be a murderer!'

'I doubt it. He's meek as they come.'

'But he might consort with murderers? *Forget* it! Look somewhere else for a stooge. I wouldn't touch something like this if you paid me. If that's a problem – if you think I owe you – tough. I don't.'

'Of course you don't owe me!' I snapped back. 'I never – '

I broke off before I said something to drive her away. I'd begun to wish I hadn't started this but it was too late to back out now.

'I've no right to ask this of you,' I muttered, 'but I'm asking anyway, because I've no one else to turn to. You wouldn't be in danger. I wouldn't ask if I thought there was any degree of risk involved. You know I wouldn't.'

Ellen sighed. 'I know.' A long pause. 'But I've work to consider. We're real busy right now. I couldn't – '

'It wouldn't interfere with your work,' I said quickly. 'You could fit it around your office hours. It would be fun. A dibbling of divertissement.' That was one of Ellen's favourite nonsensical expressions. She smiled and I knew I'd almost won her over.

She made a show of pondering my words, finally let her head roll back and sighed wearily. 'OK. I'll listen. But I'm promising nothing, got it?'

'Got it.' I wet my throat before continuing. 'All you'd have to do is go along to a couple of sessions – get your palm read, your future foretold, that kind of thing – and pretend to be interested; get to know the guy, laugh at his jokes, flirt with him a bit. Then ask to sit in on a seance and express interest in going a stage further: tell him you want to make meaningful contact with the other world and find a lover amongst the shades of the dead.'

'*What?*' she squealed, delighted in spite of her misgivings.

'That's what Nic was after,' I grinned. 'A spirit lover, a ghost she could get hot and horny with.'

'My, my.' Her eyes were sparkling. 'I bet you had some fun with *her* beneath the sheets.'

'You don't know the half of it,' I smiled. 'Made certain other parties I've slept with look like wet fish.'

'Watch it,' she growled, playfully tweaking my nose.

'Whatever your story, however crazy, act like you're serious and he'll treat you with respect. He deals with cranks all the time. If he believes *you* believe, there'll be no problem. Say you want to delve into the deep dark secrets of past incantations, mumbo-jumbo like that. Mention Egyptians and Incas – he's got a passion for Incas – anything along those lines you can think of.'

'Sounds pretty harmless so far. What next?'

'If he says he doesn't do stuff like that and turns you away, walk: thanks for the help, end of your involvement, adios. If he leads you on, play along, but push him towards a conclusion.'

'What sort of a conclusion?'

I shrugged uncomfortably: I was considering the possibility that he knew Paucar Wami and had introduced the killer to Nic, but didn't want to mention this to Ellen. 'If you press him to find you a demon lover,' I said, 'maybe he'll bring in some guy dressed in feathers and covered in paint. I want to know if he has assistants. If he has, maybe one of them – '

' – killed Nicola,' Ellen finished for me, nodding. 'If he does and I meet one, what do I do? Get names, addresses, phone numbers?'

'No. I'll do that. I have the files of Party Central at my disposal. I told you: I'm a big cheese now. You turn an assistant up; I'll take it from there.

'Another possibility is that he'll refer you elsewhere, pass you along to one of his colleagues with a penchant for the nastier things in life, who Nic may have been put in touch with.'

'That's what you're hoping for, isn't it?' she guessed.

I nodded. 'Like I said: Ziegler's no killer. But maybe one of his accomplices is. I doubt if things will pan out that simply, but it's worth a shot.'

'And if he puts me in touch with a colleague?'

'Pass the name along to me and skedaddle. I'll check it out. He'll never know about you. See? Just as I said: no danger.'

'Hmmm.' She weighed up the pros and cons, then grimaced and muttered: 'What the hell. I've been meaning to visit one of those fakirs for years. Maybe he'll direct me towards the man of my dreams. I've tried every other approach.'

'Ellen, you're a peach.' I leant across and kissed her, a chaste kiss between two old lovers who were now mere friends.

'When do you want me to start?' she asked.

'As soon as possible. Give him a ring tomorrow if you can.'

'What if he draws a connection between the two of us?'

'How could he? If you don't mention Nic and you don't mention me, he's no reason to be suspicious. Treat it like a joke at first. Don't start off serious. Let him *make* you believe. Let his act convince and propel you further along.'

'All right.' She prodded my nose with a finger. 'But you'll owe me big for this. I've a birthday coming up and this year I won't be settling for a box of chocolates and a posy of flowers you picked in a park. Understand?'

'It'll be diamond tiaras and slippers of gold,' I vowed.

'It had better be,' she snorted, then raised her glass in a toast. 'Here's to Fraser and Jeery: the Miss Marple and Hercule Poirot of the twenty-first century.'

'Marple and Poirot,' I repeated, and we grinned stupidly at one another as we clinked glasses and downed the water as though it was champagne.

12

I spent Thursday morning panning for news of Wami. The streets were teeming with stories and unsubstantiated sightings but no real leads. I toyed with the idea of offering a reward for information leading to his whereabouts, but that would have brought the crazies out in full.

I stopped in at Party Central and looked for Frank. I wanted to ask him about the Troops guarding the Skylight the night of Nic's murder. His secretary paged him: he was in a meeting but would be free in a quarter of an hour; I could wait in his office. I told the secretary I'd be back and swung downstairs to the canteen to catch up on the latest gossip.

I passed Richey Harney in one of the corridors on my way, the guy who'd originally been destined to haul Nic back from the Fridge with Vincent. I stopped to greet him.

'How'd the party go?' I asked.

'Party?' His face was a blank.

'Your daughter's party.'

'My . . . ?' The lights came on. 'Oh. Yeah.' He chuckled edgily. He seemed nervous. Guilty, almost. 'It was great. Thanks for getting me off the hook. If you ever need a favour . . .'

'Don't mention it,' I replied, wondering what he had to

feel guilty about. Maybe he'd skipped the party for a rendezvous with a mistress, or simply gone off for a beer.

No sign of Jerry or Mike in the canteen. A couple of guys I half-knew saluted me. I waved back but didn't go over: they were studying the form sections of the papers and one thing I hate is horse racing. I sat and watched TV, hoping a familiar face would walk through the door. When one failed to materialise, I took myself back to Frank's office. He arrived not long after.

'Al. What's up?'

I asked if he had a list of the guards at the Skylight. He most certainly did. Could I have a copy? Normally, no, but since I was the Cardinal's current favourite boy . . .

Thirty-six names in all. Of course, if the killer was a Troop – or in league with one – he might have been off duty at the time. But I felt thirty-six suspects were enough to be making a start on.

'Any dirt on these guys?' I asked half-heartedly.

'Every Troop's clean, Al, you know that.'

I grinned. 'Sure. Clean as a chimney sweep. You know what I mean: are there any you'd have doubts about? Any who are stuck at the Skylight because you don't want them getting in the way around here?'

Frank took the list and examined it. 'Nobody I'm at odds with,' he declared. 'Good soldiers, the lot. What are you looking for?'

I told him about Nic and how I'd learned she hadn't been killed at the Skylight. It was the first he'd heard of it. His face darkened as I broke the news.

'That bastard,' he snarled. 'Thinks he can tell me what he likes and keep the rest to himself. I can't believe I wasn't brought in on this. I'm the head of the goddamn Troops for Christ's sake! I should be the first he comes to with – '

'Frank,' I whistled, 'calm down before your head explodes.'

He glared at me, then relaxed. 'He gets on my tits, Al. You've no idea what it's like working close to that maniac.'

I thought – from my brief experience of him – that I had, but kept the opinion to myself.

'You think one of our guys might have been involved?' he asked.

'It's possible. I know everyone at the Skylight works at half cock but I can't picture them missing some guy dragging in a corpse.'

'*I* can,' Frank grunted. 'It was only her back that was cut up. The killer could have draped a coat over her, pretended she was stoned, waltzed her in brashly in plain sight of everyone. You wouldn't get away with it here, but at the Skylight . . .'

'I'd like to check on them anyway. No objections?'

'It's your time: waste it as you see fit. But have a word with me before you go hassling any of them, OK? I can do without insurrection in the ranks.'

I was on my way out with the list of names when I stopped on an impulse. 'Do you know Richey Harney?'

Frank closed his eyes and mentally searched for a face to match the name. It was one of his gifts – he could keep tabs on every one of his men – and probably the prime reason he'd been chosen to head the Troops.

'Richey,' he nodded, opening his eyes. 'What about him?'

'He said he was at his daughter's birthday party last Thursday. Could you check if – '

'Richey Harney doesn't have a daughter.'

I paused thoughtfully. 'You're sure?'

'Absolutely.'

'Is he married?'

'Was. In the middle of a divorce. No children.'

'I must have been mistaken. See you, Frank.'

Richey had left the building when I went looking for him. I was about to get his address and chase him down when I spotted Vincent Carell chatting up a secretary and decided to have a quiet word with him instead. He wasn't happy to be interrupted while courting but came when I said it was important.

'What's bugging you, man?' he hissed. 'Couldn't you see the sparks zapping between the two of us? I was this close to – '

'You recall our trip to the Fridge last week?' I'd no desire to stand around listening to his sexual fantasies.

'Do I look like a goldfish? 'Course I remember. What about it?'

'You asked Richey Harney to go with you first.'

'Yeah?' Growing guarded.

'He said he had to go to his daughter's birthday party. He missed her first communion and if he missed the party, he'd be in the doghouse with his wife. Remember?'

'Vaguely,' Vincent said, clearly unhappy.

'Richey Harney doesn't have a daughter.'

'He doesn't?'

'And he's in the middle of a divorce.'

'He is?'

I leant in closer, so Vincent had to press against the wall. '*You* can tell me what's going on,' I whispered, 'or I can worm it out of Richey. Either way, one of you will be my friend and one will be my enemy. You understand me, Vincent?'

'Harney won't say anything. He's got more sense.'

'Maybe. But he's also got less to lose than you. If he talks in exchange for my oath that I'll swear everything came from *you* . . .'

Vincent's nostrils flared. 'Don't fuck with me, Algiers.'

'I won't. Not if you play ball. Tell me what that scene

last week was about and I'll keep it to myself. Not a word to anyone. It'll be our little secret.'

Vincent took a deep breath, forehead rippling like the face of a lake during a storm: thinking never was his strongest virtue.

'If you say anything . . .' he finally growled.

'I won't.'

'Ford set me up to it.'

'Up to what?' My eyes never left his: if he lied, I'd know.

'He said to wait until you came down, then go in after you. Harney would be there, waiting, ready to respond when I said what Ford told me to.'

'*And?*' I pressed when he didn't continue.

'You were to take pity on the fool and offer to step in for him. If you didn't, we were to have an "argument" on the way out and I was to storm back in, foaming at the lips. Again I was to give you the chance to volunteer. If you still showed no sign of speaking up, I was to order you to take his place.'

'Tasso meant for me to accompany you?' He nodded. 'Why?'

'Don't know.'

'Vincent . . .'

'No shit, Algiers. Tasso didn't know either: he was following the Cardinal's orders. He was stunned as shit when I reported back and told him who we'd found there. He was gonna go to the Cardinal, then figured he probably knew already and kept his mouth shut.'

'You knew it was Nic Hornyak lying out there on the slab?'

'I'd never heard of her before you ID'd her. Ford neither. She was a Jane Doe as far as we knew.'

'The Cardinal knew better.'

Vincent shrugged. 'Looks that way.'

I stepped away from the wall and thanked Vincent for

his cooperation. He pulled a face, made light of it, warned me not to tell anyone he'd told me, and went back in pursuit of the secretary. I found a chair and sat down. The strength had gone from my legs.

I'd known the Cardinal had known about Nic from the start – the file proved that – but it never occurred to me that I'd been sent to discover the body, that he'd arranged things to make it look like it was my choice.

I recalled card tricks I'd learnt as a kid, and how important the 'force' was: a good magician could force his chosen card on a member of an audience, making it seem like that person had chosen for himself. My trip to the Fridge had been an elaborate force, arranged by the Cardinal to look like an incredible coincidence. And, sap that I was, I'd bought it.

Now that I knew about Vincent and Richey, I got to wondering what other tricks Mr Dorak might have been playing and just how far he might have gone to sucker me in. I'd been assuming Nic was the reason the Cardinal had taken an interest in me, but maybe it was the other way round: he'd confessed to having had his eye on me since I joined the Troops; perhaps he'd decided it was time to wind me up and see how I jumped. Could Nic have been killed on his say-so and planted for me to find?

Christ, I hoped not. It was common practice for the Cardinal to grab some poor unknown by the arm and spin him round, as he was doing with me, and that was fine: plenty walked away from those games, shaken but otherwise unharmed. But sometimes he set up hoops swathed in flames and goaded people through. And I'd yet to hear of anyone making it through those rings of fire unburned.

I spent the rest of Thursday and most of Friday stuck in Party Central, checking on the thirty-six Skylight Troops, scouring the files for incriminating evidence, of which there was plenty: nineteen had chalked up at least one kill; twelve had served time; four were chronic junkies (they 'guarded' the swimming pool and saunas); a further nine were being or had been rehabilitated; one had served as a covert agent in the Middle East, an authorised anarchist who suffered a moral crisis after bombing a school full of children; three used to be rent boys; two were fashioning alternate careers as pimps; most of them gambled and/or drank and/or womanised, though only ten 'dabbled compulsively', as the files put it.

But nothing to link them to Nic or Rudi Ziegler or Paucar Wami. I devoted a lot of time to the rent boys and pimps, figuring they might have moved in the same circles as Nic, but if they had, it wasn't recorded. I made a note to track them down and have a few words in private, but there was no rush: I had other fish to fry.

I wished there was some way of knowing if any of them had been to see the Cardinal during the days and weeks leading up to Nic's death. There had been no official order to Troops to turn a blind eye at the Skylight, so if he *was* behind the murder, he must have had a quiet word with whoever it was he'd chosen to assist him. Problem was, no records were kept of the Cardinal's personal appointments. Only he and his secretaries knew who came and went, and they weren't talking. I could have probed on the quiet – played up to the girls who'd been on duty and milked them for information – but I'd have been treading Lycra-thin ice: the Cardinal's standard method for dealing with folk caught snooping around his personal coterie was to have them dragged out back and executed in plain view, for all to see.

The only way to incriminate the Cardinal if he'd been in on the kill would be directly through those who'd been involved with the murder, and the chances of one of them confessing were slim. All things considered, it was better to leave my options open and continue exploring alternative avenues of possibility.

Namely: Paucar Wami.

There'd been no confirmed sightings since he annihilated Johnny Grace, though several bodies had been discovered bearing some of his numerous trademarks. I made enquiries that Friday by phone, from Party Central, which wasn't the best way: people were always inclined to reveal more face-to-face. I'd wrap up my investigation into the private lives of the Troops early Saturday morning and spend the rest of the day pounding the streets, covering every base I could think of. If nothing turned up, I'd go see Fabio on Sunday.

I cycled home Friday night, bleary-eyed, head pounding. I wasn't accustomed to all this paperwork and computer screens. I didn't know how people stuck it on a regular basis. I felt more sapped of energy than I used to feel after a full boxing bout back when I was a teenager and training to be the next Mike Tyson. I'd always been proud of my clear eyesight but if this kept up it might be time to pop along to an optometrist's and see about a pair of glasses.

I dropped into Ali's on my way up and got a couple of bagels. It was his night off, which was disappointing: I would have enjoyed a harmless, diverting chat session. That made me think of Priscilla. She hadn't called yet. I thought about ringing her but didn't: she'd said she would phone when ready. Priscilla could prove to be a most useful contact – she knew nearly all of Nic's friends and (more importantly) 'business' associates – and it would be foolish to do anything which might drive a wedge between us.

I couldn't face a book, not even a magazine, so I just ate the bagels, brewed a hot lemon-and-honey drink to soothe

the throbs in my head, and headed for bed. For once I was asleep within minutes.

The sound of dripping woke me. Soft, steady, low-pitched drips, too gentle to disturb an ordinary sleeping ear. But I'd been trained to spring awake at the faintest unfamiliar sound: alien footsteps, the creak of a door, an unexpected drip.

It wasn't either of my taps: I checked them every night before turning in, as water-conscious as any good citizen in these days of global warming. Besides, the position was wrong: my bathroom sink was on the other side of the wall at the head of my bed; the kitchen (what bit of a one there was) lay to the far right of the apartment. The drips were coming from the dead centre of the living room.

I swung my legs out, smoothly as I could. My fingers felt beneath the mattress and located the handgun I kept there as a matter of routine. Easing off the safety catch, I stood, not pausing to dress, and started for the door, moving stealthily, poised to open fire at the first sight of an intruder.

I drew up to the door and pressed an ear against it. The steady drip filled my head like a waterfall but I tuned it out and listened for other sounds: footsteps, heavy breathing, the beat of an anxious heart.

Nothing.

Leaving the light off – I wasn't going to make a target of myself – I turned the handle and let the door swing in, stepping to the left in case there was someone on the other side, waiting to barge through in the hope of knocking me to the ground.

No movement. The door reached its limit and stopped. I had the hinges oiled exactly the way I wanted and it didn't swing closed again, as some doors would. If there was anyone on the other side, he was in no hurry to reveal himself.

I stepped out, left hand steadying my right as I led with my gun. Worst mistake an amateur can make: sticking his head out for a cautious advance look. You lose your brains that way. Coming out like this, I presented a clearer target, but at least I'd have the opportunity to fire back if there was a marksman out there.

Nobody in immediate sight. The room was full of shadows but I knew after a brief once-over that it was clean. Except for the object hanging from the light bulb in the centre of the room, which was the source of the drips.

I moved towards it swiftly, head flicking left and right, arms locked in front, primed to cover either side of the room. As I closed in on the object the sounds of the drips magnified. Again I had to focus to tune them out.

Half a metre from it, I stopped. My eyes had grown accustomed to the darkness and it took less than a second to realise I was staring at the rear of a severed human head – a head which was hanging from a wire and revolving slowly.

As it spun agonisingly around, my immediate thought was that this was one of my dreams come to horrifying life: Tom Jeery's ghost head. My breath caught in my throat and the nozzle of my gun lifted. I almost let the head have a full clip, but caught myself before I fired: the head posed no threat and opening up on it would be a waste of ammunition and a sign of blind panic.

I watched breathlessly as the face crept into view, and though the sane part of me knew it couldn't be my dead father, I couldn't shake the fear that this was his spirit come to chastise me for not taking care of his mortal remains.

Then I caught sight of two twisting snakes running

down the sides of the face and all thoughts of supernatural spectres fled.

This was no corporeal phantom. It was the solid, disconnected head of the city's emperor of death: *Paucar Wami!*

13

Years of training evaporated in seconds. I froze, arms dropping, eyes widening. Wami's face filled my vision; the sound of his blood splattering the floor crowded the cavities of my ears and deafened me to all else. The city could have gone up in flames and I wouldn't have noticed. There was only the head, its eyes gouged out, the skin at the sides of the nose peeled away to create a pair of huge thumb-size holes, chin chipped in twain (hammer and chisel? a drill?) where the heads of the snakes should have met.

I was obsessed by the head itself. Not wondering how it got here, who hung it from my lamp, or where he was now.

A hand slid over my right shoulder and gripped my throat. Another hand darted around the left side of my face. On the middle finger was a ring, a ten-centimetre spike growing from its glinting underbelly. It was one stroke away from making a gooey puddle of my left eye.

'Drop your weapon; relax; do nothing stupid.' It was a soft but confidently cruel voice. Even a fool would have paid attention to it. And I was no fool. I let the gun slip from my fingers, kicked it away and allowed my arms to hang uselessly by my sides.

'Sit,' my captor said, and I felt the edge of a chair – it

must have been the one I kept by the window of my bedroom – bite into the backs of my legs. He phrased it like an invitation but I knew I had no choice, so I sat. If the head in front of me hadn't been so distorted by pain, I would have sworn it was laughing.

The hand around my throat withdrew. Seconds later, so did the hand with the ring. A fool would have dived for the gun. I sat firm.

'Where were you?' I asked, sickened to be caught so cheaply.

'Under the bed, of course,' he chuckled. 'Isn't that where all the bogeymen converge?'

It must have taken more than the few seconds I was frozen for him to slide out, fetch the chair and cross the room after me. Why hadn't I sensed him? Even a ghost would have made some kind of noise.

'Who are you?' I asked. 'What do you want?'

'In time,' he answered, then reached forward and prodded the head. It jerked away from his touch, as though repulsed. 'Know who this belongs to?'

I gulped. 'Yes.'

'Say his name. I want to hear it.'

I licked my lips. I didn't know what was happening but knew I had to play along: whoever this guy was, he'd killed the man many said couldn't be killed. He wasn't to be taken lightly.

'It's Paucar Wami,' I croaked.

'Indeed?' He sounded pleased. 'I always thought Wami was a bigger man.' There was a lengthy pause. I came close to bolting. Managed to stay in check, though it wasn't easy.

'Do you know why I am here?'

The question caught me by surprise. I couldn't answer straightaway. Then I felt something sharp scratch along the width of my bare back and the words tumbled out.

'No. I don't even know who you are. How could I – '

'Enough.' He patted my right shoulder, to calm me down. 'I am not here to kill you.' His hand crept forward and he pointed at the head with his index finger. 'I have had enough killing for one night.'

'Could I have that in writing?' My chattering teeth made a mockery of the show of bravado.

'I will write it for you in blood if you wish,' he teased. Then: 'Do not, at any stage, turn around. If you gaze upon my face, I will have to kill you.'

'Who are you?' I asked calmly this time. It was possible he was playing with me, and had no intention of letting me live, but things didn't seem quite as desperate as they had at first.

'Ask instead who I am not,' he replied cryptically.

'OK. Who aren't you?'

'I am not *him*.' The hand poked the head again. 'And *he* is not Paucar Wami. His name is – was – Allegro Jinks. A lovely name. I never knew an Allegro before. Unfortunate surname though. He was destined for a sticky end with a moniker like that.'

I frowned and focused on the tattooed features hanging from the thin wire. The face was the spitting image of how I'd pictured Wami. I began to mutter: 'I don't follow. If he isn't – '

Then the penny dropped and I groaned.

Paucar Wami – as my assailant most surely was – chuckled. 'I see I have no need to introduce myself. Good. I hate formal introductions. Much nicer to drop oneself in another's lap and simply say, "Let's be friends."'

'You've a funny way of making friends,' I noted drily.

'I am a funny sort of man,' he replied. 'Funny peculiar, it goes without saying.'

We were chatting like amiable strangers in a bar. It was crazy. But I'd rather the craziness to being speared on his ring spike or having my throat crushed by his more than capable fingers.

'Why are you here?' I asked. 'What do you want?'

'I want nothing, Al. It is Al, is it not?' I nodded. 'I come as an ally, bringing you this fine head as a goodwill token. I was going to send it by mail, then thought, "No, he will appreciate the personal touch that little bit more," and decided to lug it over myself.'

'You shouldn't have bothered.'

'Is that a rebuke, Al?' He pinched my shoulder sharply. 'I do not like rebukes. Not when I go out of my way to – '

'It wasn't a rebuke!' I hissed quickly. 'It wasn't a rebuke!'

'Good.' He released my flesh, then rubbed it with his fingers to prevent swelling. 'You were looking for me. Asking questions. Spreading nasty rumours. Said I killed the Hornyak girl. That wasn't nice. I could not stand for such slander. Normally I would have put a quick end to the lies. But you interested me. I couldn't understand why you were so convinced of my involvement. I did some checking. Discovered she had been seen around town with a Paucar Wami ringer.'

'A *ringer*?' I almost looked over my shoulder, then remembered the warning. 'It wasn't you with Nic?'

'I never met Nicola Hornyak. Never heard of the girl. Until your queries drew my attention to her.' I felt him leaning into my back. I didn't move, though the temptation to shy away from his touch was great. He leant forward and stroked the dead man's cheeks, caressing the writhing snakes, one after the other.

'These beauties belong to me and no other,' he said, barely more than a whisper. 'They are not copyrighted, true, but in this city my presence is my copyright. No other has a right to wear the snakes.

'When I heard of the impostor, I made the rounds of

various tattoo parlours. I had only the newer establishments – those which had set up shop since last I visited these environs – to focus on: older and wiser heads know better than to fashion their customers with Paucar Wami's serpentine brand, no matter how lucrative the offer.

'A slim Chinaman called Ho Yun Fen was the guilty party. A pleasant gentleman. Quite an artist. A shame to kill him, but shame and I go back a long way together. Ho Yun remembered the snakes. He remembered the customer's name and the fact that a pretty young white girl had been with him.'

'When was this?' I asked, curiosity getting the better of my fear.

'Five weeks before her death. Yes,' he said, as I opened my mouth to form the question, 'the girl was Nicola Hornyak, though that only came out when I paid a call on poor Mr Jinks. He protected her identity as vigorously as one could, given the circumstances, but in the end was forced to part with the secret, painful as it was.'

I stared at the ruined face of Allegro Jinks and made up my mind to tell Wami anything he wanted to know, the second he asked.

'Did Jinks kill her?' I asked.

'No. He had nothing to do with it. She rang him earlier that night and told him to stay in: said she would be over later on. He fell asleep waiting. Heard nothing of her until she made the papers the next week.'

'That was his story?'

'That was the *truth*.' I could feel Wami's smile warming the room. 'Men don't lie when you scoop out their eyes, then start in on their genitalia.'

I could feel my testicles retreating at the thought.

'Did he know who killed her?' I asked, driving the picture of a dismembered Jinks from my mind.

'Not a clue. He was not acquainted with her ways. She

picked him up one night, a fortnight or so prior to his tattooing. Used an alias. Never told him where she lived. No phone number. Used him as she pleased.'

'For sex?'

'That and more. The tattoos were *her* idea. He did not want them. She performed acts of wanton abandon – which I blush to think about – to win him over to her will. She also made him shave his scalp: he had a full head of black locks when they met.'

That startled me. 'Did she say why?'

'She told him it would make him look sexy.' Wami chuckled. 'Which, dare I say, is true enough. Tall, lithe, black, bare skull, tattooed cheeks: how could one go wrong?'

Once again my eyes fixed on the snakes, then took in the shaven pate and noticed it was covered by a light layer of bristle. Why had Nic encouraged such a change? Could it have been coincidence? Many of her privileged kind knew nothing of Paucar Wami. Then I recalled that she'd been a prostitute into the bargain, and had surely heard tales. It must have been an act of deliberate imitation.

'So much for my story,' Wami said chirpily. 'How about yours? Any idea why your girlfriend would have kitted Allegro out like this?'

'She knew a medium called Rudi Ziegler,' I answered, client confidentiality flying out the window. 'She took Wami – I mean, Jinks – to see him not long before her death. Said he was her demon lover. Maybe she'd heard about your exploits and description and thought this was how a demon would look.'

'You mean an actual demoniacal lover as opposed to one who is red-hot in bed?'

'Yes.'

'Interesting. Allegro mentioned her interest in the occult. Do you think I should pay a call on Ziegler?'

'No!' I said hastily. 'He's a harmless old quack. He'd nothing to do with her death.'

'Then who had?'

'I don't know,' I groaned. 'I thought it was *you* until you turned up with . . . that.' Meaning the head. 'If it wasn't you and it wasn't Jinks, I don't know who it could have been.'

'It wasn't *you*, was it?' Wami asked casually.

'*Me?*'

'Concern is a fine form of camouflage. Nobody's going to suspect a man so determined to bring her killer to justice, a hero who charges around, accusing all and sundry.'

'I didn't kill her.'

'It makes no difference to me if you did or did not. I will let you live either way. But confessing can do wonders for a man's soul.'

'I. Didn't. Kill. Her.' Through gritted teeth this time.

'Fair enough. Just thought I would ask.' There was the briefest of sighs as he stood. 'I might as well be off then.'

'That's it?' I asked, startled.

'Unless you want to share a beer and pretzels,' he laughed.

'That's all you came for? To show me the head and tell me about Jinks?'

'And to clear my name. I need not have: every unsolved murder in this city – and many of the solved – is attributed to me. I care not what people think. But I know of your connection to the Cardinal, and this was a peculiar instance of mistaken identity, and . . .' He paused, then shrugged (I knew by the rustling of his leather jacket). 'You could say it was pride. I solved the mystery and I wanted someone to share it with.'

'You only solved part of the mystery,' I reminded him. 'You didn't find out who killed Nic.'

'That part is of no interest to me. I wanted to know who was impersonating me and why. If the Hornyak girl was alive I might pay her a visit and ask why she demanded the make-over, but even *I* have never managed to pry secrets from the dead. I will be keeping an eye on developments and my ear to the ground, but my curiosity has been sated.'

'How can I trust you?' I asked. 'You might have ordered Jinks's tattoo yourself, to serve as a red herring.'

'To what end?'

'To stop me sniffing around after you.'

Wami's laughter was vibrant. 'I said you interested me, Al Jeery: you never irritated me. If you had, I would have sent you the same way as Allegro, Cardinal or no. You may enquire after me further, if that is your wish, though I would not recommend it.'

'What about Jinks?' I asked, sensing – more than hearing – Wami begin to retreat. 'Aren't you taking him with you?'

'Al,' he chuckled, '*I* disposed of the body. It's only fair that *you* should take care of the head.'

'But if I'm caught with it . . .'

'Don't be.' My bedroom window slid open and there was a slight creaking as Wami eased through it. 'Count to fifty,' he said, voice coming from the other side of the window. The fire escape at the rear had collapsed years before: he must have been clinging to the wall itself, like a bat. 'And, Al?'

'Yes?'

'Count slow,' he laughed, and then was gone, leaving me to make the slowest fifty count of my life.

My mind wanted to take Wami's words and run with them: what had Nic been up to with Allegro Jinks? Why the façade? Had she been seeking to invoke the spirit of the killer? Had it been a game, making her lover up to look like a famous serial killer just for the thrill? Or had somebody else been behind it? Had somebody told Nic to –

First things first. I drowned out the clamouring speculative voices and concentrated on the problem closest to hand: the head. I had to get rid of it and quickly. Paucar Wami could whistle carelessly while carting heads around as if they were melons but I was of a more pragmatic nature: if I was found with this, I'd be up shit's creek. There were people on the police force – Howard Kett, for one – who'd love to send me down for a long, long stretch, and this would provide them with the perfect opportunity. For all I knew, that was exactly what Wami was setting me up for, and his talk had been nothing more than distracting bluff.

I cut the head down – the knots in the wire would have taken too long to unravel – and stuck it in a small plastic bag, wrapped that in a pillow case, then dumped the package in a large black rubbish bag and tied it shut. Quickly wiped up the worst of the blood with a rag and squeezed it out into the sink (I'd make a more thorough effort on the cleaning later; right now, disposing of the head was my main priority).

I dressed in dark clothes, grabbed the bag and skulked down the stairs. I'd no carrier basket on my bike so I rode one-handed, the other holding the bag just above the knot, ready to toss it away at a moment's notice.

I arrived at the Fridge unimpeded. As I keyed in the security code I was certain a posse of cops would spring out of nowhere and bust me, but they didn't. When the door slid closed behind me, I fell against a nearby wall and relaxed, feeling safe for the first time since I awoke to the sound of drips.

A male clerk helped me check in the head. He didn't raise an eyebrow when I dumped the bag on the counter and told him I wanted to make a deposit. 'Will you be requiring a full casket or a box?' he asked politely.

'Are you taking the piss?' I growled.

'No, sir. A casket will be made available if you so desire, but in cases such as these we normally make use of our more compact storage facilities. Space is at a premium.'

I told him a box would be fine. When he asked for the corpse's details I said I'd rather not provide any. He nodded, keyed something into his computer, swivelled the terminal around so it was facing me, and handed me the keyboard. 'Do you have a clearance code, sir?' I shook my head. 'Then please type in your name and position and press enter.'

'I don't want to give my name.'

'I understand, sir. That's why I'm letting *you* key it in. I won't see your name, only your status. I need that to ensure you have the authority to command further secrecy.'

I did as he asked and pressed enter, not turning the screen back to him until I'd seen my name disappear to be replaced with a string of coded numbers. The clerk examined the data, smiled positively at me, then handed me a brief form and an envelope.

'Please fill in the name of the deceased and any pertinent details you care to include. Age, address, known relatives, etc.'

'Do I have to?'

'I'm afraid so. You have code blue clearance. That means you must fill out a form. It will then be locked away, unseen, and may only be retrieved under direct orders of the Cardinal.'

'And me,' I added.

He shook his head. 'No, sir. Only the Cardinal.'

'You mean, once I drop this bag off, I can't reclaim it or check on it or – '

'You can check on the *bag*, sir, and take or move it as you please, assuming we receive no orders from higher powers to the contrary. It's the *form* you can't touch. That remains the property of the Cardinal.'

'Where does it go?'

'I really can't say. But I assure you: none other than the Cardinal may access it.'

'I don't have to include my own name?'

'No, sir.'

'What if I made up a name for the . . . ?' I shook the bag.

The clerk smiled. 'You may play dice with the Cardinal if you wish. That is your prerogative, sir.'

I thought about it, grunted, and scribbled down the name of Allegro Jinks. Since I knew nothing about the man, I left the rest of the form blank, sealed it and passed it back to the clerk.

'I don't want the *object* taken out of the bag,' I told him.

'Very good, sir.' He made a note of it.

'How would I get it out again?'

'I'll give you a slip when I'm finished processing it,' he said. 'The box's number will be on it.'

'Will I be the only one who knows the number?'

He shrugged. 'We'll have a record saying the box is occupied but that's all the information there'll be.'

'And if somebody comes looking for a list of every box with a mystery bag in it?'

'The contents of the box won't be recorded. There'll be no way to trace your . . . *object*.'

'Fine.' I was going to leave it at that when I had a brainwave: only Wami and I knew what had happened to Jinks. If Nic had been encouraged by another to persuade Jinks to reinvent himself, maybe that party would come looking for their missing puppet.

'There's a way of tagging names here, isn't there?' I asked. 'Of setting things up so, if someone asks about a certain name, certain other people are immediately informed?'

The clerk nodded. 'For those with clearance, yes.'

'Do I have clearance?'

'Code blue?' He smiled. 'Most certainly, sir.'

'Let's do it.'

He keyed up another screen and again handed control over to me. He never once looked suspicious: they got involved in cloak-and-dagger stuff like this all the time at the Fridge.

'Type the corpse's name in at the top. Tab down, then type in your own and how you wish to be contacted: fax, phone, letter, e-mail. If anybody asks after it, you will be notified, unless their clearance supersedes your own and they demand secrecy.'

'What if they don't give their name?'

'Then we will inform you of their interest alone.'

'Is there any way they can trace the corpse to me?'

'No, sir. Contact names are never revealed, unless asked for by the Cardinal. A hacker could possibly uncover it, but such an event is extremely unlikely.'

I typed in the two names, left my mobile number, pressed enter and watched the information disappear with a beep. Minutes later it was finished. The clerk handed me the slip of paper while the bag was placed on a tray, soon to be removed and boxed. I thanked him, let myself out, cycled home and began mopping up blood.

14

If Wami was telling the truth – and, as he'd said, it would be easier for him to kill me than lie – I'd have to look for a new prime suspect. It was a drag – having to rethink my priorities and start over again – but at the same time it was a relief to know he wasn't involved. And it had done my confidence no end of good: if I could survive a confrontation with Paucar Wami, I reckoned I could survive just about anything.

I spent Saturday digging for connections between Allegro Jinks and the Troops who'd been at the Skylight. Jinks had been a bad boy: a string of arrests and convictions stretching back to his childhood, four years as a juvenile detainee, a total of eight years behind bars since he turned eighteen; hooked on crack, did some dealing when he was low on cash; affiliated with several gangs over the years – bit-players, the lot – but not recently, not since he'd tripped an alarm during a break-in and snitched on two of his 'brothers' in exchange for leniency.

There was surprisingly little violence in his history. Jinks was a coward. Avoided fights whenever possible, only wading in if the odds were stacked heavily in his favour. Stole from his women – the few there had been – but never beat them. Never killed anyone, though he'd boasted of doing so. Maybe Nic was taken in by those boasts. Perhaps the thought of bedding a killer had excited her and, when she discovered the truth, she'd made him over as Wami in the hope that some of the killer's passion would rub off on a lookalike.

No links to the Troops that I could find. One lived a couple of blocks from where Jinks had resided these past two years, since completing his last prison spell. Another six had grown up in the same neighbourhood, so might have known him as kids: I'd have to ask them in person or check on the streets to find out. A further three – one of whom was a rent boy, which sounded promising – had served time in the slammer while he was there.

I OK'd it with Frank before having words with the jailbirds. Two were on duty at the Skylight; the other was at home. He summoned all three to Party Central at my request and I went one-on-one with them in an underground holding-cell, quizzing them about their pasts, Nic Hornyak and (thrown in as an apparent afterthought) Allegro Jinks.

None had known Nic personally, though all were familiar with her name following the furore at the Skylight. Two remembered Jinks from their time as guests of the state, though they hadn't consorted with him inside. The rent boy said he bought grass from him a couple of times – Jinks had managed to smuggle in a stash, and for a while made a tidy profit, until he smoked what he had left and blew the money he'd saved on bad coke which he ended up flushing when word of its inadequacies spread – but that was as far as their relationship went.

None knew what Jinks was doing these days or where he was staying or what had become of him. Reluctantly I crossed them off my list and looked again to pastures new.

Priscilla rang late Saturday night. A long conversation. She was more open now that I knew the truth about her.

Talked freely about Nic and the tricks they'd pulled. I asked if she was prepared to provide me with a list of Nic's boyfriends. She wasn't, but said she'd take me around and introduce me to friends, colleagues and customers of theirs if I thought that would help. She also promised to get in contact with Nic's old beaus and ask them to talk to me. We agreed to make a start in the morning.

'Not too early,' she giggled. 'I spell Saturday night p-a-r-t-y.'

While Priscilla went to party, I returned to my mire of papers – at this stage they covered the floor like a plague – and once again panned blindly through them for the clue which would place me on the track of the killer.

Nic's friends and acquaintances were understandably loath to discuss their private affairs, and if I'd been alone I'd have got nothing out of them. But Priscilla sweet-talked them and chipped away and slowly got them to open up. Not that we learned anything: a few had tricked with Nic in the past but none had seen or heard from her the night of the murder; none had taken Priscilla's place in room 812 of the Skylight; none knew of any dangerous customers she'd been with; nobody recognised the name of Allegro Jinks.

A few mentioned Nic's interest in the occult. A teenager with a line of holes up his arm like a seam saw her crouched over a brown paper bag in an alley once. Her face was painted, 'like those Indians in the movies? Or the Africans? The ones with warpaint or whatever the hell. Squiggly lines, circles, triangles, that sorta shit.' She'd been naked, staggering around, muttering to herself, lifting the bag to her face and inhaling. After a while, she dumped the bag in a bin and staggered away. The kid went for a peek.

'It was a dead rat!' he squeaked. 'It'd been stabbed to

death. The paper was soaked through with blood. That's what she'd been sniffing. Freaked me out. I stuck clear of her after that.'

One of her friends said Nicola had tried interesting her in black magic. 'She was always on at me to read weird books: *tomes*, she called them. I looked at a few. Ugly, horrible things. Photos of dead animals and masks and incantations which were meant to raise the dead, only they were written in some obscure language, so I couldn't read them.'

I asked if Nic had ever invited her to spiritual meetings. 'Yes, a couple of times.' With who? 'Some Zegler guy.' *Rudi.* Any others? 'A few, yeah. I didn't go. Zegler was enough, with his smoke machine and glowing crystal ball.'

There were more like that, with similar stories. Nearly everyone who'd known her said she'd been mixed up in witchcraft, sorcery, dark magic, 'shit like that'. I'd have to give the human-sacrifice theory more thought. As a start I rang Ellen Tuesday evening and asked how she was getting on with Ziegler. She wasn't happy to hear from me.

'I said I'd ring when I had something to report,' she snapped.

'I know. I was just – '

'Don't pressure me, OK?'

'I'm not – '

'If you ring again the deal's off.' And *slam!* the phone went down. Why are women such temperamental, unreasonable creatures?

I enjoyed the couple of days I spent with Priscilla. She insisted on linking arms whenever we were out walking, and had a lovely habit of resting her head on my shoulder and mumbling in a low voice which only I could hear. I never made a pass, and she never gave any clear indication that she wanted me to, but I spent a lot of time thinking about it, imagining the two of us getting it on, undressing her with my eyes when I thought she wasn't watching.

Tuesday night, she said I'd have to make my own way for a while, at least until the weekend. She'd been neglecting her work at the salon but couldn't ring in sick indefinitely. She invited me out Friday night, to meet more of her friends in less formal circumstances. I said I'd think about it and get in touch. She favoured me with a kiss as we parted, a dry sisterly peck on the lips. There was nothing romantic or promising in that embrace, but I spent most of the night dreaming about it nonetheless.

I meant to dive back into the paperwork Wednesday morning – looking for links between Ziegler and Jinks and/or the Troops – but when I woke up and stared around at the opened files and their bulging data-stuffed intestines, a switch clicked off inside my head. I couldn't face it. I'd been cramming my head with profiles, theories, facts and figures for nearly two weeks straight. I needed a break. And, since I was my own boss and directly answerable to nobody, I took one.

I cycled to Shankar's for breakfast, a full meal to set me up for the day. Ate by myself, not wanting anything to distract me from my day of rest. Went for a long walk by the river afterwards, a good two hours at medium stride. The scenery wasn't up to much but it was nice to watch the boats drifting by. I'd always dreamed of owning a boat. If I cracked the case, maybe I'd ask the Cardinal for a small yacht by way of a reward, take a few months off and sail up and down the coast. (Grinning as I thought:) Bring Priscilla along as first mate.

It was a sweltering day – the roads shimmered and poorly tarmacked paths were melting in places – and I was soaked with sweat by the end of the walk. I was heading for home and a shower when I had a better idea, located a public swimming pool and went for a swim. Did forty lengths of the pool, changing strokes at regular intervals. Felt like a fish by the time I got out.

The movies after that. A Bogie double bill: *The Maltese Falcon* and a creaky old piece called *The Petrified Forest*, which would have been unbearable but for the presence of its rising young star. Bogie, Edward G. Robinson and Cagney: I could watch them in anything.

A pub called the Penguin's Craw after the flicks. A quiet drinking hole, no music, no TV, no fancy gimmicks or promotions. Just alcohol, a bar and plenty of chairs. The sort of place you went for a discussion or to play chess. I ordered a cup of coffee and went for a wander round the two-storey establishment. I stopped to watch a couple of guys in their fifties or sixties playing darts and got chatting to them about their children and what they'd worked at before retiring and how they spent their time these days.

Students poured in later – gangs of them were constantly 'finding' the pub and annoying the regulars – and soon the air was awash with their monkey-like chattering: majors and minors, tutors, dissertations, the Big Game, inadequate library facilities, overdue essays, how much they'd had to drink last night. The usual student gibberish. I stuck it for an hour, hoping they were on a pub crawl and would move on. When I saw they were settling in for the night, I upped stakes.

Cruised the city for a couple more hours, just cycling or walking aimlessly, mingling with the late-night crowds; popped into a twenty-four-hour bookshop and picked up a James Ellroy page-turner; wandered down to the river again and observed the boats, now lit up and filled with drunken revellers; went for a very late supper in a pirate-themed restaurant called Blackbeard's Galley; got home about one in the morning and went straight to bed.

I enjoyed the break so much, I took Thursday off as well.

Why not? I'd be busy come the weekend, interviewing more of Nic's companions, compiling more stacks of files, shuffling through them like a card-shark desperately trying to conjure up a winning hand. I didn't think two free days per fortnight was too much to ask.

Alas, my second day of rest was cut short when my mobile went off halfway through *Little Caesar* (with *The Roaring Twenties* – Bogie and Cagney together in the one film! – to follow). I cursed quietly and quickly retired to the foyer before the tutting film buffs bludgeoned me to death with their ticket stubs.

'What is it?' I snapped, angrier at myself for forgetting to leave the mobile switched off than I was at the caller.

'Mr Jeery?' A female voice. Unfamiliar.

'Yeah?'

'My name's Monica Hope. I work at the Fridge.'

'Oh?' I suddenly lost all interest in Edward G.

'You wished to be notified if we received any enquiries regarding a certain Allegro Jinks?'

My heart beating fast: 'Yes?'

'There's been one.'

'Could you hold a moment, please?' I checked to make sure nobody was eavesdropping, pressed the phone closer to my face and lowered my voice. 'Did he leave a name?'

'Yes, sir.'

Through a victorious grin I bid her, 'Continue.' She did.

His name was Breton Furst and he was one of the Troops who'd been guarding the Skylight the night of Nic's murder. One of the cleaner of the clan: never served time, no nasty habits, married since the age of nineteen, three kids (ten, six and two), trustworthy; no visible connection to Nic, though it wouldn't surprise me if one came to light.

I didn't ask Frank for permission to interview him: I'd have had to tell him about Jinks, and that was something

I'd prefer to keep between myself and Furst. I checked with Party Central after the phone call from the Fridge and learned he was at home on a day's leave. I got the address and shot across town.

He was out on the street when I arrived, loading a basket into the back of a red Nissan, preparing for a picnic. His two oldest kids – a boy and a girl, chronologically – were in the back seat, leaning on the headrests, watching their father. His wife emerged, youngest kid in tow, and asked if he had everything. He said he did and she shut the door and started for the car.

'Mr Furst! Breton!' I yelled, propping my bike against a lamp-post and hurrying over, not pausing to chain it. He glanced at me suspiciously, right hand edging towards the pistol I could see strapped to his left side. I smiled and showed my empty palms. I recognised his face from the photos in the file but he didn't know me from Adam.

'Can I help you, friend?' he asked. His wife had stopped on the pavement and was passing a small bag to the kids on the back seat. The two-year-old had wandered towards his daddy.

'My name's Al Jeery, Mr Furst. I have to – '

'I've heard of you. Party Central, right?'

'Right. I have to talk to you. Now.'

He frowned and looked at his wife and children. She was staring at him, a look which was easy to read: 'Go off on business, Buster, and you'll be cooking your own dinners from here till Christmas.'

'Can't it wait? We're on our way to – '

'It's about Allegro Jinks.' His face dropped. I glanced around. This was a quiet, respectable neighbourhood. An elderly gentleman was on the sidewalk further up, washing his car. A woman pushed a pram along the opposite side of the street, a kid following slowly behind. 'We can do it out here if you want,' I said, 'or we can go in where it's nice and secluded, out of the way of your family and friends.'

'You're just here to *talk*, aren't you?' He looked nervous.

I smiled. 'That's all.'

He sighed unhappily. 'I don't think I can help you, Mr Jeery, but come on in and we'll see what we can do. Just give me a moment to clear it with – '

He was turning to tell his wife about the delay when he staggered and took a couple of steps back. I thought he'd lost his footing, but then spotted the red stain spreading down the front of his shirt and realised the twitching in his hands was the start of a death rattle, not a feeble attempt to regain his balance.

'Breton?' his wife asked sharply, sensing something bad. She moved towards him, arms lifting to steady him on his feet, but he hit the ground before she cleared the rear of the car. 'Breton!' she screamed and darted forward. She opened her mouth to scream again. Before she could, a bullet made a fleshy rag of her throat. She collapsed to her knees, then began crawling to her already dead husband.

'Stay back!' I roared. Stunned as I was, my gun had leapt into my hand and I was covering the rows of houses across the road. But the assassin had struck too quickly and I hadn't managed to pinpoint his location. 'Mrs Furst! Don't come any – '

The top of her head fanned out in a cloud of blood and hair and she fell face-down onto the pavement. The two kids in the back seat had witnessed all this and began to scream their lungs out. The girl hammered at the window, yelling, 'Mummy! Mummy!' The boy kicked and pounded at his door, which must have been child-locked.

'Stay down!' I shouted at them. 'Get your heads the fuck down!'

Ignoring me, the boy abandoned the lock and rolled down the window. He was halfway out when his chest erupted in a forest of red, bony splinters. His head flew back, connected harshly with the roof – not that it mattered by this stage – then slumped forward.

I'd spotted the marksman – two houses along to the left, second-storey window – and fired on him. But I was on the ground with a handgun; he was in an elevated position with a rifle. I might as well have spared my ammunition for when I needed it.

The glass in the rear window of the car shattered over the girl. She shrieked with pain and covered her face with her hands. She fell out of sight and for a few seconds I thought she was going to stay there, under cover, out of harm's way. Then she sprang up like a jack-in-a-box, yelling about her eyes, pleading for help, calling for her mummy. There were two soft popping sounds – like damp lips peeling apart – and she cried no more.

I was on one knee now, gun hand braced, focused on my target. I hit the window – no small feat from where I was – and the sniper drew back to avoid the shards of broken glass. My eyes swivelled to the youngest of the Furst children, the sole family survivor. He was by his father, tugging at the dead man's bloodied shirt, bawling his eyes out. Two years old: too young to understand what was happening, but old enough to realise something was seriously amiss.

I should have held my position or ducked behind the car – that would have been the correct procedure – but how could I leave a two-year-old kid out in the open, at the mercy of a killer who had thus far shown none?

Praying the sniper hadn't recovered, I dived towards the boy, grabbed him round the torso with my left arm, pulled him off his feet and spun around, gun coming up protectively.

A bullet nicked the top of my right arm. Red spray arced up into my eyes. I held on to my gun, useless though it was now that I was temporarily blind. Stumbling backwards, unaccustomed to the weight of the child, I fell on my posterior, presenting a soft, ridiculous target. I started to pull the boy into my chest, planning to turn over and shield him with my body, so at least one of us might walk away from this, but before I could make the ultimate sacrifice his face disappeared in a howl of red and I found myself staring down into a nightmare mask of blood, bone and brains.

Cradling the boy in my arms, I let my gun drop and waited for the killer to finish the job. Seconds passed. I thought the sniper must be reloading but eventually, as stunned neighbours crept from their houses like frightened Munchkins, it dawned on me that he'd wrapped up for the day, that I had been spared.

As I gazed around at the plethora of bodies through blood-filmed eyes, I found little to be grateful for. In the face of so much tragedy it seemed to me that this must be the most cynical act of charity since God let Lot go but turned his wife into a pillar of salt for daring to look back.

I refused to surrender my hold on the boy until the ambulance arrived and it became necessary to give him up. I sat in a cooling pool of blood and rocked him lightly to and fro, unaware of the pain in my arm, heedless of the crowd forming around me, staring dead ahead at nothing.

The first cops on the scene approached me warily, eyeing the gun, shouting at me to kick it away, thinking it was the murder weapon. An old man – the one who'd been washing his car when the madness began – stepped into their path and told them what had happened, how I'd acted heroically and been injured trying to save the child. They relaxed after that and lowered their guns. One asked if I was OK. I nodded. Did I want to let go of the kid? I shook my head and tried telling him I'd wait for the ambulance, but my mouth wouldn't work.

When I eventually handed over the boy – they covered his body with a sheet and wheeled it away – a medic crouched beside me and attended to my arm. A light graze. Nothing a spot of cleaning, a bandage and a few days' rest couldn't cure. The supervising officer checked to make sure I didn't require hospitalisation, then had me gently loaded into the back of a squad car and escorted to the local precinct for questioning.

They went easy on me, allowing for shock, asking if I wanted anything, a drink, something to eat, a lawyer. I replied in the negative to all offers, concentrating to make my vocal cords work, and told them I just wanted to tell my side of the story and go home.

Three cops handled the interrogation (and, polite as they were, that's what it was). One was in uniform, one in a suit, the third in casuals. They gave their names but I found it easier to identify them by their clothes. The one in uniform was a meathead, and though he refrained from harassing me outright, he was the least sympathetic of the three. They noted my particulars: name, address, occupation. Their ears perked to attention when they heard I was in the Troops. I could see Uniform's eyes narrowing suspiciously.

'Do you have a licence for that gun?' he asked after a while, even though he could tell by the make that it was standard Troop issue.

'Of course.'

'Breton Furst was in the Troops too, wasn't he?' Casuals asked.

'Yes.'

'Were you good friends?'

'I never saw him before today.'

They glanced at one another, then Casuals gave Uniform

a nod. 'So what were you doing at his house?' Uniform blurted out, and I knew he was the flunkey, here to ask the other pair's dirty questions and take the heat if I created a fuss.

I had to think quickly to come up with a lie that would sound legitimate. It wasn't easy after what I'd been through, but Troops are trained to separate their thoughts from emotions, to function like automatons, regardless of their feelings.

'Breton works – worked – at the Skylight. My post's at Party Central but I was thinking of changing. I've been asking around, trying to find out whether the Skylight is a good career move or not. One of my friends said to give Breton a ring: he'd been at the Skylight nearly six years, so if anyone knew the set-up, it was him. I called earlier today. He said he was going on a picnic with his family but I could tag along if I liked and we'd discuss work over a hot dog and a beer.'

'Do you drink a lot?' Uniform asked.

'Used to. I'm teetotal these days but Furst didn't know that. As I said, we hadn't met before today.'

'Go on,' the cop in the suit encouraged me softly.

'There's not much more to say,' I answered honestly. 'I arrived, walked over to greet him, next thing I knew . . .' I drummed my fingers on the table top, putting sounds to the volley of bullets which the marksman's silencer had muted.

'You didn't see the assassin?' Suit.

'I saw where he was but couldn't get a make on him.'

'Any idea who'd have it in for the Fursts?' Uniform.

'How could I? I didn't know them.'

'You don't think it was connected to your being there?' Suit.

'No.' A barefaced lie. 'I went over to talk shop. Whatever this was about, it had nothing to do with me.

228

It was bad timing, that was all. I wandered in at the wrong moment.'

'Any chance the sniper was after *you?*' Uniform asked, and even his colleagues looked embarrassed by the ridiculous question.

'Yes,' I said, smiling grimly, 'but he was a lousy shot. An accidental ricochet accounted for the five others.'

'Must have been the same rubber bullet that killed Kennedy,' the casually dressed cop chuckled, then looked immediately contrite when Uniform turned on him and glared.

It went on in that vein for hours, the uniformed heavy asking most of the questions, Casuals making the occasional observation, Suit saying little, judging my answers. I was happy to cooperate: focusing on the three men and their enquiries kept my mind off the Fursts. I knew the images of the family in the blood-soaked dust of the street would return to haunt me later, but right now I was only concerned with getting through the rest of the day intact.

Having made up their minds that I was either unbreakable or simply innocent, they drew the interrogation to a close and prepared me to leave. New clothes had been purchased for me during the interim and I was led to the showers to wash before changing. I could hear reporters outside, clamouring for news. Suit stepped into the locker room as I was slipping on my socks and asked if I wanted to confront the media. I said definitely not.

'What about my name?' I asked. 'Has it been released?'

'No, but it'll probably leak soon.'

'Any way of holding it back?'

He shrugged. '*We* won't be able to keep the press quiet, but your guys might. The Cardinal's more accustomed to glossing over scandals than we are.'

'What happens when I leave? Am I free to do as I please?'

'Sure. Stick around the next few weeks, in case we need to get in touch, but I doubt you'll hear from us again, not unless we catch the guy who did this.'

'Think you will?' I asked.

He snorted. 'Get real.'

When I was ready to leave, he told me there was someone waiting to escort me home. I'd been expecting one of the Troops but it was Bill.

'Tasso rang and told me,' he said by way of greeting. 'He thought you'd rather I came to pick you up than one of the party faithful. It would look better too, I suggested, but he said that had never occurred to him.'

I smiled. 'He was right. About preferring you.'

'Want to go back to your place or mine?'

'Yours, if that's OK. I can't face home.'

'Sure. Give me a moment to clear it with the staff.' Bill told the officers on duty where he was taking me, gave them his number if they wanted to get in touch, and asked them to let him know if they turned up any evidence. A few knew him and he had to spend a couple of minutes chatting with them, smiling mechanically, answering questions about himself and life at his precinct. He made his excuses as soon as was politely possible, led me out by one of the side doors, tucked me down in the back seat of his car and started for home. As we turned our third corner, I got up and joined him in the front, switched on the radio and spent the entire journey listening to some MOR station, not saying a word, thinking about the boy and how light his lifeless body had felt in my arms.

Bill lived in a crumbling old house in the suburbs. A wreck of a place, but it was his family home and he loved it. I entered ahead of him while he parked the car and ran my eyes over some of the bookshelves in the hallway. Bill was a bibliophile. He owned thousands of books, rare first editions, some hundreds of years old and signed by their authors. He spent a small fortune on them. Had most of Dickens, Hemingway and Faulkner – his three favourite writers – and a fabulous collection of mystery novels.

Bill kept his books neatly stacked on innumerable shelves throughout the house. They were valuable, even in these days of mass illiteracy and plummeting sales, but he didn't believe in locking them up. He kept them around, where he had ready access to them. He read and reread them all the time; even thumbed down the corners of pages to mark his place. Librarians and fellow bibliophiles would have shot him if they'd known of his irreverent handling but Bill didn't care. He collected for himself and didn't give a hoot what happened to the books when he passed on. 'When I die and go to hell, the books can too,' he often declared. 'Let them rot, or let the neighbourhood kids cart them off. I'll have protected them as long as I've a mind to.'

'I got an Ellroy book last night,' I said as Bill entered and shut the door. 'Didn't start it yet.'

'Ellroy's cool,' Bill grunted. 'I'm reading *The Black Dahlia* at the moment.'

'I loved that book. Figure out who the killer is yet?'

'You know I don't go in for detective work in my spare time,' he laughed, trying to sound natural, failing.

We moved into the front room and I took my customary place in the large rocking chair opposite Bill's. My back was directly to the huge front window and I could feel a draught. This place should have been double-glazed years ago but Bill wouldn't hear of it.

'Coffee?' he offered.

'Later, perhaps.'

A few uneasy seconds ticked by.

'You had a lucky escape,' Bill muttered, broaching the subject diplomatically.

'*Escape* my ass,' I sighed. 'I was spared. He took them out one by one. Gave me this' – I tapped my wound – 'when it looked like I might save the child. It would have been simpler to kill me at that stage. He didn't because he wanted me alive.'

'Any idea why?'

I shook my head glumly.

'Could it have anything to do with Nicola?' He spotted my wary look and shrugged. 'I'm a cop, Al. Part of my job's talking to people and keeping up with what's going on. I couldn't help but hear about you and the Cardinal and what he's set you up to.'

'How long have you known?'

'A week or so. Didn't say anything because I hoped you'd come to me about it. When you didn't, I figured it was a deliberate snub and I should keep my nose out.'

'It wasn't a slight, Bill. I just didn't want to bother you with it. If I find her killer, he won't be brought in for trial. He'll be subject to justice as the Cardinal sees it. Didn't think you'd want to get mixed up with shit like that.'

Bill smiled drily. 'Well, I'm involved now. So tell me: any link between Nic and the Fursts?'

'I think so,' I said guardedly, not wanting to draw him in too deeply. 'I went there to ask questions about her. It would be a coincidence beyond belief if the executions weren't related.'

'The killer didn't want Furst speaking to you?'

'Guess not.'

Bill frowned. 'But why take out the others? Afraid he'd discussed it with them?'

'I guess. Husbands tell their wives things. Kids overhear.'

'Would have been a lot simpler just to shoot *you*,' Bill mused. 'Or to shoot you along with them. This way it's as if he was playing with you.'

I nodded slowly.

'Any idea who it might be?' he asked.

'Wouldn't be here if I did. I'd be out nailing the bastard's balls to the clouds.'

'Word on the street was you were looking for Paucar Wami. Think he could have – '

'No,' I interrupted. 'Wami's clean.'

'You reckon?'

'He told me he didn't kill Nic. I believe – '

'He *what?*' Bill almost leapt out of his chair. 'You've met him? You've met Paucar Wami?'

'He paid me a visit a while back.' I told him the story of my midnight encounter with the angel of death.

'Jesus Christ,' Bill gasped, sinking back into his chair. 'If that was me, I'd have run for the hills, down the other side and on to the ocean. What were you thinking? I know you don't mix with the fair and timid, but Wami!'

'Don't give me a hard time about it,' I pleaded.

'I won't, but surely this implicates the son of a bitch. Whoever slaughtered those kids was a monster. There aren't many that cold-blooded. I think we should – '

'Bill, *please.*' I dropped my head to hide my tears.

'Al?' He came over and knelt by my side. 'Are you OK?'

'I was holding him,' I sobbed. 'I had him in my arms. I saw his face explode and then he was dead. Two years old, Bill. Two . . .'

I broke down, emotions rushing to the surface in one overwhelming tide. Bill paused a moment, then wrapped his arms around me and whispered in my ear: 'There, now. It's OK. It's over, Al. You're all right. It's OK.'

Bill had held me like this once before, when I was seventeen. I'd just lost the biggest fight of my fledgling career on points to some skinny nobody who anyone with a touch of class would have knocked to the floor in the first round. Until that night I'd believed I was destined for greatness in the ring. I thought – as Brando had put it – I could be a contender. Sitting in the dressing room afterwards, hiding my bruised mess of a face behind an ice-bag, I'd realised that I didn't have the power, speed or intelligence to make it. The knowledge destroyed the dreaming child within me and I'd wept like a baby.

Bill stepped forward to hold and comfort me that night, as he was holding and comforting me now, and he hadn't let go till I'd ridden out the storm, just as he didn't let go now.

It took a long time for the fit to pass. An age of sobbing into Bill's chest, cursing the unknown killer, then myself for not moving quicker. I tried explaining it step by step, so he'd know I wasn't to blame, so I could prove – to myself as much as him – that I'd done everything I could. But Bill only patted the back of my head and whispered softly over me, 'Easy, now, easy,' like I was a shy horse in need of calming.

When, late into the night, I'd recovered and dried the tears away, I told Bill I'd like that coffee now. We made coffee and sandwiches and broke open a pack of biscuits. Spent the next twenty minutes tucking in. We didn't mention Nic or the Fursts again.

Later, Bill led the way downstairs to the cellar. It was a huge room and the only one in the house he'd modernised. It was full of crates and boxes, packed with every kind of firework imaginable, barrels of gunpowder, even real explosives he'd bartered with the bomb squad for: Bill had plenty of contacts on the force and could get almost anything he wanted; he could have made a killing on the arms market if he'd been so inclined.

Bill was one of the city's chief pyrotechnic experts. He'd been staging firework shows for decades. If he wasn't putting one on, he was acting as safety inspector for somebody else's. It was his only real hobby aside from his books and the occasional fishing trip.

He was getting ready for a big show, an annual event for orphaned kids. There'd be film stars, the mayor, everybody who was anybody in attendance, so he wanted to make it a good one. He was buzzing with excitement.

We spent a few hours examining the boxes. They were brightly illustrated and Bill explained how they'd work, the shapes they'd make, the way he'd interweave them. I preferred his speeches to the actual displays: he brought things to life in a way reality couldn't. His face lit up when he spoke of the animals and caricatures he would build in the air. Timing was everything, he'd say. If you timed it right, you could make marvels out of a sack of gunpowder, cheap cardboard, a child's chemistry set and a pocketful of tinsel. If you got it wrong, all the money and technology in the world wouldn't help. I think Bill was wasted on the force. He should have been designing magical aerial shows somewhere beautiful and exotic, like China or Japan, where he'd be appreciated and revered.

'Will you come to the show?' he asked.

'Maybe,' I said, knowing I wouldn't: after my brush with disaster today, I'd be too busy to bother with fireworks. I'd decided, while sitting in the gutter with the remains of the youngest Furst boy in my lap, that I was going to get this killer. It hadn't been personal before, regardless of my connection to Nic. Now it was.

'Come on, Al,' he groaned. 'Make time. It'll be great. I'm getting in a couple of big model planes and I'll fly them through the middle of a huge shower of rockets. Rockets will be exploding all around, inches to the left, inches to the right, above and below, but they won't even rock the planes.'

'What about air turbulence?'

'Got it covered. Like I always tell you, with explosions

you can account for everything. You wait and see. It's going to be like those old war movies, where the planes fly through seemingly impassable barrages, only this time there'll be no special effects, no whizz-kid pulling the strings in a lab.' He tapped the lid of a box lovingly. 'It'll be my best performance yet.'

When we emerged back upstairs the clock hands were hovering near the two-thirty mark. I was tired but this was an ordinary time for Bill to be up and about: he was an insomniac and rarely went to bed before three or four. He offered to make more coffee. I refused and told him I should be getting home.

'Home?' He blinked. 'I thought you were staying here.'

'So did I. But now . . .' I smiled shakily. 'I think I'd be better off by myself. It's been a long time since I cried that hard and I'm kind of embarrassed.'

'Don't be stupid. After what you've been through, a few tears were the least anyone could expect. Stay, Al. The spare room's ready. You won't sleep much anyway tonight. It wouldn't be healthy, going off by yourself.'

'It's what I want to do,' I assured him.

'Well, let me drive you over. I'll come in with you and – '

'No. Thanks, Bill, but no. The walk will do me good. Who knows: I might cry a bit more on the way.'

He didn't like it but knew better than to argue with me. 'Give me a ring when you get there?' he asked.

'If it's not too late. Otherwise in the morning.'

'Al?' he called me back as I started for the door. His face was grave. 'Be careful. You had a fortunate escape today. Next time – and we both know there'll be *some* kind of next time – you might not be so lucky.'

'I know,' I sighed.

'I'd hate to bury you, Al.'

'Wouldn't be too keen on it myself,' I grinned sickly, then let myself out. It was a long walk home and the night was cold, but that didn't bother me. While I was awake and walking, I couldn't dream about the boy and the gap where his face should have been.

15

I was eager to launch myself back on the case but kept my head down the next day, for fear of being rumbled by reporters: I didn't want any grubby paparazzi tagging along after me while I was trying to interview suspects. It would be bad enough being in the spotlight, but if they discovered I was working for the Cardinal and investigating the deaths personally I'd never get rid of them.

As it turned out, I'd nothing to fear. The Cardinal's people must have been hard at work because though the news bulletins on the radio made heavy mention of the Fursts throughout the course of the day, my name never cropped up. They didn't even report that there had been a survivor, and only a few of the papers commented on it.

I ducked down to Ali's later in the day for bagels. Passed a beggar on my way, going from door to door, selling photos of one kind or another. Ali was discussing the Furst slaughter with a customer when I entered. It was a disgrace, in their opinion, and the man who killed so immorally deserved to be roasted alive without a trial. I didn't want to join the conversation – afraid my emotions might betray me – so I paid for my bagels and made a hasty departure. Passed the beggar again on my way up. He was close to my apartment and would be calling on me within minutes. Inside, I got some change ready – it was easier to pay these people off than not answer when they knocked – and stood by the door, waiting.

The beggar knocked twice, politely. I opened the door and held out the coins. 'Here you go,' I started to say, but stopped when I saw his walking stick and dark glasses: he couldn't see the hand and so couldn't take the money. I immediately thought of the blind men I'd seen at the funeral and later at the building site, but this guy looked nothing like them: younger, shorter, no mole, dressed in ordinary shabby clothes.

The beggar smiled and held out a small group of photographs bound together by an elastic band. 'Visions of the city,' he intoned. 'Can I interest you in visions of the city – ' a moment's pause while he sniffed the air ' – sir? Best snapshots money can buy. Swiss Square at night. Peacock Wharf. Pyramid Tombs. Very scenic postcards. Ideal for framing or sending to – '

'How much?'

'Donations are voluntary. When the gods took my eyes, I learned to trust myself to the generosity of others. I place myself at your mercy. You may – '

I dropped the coins into the tin hanging by a string around his neck. He listened, head cocked, judging their worth by the sound they made, then smiled happily and pressed the photos on me. I had no use for them but took them anyway, to satisfy him.

'May the gods bless you, kind sir,' he said, bowed politely and moved along to the next door. I glanced at the top 'vision' – a tacky shot of Pyramid Tombs, where wealthy fools paid to be buried in the manner of ancient Egyptians – then tossed the package to one side and got busy on my bagels.

I started the Ellroy book in the afternoon, radio on as I read, to keep abreast of developments in the Furst case. The pages flew by in a blur, as Ellroy's pages always did,

239

and I was soon caught up in his reconstruction of earlier times – supposedly more innocent, but as he wrote it, just as twisted as today's – and two hundred pages in before laying it down to rest my eyes.

I listened to the six o'clock news programme and, satisfied that my name wasn't going to emerge, stuck a bookmark into the novel and went for a walk. Strolled to the end of the street, chose a direction at random and took off. It was a surprisingly cool day and I was glad of the light jacket I'd brought. The exercise stimulated my appetite, so I bought some fruit from a street stall and chewed on it as I walked. Tossed the remains to a couple of magpies which were rooting through a rubbish bin. They cawed their appreciation and tucked into the scraps.

Back home I spotted the postcards on the floor as I was shrugging off my jacket and decided to take a closer look. I picked them up and removed the elastic band. Studied the photo of Pyramid Tombs and read the blurb on the back: when the cemetery opened for business, who built it, how it was an exact replica – albeit on a smaller scale – of the Egyptian originals, some of the famous names housed on the premises.

The villas of Versailles were next. This was a part of the city I was familiar with by reputation only: it had been colonised by a band of fleeing French aristocrats shortly after their big Revolution and to this day the language favoured by its inhabitants was French. The ornate houses were walled off from the surrounding suburbs and many had been converted into hotels, even though tourist trade in the city had never been brisk.

As I turned the card over to read about its 'glorious' history I spotted the face of the third and slowly let the first two flutter to the floor. I checked the final pair – Swiss Square and Conchita Gardens – before disposing of them and concentrating on the middle joker of the pack. Unlike the others, this was an ordinary photograph, not a card, and the setting and figure in it could have been of interest to nobody but me.

It was the lobby of the Skylight. Impossible to tell whether it was day or night: the photographer must have been standing with his back to the windows. A couple of people in the background, but they weren't important. It was the man at the centre, caught unawares as he turned from the register, who mattered. He was heavily made up, wearing a veiled hat which obscured the finer details of his features, but the face was unmistakable: Nicholas Hornyak.

Turning the photo over, I discovered printed letters on the back and a short, mocking message: 'Guess the date, Clouseau – win Furst prize!'

It was easy to confirm that the photo dated from the night of Nic's murder (which I assumed was what I was meant to deduce). I had a copy of the Skylight's register and there were copious samples of Nick's handwriting in the file on him. It took less than five minutes to make a match. He'd booked in under a false name – Hans Zimmermuller – but the writing was unmistakably his. And the room number for 'Mr Zimmermuller'? 814: *the room next to Nic's.*

I couldn't find Nick. I tried all over – his home, the Red Throat, a string of gay pubs and clubs he was known to frequent – with no success. Lots of people I spoke to knew him, and a few had seen him earlier that day, but nobody had spotted him within the last several hours. A grinning drag queen told me he often made early nights of the weekend, dragging a lover home or striking out for some hotel or other; he preferred to do his socialising during the week, when things were quieter.

I didn't sleep much – still afraid of nightmares about the

boy – and spent most of the night and following morning pawing through my files, trying to link Nick to Allegro Jinks and Breton Furst. I came up with squat. When evening dawned, I changed clothes and hit the streets, resuming my search.

The Red Throat first. No sign of him, but the barman said he might be in later: few Saturdays went by without him making some kind of an appearance. I traipsed around more of his favourite watering holes, then returned, determined to grab a table and wait him out. He'd have to pop up eventually and when he did . . .

I parked round back and nipped in by the fire escape when someone staggered out to be sick in the alley. The Red Throat was busier now, filling up with the late-evening rush. I was heading for one of the few remaining vacant tables when by chance I spotted Nick propping up the jukebox, looking immaculate in a kilt and matching tartan top, chatting to a short, pudgy man. I barged my way over and rudely squeezed between the two. 'Hiya, Nick,' I greeted him. 'How's tricks?'

He stared uncertainly at me, then placed my face and broke out in a smile. '*Al!* You came back. How perfectly charming.'

'Who is this man, Nicholas?' his companion asked, peering indignantly at me. 'I've not seen him before. Is he a friend of yours?'

'Beat it,' I said, nudging him aside. 'Nick and I go a long way back. I'm stealing him for a while.'

'Nick?' he asked uncertainly.

'Run along, dear,' Nick told him. 'I'll catch up with you later.' He grinned slyly. 'If nothing better comes up.' His companion pulled a sour face and clacked away in a huff. 'So,' Nick purred, 'what can I do you for, Mr Detective?'

I came straight out with the accusation. 'I know you killed your sister, Nick.'

'Really?' he drawled, unfazed. 'How dreadful of me. It's so unpleasant when siblings turn on one another.'

'You were at the Skylight the night of her murder,' I growled, 'in the room next to hers.'

His face blanched and his lips twitched nervously. 'You can't prove that,' he gasped.

'I've a copy of the register. Your name's different but the handwriting's the same.' I grinned. '*Mr Zimmermuller.*' His left eyelid jumped guiltily at the name. 'Want to tell me about it, Nick?'

'You can't prove anything. I was with a date. I never saw Nic. I wasn't there when the murder took place.'

'No?'

'No! I swear it wasn't me. I was with a guy called Charlie Grohl. He'll vouch for me. We left the Skylight about midnight, hours before Nic was killed.'

'Hours before she *died*,' I corrected him. 'The attack took place earlier.'

He shook his head vehemently. 'It wasn't me.'

'You know I work for the Cardinal, Nick. If I tell him it was you, he'll take my word for it, and then . . .' I smiled tightly.

Nick took a deep breath. 'You want the truth? All right. I *was* there that night. With Charlie, as I said. I ran into Nic in the lobby. She told me she was booking in for the night as well. We decided to get adjoining rooms, for the hell of it. She said to rap on her door when I was leaving and if her date had left she'd let me in and we'd have a chat.'

'She was there with a date?'

'Sure.'

'Not a john?'

'John who?' he asked. I let it pass.

'I don't believe you.'

'It's true.'

'You're lying.'

243

'Why would I – '

'Nic didn't sign for her room.'

His face caved in. 'What?'

'Her *date* booked the room.' I kept Priscilla's name out of it.

'But . . . I thought . . .' He trailed off into silence.

I said nothing for a minute. Then, earnestly, 'Why'd you do it, Nick?'

His expression was one of sheer confusion. 'I didn't!'

'You lied about meeting her in the lobby.'

'No. I mean . . . yes. Yes, I did. But only because it sounded more plausible. The truth is, it was an accident, us ending up in rooms beside each other. But I didn't think you'd buy that, so I lied.'

He was lying again. A child could have seen through him. But he was telling the truth about not killing her.

'Maybe you helped,' I suggested. 'Maybe you set her up – accidentally, perhaps – for the killer?'

'No! I had nothing to do with it. I didn't see her. I'm not the killer. I don't know who is.'

I considered pushing him for more details but there seemed little point: he was panicky but not hysterical. I wouldn't get more out of him tonight, apart from lies. Better to feed him some rope, let him wander away and think things over, hit him later, when I had more evidence.

'OK,' I said. 'I'll drop it for now. But you haven't fooled me and you won't. I know you were at the hotel: it's only a matter of time before I prove you were in her room. I'll be back.'

I looked for the exit sign. Nick grabbed my shoulder. I glanced back at him. 'I didn't kill her,' he hissed. 'She was my sister. I loved her. I couldn't have had any part in something like that. You have to believe me.'

'Tell me the truth – why you were there and how you ended up in the room next to hers – and I might.' He bit his lip and shook his head miserably. I brushed his hand away and started for the exit. 'Be seeing you, Nick.' He didn't stop me this time.

The dark alley was deserted. I stood over my bike, thinking hard, head bowed, eyes closed. I didn't think Nick was the killer but he was implicated at some level. The question was: how deep did his complicity run? Was he covering for someone, maybe this Charlie Grohl he'd name-checked, or was he afraid of –

An arm snaked around my neck, suddenly, sharply, cutting off my air supply, throwing my thoughts into disarray. As my hands rose defensively, another pair clutched around my midriff and jerked me backwards. I connected hard with the floor. My assailants were on me before the stars cleared from my eyes. One kicked me in the ribs. The other swung something short and hard at my head.

I dodged the club but not the foot that scythed in at my face. It caught me full on the chin. The one with the pipe dug the point of it into my stomach. I struck at him blindly, but met fresh air.

A second later, I felt the weight of the pipe slamming down on my back. I grunted, hurt, and writhed on the floor. One of the attackers went for my face with his boot again, only scraping it this time, and then a barrage of fists and feet followed and it became impossible to tell one strike from another.

My body rocked between the blows. The men – laughing and panting like dogs – were clumsy and missed with a lot of the shots. If I'd been in better shape, I could have struggled to my feet and dealt with them. But their earlier efforts had sapped me of my strength. I couldn't move or react, only lie there, take it and pray they didn't do any serious damage.

Finally, one had a brainwave. Picking up a glass bottle,

he smashed the top off and waved it underneath my nose. His partner yanked me to my knees and giggled as I moaned.

'Gonna slice you, nigger,' the one with the bottle whispered. 'Cut you so bad, you ain't gonna have a face left.'

'I wanna cut him too,' the other pleaded.

'You'll get your turn,' came the promise.

I watched in sickened fascination as he drew the glass back for the first cut. It wasn't the slicing I was worried about. What terrified me was the thought that he might go too far. Plastic surgery can do wonders for a destroyed face but nothing for a corpse.

There was movement to my right. I glimpsed it out of the corner of my eye. A figure darted forward, silently, swiftly, almost invisibly. There was a lightning blow to my assailant's wrist, and suddenly he wasn't waving a bottle any longer, but was backing off, screaming about a broken hand, cradling it across his chest.

The thug holding me didn't know what to do. He shoved me at the mystery man, but not hard enough to create a problem. The Good Samaritan leapt over me and drove after his prey like a tiger.

My head was spinning. I could feel consciousness slipping away. Rolling over onto my back, I glanced up and saw my saviour disarming the one who'd been holding me, clubbing him to the floor with his fists, turning to wrap things up with the disabled bottle-wielder.

My laboured breath caught in my throat. Though it was dark back here, I could clearly see the colourful, coiled snakes running down the sides of his face and knew it must be Paucar Wami. But that wasn't what stunned me: in my pitiful state, a revelation of that nature could elicit only mild surprise. It was the face itself which sent me spinning into shock before I blacked out. Because I *recognised* that face. It had been many, many years, and there had been no snakes, and a thick mane of hair had adorned the now bare skull. But I knew it. Without a doubt, as surely as I knew my own, I knew it.

It was the face of Tom Jeery. *My father.*

part four

'the red fingerprints of death'

16

I could tell, as I returned to consciousness, that I'd been out a long time. I was in a pitch-black room, so I couldn't check, but gauged by my internal body clock it had been anywhere between twelve and eighteen hours, making this early-to-late Sunday afternoon.

I ran my fingers over my scalp, assessing the damage. Painful – every touch produced a sting – but nothing broken. And although my stomach was a cauldron of bruised agony I didn't think any of my ribs had snapped. All things considered, it could have been a lot worse.

Then I remembered Wami.

I might have been mistaken: I'd only barely glimpsed the face in the alley, and I'd been thinking a lot about my missing father, and I wasn't at my most coherent at the time; maybe all I'd noticed was a vague similarity and the rest was conjecture. But I knew better. You don't make mistakes of that nature, no matter how extreme the circumstances.

I got to my feet and almost fell down again as rockets of pain exploded all over. I thrust out an arm, found a wall and propped myself against it, breathing hard, letting my head clear, groaning softly.

'Up at last,' came a voice from the shadows. 'I thought you would snooze for ever.'

I stiffened and peered vainly into the darkness. It was

Wami's voice but I couldn't see him. Not even the vaguest outline.

'Where are you?' I asked.

'Around,' he replied and now the voice came from another location. He was circling the room, silent, unseen. I was vulnerable as a baby and there was nothing I could do about it.

'You saw my face in the alley, didn't you?' He sounded petulant.

I thought about lying but felt he'd sniff it out. 'Yes.'

'You know who I am? Who I *was*?'

Again I considered the lie. Again I opted for the truth. 'Yes.'

'I thought so.' The light went on.

It was painfully bright and I had to close my eyes and shield them with my hands. Counted to twenty inside my head before opening them again, slowly. Saw I was in a small room, white walls, approximately five metres by five, low ceiling. Nothing in it apart from the mattress I'd been lying on, me and . . . Paucar Wami.

Or Tom Jeery, as he used to be called.

Now that I saw him up close all doubt evaporated. The years had barely touched him and he was pretty much exactly as I remembered – except now he was bald and had tattoos. He said nothing while I ran my incredulous gaze over him, taking in the lean, muscular frame, the slender hooked fingers, the cat-green eyes, the snakes, the casual jeans, T-shirt and leather jacket. Spreading his arms, he grinned.

'Got a hug for your dear ole pappy?'

'This is a nightmare,' I groaned, sliding down the wall. 'This has to be a fucking nightmare.'

'Language,' he tutted, squatting so we were on level terms. 'Your mother never approved of foul language. Even complained when I swore during sex.'

252

I stared at him, appalled. How could I be related to this grinning monster, this creature of evil? It was like discovering you were the bastard offspring of Adolf Hitler. Except I wasn't a bastard. He'd married my mother. It was one thing for a young woman to fall for a sly killer's charms and have a fling with him, but my mother *married* this fucker!

'Did she know?' I gasped. 'Mum. Did she know who you – '

' – really were?' He nodded. 'But not right away. I held that back for the night of our honeymoon.' He laughed with delight at my expression. 'I'm joking!' he roared. 'It was years before she found out, long after you came along. A nosy neighbourhood biddy spotted me without my make-up one dark night and recognised me from word-of-mouth descriptions. Wasted no time sharing the news with poor befuddled Mrs Jeery. Needless to say, I slapped the interfering old bitch's wrists.'

'You wore make-up?'

'Face paint. A wig. Contact lenses to disguise my beautiful green eyes. This is my natural countenance: the man you knew as Tom Jeery was a façade.'

'What did she do when she found out?' It was important to me to know my mother hadn't been involved with his crimes. Getting my head around the truth of my paternal parentage would be a long, unpleasant process, but far messier if my mother was also implicated.

'Kicked me out of the house,' he laughed, sounding almost human. 'Knew who I was and what I could do to her but took no notice. Batted me round the head with a frying pan, tore the skin off my shins with her shoes, nearly took an eye out with the poker. She was a feisty woman, your mother.'

'Yes,' I said proudly. 'She was.' I stretched my legs out

and began rubbing the aching flesh around my middle. 'Is that when you left us, when you *died*?'

He shook his head. 'I kept Tom Jeery on the go for two or three more years, but kept out of your way most of the time. I dropped by occasionally to see how you were progressing – as my first-born, I've always had a soft spot for you – until my position became untenable: your mother threatened to flee the city and go into hiding if I did not stop visiting.'

'Why didn't she do that as soon as she found out?' I asked.

'The same reason she never told anyone the truth about the man she married, not even her son: I vowed to track the two of you down and kill you if she did.'

'Kill *me*?' He nodded. 'But you just said – '

' – that I had a soft spot for you, yes. But business is business. One cannot let sentiment interfere with one's other interests.'

'You'd really have killed me?'

'Of course. I never lie about the important things. Your mother knew that. It is why, even if she had lived to be a senile old woman, given to spurting out her darkest secrets to all and sundry, she would never have told about me.' He tapped the floor. 'Fear is a great silencer, Al m'boy, especially if it is fear for one you love.'

He got up and offered me his hand. I refused it and struggled to my feet on my own. He smiled cynically, asked if I could walk, opened the door when I said I could and gestured me through to a long, sterile corridor.

'Where are we?' I asked, glancing up at the flickering luminescent tubes overhead.

'A building,' he answered vaguely. 'One of my many places of work. I do not think you need know any more.'

As we walked, Wami in front, me struggling to keep up,

254

something he'd said struck me and I stopped. Wami halted immediately and looked back.

'You said I was your first-born.'

His face split into an approving smile. 'You are quick.'

'You have other children?'

'Many. By many different women.'

'I have brothers? Sisters? I'm not an only child?'

'You are the only child of Lorna Jeery, née Richardson, but of half-brothers and sisters: you have plenty. Thirty or forty at last count. Quite a few half-nephews and nieces by this stage too.'

The news left me reeling. I'd always believed I was alone in the world. It had never even occurred to me that . . .

'Where are they?' I asked. 'Here? In the city?'

'The majority, yes, though I have sown my oats in ports of strange and distant lands. You even have an Eskimo half-sister.' It was hard to tell if he was joking or not.

'Do you keep in contact with them?'

'I keep *tabs* on them. I do not have much time for personal relationships.'

'Is that why you were following me? Why you were outside the Red Throat when I was attacked?'

He pondered his answer, then turned sharply on his heel and beckoned me to follow, opting for silence.

'What happened to that pair?' I asked, shuffling along after him.

'They await our pleasure.'

'They're *here?*'

'I told you this was a place of *work.*'

We passed several doors before he stopped at one and entered. It was another dark room. He didn't turn on the light until I was standing beside him and the door was closed. When he did, I wished he'd left it off.

The two men from the alley hung by chains from the ceiling, one upside down, the other horizontally. The latter had been disembowelled and his guts trailed over his sides like some long pink mess which had been dumped there; his eyes had been neatly gouged out and nailed to his nipples so he looked like an obscene alien from a cheap sci-fi movie. Most of the other's face had been sliced away and a pin had been driven through his genitals, which stretched upwards tightly, suspended by a shorter chain, so that every time he moved he was in agony.

Both were still alive.

Though the motion hammered at my guts like a drill, I turned aside and retched. Wami warned me not to vomit on his shoes but I made no response to his mocking jibes. When I'd recovered, I kept my face to the floor and asked who they were.

'That was my first question too,' he replied. 'When I saw them follow you outside and lay into you, I thought they might be the killers of Nicola Hornyak or else hired henchmen. But when I saw the clumsy way they set about you, I began to have doubts.

'Tell me: did you *really* take a white woman to the Ku Klux Klub?'

I didn't know what he was talking about, then remembered my first date with Priscilla and nodded warily. 'Yeah. So?'

'*So* these two fine Caucasian queers were there that night and took umbrage at your uppitiness. By chance they noticed you in the Red Throat yesterday and decided to – as one so poetically phrased it before I removed his tongue – "teach that fucking nigger some goddamn respect for his betters".'

My feeling of bitter disappointment was greater than my sense of disgust at what Wami had done to my assailants. 'They had nothing to do with Nic or the Fursts?' I asked, examining the face of the man who still had one, in case I could identify him from that night at the KKK. I couldn't.

'Nothing,' Wami said, sounding as disappointed as I felt. 'A major let-down, all things considered. Still, I thought it too good to be true. Nicola Hornyak's murderer would hardly pick the back alley of a gay pub to try his hand at another: far too much could go wrong.'

The man with no face groaned and twitched on his chains. Something – it may have been the remains of his nose – slipped from his chin and landed in the pool of blood beneath with a gentle plop.

'Will you for Christ's sake make an end of those two?' I moaned.

'You think I should? I have grown rather fond of them. I was thinking of keeping them around awhile.'

'Just kill them!' I shouted.

Wami regarded me coolly. 'Do not adopt such tones when addressing your father, young Albert. You are not too old for a good spanking.'

'Please,' I said sickly. 'They can't tell us anything and I can't bear looking at them like this.'

Wami produced a knife and held it out. 'Care to do the honours?' I stared at the knife, then the two men, and slowly shook my head. 'You have killed before. Why shy away from these two?'

'I killed when ordered, when there was a reason.'

'You will be putting them out of their misery: is that not reason enough?'

'I can't do it. Not in cold blood. Not like this. They were a pair of fools but they didn't deserve to be – '

Wami spun the knife around and reholstered it in the twinkling of an eye. 'Then make no further entreaties of me. If you are incapable of wielding the final cut, I must and I shall, in my own good time. One should never expect another to extend the hand of mercy on his behalf.'

He strolled past the stricken pair – who sensed his presence and started groaning and writhing anew –

towards a door set in the far wall of the room. Reluctantly, I followed, steering as far clear of the anguished slaves as I could. I found myself in a cosy room with a mahogany desk and two leather chairs, one on either side. There was a computer in the corner and shelves filled with books behind the desk. I glanced over them, expecting tomes on torture and sadism, but they were mostly computer manuals, the odd thriller strewn amongst them.

'Sit,' Wami instructed, taking his place on the far side of the desk. I was glad to take the weight off my feet. 'You will not like what I have to tell you,' he informed me. 'From what I know of you, you are overly sensitive and given to rash reactions. The way you tried to protect the Furst boy is proof enough of that.'

'How do you know about – ' I started, then stopped when I saw the pistol Wami was carefully laying on the desk.

'I will use this if provoked,' he warned me. 'I will not shoot to kill – it should be obvious by now that I have no wish to harm you – but I will disable you without a second's hesitation.'

'I'll be still as a mouse,' I promised, stomach clenching in anticipation.

'You asked why I was at the Red Throat. It was not because you are my son. I was there in search of answers, hoping to trace a client through you.'

'What client?' I asked, frowning.

He paused a second, then said quietly but evenly, 'The client who hired me to eliminate the Fursts.'

In the silence which followed I came dangerously close to disregarding his warning and going for his throat. If I'd had a weapon of my own, I might have. As it was, the cold, sensible, Troop-trained part of my mind held me in check.

'You bastard,' I muttered, feeling tears course down my cheeks as I thought of the two-year-old I'd held in my arms. 'He was a child. Little more than a baby. How could you – '

'Please,' Wami yawned, 'spare me the sermon. Would you rather I waited until he was grown-up to kill him? Would that make it OK? The men you have killed were children themselves once. Do not get sanctimonious, Al m'boy: hypocrisy is not your strong suit.'

'Why did you do it?'

'I was paid.'

'Why *them?* Why Breton Furst?'

He shrugged. 'That is what I was hoping to find out. There was no direct contact between my employer and me. Via one of my many sources of contact I received a cryptic message: to shadow the Fursts but only kill them when "the one I would know" appeared. My curiosity was instantly piqued. I picked my spot and patiently waited for "the one I would know". Then you turned up.'

'Somebody knew I'd make contact with Breton?'

'It appears so.'

'And they didn't want me talking to him.'

'Apparently not.'

'But they didn't want you to kill him before I met him.'

'If you continue stating the obvious, I shall have to administer a slapping.'

'They wanted me to witness the execution,' I went on, ignoring him. 'I was set up. We were *both* set up.' I stared at the killer, sympathy for the Fursts momentarily eclipsed by bewilderment. '*Why?*'

'If I knew, I would not have been shadowing you around the city like a run-of-the-mill detective. Whoever it is, he is desperate to throw the two of us together: this is the second time he has deliberately arranged things so our paths would cross. Men with such playful imaginations annoy me. I would unmask him and put an end to his machinations.'

I thought about it in silence. Whoever was behind it must have known Wami and I had met, or else couldn't have been sure that Wami would recognise me; that Breton Furst was connected to Allegro Jinks; and that I would find this out and go after Furst. It escaped me how anybody could be that clued-in to what was going on, but more worrying was what else the mystery puller of strings might be arranging.

Wami and I discussed it at length but neither of us could pin the tail to a viable suspect. I told Wami what had been happening with my investigation, how Nick had been at the Skylight the night of his sister's death, but we both agreed that the Hornyak brother couldn't have set up something this elaborate. Wami was half-tempted to pay him a call and find out exactly how much he knew, but doubted it would lead anywhere: the person who put Wami onto me at the Fursts' was certainly the same one who put me onto Nick; only a lunatic would have passed on such information if he could be traced through it. Nick might be a stooge but he wasn't the mastermind. More might be gained by shadowing him than torturing him.

With night falling, Wami returned to the killing chamber and told me to wait for him in the corridor outside unless I wanted to sit in on the finishing-off of the Red Throat pair. I passed on the offer and took my place in the hall. He didn't spend long on them – I had the feeling he made a quick job of it on my account – and when he came out he was dragging two black body-bags, one of which he nudged with his knees over to me. We hauled them through the building to a vacant parking lot. Wami disappeared into the neighbouring streets, returning with a hot-wired car, into the boot of which we lumped the bodies. He then tied a blindfold over my eyes so I wouldn't know the location of his hideout and off we set for the Fridge.

Five minutes into the journey, Wami stopped, removed my blindfold and swapped places with me. He didn't like driving, he told me: took too much time to free his hands in case of an emergency. Motorbikes were his vehicle of choice. He commented wryly on how endearing it was that his son's favoured mode of transport so nearly mirrored his own, but I saw nothing cute in the comparison.

As we neared the morgue my mind turned to Tom Jeery's empty casket and I asked when he'd left the note. He didn't know what I was talking about.

'The "Out to Lunch" note,' I reminded him.

'I have no casket in the Fridge,' he said.

'Sure you do. When you killed off Tom Jeery you hired a casket and pretended . . .' I trailed off. 'Didn't you?'

He shook his head shortly. 'I acquired a fake death certificate to present to your mother – sentimental romantic that I am – but never a casket.'

I slowed down and pulled over, despite the fact that we were within rifle range of the Fridge. 'But . . . it's there. I checked on it. There was a note inside: "Out to Lunch".'

Wami sniffed uninterestedly. 'A staff prank. The ghouls of the Fridge do many strange things with the bodies in their care.'

'But there wasn't a body! Only a name: *your* name.' I corrected myself. '*Tom Jeery's* name.'

He frowned. 'Different person, same name?'

'No. The Car – ' I stopped. An empty casket. Tom Jeery's name. Somebody eager to throw my father and me together. Was the note one more device to set our destinies a-clash?

'How many people know about you and me?' I asked.

'One or two from the old neighbourhood may have pieced it together but I never heard anyone mention it. Apart from your mother, the only one who knows is . . .' He pulled a disgusted face.

I waited for him to say the name. When he didn't, I did, to have it out in the open.

'It's the Cardinal, isn't it? The Cardinal knows.'

'Yes,' he sighed. 'He knows of all my children. It was on his advice that I first began to propagate: he thought it would be amusing to create a horde of baby Paucar Wamis.'

'The Cardinal told me about the Tom Jeery casket,' I said, and at that the killer turned to stare at me. For one short instant I saw the poise and certainty evaporate from his eyes, and realised that he was just as shaken by this twist as I was.

We agreed that I'd have to confront the Cardinal. Wami would do his own checking-around in the meantime, but the Cardinal was a master at covering his tracks and if he had staged Nic's death, the execution of the Fursts, and our meeting, in all likelihood the only way to reveal the truth would be to take our findings directly to the ogre and challenge him with them. I was less than thrilled by the thought.

'What if he doesn't take kindly to my intrusion?'

'If this is one of his games, he will expect a confrontation: he hired you to unmask the killer and will be tickled pink if you do. If you treat him respectfully, nothing untoward should come of it.'

'And if he says it wasn't him?'

'We shall take it from there.'

'You still think he might be innocent?' Wami wasn't convinced the Cardinal was our man.

'The game is indicative of the Cardinal,' Wami said meditatively. 'Were *I* not involved, I would be quick to point the finger at him. But the Cardinal and I go back. We respect one another. Hiring me to kill the Fursts and thus collide with you was an act of contempt. The Cardinal I

262

know would not behave so rashly. It is why I did not suspect him before.'

I'd taken too much of a battering to step into the ring with the Cardinal straightaway, so Wami drove me home – once we'd dropped off the bodies and collected my bike from behind the Red Throat – and set me down outside Ali's bakery. He kept the engine running while I got out and didn't linger once I'd closed the door, pausing only to roll down the window and remind me that he'd give me a ring late tomorrow. Then he was gone.

I took my time mounting the stairs. My system had grown accustomed to the pain but I knew it would return to haunt me the next morning. If it was especially bad, I might put off visiting the Cardinal until Tuesday. Maybe even Wednesday.

Somebody was waiting for me outside the door of my apartment. My first reaction was: *trouble!* I began to retreat before I was spotted. Then I recognised the short, shapely legs of Priscilla Perdue.

'About time!' she snapped as I mounted the final few steps. 'I've been waiting for ages. Ten more minutes and I'd have . . .' She trailed off as I hobbled into view, displaying my battered features. 'What on earth happened to you? You look like you fell through a shredder.'

'I should be so lucky,' I chuckled, grimacing as the laughter made the pain flare back into life.

She hurried forward and ran a quick eye over my body, taking in the gentle way I was cradling my ribs with my hands, my stiff gait, the stoop of my injured left shoulder.

'Give me the key,' she commanded, opened the door and guided me through. I just wanted to collapse into bed and sleep but she was having none of it. She henpecked me into the bathroom and had me disrobed down to my boxer shorts before I knew what was happening. She wet a sponge and wiped at the worst of my cuts and bruises. It would have been highly erotic if each swipe hadn't elicited a stream of gasps, winces and curses.

'Why don't you run a cheese-grater over me!' I roared.

'Don't be such a big baby,' she replied calmly. 'You know this has to be done. By rights you should see a doctor. There could be internal injuries.'

'There aren't.'

'You can't *know* that.'

'I'll take a gamble. Shut up and rub.'

Next came the antiseptic – my roars must have been heard in Zimbabwe – then the bandages. After that she wrapped a robe round me and ordered me through to the living room, where she laid me out on the couch, took my temperature and brewed coffee.

'You should have been a nurse,' I mumbled.

'I would have been if it hadn't meant facing cry-babies like you every day of the week.'

'If you'd been through the beating I have . . .'

'Yes, well, we can't all be big brave boys who go around settling our differences with our fists, can we? Let me guess: somebody insulted your mother? Passed adverse critical comment about the colour of your socks?'

'As a matter of fact, *you're* due the credit.'

'*Me?*' She laughed. 'Don't tell me you were defending my honour.'

'Not exactly. A couple of your friends from the Kool Kats Klub decided to teach me a lesson that would deter me from setting foot on their hallowed turf again.'

'No!' she gasped, immediately contrite. 'Oh, Al! The dirty sons of . . . Give me their descriptions. I'll find out who they are and have them disbarred for life.'

'Hardly,' I laughed. 'If word reached their superiors it'd probably mean medals. Besides,' I coughed guiltily, 'they won't be doing it again.'

'Was this why you skipped our date?' she asked.

'Date?' I stared at her blankly.

'We were *supposed* to be stepping out together last night,' she reminded me. 'You *said* you'd ring.'

'Oh.' I smiled sheepishly. 'Sorry. I forgot.'

'You *forgot*?' She slapped me round the back of the head. 'You're a no-good son of a diseased mongrel, Al Jeery. I should have left you as you were. That's the last time I'll do a good deed for – '

'Please,' I interrupted as she stormed for the door. 'Don't go. I've had things on my mind.'

'Really?' she sneered. 'Such as?'

I silently debated how much I should tell her and decided a morsel of the truth could do no harm. 'You heard about the family which was wiped out last Thursday? The Fursts?'

'Of course,' she said, face softening. 'That was awful. Those poor children. Whoever did that should be taken out and . . .' Her lips shut slowly, then opened to form a fascinated O. 'Some of the reports mentioned a survivor. A man who tried to save the . . .' She looked at me questioningly. I nodded. 'Mother of God,' she whispered, covering her mouth with a hand. 'You were there?'

'Breton Furst was on duty at the Skylight the night of Nic's murder. I believe he was connected. I went there to question him. Before I could . . .'

Priscilla sank to the floor and took my hands in hers as I briefly ran her through the horror of that nightmarish day. When I drew to the end she said nothing right away but lowered her head and squeezed my hands tightly. When she looked up there were tears in her eyes.

'I'm sorry, Al. I never stop to think, that's my problem. I jump right in and say things I shouldn't.'

'Don't be silly,' I smiled. 'You couldn't have known.'

'But I should have guessed something was wrong. I assumed you stood me up out of spite, thinking – like usual

265

– that I was the centre of the world and nothing happened that didn't revolve around me. God, Al, it must have been awful. Then you get hammered by a pair of my ignorant *friends*. Then I turn up and . . .' She took her hands from mine and stood. I was amazed and rather flattered by how upset she was. 'I'll leave,' she muttered. 'I'll let you recuperate in peace.'

'No,' I said quickly, pulling her back. 'You don't have to. I want you to stay.'

She stared down at me, then wiped around her face and said in a voice as soft as velvet, 'The night?'

My heart almost exploded in my chest, but I knew I was in no shape – either physically or mentally – for sexual entanglement. 'Well, a couple of hours at least,' I said, smiling shyly.

Priscilla sat on the couch, leant forward and pressed her lips to mine, gently, mindful of my fragile condition. 'All right,' she sighed. 'I'll stay. For a while. And we'll see how things go. OK?'

'Sounds good to me,' I agreed, then kissed her back just as gently as she'd kissed me.

17

I felt a lot better Monday morning than I'd feared. The worst of the bruising had subsided and though I was tender from top to toe it was nothing I couldn't live with. Some light exercising, a healthy breakfast, a brisk walk around the block and by eleven I was flying, ready to take on God himself. Since the supreme being wasn't available, I settled for the next best thing and caught a cab to Party Central to see the Cardinal.

I was in luck: his secretary could fit me in at two. I spent the in-between hours wandering the halls of Party Central, catching up on what had been happening during my absence. Breton Furst was the talk of the establishment, but hardly anyone knew of my involvement with him. I asked if Furst had had any close friends in Party Central: I wanted to learn more about him. Nobody I spoke to had known him personally. Mike, who was on his lunch break, said Jerry and Furst had been buddies, but Jerry was off on sick leave. Mike said he'd tell him to give me a call when he returned.

When it was time to meet the Cardinal, I turned up at his office, only to be led down the corridor by his secretary and shown into a private gymnasium. The Cardinal was within, alone, jogging on a treadmill, bare-buttock naked. 'Come in,' he said, gesturing amiably. I advanced halfway, cleared my throat and averted my eyes. The Cardinal laughed pleasantly. 'No need to be embarrassed. I can't tolerate sweaty clothing. It chafes the skin.'

'Most people use tracksuits and change when they're finished.'

'*I* can't afford to spend half the day changing in and out of various costumes. Much easier this way. Besides, it's good for the penis: poor fellow spends so much time locked away, he must feel like the Man in the Iron Mask.'

'Will you be much longer?' I asked, staring furiously at the floor while my ears burned. This was one for my memoirs: publishers would pay through the nose for a blow-by-blow account of a nude Ferdinand Dorak's less public characteristics.

'Yes,' he said, upping the tempo. 'We can talk while I work out, assuming you don't find yourself tongue-tied in the face of my nakedness. Most people are. Mr Tasso was the only one to walk in on me in my natural state and not bat an eyelid. First time he saw me, he took a good long look and said, "I never thought such a big man would have such a small prick".'

At that, I was unable to prevent my head from lifting and my gaze darting across. The Cardinal had been waiting for this and howled with glee. He pointed a long bony finger at me and sang out like a schoolkid, 'Made you look! Made you look!'

I swiftly turned my head away, then decided I wouldn't be intimidated in such a moronic fashion, faced him, glared straight at his manhood – more developed than he'd led me to believe – then up into his eyes. He nodded, amused by my actions, and continued jogging.

'I heard about your unfortunate encounter with the Fursts,' he commented. 'A nasty business. It had something to do with the Hornyak investigation?'

'You tell me,' I replied evenly.

'A curious answer,' the Cardinal grunted. 'Why should *I* know anything about it?'

'You hired Paucar Wami to do it, didn't you?'

The Cardinal trundled to a slow halt, sat down on the mat of the machine, swung his legs over the side and gazed at me with interest. 'Wami killed them? I thought you didn't see the assassin.'

'At the time I didn't. Things have moved on apace since then. The two of us had an enlightening encounter yesterday evening.'

The Cardinal mopped at the back of his neck with a towel. 'You've met him? In person? Face to face?'

'Oh yes.'

'Then you know . . .'

' . . . that he's my father?' I nodded.

'*There's* a family reunion I'm sorry I missed. I bet you had a lot to talk about. So much to catch up on.'

'That's not the half of it. We were going to dig up the old family photos but got kind of sidetracked wondering who went to all the trouble of pitting the two of us together.'

'And you think it was me?'

'You seem the obvious choice.'

'You think I knew about Allegro Jinks and how he was masquerading as Wami, that I killed Nicola Hornyak – perhaps set you up with her – to get you involved, let you find Jinks, then slaughtered Furst when you traced him to Jinks, using Wami to throw the two of you together. Correct?'

'Something along those lines.'

The Cardinal tilted his head sideways and considered his own proposal. 'A neat solution, Mr Jeery, but not, I'm afraid, correct. I knew nothing about Nic Hornyak, Jinks, Furst or Wami in advance of their introduction to the game – and, the more it develops, the more certain I am that it *is* a game, twisted and unpalatable as it is.'

'If you didn't set it up, how did you know about Jinks and his link to Furst?' I challenged him.

The Cardinal stood and started drying around his groin. 'Return to the waiting room, Mr Jeery. My secretary will fetch anything you require in the line of refreshments. I'll be with you shortly.'

I departed promptly – if I appeared pushy he might turn obstreperous – and passed an anxious ten minutes waiting for him. When he appeared he was in his usual baggy clothes. He cocked a finger at me and made his way to a console room filled with TVs, computers and video equipment. He located a disc and inserted it into one of the many machines.

'I've been keeping an eye on you, Mr Jeery,' he started, fiddling with the control as he talked. 'Since I'm a voluntary captive of Party Central, this means employing others to watch out for you and keep me informed of your activities. One of my spies at the Fridge rang the Friday before last and said he had something interesting to show me.'

He hit *Play* and one of the screens flickered into life. It was a recording of me in the Fridge, the night I dropped off Jinks's head. The Cardinal turned up the sound and I heard myself asking the clerk about keeping tabs on the corpse.

'Enough?' the Cardinal enquired.

'Enough,' I sighed.

He turned it off. 'It was a simple matter to trace the head after that and get a make on Allegro Jinks, though I was able to find nothing to connect him to Breton Furst until Furst went looking for him by name.'

'Is that when you hired Wami to kill Furst?'

'I didn't hire Wami. Why should I? I *want* to know who killed Nic Hornyak; whoever ordered Furst's death *already* knows.'

'You didn't kill her?' I asked sceptically.

'No.'

'So how come you had a full file on her when nobody was supposed to know her name? And why involve me?'

'It took only a couple of hours to identify her body,' he said by way of answer. 'I recognised her name as soon as I was informed: I've been observing your progress and personal life ever since you were a child, as I have all the children of Paucar Wami.'

'I've been under surveillance all my life?' I asked, not a little alarmed.

'Discreet surveillance. I haven't tapped your phones or had you shadowed or staked out your house, but I have a network of informers, friends and neighbours and colleagues of yours, who tell me how you're getting along, what you've been up to, who you've been seeing. I knew of your involvement with Nicola Hornyak but read nothing untoward into it until she turned up dead in the Skylight.'

'Why not inform me immediately? Why the subterfuge?'

'I wanted to clear your name before I contacted you, in case you had killed her.'

'*Me?*' I was stung by the accusation.

'Please, Mr Jeery, do not be offended. You are the son of Paucar Wami. It was possible that your father's evil genes had bubbled to the surface: I'd been expecting them to for years.'

'I'm nothing like *him*,' I snarled. 'I'm not a killer.'

'I know,' he sighed. 'I have a lot of admiration for Paucar Wami. He has served me loyally and well. But he is getting old – as am I, come to that – and soon I'll be looking for a replacement. What better prospect than one of his own flesh and blood, trained by my very own men?'

'You thought . . .' I sputtered indignantly.

'I *hoped*,' he corrected me. 'If you *had* killed her, it would have been your first vengeful act and I didn't want to do

271

anything which might stunt your potential growth. Men of your father's calibre are damn near impossible to come by. Many come unstuck in the early days of their criminal careers. It would have profited me none to expose you as the killer.'

'And when you found out I hadn't killed her?' I growled, disgusted that anyone could think so low of me.

'Disappointment. Then curiosity: it *could* have been a coincidence, her being seen around town with a Paucar Wami lookalike, then taking up with his son, then being murdered; but not very likely.'

'Then you knew about Jinks before I turned up at the – '

'I knew of the *lookalike*,' he interrupted. 'My detectives hadn't yet ascertained his identity when I was forced to withdraw them prematurely from the chase.'

'*Forced?*' I couldn't imagine anyone forcing the Cardinal's hand.

'Perhaps *invited* would be a more accurate description. Here: have a look at this. I found it on my desk one morning.' He handed me a picture postcard. Four lines of print adorned the back:

> *Howard Kett knows about Nic Hornyak*
> *He will be demanding her return*
> *Remove your current investigative teams*
> *Install Al Jeery in their place*

I read the words several times, then flipped the postcard over and studied the front. A grotesque three-breasted statue stretched the length of the card; underneath its breasts was printed a calendar, although the names of the months were in a language I couldn't identify; at the bottom was the following caption: 'Early Incan fertility symbol and calendar.' The eleventh month – represented by the word *Ayuamarca* – was highlighted in green.

'What's this about?' I asked, tapping the card.

'I am interested in our Incan past,' the Cardinal said, dismissing it with a wave of a hand. 'I suppose the sender thought it would grab my attention. He was right.'

'How did it get on your desk?'

'Somebody must have sneaked in while I was asleep. That's why I went along with the request: a man who can slip in and out of Party Central unseen is not to be taken lightly.'

I turned it over and read the message again. 'When did it come?'

'Two days before Kett came looking for the body.'

'Then he knew about it before he claimed to?'

'Possibly.'

'It says here he did.'

'That may have been an error of phrasing.'

'You've investigated Kett?'

'That's *your* area of expertise.'

'Did you have the card analysed? For fingerprints and the like?'

'Naturally.'

'Find anything?'

'Nothing bar the fleas, as my dear old mother used to say.'

'I received a similar card not so long ago,' I told him.

'Oh?' He leaned closer, intrigued.

'A blind beggar came selling cards in my apartment block. I purchased a packet. One of them was a picture of Nicholas Hornyak in the lobby of the Skylight, the night of his sister's murder, with a note on the back inviting me to make the connection.'

'A blind beggar.' The Cardinal was troubled by my words.

'I've spotted a few blind people recently,' I mused, recalling my vision at the site of the Manco Capac statue.

'This city has its share,' the Cardinal said.

'You think they might be behind the murders?'

He hesitated. 'I wouldn't like to say. Chances are your blind man was a hireling, while the man who made a mockery of Party Central's defences could hardly have done so without the use of his eyes. Not to forget the fact that a blind man wouldn't know a photograph of Nicholas Hornyak or an Incan fertility god from a snapshot of Paucar Wami's black ass.'

'Rudi Ziegler would know an Incan fertility god if he saw one,' I suggested.

'He would indeed,' the Cardinal agreed. 'It is something I thought about myself whilst perusing your reports – which have been arriving rather slackly of late, now that I think of it.'

'I've been too busy to write everything down.'

'Or you just didn't trust the old Cardinal?' he countered, a gleam in his eyes. 'You didn't want me knowing that *you* knew things which you thought *I* did too? Because you believed I was setting you up?'

I grinned guiltily. 'A bit of that too.'

'We must learn to trust one another, Mr Jeery.'

'I'll trust you when you start playing straight with me,' I said.

'Are you suggesting I haven't been?'

'You went on letting me think Nic had been murdered at the Skylight when you knew she wasn't.'

'Ah. You found out.'

'Why didn't you tell me?'

He smiled apologetically. 'I'm ashamed to say I was testing you. This game is not of my making but it's one I have attempted to profit by. As I told you at the start, I believe you have the potential to be more than you are. You now know the genesis of my faith in you. I guessed this investigation would turn nasty when I read that note;

274

I suspected you were being set up, though I didn't – and still don't – know why. I could have protected you.

'But I wanted to see how you'd react. This was a chance to watch you stretch your wings and fly. I found it impossible to resist. So I set you up to *find* the body, and I held back certain key details – such as the Wami lookalike and that she'd been murdered elsewhere – in order to make your work more of a challenge. It was cruel to toy with you so, but cruelty, as they say, is my middle name.'

'And now?' I snapped. 'Have you come clean or are there more secrets you're keeping from me?'

'Ah,' he clucked, 'that's for me to know and you to find out. I will say this: I don't know who killed your girlfriend and I don't know why they're interested in you.'

'You wouldn't tell me if you did,' I replied bitterly.

'Probably not,' he agreed. 'But you've been trained to tell a lie from the truth. I am, of course, the king of liars, but one of your standing should be able to make an educated guess. Judge for yourself: do I lie or not?'

From what I could read of him, he didn't. I decided to keep an open mind on the subject but – for the time being – take him at his word until I learned different.

'Where do we go from here?' I asked.

'Wherever you decide. I have full faith in your abilities.'

'Maybe it would be best to let things lie. A lot of people have died on account of this *game*. More might follow. If we drop the investigation and I jump town . . .'

The Cardinal frowned. 'Round here we call that chicken talk, pilgrim,' he growled in his best John Waynese.

'Call it what you like: do you think it would work?'

He shook his head firmly. 'The only one who can change the rules in a contest of this nature is the gamesmaster. Any attempt by either of us to cut short the frivolity would be met with a suitably harsh countermeasure. I won't force you to continue but I think you should.'

I nodded slowly, then followed him out as he headed back for his office. He paused outside the door and took a sheaf of notes from his secretary. 'Anything else?' he asked.

I thought a moment. 'No.'

'In that case . . .' He disappeared into the office without a word of farewell. I caught the eye of his secretary and we shrugged simultaneously at one another, then smiled. I tipped an imaginary hat to her and she waved back, then I caught the elevator down and went home to wait for 'Daddy' to call.

He came round in person, shortly after eleven, and we discussed my conversation with the Cardinal late into the night. Wami was now satisfied that the Cardinal wasn't the one toying with us, and though I still harboured doubts, I agreed that we should broaden our horizons.

He was fascinated by the postcard the Cardinal had received and the possibility that the blind beggar might be involved. He chastised me for not mentioning the beggar before but I told him I couldn't be expected to reel off every last detail at the drop of a hat. Besides, as the Cardinal had said, a blind man couldn't have penetrated Party Central's defences or identified Nick Hornyak.

'I would not be so sure of that,' he snorted. 'I know of a collection of blind enigmas. They haunt the streets. I have never paid much attention to them – they do not interfere with me – but have tortured a few over the years, out of interest's sake. Not one of them uttered a single word, even under the greatest duress.'

'Well, this beggar had plenty to say, so he couldn't have been – ' I stopped, remembering the blind man at the building site and the vision he'd thrust me into. 'These

276

blind men,' I said. 'They don't dress in white robes, do they?'

'They do. You know of them?'

I told him about that day at the site.

'Most strange,' he mused. 'I envy those privy to visions. I would love to be able to slip between worlds at will. Perhaps I should ask those Incan eyeless wonders to – '

'*Incan?*' I interrupted sharply.

'I believe they are of Incan extraction,' he nodded. 'Why?'

I told him about the flip side of the postcard. He became agitated when I spoke of the highlighted eleventh month.

'*Ayuamarca,*' he hissed, though I hadn't mentioned the name.

'It means something?' I recalled the way the Cardinal had quickly dismissed my query about the calendar.

'You know of the Cardinal's many files and dossiers.' Wami spoke hesitantly. 'One of his most secretive is headed *Ayuamarca*. It is, primarily, a list of ghost names, people who have been written out of existence and memory.'

'I don't understand.'

'Nor do I, completely. But I know it is a list of great importance to the Cardinal. No wonder he jumped when our mystery killer snapped his fingers.' I started to ask about the list, only to be silenced by an angry gesture. 'Be quiet. I am thinking.'

Moments later, he nodded unhappily. 'A sacrifice,' he sighed. 'It must be. Nothing else makes sense.'

'You're talking about Nic?'

'I am talking about *you*.' He paused. 'And *me*. The Cardinal said he was holding information back in order to test you: that might be the truth, but I bet it is a lie. He played dumb because he was afraid.'

'The Cardinal? Afraid? Of what?'

'Of being exposed or eliminated: I am not sure. This list of his seems to matter more to him than the rest of his empire put together. He goes to extraordinary lengths to remove all trace of those on it. I believe he would sacrifice anything in the name of that list. Any*thing* and any*body*.'

'You're not making sense,' I groaned.

He leaned in close to me and there was a cold fire burning in his eyes which I thought would turn my hair icy white. 'Let me put it to you this way: that note to the Cardinal was a warning. In effect it said, "We want Al Jeery: give him to us. We know about *Ayuamarca*, so play ball or else."

'You are being sacrificed, Al m'boy. Somebody wants your head and the Cardinal – wary as only one with so much to lose can be – is delivering it, no questions asked. He has no interest in testing you or seeing you surmount the obstacles strewn in your path. He only wants to see the back of whoever it is that is threatening him.

'You have been cast aside like a pawn to protect a queen. That is the bad news. The good news is – ' here he grinned grimly ' – you are not alone. I am part of this game too, and *I* have no Achilles' heel. I will stick by you to the sweet or bitter end.'

He clasped the back of my neck and winked. I forced a shaky grin, though in truth the thought of having a monster like Wami on my side depressed more than comforted me.

18

The more I thought about it the next handful of days, the more it seemed like a paranoid delusion of my father's. It wasn't that I trusted the Cardinal more than his hired killer: I just found it impossible to believe he could have his arm twisted the way Wami believed.

Wami's presentation of the *Ayuamarca* file failed to assuage my doubts: it amounted to nothing more than a few sheets of paper with dozens of names, most crossed out. According to Wami, these were people he'd once known but no longer had any memory of, people who had vanished from the public psyche, who to all extents and purposes had never existed. I agreed it was most passing strange (as he put it), but behind his back I was starting to think that maybe I was dealing with a schizophrenic psycho who'd murdered Nic and then forgot he killed her.

He was a strange man, my father. He must have been in his late sixties – he grew coy the few times I mentioned his age – but was in incredible shape, fitter than I had ever been. The lethally assured grace with which he moved, the speed of his thoughts and his capacity for taking in everything in an instant made me feel as if my years with the Troops had been nothing more than kindergarten training.

No matter how friendly a front he put on for my sake – and most of the time he treated me with a semblance of warmth – he was at heart as cold and distant as the stars. He had time for talk of nothing but death. If I mentioned the weather, he'd sigh and remark, 'It was on a night such as this that I killed my first nun.' If I asked for his recollections of our time together when I was a child: 'Those were wonderful days. I'd bounce you up and down on my knee in the morning while your mother was out working – I was pretending to be on night shifts – tuck you in for a nap, nip out to slit the throat of one of the Cardinal's rivals or just to keep my hand in, return in time to change your nappy, feed and burp you.'

His stylised way of speaking took some getting used to. He treated the language with undue respect, rarely running his words together. It was almost always 'do not' instead of 'don't', 'cannot' instead of 'can't'. He said that was his natural way.

I asked him for the names of my siblings one night but he refused to divulge any: none of his children knew of the others and he preferred it that way. I argued with him – what if, unknowingly, I started an affair with a half-sister? – but he laughed and teased me: 'Maybe you already have.'

We were concentrating on Nick Hornyak. Ellen still hadn't got back to me about Ziegler, the blind Incans wouldn't say anything even if we found them, and there was nothing in Breton Furst's files that was of any use. Nick was our boy. Wami wanted to snoop around after Priscilla too, but I warned him to stay away: I said I'd keep my own tabs on her.

We dug up every clipping on Nick that we could find and scoured them for any hint of scandal. Nothing. He was hardly clean, but his vices ran no further than sexual kinks, soft drugs and friends with dubious pasts: which was about par for the course around here.

So we shadowed him. Followed him everywhere, covering the front and rear of every building he entered, Wami trailing after him on his motorbike, keeping me informed of his position over the phone as I cycled along behind.

He was easy to keep up with by day, since he spent most days in bed. When he occasionally arose he'd mope along to the Red Throat or a similar establishment and pass the time socialising, drinking and playing pool.

Nights were trickier: he bounced from one club to another like a pinball, rebounding round the city in search of laughs and a partner. We lost him a few times, in cabs and ducking out unseen amidst a crowd, but he was always easy to pick up again. When he'd retire for the night – be it home or an hotel – one of us would leave to catch some sleep while the other waited an hour or so in case he emerged again, before heading off himself.

We stopped taking notes and photographs after the first night. No point: he moved in loose circles and met scores of people. We couldn't process those sorts of numbers. Unless we saw him with somebody who looked especially dangerous or someone we recognised, we took no notice.

He didn't go anywhere strange or act suspiciously. Just pubs and clubs, parties and orgies. After four days I knew it was hopeless: if he was in league with the killers, he was being kept at arm's length from them. Shadowing him would lead nowhere.

Wami agreed with me but was more philosophical about it. Time, he said, was a great provider. Trailing around after Nick left our conspiring opposition with time on their hands, time to plot and grow restless and reveal themselves.

Nevertheless, for all his patience, by the coming of the weekend he was leaving me alone more than he was partnering me. He said he was exploring alternative avenues of enquiry, but I think he was tired of the lack of bloodshed and was using the time to do a bit of freelance killing, of which the less I knew the better.

I kept in touch with Priscilla by phone all week, even managed to drop in on her at work a couple of times. We didn't talk about that night in my apartment, when we could have so easily become lovers, but we discussed all sorts of aspects of our lives: dreams, aspirations, pasts; stuff on-the-verge-of-courting couples the world over know about. It was early days, but I had the feeling something strong was growing between Priscilla and me. I didn't know if that was good or bad – things were complicated enough as they were – but I couldn't control it, so I rolled along loosely with my emotions and let things develop as they dared.

Ellen invited me over to her place Sunday afternoon. I rang Wami and told him I wouldn't be tracking Nick, and why.

'My ex-daughter-in-law,' he chuckled. 'Perhaps I should come with you and introduce myself.' I knew him well enough by now to know he was joking. I asked if he'd cover Nick for me. He said he wouldn't bother, then changed his mind: 'Laws of Fate,' he muttered. 'Something's bound to happen if we aren't following him.'

Ellen had a lovely pad overlooking the river. She'd only moved in six months before so it still smelt new and didn't feel lived-in. It would have driven me mad if I'd had to share it with her. She looked divine, dressed in white, a blue ribbon through her hair. I used to love combing that fine blond head of hair. If I had to say what I missed most about her, it would be waking up in the early hours of the morning to find her hair spread out on the pillow beside me, and gently combing through it with my fingers to discover her sleep-puckered face.

She'd cooked a light pasta dish, which we quickly chewed through. Stuck the dishes in the washing machine and retired to the veranda, making the most of the glorious weather. She noticed the faint scars on my face – a memento of my run-in with the KKK boys – and enquired about them. I made up a story.

'Now then,' she said when I finished. 'Rudi Ziegler.' She pulled a file out from beneath the veranda chair. Licked the tips of her index and third fingers and flicked over the first page. 'That's his real name, by the way, not an alias.'

'I know.'

'You do?' She glared reprovingly at me. 'You might have told me. I spent days tracing his roots because I was sure it wasn't kosher.'

'Sorry. Didn't think.'

'Well,' she sniffed, 'you probably know the rest as well, but I'll reel it out anyway. No police record, never in trouble. Fills out his tax forms, operates above board. Worth a small fortune. He started out with little: a small inheritance when his father died, which he used to launch and advertise the business. A couple of office jobs when he was younger, but most of his life has been devoted to magic. I tried finding out who he studied under but he seems to have picked it up from a variety of sources, fairground fortune-tellers and the like. Never married. Hasn't sired any children.'

She zipped forward a few pages. 'Let's get down to the juicy details. I attended four meetings. The first time, it was just the two of us. I told him I'd been having odd dreams and wanted to explore the spiritual plane in an attempt to reconcile myself with my hidden interior soul.'

'Nice.'

'I got it from an article in *Life*. He read my palms, the tarot, the usual rigmarole. I acted intrigued. Said I wanted to try a seance. He took my number, said he'd phone when a suitable group place came up. Said it might take a few weeks: my karma had to be compatible with the group's, or some such hogwash. Rang a couple of days later to say he'd found the perfect companions. One of their number had dropped out and I was mentally and spiritually ideal. I went along to three of those sessions.'

'Anything happen?'

She chuckled scornfully. 'Lots of fog, strobe lights, eerie noises and table-shaking. He's got a crystal ball and he conjured up some images. Spoke in voices. Loads of mystical Incan crud. I was disappointed: it was blatantly fake. The others seemed to enjoy it but I'm not sure they believed it was real any more than I did.'

'Nothing dark or magical?'

'No. I asked after the third seance if there was anywhere further to go. Said I was enjoying myself but wished to make meatier contact. Told him I wanted to dance with the demons.'

'You didn't!'

'*You* told me to say it.' She couldn't hide an impish grin.

'How did he react?'

'He was understanding. Said he wasn't that way inclined – Incas were more concerned with gods of light than demons of the dark – but he could pass me on to people who were. I told him I'd be grateful if he would, that I was looking for thrills and didn't mind how extreme they were. He gave me a few names. Said they were reliable, classy, discreet. He wouldn't recommend their methods but none of the people he'd sent their way had expressed regrets.'

'This sounds more like it.' I rubbed my hands together briskly. 'I hope you didn't go visit these guys.'

She shook her head. 'Like you said, one of them could be a murderer. I've got your leads, Al. The rest is up to you.'

'Where are they?' She handed me a sheet of paper with two names and addresses. They meant nothing to me, so I laid the sheet aside for later. Probably red herrings, but I'd put them through the link-the-suspects-to-Nicola paces anyway, on the off chance that one might pan out.

We discussed the case and how I'd been progressing (I told her as little as possible, nothing about Paucar Wami or the Fursts) and then talk turned to love. Ellen asked if I'd been seeing anyone lately. I told her I had. Was it serious? I thought of the way my heart leapt when Priscilla kissed me, and said it might be.

'How about you?' I asked, as you do in return when someone makes enquiries of that nature. 'Been getting it on?'

She smiled nervously. 'Actually, I have.'

'Oh?'

'I think I might be in love, Al. I think I'm falling.' She gazed into my eyes uncertainly, awaiting my reaction. I stared out over the river and considered my feelings. It was a surprise: there'd been nobody meaningful in Ellen's life since our marriage dissolved and I'd kind of forgotten that she was unlikely to stay true to the memory of me. A month ago the news would have upset me – might even have sent me running back to the bottle – but after all that had happened these last few weeks it didn't seem as world-shattering as it once would have.

'Anybody I know?' I asked.

'Yes.'

'You going to tell me the name or do I have to guess?'

She hesitated. 'Not yet. It's not the right time. I don't know how involved things are going to get. It's sped along nicely so far, but I'm not at the stage where I want to make a public commitment.'

'So why mention it?'

'In case word leaks. So you know there's somebody

special. So you don't feel like I've been going behind your back.'

'We're divorced,' I reminded her. 'You're a free agent. You can do what you like.'

'I know. Still, if it was *you* and things were getting hot and you didn't tell me, I'd be hopping mad.' I knew what she meant: as far apart as we'd drifted, we could never truly separate. There would always be something warm between us.

'Well?' she asked when I said nothing. 'What do you think?'

'Does it matter?'

'You know it does,' she said softly.

'I don't know the guy,' I protested. 'How can I form an opinion if I don't know who he is?'

'Who says it's a guy?' she smirked. 'Maybe I've gone for the buttered side of the bread.'

'Oh, sure,' I laughed. 'I can just see you setting up house with another woman. You get irritable if a female comes within fifty yards of this place.'

'Hmmm. Maybe I'll surprise you one day. But seriously, Al, what do you think? Are you jealous?'

'No,' I answered truthfully. 'I'm surprised but not jealous. Truth be told, I'm delighted. I *mean* that. It's great. I wish you all the best.' I cocked a finger. 'Subject to final approval: I want to meet this love of your life, and soon.'

'You will,' she promised, relieved by the way I was taking it. I was rather pleased myself, to know that she still thought so much of me.

'Can I give you away at the wedding?' I asked cheekily.

'There won't be a wedding,' she replied. 'One was enough. Besides, it wouldn't be appropriate.'

'Why not?'

'You'll see,' she grinned, and said no more.

286

She kissed my cheeks before I left and rubbed my nose with hers. In the old days, that would have been the sign for our lips to meet and matters to progress. Now, it was simply a nice way for two close friends to say goodbye.

'Give me a ring if anything comes of the Ziegler tips,' she said.

'I'll be sending over the grandest bouquet of flowers I can find if one of these names leads anywhere,' I vowed.

'And be careful: I don't want the killer carving you up like he did that poor girl.'

'I'll watch my back, kemosabe.'

'See you round, grasshopper.'

We smiled at each other, then I slipped away, to spend the rest of the day wondering about her new beau. Whoever he was, he'd better treat her well – better than *I* had – or I'd be after him. No matter how hot and heavy things got between Priscilla and me, Ellen would remain the one true love of my life. Nobody would harm her as long as I was around.

The names of the two mystics led nowhere. No outstanding connections to any of the key players, though Priscilla had been a customer of one of them. I asked her about him: she said he was a fakir, graver than Ziegler but no more genuine. Nic had never been to him.

Apart from the two names, there was nothing in Ellen's report of any great use. I hadn't expected much – it wasn't like I thought Ziegler would talk openly of human sacrifice – but was disappointed all the same: I'd agreed with Wami that if nothing happened with Nick over the next few days, we should shift our focus onto Ziegler; since Ellen's report and our files had produced no dirt, that would mean more shadowing, more long hours of hanging around, doing little.

The depression was still with me Tuesday when I rolled

home shortly before midnight and hit the sack. I was sleeping soundly these times, too exhausted to dream, and usually didn't stir till morning. So when I jolted awake in the middle of the night, I thought something was wrong. I couldn't hear over the sound of my pounding heart for a few seconds. Then, when my hearing returned, I realised it was only the buzzing of my mobile phone which had disturbed me. I checked my watch – 3 a.m. for Christ's sake! – groaned and reached blindly for the annoying communicator.

'This had better be a matter of life or fucking death,' I yawned/snarled into the mouthpiece, expecting the mocking tones of my father. But the voice, when it came, wasn't Paucar Wami's.

'The public phone in front of the library, three blocks up. Be there, ten minutes from now.'

'Who – ' I began, but the caller had hung up. I sat on the edge of my bed a few moments, trying to place the voice. When I couldn't, I sighed, rolled off and got dressed. I might be walking into trouble but was too tired to care. I thought of ringing Wami for back-up but he'd be asleep and I didn't want to disturb him.

Heading for the door, my eyes flicked to the mantelpiece and I slowed. The black, gold-streaked marble I'd found in the trout's mouth and placed there was missing. For a moment I was sure someone had stolen it. But that was silly. More likely it had rolled onto the floor. I didn't have time to look for it, and anyway, it wasn't important. I'd forgotten about it by the time I'd unchained my bike.

I arrived at the kiosk with a couple of minutes to spare. Stood in out of the cool night breeze, yawning. A patrol car passed, two night officers giving me a suspicious once-over. I half-waved at them and they carried on without stopping. Then the phone rang and I answered immediately. 'If this is a joke, I'll come over and kick you – '

'There's a phone outside the post office in Marlin Street,' the voice interrupted. 'Know where that is?'

I ran the name through my memory banks. 'Yeah,' I said cautiously.

'How long will it take you to cycle there?'

'Fifteen, twenty minutes.'

'I'll ring in twenty-five. If you're being tailed, pass it by and I'll get in contact another time.'

'Who is this?' I snapped. 'Why should I – ' He was gone again.

I considered my next move. It could be a trap but it seemed unlikely: just as easy to strike at home or here outside the library as it was across town. This way I had time to call for assistance and prepare. Besides, the caller had sounded scared.

With hardly any traffic on the streets, and jumping red lights, I made Marlin Street in seventeen minutes. As far as I could tell, I wasn't being followed, though from my experience with Nick I knew how simple it was for a cautious hunter to track his prey undetected.

I'd been thinking hard about the voice and this time, when the phone rang, I spoke before the caller could. '*Jerry?*'

There was a nervous pause, then: 'No names. This phone was safe a couple of hours ago but we both know how quickly certain people move. There's an all-night diner at the top of this street. Come on up. I'll be waiting.'

I was sure when I hung up: it was Jerry Falstaff, from work. I'd seen virtually nothing of him since the Cardinal took me off regular duty. What was he doing, ringing me now, in such provocative fashion? Only one way to find out . . .

A handful of late-night souls were scattered around the diner, eating silently, reading or staring out the windows. Jerry was near the back, close to the rear exit. From the way he was sitting I knew he was cradling a gun under cover of the tablecloth. I glanced around at the other diners again, searching for danger, but they seemed oblivious to all but themselves.

I strolled across but didn't sit.

'That a gun in your lap or are you just pleased to see me?' I quipped. Jerry didn't smile.

'Get something to eat,' he ordered, voice low, panic tainting it at the edges. 'Make it look natural. Sit opposite me and cover the area to my back. First sign of trouble, open fire and make a run for the kitchen: there's a door, leads to a set of stairs running down to an alley. It's our best bet if we're rumbled.'

'I'm sitting nowhere and doing nothing till you tell me what this is about,' I replied bluntly.

Jerry looked up at me, briefly, then cast his eyes back over the diner. 'You trust me, Al?'

'I've never had reason not to,' I answered indirectly.

'Then listen carefully and do what I say.' He took a bite out of a large roll and, using it for cover, muttered out of the side of his mouth, 'It's about Breton Furst.'

To my credit, I froze only momentarily, then forced a smile, took my jacket off, draped it casually over the back of the chair and went to order a slice of pizza. When I returned, sat and started to eat, Jerry let me have it.

'I graduated from basic training with Breton. We kept in touch. He drew me aside at Party Central a few weeks ago and asked me to be his Tonto.' That was a phrase we used in the Troops when one of us passed a message to another to be opened in the event of his disappearance or death. Such messages were usually issued when someone found himself getting in over his head, to serve as a warning: 'If you knock me off, you'll unleash my Tonto.'

Tontos were strictly forbidden – if you were found holding a note from a colleague which contained the merest hint of classified information, you were dismissed from the Troops without benefits, and that was the most *lenient* reprisal – but common practice all the same. I'd never had to hire a Tonto but I'd been one for three of my associates, none of whom met the sticky end they'd been fearing. We looked out for one another in the Troops.

'I fled as soon as I heard about the execution,' Jerry continued. 'Called in sick and did a runner. Been sleeping in my van. It wasn't Breton's death that set me running: it was what happened to his wife and kids. I've got family too.'

'You think whoever killed Furst knows about you?'

'Probably not,' he grinned nervously, 'but would *you* chance it?' One of the customers rose and Jerry's body tightened. I thought he was going to start firing, but then the guy tossed a tip down and ambled away. Jerry relaxed.

'Do you have the message on you?' I asked.

'You crazy? I read it, memorised it – figured I owed him that much – then burnt the fucker. Laid low and let some time pass before getting in touch with you.'

'I was mentioned in the message?'

'No. But I heard you were with him when he was killed and I guessed you were as good a person to turn to as any. Don't trust anybody else.'

'What makes you think you can trust *me*?'

He shrugged. 'It's *your* girlfriend he died for.'

'Nic Hornyak?' He nodded. I swallowed a stale mouthful of pizza and said, 'Go back to the start. What was in the message?'

'Breton was on duty the night she was killed, monitoring a side door. Some guy bribed him to go buy cigarettes at ten o'clock: said he wanted to sneak in a friend without anyone seeing. According to Breton, that shit happens all the time at the Skylight. After a while you learn to take the money, keep your mouth shut and let it slide.'

'Did he know the guy?'

'Not straight off.'

'But he found out?'

'I'm coming to that. There was more to the bribe: the guy wanted Breton to come up to his room early the next morning – between two and three – and let the mystery "friend" out. Said he'd be chained to the bed and wearing a mask which Breton wasn't to remove. Breton was reluctant to get that deeply involved but the guy upped the tip, told him the room number, and Breton relented.'

'It was Nic's room?' I guessed.

'No. The room next door, 814.'

'*Nicholas* Hornyak's,' I sighed.

Jerry looked surprised. 'You know about him?' I nodded. 'Breton only found out when his picture turned up in the papers. Said it was one of the reasons he kept quiet: if he'd spoken up after a week of silence, it would have looked like he'd been in cahoots with the brother.'

'Why not spill the beans as soon as he heard about the murder?'

'He wasn't thinking clearly. See, he went up and let the guy out in the middle of the night like he'd promised. He was masked, chained to the bed and naked, as Breton was expecting, but also mad as hell. He attacked Breton, wanted to know where the bastard who'd tied him up and left him was hiding, threatened to have both their heads. Breton told him to shut up or he'd remove his mask and drag him down for everyone to see. That worked – he got dressed and left after Breton did.'

'Furst didn't see his face?'

'No. He'd no idea who he was.'

But I did. Nick's lover of the night: Charlie Grohl. I hadn't gone looking for Grohl – to be honest, he'd slipped my mind – and now I cursed myself for the oversight.

'Breton didn't see or hear anything of the folks in 812,' Jerry went on, 'but felt guilty when news of the murder broke: he thought the two events were connected, that the guy who'd bribed him also killed the girl.'

'Why should he think that?'

Jerry shrugged. 'Would *you* have thought it was coincidence?'

'Probably not,' I admitted.

Jerry continued. 'Remember I told you how crazy Frank got when the body was discovered? The way Breton saw it, his ass would have been grass if he talked. First, he'd have had to explain why he was in 814 and you know how Frank reacts to Troops who take bribes. Second, if the guy he let in *had* murdered the woman in 812, he'd be accused of being an accomplice. Third, he'd have to admit that he'd untied and released the one man who could identify the possible killer, so he'd look like a fool on top of everything else.

'He decided to keep his mouth shut.'

'I can understand that,' I said, pizza forgotten, focusing on the tale. 'He fucked up, then covered up. Dumb, but human. But he wasn't killed for keeping quiet. What happened afterwards?'

'For a long time, nothing. Her body was found, he kept quiet, probably walked on his toes for a while, started to relax when it looked like he was in the clear. When he saw Nick Hornyak's photo in the paper and recognised him, he almost turned himself in. But didn't.

'Then, nearly two weeks after she'd been returned to the Skylight, someone rang. The caller knew everything, how Nicholas Hornyak had tipped him off, that he'd been in the room next to the girl's, that he'd kept quiet. Said he needed a favour and arranged a meeting. Breton didn't want to go but had no choice.

'They met in a cinema. It was dark and the blackmailer

tried not to show his face, but Breton ID'd him anyway. He didn't let on at the time, but he put it in his message.'

'Who was it?' I snapped, thinking it must have been Charlie Grohl.

'In a minute. I'm almost finished. The blackmailer said he was looking for the body of a certain Allegro Jinks. He thought it might be in the Fridge. He wanted Breton to go there, find it if he could, and tell him the next time he called. If he cooperated, his secret would be safe.

'Back home, Breton wrote up his confession, sealed it and passed it along to me. He said at the end that he was on his way to the Fridge. He didn't know what would happen, but wanted to make sure – if something went wrong – that the man who'd set him up didn't waltz away unpunished. It was a bit late in the day to do the right thing, but if he was killed for being a fool, at least he'd have the satisfaction of redeeming himself from beyond the grave.'

'Very noble,' I snorted, leant forward and hissed: 'The *name*.' I was afraid someone would burst in and pump a round of bullets through his head before he could spit it out. 'Who the hell was it?'

Jerry smiled thinly, glanced around, then lowered his voice and said, 'Does the name *Howard Kett* ring any bells?'

19

It was a three-hour train ride to the lake resort. I grabbed a window seat and spent the journey reflecting.

I'd run Jerry through his tale a couple more times, in case he'd missed anything. Put the names of Charlie Grohl, Rudi Ziegler and Priscilla Perdue to him, none of which were familiar. If Breton Furst had seen anyone loitering on the eighth floor or in the vicinity of the door he was meant to be guarding, he hadn't included it in his letter.

Jerry felt better by the end of the conversation. He'd been dreading the contact, afraid the same thing would happen to him as to Furst. Now that it was over, and he had my word that I wouldn't mention his name, no matter what transpired, he could relax. He'd lay low a few more days before reporting back to work, then do his utmost to drive all memories of Breton's message and this meeting from his mind.

He left ahead of me, visibly less tense than he'd been when I arrived. I hadn't thanked him, as thanks were unnecessary: we both knew the risk he'd taken and the debt I owed, and it went without saying that if he ever needed a favour he had only to call.

I stayed on at the diner awhile, thinking about Nick and Charlie Grohl. Nick had said he'd been with his lover the whole night, but according to Breton's testimony Grohl had been trussed up and alone when Breton found him. Where had Nick been? In the next room, slicing up his sister? Plotting with Howard Kett?

Kett . . .

Where did he fit in? Earlier he'd warned me away from Nick. Now I knew he'd sent Breton Furst to the Fridge in search of Allegro Jinks, which meant he knew about the Wami imitator. Had Kett killed Nic or conspired with her killer? Had he set Wami on the Fursts?

The evidence against him was strong, but I couldn't bring myself to believe the worst of him. Kett was an insufferable son of a bitch by all means, ignorant and cruel, but *crooked*? I didn't think so. He was surly, but straight.

Besides, he wasn't a good sport. Kett wasn't the kind of man who got his kicks from twisted games, who'd think of pitting a killer like Paucar Wami against his son, or calmly play the Cardinal like a patsy. It would be nice to think everything ended with Kett's exposure but that would surely be a case of naive wishful thinking.

I rang his office early the morning after my meeting with Jerry: they said he was on a week's holiday, not due back until the weekend. I thanked them, hung up and rang Bill. Pretended I was ringing to say hello. Manoeuvred the conversation round to talk of Howie. Expressed surprise when Bill told me he was on holiday; asked where prigs like Kett went in their spare time; idly wormed the name of the resort and Kett's hotel out of Bill; moved on to a discussion of one of his big fireworks shows; drew the chat to a close and quickly got in touch with the train station to book an open return ticket.

It was early afternoon when I reached the hotel, to learn Kett and family were out for the day. I booked a room, so I had an excuse to hang about, then positioned myself out front at a shaded table, pulled on the hat and dark glasses which would serve to disguise my identity from all but the actively curious, and spent several hours sipping non-alcoholic drinks while watching the street for the Ketts.

They turned up not long after seven. Howie, his wife, and five of their eight (or was it nine?) kids. Howie was in a pair of shorts, a flash Hawaiian-style shirt and a cardboard ten-gallon hat. I cursed myself for leaving my camera at home. The kids were arguing about what to do next. As they drew closer and entered the hotel, I heard Howie say they'd change clothes, then head down to the jetty to unwind and take the night from there.

A quarter of an hour later they re-emerged – Howie in more sombre attire this time – and started down for the jetty. I let them get a bit ahead, rose and slowly followed, making up my mind as I walked about how to play this.

The kids started to pester an old guy on a small yacht down at the jetty. I gathered he knew them by the way he didn't lose his rag when they clambered aboard. Mrs Kett wandered over to keep an eye on them. Howie stayed where he was, gazing out over the water at the setting sun, shirt rippling in the cool lake breeze.

I stepped up behind him and said, 'Beautiful, isn't it?'

'Yes,' he agreed, turning with an appreciative smile which disappeared when I raised my glasses and winked. '*Jeery?*' he gawped. 'What the fuck are you doing here?'

'Came for the fresh lake air, same as you.'

He stared at me suspiciously. 'Bullshit.'

'You're right,' I grinned. 'I came to ask you to connect the dots between Nicola and Nicholas Hornyak, Charlie Grohl, Breton Furst and Allegro Jinks. I heard you were the man for the job.'

He turned ghostly white. 'You scum,' he snarled. 'I'm on holiday, with my wife and children, and you have the goddamn fucking nerve to follow me here and – '

'If you want to create a scene, I'm game,' I interrupted softly. 'I don't mind having it out in front of your family.'

I thought he was going to hit me but then his shoulders sagged, he turned and yelled at his wife that he'd be with her soon, regarded me contemptuously, jerked his head towards the far end of the jetty and struck for it. He walked fast and I only caught up with him at the very edge, where he stood rooted to the boards like a guardian statue overlooking the lake.

'Make it quick, asshole,' he snapped. 'I'm only here for a week. I want to waste as little of it on you as is humanly possible.'

'Tell me about Nicholas Hornyak,' I said pleasantly. 'Why did you warn me off?'

'I told you: he's got friends who look out for him.'

'Name them.'

'No.' Bluntly, no room for argument.

'OK. Let's forget about Nick for a while. What about Breton Furst? You sent him after Allegro Jinks. That enquiry led to his death. His wife and kids too. Care to tell me what they died for?'

'I'd nothing to do with that,' Kett said quickly. 'I was trying to locate a missing person. I'd no idea it would end up the way it did. I wouldn't have sent him if I had.'

'Why send him at all? How did you know about him and Nick? Come to that, how'd you know about Jinks?' When he didn't respond I sat and hung my head out over the water, studying my reflection. 'This is a lovely spot,' I remarked. 'Come here a lot?'

'Every year, nearabouts,' he answered guardedly.

'Tell me what I want to know or it'll be a long time before you come again. How long do you think they'll send you down for if I go public? Nobody would have raised much of a fuss if it was just Nic and Breton Furst. It's the children: people are outraged, thirsty for blood. They want someone to vent their fury on. The killer, ideally, but I'm sure an accomplice would do. You might even get the chair, though life imprisonment's likelier.'

The grinding of Kett's teeth was louder than any motor on the lake and I was half afraid he'd chew his way down to the gums. But, with great effort, he parted his lips and said with a snarl, 'It all goes back to Charlie Grohl.'

I hid my smile and waved for him to continue.

'Grohl got in touch with me shortly after the press ran details of Nic Hornyak's death. He'd been in the room next to hers with her brother and was afraid his name would surface. He didn't know Nicholas Hornyak very well: he was only in town a couple of days, they hooked up at some gay joint and went to the Skylight for a night of passion. Nick did a runner during the night, leaving Grohl tied to the bed. A guard turned up the next morning and let him go. Grohl was furious, went looking for Nick, didn't find him, left the city without seeing him again.'

'He knew nothing about the murder?'

'No. Nor Nick's sister: he never saw her.'

'What did he think when her name turned up in the papers?'

'At first, nothing: it was a week after the event and he didn't connect it to his night there. Then he heard a half-rumour that she'd been murdered the week before – the Cardinal doesn't have so tight a stranglehold on the media outside the city – and concluded that Nick had killed her while he was tied to the bed, and that he was being set up to take the rap further down the line. That's why he hurried to tell me his story, before somebody dropped him in it.'

'Why come to *you?*' I asked.

'He'd made enquiries. Knew I was handling the case. Knew he could trust me to keep his name to myself.'

That sounded dubious but I let it pass. 'So he pointed the finger at Nick. Fine. Why didn't you go after him?'

'I did,' Kett sighed. 'That's when I was told to keep my nose out. My kids were threatened. I didn't like it, but I backed off. When *you* started sniffing around, Hornyak's friends sent me along to have a word. That's the bitch about these fuckers: give in to them once and you're giving in the rest of your life.'

'We keep coming back to these so-called *friends*. Names, Howie.'

'And wind up like the Fursts?' He laughed bitterly. 'If you put a gun to my children's heads and tell me to talk, and I believe you'll shoot if I don't, *then* I'll yap. Otherwise, go whistle.'

I wasn't happy. Not because he wouldn't tell me their names, but because I doubted they existed: Kett wasn't the sort of cop who bows to pressure. I didn't think threats had anything to do with his decision to keep mum about Nick. But there are times when it's easier to accept a lie than push to expose it.

'Tell me about Allegro Jinks,' I moved on.

'First you've got to understand,' he said. 'Grohl told me everything about that night, including the name of the guard who freed him. Also, though I'd kept Nick Hornyak out of my investigations, I hadn't let the case die: I'd been pursuing other angles, asking questions about Nicola. I knew she'd been seen with a guy answering Paucar Wami's description.'

'You found that out?' I was mildly surprised.

'I know a *bit* about detective work,' he sneered. 'So, I'm busy with that. Then my leads peter out, I've other cases, I figure if Nick was the killer, I won't be able to bring him in; if it was Wami, I won't be able to bring *him* in; and if it was some nobody freak she picked up, chances are I won't find him, so I won't be able to bring *him* in. It begins slipping down my list of priorities.

'Then a woman turns up looking for her missing son.

Sobbing her eyes out, begging for help. He's had problems in the past but he was settling down. Then, the past few months, he's shaved his head, tattooed his face with snakes, split from his friends and taken up with some rich snip of a white girl.'

'Allegro Jinks,' I guessed.

'Of course. The bald head and snakes tipped me off. I looked for him but, as his mother had said, he'd vanished. One evening he'd been seen going up to his room. After that: nothing. Then I heard about a Chinese tattooist who'd been ripped to pieces shortly before Jinks went missing. Word on the street was Paucar Wami did it. I put two and two together – '

'You've learned to add, Howie,' I interjected. 'Congratulations.'

' – and came up with the Fridge,' he finished, blushing angrily. 'I know Wami leaves a lot of his kills there – or so rumour has it – and I figured that was the only chance I had of finding Jinks. His mother was ringing me every other hour – worst mistake I made, showing some sympathy – and the only way to shut her up was to find his body and deliver it to her for burial.

'But I couldn't trot along to the Fridge and ask if they had an Allegro Jinks on ice. It doesn't work that way. I had to go through someone who was part of the system, who wouldn't be questioned, someone like – '

' – Breton Furst,' I finished for him.

'Exactly. There were others I could have used, but I'd recent dirt on Furst, I reckoned he'd still be shaky about not coming clean when he should have, and thought he'd be as easy to manipulate as anyone.'

'You met him in person,' I noted. 'That was foolish.'

'Couldn't discuss it over the phone,' Kett countered. 'It could have been bugged. Besides, it was dark in the cinema and I didn't think he'd recognise me. Obviously – since you're here, and you could only have learnt about me through Furst – I was wrong.'

'He left a note,' I said, quietly analysing Kett's story. 'So you sent him to ask about Jinks. What next?'

'Nothing next. I was going to ring him later that evening. Heard about his murder at work. Figured it tied in and that if anyone knew I'd set him up to it, I was fucked. Kept my head down and booked a holiday as soon as I could. Thought I'd left the mess behind till you turned up.'

A neat story. I'm not saying I believed it, but it was neat.

'You think Nick arranged Furst's murder?' I asked.

'I neither know nor give a shit,' he answered. 'I feel lousy about what happened to him – especially his wife and kids – but what can I do? Step forward and risk my own family? Nuh-uh. I've had my fill of killing. You go on and investigate if you want. Me, when I'm finished down here, I'm going back to proper detective work.'

'You're a coward, Howie.'

'So was Breton Furst. Difference is, I'm a *live* coward.'

I raised myself, shook the dust from the back of my trousers and wondered how much of his story was true. It was easy to call Kett a coward – and easy for him to admit it – but we both knew that was a crock. He'd gone after tougher fish than Nick Hornyak – *friends* or otherwise – regardless of risk to himself or his family. Bill had often told me – usually when I was belittling his boss – of the extra hours Kett put in, the time he'd crawled out onto the top of a train to take on a couple of teenagers stoned out of their heads on PCP, how he'd kept after a gang boss till he got him, in spite of bomb-mail and an attempt on his eldest son's life.

'You'll save us both a shitload of trouble if you play straight with me,' I said. 'Nobody need know. Tell me the truth and I'll leave you be.'

302

'I've told the truth,' he stubbornly insisted.

'Some of it, perhaps, but not all. I'm not a fool, Howie.'

'I think you are,' he said softly. 'A fool to come down here. A fool to keep pressing. I can't say for sure, but it looks to me like Paucar Wami killed Jinks and the Fursts. You keep on with this shit and next thing you know he'll be coming for *you*. What'll you do then, Jeery, huh?'

I smiled as I thought of what he'd say if I told him about my working relationship with my long-lost father, but – sweet as it would be to watch his face drop – that was information best not shared.

'See you back in the city, Howie,' I said, taking my leave.

'Not if Paucar Wami sees you first,' he retorted, then scurried off to collect his family and shepherd them back to the hotel.

I could have caught the last train home, but why hurry? This was a nice little town, I'd a room booked for the night, there was nothing to draw me back to the city and the game. I was due a night off.

Mention of Wami had set me thinking about him. I hadn't forgotten about my father in my haste to catch up with Kett, but I'd conveniently let him slip my mind: if I'd told him of my meeting with Jerry, he would have insisted on coming with me to *assist* in the interrogation, and though I bore no love for Howard Kett, I didn't want to see him winding up as bait on the end of a fish-hook.

I rang Wami from my room. No answer, so I went for a walk, found a cosy restaurant, tucked into a fish so fresh I expected it to leap off my plate, and tried his number again from a phone box.

'Al m'boy,' he answered. 'Was that you ringing earlier? Sorry I couldn't come to the line: my hands were full.' There was a groan in the background.

'What was that?' I asked.

303

'Our friend Nick,' he replied. 'I tired of trailing him, so I – '

'No!' I roared, gripping the phone furiously.

Wami chuckled. 'Relax, Al. I was pulling your leg again. Nick is perfectly safe. This is some poor nobody I picked up off the street. Would you care to share a few last words with him?'

'You're a sick son of a bitch,' I moaned.

'And you are the son of a son of a bitch. No matter. Where are you and where have you been? You were supposed to be shadowing Nick this afternoon.'

'I've been busy. A lead fell into my lap.'

'Do tell,' he said eagerly.

'Not over the phone. It's too long.' And I didn't want him going after Nick without me, which he might if he knew I wasn't around to stop him. 'Listen, I want you to see if you can find a guy called Charlie Grohl. He's a friend of Nick's, the lover who was with him in the Skylight. He lives out of town.'

'Any idea whereabouts?'

'None whatsoever.'

'That might take some time.'

'It'll be time well spent.'

'This has to do with your new lead?'

'Yes.'

'Very well,' he sighed. 'I shall wrap things up sooner than I had planned and apply myself to the tiresome task. Will you be joining me in the quest or must I cast my nets alone?'

'Tomorrow. I'll give you a ring.'

'Very well. Good night, my son.'

''Night,' I threw back gruffly, hating him for his sarcastic politeness, hating myself more for turning a blind eye to his murderous ways. There were times, trailing Nick, when Wami was vulnerable. The opportunities to take a shot at him had been ample. Maybe I could have put him out of the city's misery by now.

But I needed him to crack the mystery and find Nic's killer. I was putting my own selfish motives before the welfare of a city of millions, any one of whom could be next on Wami's hit list, and sometimes it churned my stomach to think of it.

A long late-night walk to clear my head, lapping up the small-town atmosphere, breathing in the fresh lake winds. I wondered what Kett was up to: sitting alone, brooding, cursing, ringing a partner and telling him about me? The light in his room was still on when I returned but that may have been his wife or kids, staying up late to read a book or watch a movie.

I tucked myself into the soft hotel bed and stared out the open window at the unusually clear sky. Living in the city, it was easy to forget about the untold number of stars up there. I recalled the old myths that our destinies were written in the skies and fell asleep thinking how much simpler life would be if that was the case.

I caught an early train back and arrived home before ten in the a.m. Bounced up the stairs, bright and frisky, only to find my front door key wouldn't turn. Taking it out, I got down on one knee and peered into the keyhole. Some clever bastard had been here while I was away and filled it with glue. It was the third time this year. Some bored kid, no doubt. One day I'd catch him at it and . . .

No use crying. Only one thing to do. I got to my feet, took aim, counted to three, and kicked sharply at the lock. It busted and the door burst open first go. I trooped in, dumped my overnight bag on the sofa and croaked to the stale, ill-lit room, 'Welcome home.'

I brewed a mug of coffee and drank it slowly, then started out again, swinging the door closed behind me. I cycled over to my friend Danny's hardware store. It was out of my way but I didn't care. Danny was an old pal and welcome to my custom. I'd met him through Bill, who used to work for him when he was a kid, many years ago.

Danny was behind the counter. He was getting on in years and was found more often in the back these days, pestering the staff. He'd been threatening to retire for ages but everybody knew he wouldn't.

He laughed when I walked in with a scowl on my face. 'Not the lock again!' he hooted.

'If I ever catch that son of a bitch . . .'

'Maybe it's a locksmith,' Danny grinned. 'The guy who owned this place before me used to pull that trick when business was slow. Glued up locks of people he knew and waited for the calls to flood in. He got busted a couple of times but that didn't stop him. He was a mad old buzzard.'

'You never tried it yourself, of course,' I smiled.

'Certainly not,' he said indignantly, but I could see him reddening guiltily around the throat. 'Same make as before?'

'Unless they've started making glue-resistant models.'

He asked about Bill as I was paying for the lock. I told him he was fine and mentioned the fishing trip we'd been on. Danny used to come fishing with us before his health deteriorated. He sighed and asked me to let him know the next time we were going: he'd come along if his doctor OK'd it. I promised I would, waved away my change and wished him well.

Back home, there were two squad cars outside the building and cops in my apartment, talking softly among themselves. I hesitated in the hallway, unseen, wondering whether to proceed or beat a retreat. I decided to face them: maybe someone had noticed the busted lock and called them in to check on it.

I knocked loudly as I entered. I didn't recognise the three

young officers but smiled at them as if they were old friends. 'Howdy, boys. Help you any?'

'You Al Jeery?' one of them asked.

'Yes.'

'Yes, *sir*!' another snapped.

I sighed inwardly: an asshole. 'Yes, sir,' I mumbled.

'We'd like you to accompany us across town.' The one who'd first spoken.

'What for?'

'I'd rather not say.'

'Am I under arrest?'

'Not yet, punk,' the asshole snarled.

'What if I don't want to go?'

'It would be better if you did.' The first cop. Earnest.

I yawned theatrically to show I wasn't worried.

'Come on then,' I said. 'Let's go see what you want.'

'Thank you,' the first cop said.

'Jerk,' the asshole added.

The third stayed silent.

I peered in the window of the bagel shop as I was passing. Two more cops inside, talking with Ali, taking notes. Ali looked numb. He was shaking his head and appeared to be crying. A bad sign.

They ran me across town, sirens blaring, saying nothing. They avoided the roads to the station, which surprised me. I checked their uniforms in the dim glow of the street lights: they looked real but I had a bad feeling about this. Maybe they were in disguise. I was between two of them on the back seat but wasn't cuffed. I should be able to make the door handle before they could stop me. Tensing my muscles, I leant over . . .

. . . then relaxed as they pulled up at the Skylight. I knew now the uniforms were real, and had a pretty good idea of what lay in store. The dismayed faces of the customers and staff in the lobby – I spotted Terry Archer hovering behind his underlings, wringing his hands together miserably – confirmed my suspicions. By the time I reached room 812 and saw the corpse draped across the bed it was something of an anticlimax.

The ranking officer was a guy called Vernon Ast. Bill had introduced us on a couple of occasions. A pleasant man, but his face was grim when he stepped in front of me and asked if I could account for my whereabouts last night. I told him I'd been out of the city and could produce witnesses if required (I grinned as I thought of Kett's apoplexy if he was forced to take the stand in my defence).

'I hope that's true,' Vernon sighed, massaging the bridge of his nose. 'For Bill's sake. I know he thinks highly of you.'

'Who is it?' I asked directly, nodding at the naked female body.

'You don't know?' I shook my head. 'We found some stuff: a credit card, a pair of sunglasses, a single sock. No prize for guessing whose name is on the card. The rest of it's probably yours too.'

'A thorough frame,' I noted, smiling grimly. Was it Priscilla? Had the bastard who'd murdered Nic now made an end of her sometimes partner?

'You want to ID the body?' Vernon asked. 'You don't have to. If you want to consult with a lawyer . . .'

'The suspense would be the end of me. I'll take a look.'

I walked slowly over to the body, feeling time and space contract, barely aware of the police clearing a path, drawing back from me as though I had the plague. She was lying face-down. The killer had been even more brutal this time. It looked to me as if they wouldn't be able to make an accurate count of the puncture wounds on her back.

I stopped at the foot of the bed, noting something shining amidst the pools of blood. My right hand darted forward before anyone could stop me. My fingers brushed aside jagged fleshy folds and closed around a hard, cool ball. Raising it to the light, my suspicions were confirmed: the black, gold-streaked marble.

'Recognise it?' Ast asked quietly.

I nodded. 'It's from my apartment. I don't know how it got here.'

'You'd better put it back,' he said.

Replacing the marble – which had unnerved me more than the body – I rounded the bed, into a position where I could view the face. It was half-smothered by a pillow, which obscured the corpse's features. I had to kneel down for a decent look.

I was expecting Priscilla and preparing my reactions with her in mind. But as I knelt I realised the hair was wrong and the legs were too long. My heart leapt gratefully: it wasn't Priscilla! This woman was entirely the wrong shape, taller, broader, thicker legs and arms, a long capping head of beautiful . . . blond . . . hair . . .

My stomach dropped. I no longer had to see the face to make an identification. I knew by the hair, that magnificent hair, so strong yet soft to the touch. The hair I'd combed a thousand times.

I tried not to think her name. I focused on the hair, driving all else from my mind, for fear the truth would madden me. Fanned out on the pillow the way I remembered so well. Flowing, vibrant, perfect, flecked with the red fingerprints of death but otherwise unharmed.

Her hair was all I thought about as they read me my rights and led me down the stairs. Her hair, as I was bundled into a car and driven to the station. Her exquisite, gleaming, blood-smeared hair, as they locked me away and swamped me with questions, none of which I could answer.

And then, when I was alone and the hair couldn't keep

the name at bay any longer, I whispered it to myself, under my breath, feeling my world ignite at the edges and burn swiftly as I said it '*Ellen . . .*'

part five

'the blood of dreams'

20

The isolation of the cell suited me. It was good to be cut off from the cruel world and its hideous sounds. I could have hidden in here forever, undisturbed, thinking about nothing.

A cop entered and shattered the silence with: 'You want something to eat? To drink?' I shook my head. 'What about your phone call?' A careless shrug. He hesitated. 'I know you and Bill Casey are friends. We're trying to contact him, but he's out. We'll keep trying. If you want anything . . .'

'Thank you,' I said softly, since my response was obviously the only thing that would shift him.

He smiled, gratified. 'No problem. We all know the *evidence* is so much shit in a sack. We won't be long cleaning this mess up.'

Then he was gone and I was alone with the soothing silence again. But the interruption had jolted me. My thoughts started to churn. I was dragged back to the world of memories against my will.

When I first met Ellen. She was a friend of my then-current amour. Ellen didn't like me: she'd heard I'd been cheating. Came over to my flat and berated me. Subjected me to a tongue-lashing of epic proportion. I listened calmly, watching the bob of her hair, and when she finished, asked if she'd like to come in and make the beast with two backs. She slapped my face, stormed off, rang her friend, and I was down one belle.

A park, some years later. Relaxing by an artificial pond, wondering what to do with the rest of my life. A weeping woman sat down close by and cried into the water. I studied her quietly, out of the corner of my eye. I thought I recognised her and, inquisitive infidel that I was, edged over and asked if we knew each other.

She lashed out at me blindly and I remembered her immediately. She apologised moments later and asked me to sit. She hadn't yet checked my face. Didn't know who I was. Proceeded to tell me about her hardships, the man she'd loved for two years, who'd just walked out and said he was never coming back. Her father had died a couple of months before and she was still aching from that. She was lonely and frightened and didn't know where she was going to end up.

I said she wasn't alone. I was lonely too. Worried about where I was heading. Told her life was hard, there were no smooth rides, we had to do the best we could and hope to Christ we didn't get screwed over too often. She empathised with that.

We spoke for ages. She didn't look at me once. I told her loads of stuff about myself, even the last time I cried, after my final fight, when I realised I'd never make it in the ring. By the end of our chat she was smiling and we both knew something special might blossom between us, given time. Then she turned and took in my face.

'Hey! You're that bastard Al Jeery!'

The door opened and shut softly. A large man sat down opposite me and said nothing for a while. When he finally spoke, it was through vocal cords constricted with sorrow.

'I don't know what to say.'

I saw a pair of fists clench viciously on the table.

'All these years of comforting the bereaved and I can't think of a single fucking thing to say.'

I concentrated on the fists, tracing the angry red knuckle lines with my eyes, noting the quiver in the fingers.

'I thought it was a sick joke when they rang. Refused to believe it until I saw the body. Oh, Christ, the body . . .'

'A piece of work, wasn't it?' I looked up into Bill's sad, red eyes. I hadn't cried yet. Couldn't.

'Who did it, Al? Do you know?'

'What would you do if I said I did?'

'I'd find the bastard and . . .' He gripped the edge of the table, tears falling thickly, shoulders hunched forward painfully.

'I don't know who did it, but if I did, I wouldn't tell. She was *my* wife. I'll deal with it.'

Bill nodded, wiped at his eyes, then produced a bottle of whisky, set it in the middle of the table and cleared his throat. I stared at the bottle, then Bill.

'Take it,' he said sombrely.

'No.' The word was barely a sigh on my lips.

'Don't fight, Al. If the thirst's in you, sate it.'

'You know what that does to me, Bill.'

He nodded slowly. '*I* weaned you off it, remember? *I* said I'd kill you if I saw you touching it again.' He leaned forward and gripped my hands. 'But things change. Situations alter and we have to alter with them. All I care about is getting you through the next few days, and if you have to be steaming drunk to do that, so be it.'

'And after?'

'Fuck after!' Bill roared. The cursing was unusual for him. 'We'll deal with that when it comes. Drink!'

He let go of my hands and sat back, looking ashamed. I knew this offer was tearing him apart. He must think I was

315

precariously close to the edge of madness if he was willing to resort to such desperate measures. Maybe I was.

I reached out to caress the bottle. Unscrewed the top, bent over and inhaled. He was right: I did need it. More than anything else in the world. A couple of good swallows and all would be right with me. I'd cry and mourn for Ellen, drink myself to sleep at night, and curl up into a safe, drunken ball by day.

I sat back, leaving the bottle.

'No,' I said. 'I can't. The pain's bad but it keeps me going. I'll find her killer but only if I stay sober. There'll be time for drinking later.'

'Al, you mustn't – '

'No!' I stopped him. 'There's nothing without her. It's not just that she was killed: she was killed because of *me*. I'm the reason she's dead.'

'You can't be sure of that.'

I stared at him coldly until he dropped his eyes.

'OK,' he sighed, pocketing the bottle. 'I can't tell you what to do. But, if you change your mind, don't be afraid. No man should have to face something like this alone. Screw the consequences: I pulled you back from the brink before; I can do it again.'

We sat listening to the silence when he was done talking. I kept thinking about the bottle in his jacket. I wanted him to take it out and make the offer again. If he had, I might have been tempted.

'What about this evidence against me?' I asked, focusing on the issue immediately to hand.

'It's bullshit. If Kett was here he might make something of it, just to be ornery, but nobody's going to chase it. All the same, I rang Ford Tasso and he'll send along some hotshot lawyer to bail you out quickly, with the minimum of fuss.'

'Anybody contact Kett yet?'

'No. He'll hear about it sooner or later. If I have my way, it'll be later.'

Kett could have cleared me instantaneously but I'd rather keep him out of it: if I brought him into this mess, I'd have to explain what I was doing down there. It might complicate matters. Right now, as I'd told Bill, I didn't want anyone taking an interest. The bastard who killed Ellen was *mine*.

'When did it happen?' I asked.

'Early hours of this morning.'

'Was she killed in the hotel?'

'I assume so.' He glanced at me suspiciously. 'Any reason to think she wouldn't have been?'

I didn't reply: I could find that out later.

'Anybody see anything?'

'No.'

'Who was the room checked out to?'

'Nobody. It was supposed to be empty. It hadn't been put to use since . . .' He coughed discreetly.

We talked some more and then he had to go. I was alone again, just me, the silence, the fumes of the whisky, and the memories. There was no escaping the memories.

Ford Tasso stormed the station within an hour of being alerted, Emeric Hinds and a posse of lawyers in tow. Shell-shocked as I was, I couldn't help being impressed: Hinds was the Cardinal's sharpest legal mind, usually reserved for the elite. Sending him was a mark of enormous respect, though his presence probably wasn't required: anyone with a tenth as much experience would have done. As Bill had said, the evidence against me was risible, more an insult than anything else.

I asked Hinds if he could get the marble for me. That marble had set me thinking and I wanted it back, so I could gaze into its dark heart and think some more. He

317

said he could get it later, not straightaway. I had to settle for that.

Tasso said the Cardinal sent his regards and would receive me any time I chose to drop by. He'd also told his henchman that I could now proceed with the Nic Hornyak investigation or drop it: whichever I chose, it wouldn't be held against me. As if I could quit *now*!

I moved in with Bill until the funeral. He was going to take time off work but I told him not to: I preferred being alone. I sat in his big old house, staring out the huge front window. It wasn't as quiet as the cell had been but it was quiet enough. I thought about Ellen and Nic and what I would do with the killer when I caught up. I also thought about the marble, its black sheen and golden streaks, the smears of Ellen's blood.

The days blurred into one another. I didn't take much notice. Didn't stop to think about Nick, Kett, the blind priests, or if any of them had anything to do with Ellen's murder. Didn't ring my father or hear from him. All that could wait. This was a period of mourning. A time for Ellen.

The drinks cabinet in the living room obsessed me. It was full of familiar old friends. Alcohol was the only thing that could stop me, the only way I might be sidetracked. If I hit the bottle, I'd forget about Ellen, her killer, the rest, and escape to the blessed sanctuary of drunken oblivion.

Finally, when it seemed I must burst or give in to temptation, I took to the streets. Grabbed my bike – Bill had brought it over – and spent hours cycling around, losing myself in a maze of city streets, stilling the memories, the demons, the needs.

I covered most city sectors but lingered in none, stopping neither for rest nor refreshments. Nobody paid any notice: slipping by them, I might have been invisible. I felt like I could have done anything, as though I'd stepped outside the boundaries of the real world, into a realm where I was master. But I didn't *want* to do anything except ride and blot out the memories.

My wanderings led me in the end to the Manco Capac statue. I'd passed it several times without stopping, but finally drew up at the building site, tied my bike to a fence and ambled in. I wasn't sure what brought me here but it seemed like the right place to be. The site was teeming with workers but none paid any attention to me. The giant statue looked to be in much the same shape as before: if they'd made progress, it wasn't of the immediately visible kind.

The cool shadow of a crane passed overhead. I raised my eyes and followed the arm of the machine as it rotated from one side to the other. A dim part of my mind wondered once again how they got these monsters up, but I wasn't in the mood for childish riddles and the question rapidly slipped from my thoughts.

When my gaze returned to the ground, a tall man in white robes was standing directly opposite me. His eyes were round and blank. He was smiling. By the mole on the left side of his chin, I recognised him.

I wasn't surprised: part of me had been anticipating something along these lines from the moment I made the decision to stop.

I started across to confront him. I didn't know what I'd say: I was playing this by ear. As I closed in on the blind man he extended his arms to the left and right, said something in a language I couldn't understand, turned and darted behind a Portakabin. I sped after him, only to find the area deserted. Spinning around, I spotted a flash of white near the base of the statue. Not pausing to wonder how he'd crossed so much ground so quickly, I raced after him.

No sign of him when I arrived. I circled the statue twice

before noticing the ladder leading up the calf of one huge leg. I climbed up, taking the rungs two at a time. Emerged onto a flat platform dotted with protruding ends of thick steel girders. In the centre a trapdoor had been flung open. I caught a glimpse of the blind man's head as he disappeared through the floor.

When I reached the opening I discovered a thin ladder set inside. For the briefest moment I hesitated – the Troop in me screaming: 'Not a good idea!' – then dispensed with logic and started down.

After six or seven metres I'd almost caught up with my prey, when all of a sudden he let go of the ladder and vanished into the darkness of the vertical tunnel beyond. I scuttled down a few more rungs, only to learn he hadn't let go for fun: the ladder ended here. I peered down into the tunnel, wondering if I dared proceed, when the trapdoor overhead slammed shut, pitching me into complete blackness.

My heart leapt wildly and my head filled with visions of dread. I sharply reprimanded myself – I was too old to be afraid of the dark – and focused on my options. I could ascend the ladder and try the door or I could follow the blind man. Since I saw no sense in retreating, I explored the tunnel with my feet and hands, realised it was narrow enough to wedge myself in and proceeded to do so. Back jammed against one wall, knees and hands braced against the other, I shuffled down.

It was stuffy; the air was poor; the darkness was oppressive; but I went on. When I appeared to be getting nowhere, I extracted a coin and dropped it. It rolled and clanged for what seemed an age before trickling to a stop. Taking a deep breath, I did what had to be done if I was to stand any reasonable chance of catching up: pulled in my legs, removed my hands from the wall, lay back and slid.

At first it was a virtual straight drop and I thought that I was falling to my death. Then the tunnel angled outwards and I gradually slowed, more with every passing second, until I came to a stop in what seemed from the sounds to be an enormous barren cavern. I put my hands out but couldn't see them. Got to my feet and took a few cautious steps forward, testing each new section of ground with my toes before settling my weight on it.

The sound of swishing robes pierced the silence. I froze, alert, relying on my ears. Drew my pistol but held it by my side until I had something to aim at.

'Welcome, Albert Jeery,' came a voice from the darkness. 'Welcome, Flesh of Dreams.' Smothered in echoes, it could have originated anywhere in the room.

'Where are you?' I snapped, only to have my own words echo back at me: ' . . . are you? are you?' 'Show yourself,' I shouted. ' . . . self, self.'

'You seek answers, Flesh of Dreams. You seek truth. Death stalks your every move and you wish to know why.' The speaker paused between sentences to let the echoes die down.

'What's with the Flesh of Dreams shit?' I retorted, but my query was ignored.

'Only through us may you access the truth. We know all that occurs in this city and why. Accept us, and we will share our knowledge. Deny us, and so shall you be denied.'

'Quit with the riddles and get to the point,' I growled, at which a match flared in the distance and a torch was lit. I brought my gun up and trained it on the light, but there was nobody in sight.

Cautiously I edged towards the torch, awaiting further communication. When I reached the source of the light I discovered the torch was set in a wall and couldn't be moved. Underneath it hung a small pouch. I glanced around the cavern: rough-hewn walls, Gothic shadows, no sign of life.

'We are of Dreams,' came the voice, filling the cavern, once again appearing to come from everywhere at once. 'You are Flesh of Dreams, but more Flesh than Dreams. To move beyond these walls, you must move beyond Flesh. In the pouch lies dust. You must inhale it. Place the mouth of the pouch to one nostril. Squeeze the pouch sharply. Repeat the procedure on the other side.' With the pauses, the instructions seemed to take forever.

'The hell I will,' I laughed once the echoes had subsided.

'You must.'

'What's in it?'

'Seeds of Dreams.'

'Some kind of drug?'

'Dreams come by many names.'

'What if I refuse to play along?'

There was no answer, which was answer enough.

If I'd been in full control of my senses I wouldn't have done as they suggested. I'd have scouted around for tunnels leading from the cave, or tried making my way back up the sliding tunnel to the surface, long and painful as the climb might be. But I hadn't been in full control since I found Ellen's body in the Skylight. I'd given myself over to the city and this was what the city had tossed back. It was easiest to surrender completely, the hell with reservations.

The first inhalation blew my mind away. I don't know what was in that pouch, but it was as strong as any shit you'd find on the streets. Rockets went off and the light from the torch intensified a thousand times. By themselves, my hands raised the pouch again, located my left nostril and injected more dust. The walls of the cavern dissolved, I lost all sense of body and time, and became part of an immense sphere of light which was brighter than the sum of all the torches in the world put together. I swam in that light, and felt the light swim in me, and was as delirious for the duration as it's humanly possible to be.

Minutes – hours – later, the effects of the dust diminished, and though the vision of light persisted, it wasn't absolute. I flickered in and out of reality, one moment fully aware, the next immersed in the dreamy light. I recall descending a narrow staircase, dark as a coal-pit, which seemed to drop to the very bowels of the earth. When we hit bottom there was a long walk through a dark maze. Some time later I became aware of a dimly lit room. The walls were draped in curtains the colour of blood, and skeletons dangled from the ceiling, some low enough to touch.

'Pretty,' I murmured through numb lips.

'They are the remains of the lower servants of Dreams.' Looking around, I realised there were two men with me, both in white robes, both blind. I started to ask where we were and who they were but before I could speak I was swept away on another wave of light.

The next I knew, we were in a small antechamber and they were removing my clothes. There was nothing sexual in their actions and I didn't resist as they stripped me naked and daubed my body with painted symbols.

'Your eyes,' I said dreamily to one of the men. 'I can see clouds. And yours,' to the other. 'Mountains. Poking up through the clouds. I've seen them before. Mountains and rivers. Rivers of blood.' It was only later that I remembered where I'd seen them: in the rain-induced vision.

The blind men looked startled, then smiled approvingly. 'That is good,' one commended me. 'Very good.' I beamed proudly, absurdly delighted by the praise, then slipped down another corridor of light to explore the glowing clouds of illumination inside my head.

I was brought back to the real world sharply this time. One of the men blew something into me which shattered

323

the wondrous universe of light and jolted me back to semi-consciousness.

'We must present you now,' I was told. 'Try to stay with us.'

I nodded wordlessly and concentrated on making my feet move as they guided me through a door and into an immense cavern which made the first I'd fallen into seem like a cranny. Thick candles dotted the walls and ceiling, dripping wax which was left to form sculptures of its own making on the floor. The cavern receded into the distance as far as I could see. Symbols – similar to those I had been painted with – adorned the walls, many of them representations of the sun. I thought they were beautiful, though part of me (which remembered the spoiled bodies of Ellen and Nic) recoiled.

Directly in front lay a circular stone platform, roughly half a metre high, maybe forty in diameter. A huge gold sun medallion hung suspended overhead. The circumference of the platform was dotted with the stiff remains of preserved human corpses: they sat upright in plain chairs, facing inwards, mummified – it appeared – by some sort of fluid or balm. Three grander, ornate chairs – thrones – decorated the centre of the circle, set about a metre apart from one another.

The robed white-eyed man with the mole occupied the middle throne. Similarly blind and clad men stood behind the other two, faces just visible over the tops of the high backs. They looked almost identical, except the one in the middle had that mole and a few years' march on the others.

In front of the trio, a young man sat on his haunches, crouched at the feet of the sitting white-eyed man like a dog. He had long silver hair, brown eyes, and was naked as myself, his body also covered with intricate designs. He was the one who addressed me throughout.

'Welcome, Flesh of Dreams,' he greeted me. I blinked nervously in reply, lost for words. The man on the throne said something in a language I couldn't place. The younger man nodded. 'Do not be afraid. You have nothing to fear. We shall not harm you.'

'Thank you,' I replied, then found myself fixing on the huge sun ornament. One of the men who'd accompanied me from the first cavern gently redirected my head so that I was facing the platform again. The young man waited to speak until he was sure I was lucid.

'We are *villacs*: the priests of the sun,' he intoned. 'We are the builders of this city, the architects of its future. What we do, we do for the city. You are a spirit of destiny, Flesh of Dreams, of our planning and making. Great things will come of our union.'

'That's nice,' I giggled.

'We would tell you of our plans but it is not time. First you must be cleansed. You cannot join us as you are. Only the pure may serve.'

The man on the throne spoke again. The young man listened, nodding intently. I staggered on my feet and tuned into the sound of water dripping somewhere. This was further beyond my level of comprehension than quantum physics or Joyce's *Finnegans Wake* (which Bill had once pressed on me), but I was druggedly determined not to let my confusion show.

'Unclean as you are,' the naked man on the platform resumed, 'it is time to draw your blood. That is why you are here. This city was built on blood and is sustained by blood. The blood of man, the blood of the sun, the blood of Dreams. For centuries, these blood-streams have run separately. Soon the three will merge and there will be but one blood, which will feed this city eternally and secure its fixture in the firmament long after the marvels of man have crumbled to dust.

'You are here because yours is the blood of the union: you are the son of Dreams Made Flesh, the offspring of the waking and sleeping worlds. We have guided you since birth; quietly encouraged your talents, working through others so that no harm befell you. We bring you here to prepare you for the day of the union, to make you aware of the glorious destiny to which you were born.'

Though I took in what he was saying, I couldn't make much sense of it. Nor did I try: I was thinking about the pouch of dust and hoping they'd offer me some more to transport me back to the world of light.

'*Blood*,' he hissed. 'All revolves around the sap of the living. You thirst for blood, do you not? Your women have been murdered and you live to avenge their deaths, yes?'

My eyes narrowed, the world of light dwindled from my thoughts and sobriety laid hold. 'Ellen,' I sighed.

'She was killed for the sun. Your other lover too. Sacrificed for *your* destiny. Slain, that *you* may grow in spirit and move towards – '

'You killed her!' I screamed madly, surging forward, only to find my way blocked by the two men who'd been my earlier guides.

'We did not kill your women,' the man on the platform vowed. 'The murderer you seek resides elsewhere.'

'Who killed them?' I shouted. 'Tell me or – '

'That is for you to discover,' he interrupted. 'Answers must be earned. Blood must find its own way.'

'Fuck blood!' I screamed. 'Tell me who killed Ellen or I'll – '

The blind man on the throne barked a sharp order. I don't know what he said, but it was commanding enough to silence me. He got to his feet and walked to the edge of the platform, passing the naked man, who bowed low and averted his eyes. The blind priest continued speaking as he advanced, empty eyes fixed on my form.

'My master says you must show respect,' came the translation.

I was afraid of this sinister man but the memory of Ellen drove me to snarl, 'Fuck respect.'

The blind man at the fore of the platform stiffened, then chuckled and mumbled something to his servant, who smiled in reply.

'My master says your blood is hot, and that is good. Respect will come later. He can wait. For now, you must lend us your hands.'

'My . . . ?' I stared down at the two extremities. The blind priest reached into his robes and produced a long curved dagger. I took a nervous step backwards. 'You're not taking my hands,' I moaned.

'We don't intend to,' the young man laughed. 'We need only your blood, and precious little of that. Step forward.' I shook my head and jammed my hands behind my back. The priest with the mole began to chant quietly, then made a beckoning motion with his knife. Suddenly I was stumbling towards him involuntarily.

I stopped at the edge of the platform. I wanted to turn and flee, but was under the blind priest's spell. He knelt and leant forward, took my left hand, laid it gently on his head, said something under his breath – it sounded like a prayer – lowered my hand and kissed the palm. Next he made a quick slice with the knife across the centre of my soft flesh and drew blood. Maybe because of the drug, I felt no pain.

I thought he was going to lick the blood off but he didn't. He let it drip to the floor of the platform, where it disappeared, as though sucked up by the stone, then repeated the ceremony on my right hand. Finished, he stepped back, handed the dagger to one of the priests behind the empty thrones and resumed his central position.

'It is done,' the naked man said. 'The blood of Flesh of Dreams is diminished. To replenish it you must take blood in anger: in doing so the way for the union will be open.

'Take him back,' he said to my guides. As they stepped forward to escort me away, he addressed me a final time: 'We will contact you again. When next we bring you here, it will be to celebrate the union of the blood-streams. On that day, all shall be revealed, and every question answered.'

'No,' I mumbled, shaking my head. 'No!' I bellowed. 'I want to know *now*. You're going to tell me. I won't leave until you do. I'll tear you apart, the lot of you if I have to, but I won't – '

As I was making the threat, I stepped up onto the platform, only for a shock to course through my body like a flood of electric eels as soon as my bare feet made contact with the stone. It was as though I'd rammed my fingers into a live socket. I was hurled backwards through the air. The world went momentarily white, then red, and then I knew nothing except dreams.

Bill was standing over me when I returned to the land of the living, slapping my face lightly. 'Al?' he asked softly. 'Are you OK?'

'Where am I?' I groaned, sitting up. I was anticipating a headache but there was none.

'My place, of course,' he said. 'You've been asleep for two whole days. I thought you'd never wake. I was about to ring for a doctor.'

'The cavern,' I sighed, remembering parts of my under-world adventure, though full recollection wouldn't come until later.

'What was that?'

'The cavern. The platform. I was . . .' I bent forward and examined the soles of my feet, expecting to find burnt

328

patches, but they were unmarked. 'Where was I found?' I asked, wriggling my toes.

'*Found?*' Bill frowned. 'You've been here, sleeping.'

'Not two days ago. I was out cycling.'

Bill shrugged. 'You were here when I got back that night, dead to the world, tucked up in bed like a baby.'

'That can't be. The cavern. The priests. They took my blood. They told me I was – '

'You've been dreaming,' Bill chuckled.

'No!' I barked. 'It was real. I was – '

'OK, OK,' he said, taking a quick step back. 'You were cycling in a cavern. I believe you. Now, are you gonna get up and dress or do you want to cycle some more?'

'Later,' I muttered, scratching my head and trying to remember all that had occurred. 'I'm hungry. I'll have breakfast first, then – ' I stopped. My best suit was hanging from the back of a chair near the foot of the bed. 'What's that out for?'

'You don't know what day it is?' When he realised I didn't, he took my hands and squeezed tightly. 'It's Thursday.' When that didn't register, he added sorrowfully: 'Ellen's being buried today.'

21

The funeral was a devastating affair. Ellen's mother was a vibrant, forceful woman, in the normal run of things capable of taking anything life threw at her square on the chin. She lost her first child to cot death: came to terms with it. Cancer drove her husband to an early grave: survived that too. But Ellen's death was one blow too many. Hysteria had descended. She wept throughout the service, keening like a professional wailer, pounding her knees with bunched white fists.

(Later, at the wake, I asked Bob – one of Ellen's brothers – why they hadn't given the old lady something to calm her down: he looked me straight in the eye and said they *had*.)

Ellen was buried on Glade Hill, a carefully tended cemetery perched above much of the city like a bird's nest. The cost of burial here was outrageous – nearly everyone went in for cremation: cleaner and more economical – but Ellen had feared fire and often expressed her desire to be buried in her natural state.

None of her family knew about Nic Hornyak. None knew she was dead because I'd drawn her into my sordid little world. I had that much to be grateful for: I couldn't have attended otherwise. But being blameless in their eyes did nothing to ease my conscience. If anything, it made matters worse. There I was, mixing with the innocent, hiding my complicity, accepting their genuine condolences with wan smiles and sad shrugs. I felt lousy. Hypocritical. *Guilty*.

The service drew to a close and the cars began pulling out of the drive. I'd have been happy to stay by the grave – it was a warm day and solitude suited my mood – but I was expected at the house for the wake.

As I hunted amidst the crowd for a lift – Bill had driven me here, but had kept to the back of the crowd and slipped away before anyone else: though he was of Irish descent, he didn't enjoy funerals and couldn't bear wakes – a team of five black Cadillacs wound their way up Glade Hill, entered the cemetery and came to a halt not far from the car I was about to get into. A familiar tall, bony figure stepped out of the middle car, and I had to double-check to make sure I wasn't imagining things.

It was the Cardinal.

He blew into his cupped hands, as though there was a chill in the air, then nodded at me to advance and got back in the car. I told my driver – one of Ellen's cousins – to proceed without me and went to see what was going on.

I stood by the open door of the Cadillac and stared in at the Cardinal, who was rubbing his arms and gazing out the side window, a picture of unease.

'Get in,' he snapped. 'I hate the great outdoors. I can't stand fresh air.' I sat in without a word. 'Take you anywhere?' he offered.

'You know where the wake's being held?'

He nodded, informed the chauffeur, who passed word on to the other cars, and off we set. He said nothing until we were off the hill and shadowed on either side by tall grey buildings, whereupon he regained some of his composure and relaxed.

'The city looks much prettier from the fifteenth floor of Party Central,' he noted, nose crinkling as he took in the dusty streets. 'I'd forgotten how seedy it is. Bit of a dive, all things considered, isn't it?'

'It's home,' I said softly.

'Hmmmm.' He opened the mini-refrigerator and produced two bottles of mineral water. I accepted one wordlessly. 'If you have to travel, this is the only way,' he grunted.

'What are you doing here?' I asked, dispensing with the chit-chat.

'You didn't come to see me. I wanted to check that everything was all right between us.'

'*All right?* I've just buried my ex-wife. How could everything be *all right?*'

'I said "all right between *us*",' he reminded me. 'I'm aware of your grief. I share some of it: though I didn't know the woman, I know how much she meant to you and I feel partly responsible for what happened.'

'So you should,' I snarled. 'You as good as murdered her.'

'No,' the Cardinal sighed. 'I didn't. That's what I came to tell you. I had nothing to do with Ellen Fraser's death. I know you've teamed up with your father behind my back – that was hardly likely to go unnoticed by my network of spies – and I suppose you must have developed suspicions of me, given the degree of secrecy you've sunk to. But I don't know why your ex-wife was killed, or Nicola Hornyak, and I certainly don't know who did it.'

'Wami thinks you allowed us to be set up,' I said. 'He thinks you were spooked by that Incan card you got and played along because you were afraid.'

'As usual, he's not far off the mark.' The Cardinal sipped contemplatively at his drink. 'I've never run from a challenge or retreated out of fear. It's not in me to back down. But I've learnt to box clever, and sometimes it suits my purposes better to lie low rather than attack. This was one such instance.

'When the postcard came, I was furious at the thought of some brazen fucker trying to force my hand. If I'd been twenty years younger, I'd have torn the city apart till I'd found and punished him. But I'm old and wise and my blood doesn't run as recklessly as it once did. I had more pressing matters on my mind. This was a distraction I could do without. Though it galled me to play along, it was the right thing to do. So, yes, I threw you in at the deep end and left you to swim or sink. But I'd no idea it would end like this.'

'Would it have made a difference if you had?' I asked.

'It might. I know the pain that comes of losing a wife, even an ex. I would wish it on no one.'

'That's right,' I murmured. 'You were married once. Drove her crazy, according to the rumours. Walled her up in the Skylight.'

'You're treading on thin ice, Mr Jeery,' he growled.

'Do I look like I'm worried?'

'You should be. I could have you – ' He stopped with a muted curse. 'I didn't come to make threats,' he sighed. 'I came to clear my name, before you did something stupid. I'm not your enemy, Mr Jeery, and you'll only waste your time treating me as one.'

That was debatable but I had sense enough not to provoke him. 'The blind priests say they know who killed her,' I told him instead.

'You've had contact with them?'

'Yes.'

'They spoke to you? In English?'

'Yes.'

The news startled him. 'I did not know they were capable of common speech. Tell me what they said.' I gave him an abbreviated version of my encounter with the *villacs*.

'Of course, they could have been lying,' I concluded. 'About not killing Nic and Ellen themselves.'

'Doubtful,' he replied. 'I don't see why they should drag you all the way down there just to lie to you.' He stroked his chin with his twisted little finger and looked away from me. 'Did they explain why they referred to you as Flesh of Dreams?' Though he phrased the question casually, I could tell it had hidden significance for him.

'No. They babbled on about my blood, and how it was the blood of Dreams. They explained nothing.'

'Three blood-streams,' he mused. 'And three thrones. One occupied, two vacant.'

'Does this mean something to you?'

'No,' he lied, then grinned sheepishly when he realised I could see through him. 'Yes,' he switched answers. 'I can't say for certain what it means, but I have a few theories.'

'Care to share them?'

'You wouldn't believe me if I did. Besides, they have no direct bearing on the issues to hand. You've enough on your plate without taking the mysteries of the Ayuamarcans on board as well.'

'Ayuamarcans?' I faked ignorance.

'I'll tell you about them some day,' he promised, 'if our blind friends don't break the news first.' He sat up straighter and made a dismissive gesture. 'Enough. Let's get back to the investigation. Do you wish to continue or shall I free you of your burden?'

'It's too late to free me,' I responded.

'Nonsense. I can remove you from the case and reinstall the professionals. I withdrew them because – as I said – I didn't want this ruckus interfering with other affairs. Now it seems I can't keep the two apart. I'm through running from my blackmailers. If you say the word, I'll whisk you off the case and out of the city, and you won't have to return until everything's been sorted and cleared.'

'I'm not running,' I told him. 'And I don't want you interfering. Ellen's killers are mine. I've warned the police off: now I'm warning you. I'm going after them, and if anyone gets in my way . . .'

'Sounds ominous,' the Cardinal chuckled, delighted by my anger. 'I was right about you, Mr Jeery: you *were* wasted in the Troops.

'Very well: the case is yours. I grant you unequivocal freedom. My files, my people, my services are at your command.'

'Is there anything in the files of import?'

'Not really,' he shrugged.

'Then I'll do without the rest as well. The only thing I need to get even with Ellen's killer is this.' I opened my jacket to show the Cardinal my .45. I didn't like carrying a weapon to the funeral but I was taking no chances.

'As persuasive a tool as any,' he noted ironically, and said nothing further of note during the remainder of the journey.

The wake was held in a large house belonging to one of Ellen's cousins. Family and friends milled about, talking in low voices, drinking heavily, smoking as though the tobacco industry was about to go out of business.

There was a huge grate for an open fire in the main room. Somebody lit it late in the afternoon, in spite of the weather, and it was there that I retreated when I'd run out of things to say and couldn't take one more comforting pat on the back. I would have left, but that wouldn't have been polite, and for once in my life I wanted to do the decent thing. For Ellen's sake.

I sat by the hearth, watching the flames, cold as I'd ever been, passing as few words with the others as I could. After a slow, lonely half-hour, Deborah – Ellen's elder sister – approached. 'Holding up?' she asked, dabbing round her eyes with a much-used handkerchief. I nodded numbly. 'Mum's taking this badly. We're all worried sick about her.'

'Some people take things like this worse than others. She'll come to terms with it eventually. You just have to make sure you're there for her when she needs you.' The platitudes came naturally. '*You* seem to be bearing up OK,' I noted.

She glanced around to make sure we were alone, then spoke quietly. 'You remember Donny, my son?'

'Sure. He used to be a real terror. Must be thirteen, fourteen by now?'

'Fourteen,' she confirmed.

'Is he here?'

'No. He's in . . . hospital.'

'Oh?' I got the feeling something very bad was coming.

'It's cancer.' A confidential whisper. 'Just like Dad.' I stared at her, unable to speak. I hadn't cried since finding Ellen dead at the Skylight, but I came close to it then.

'Is it serious?' I asked stupidly.

'He's dying.' Eyes glued to the floor. 'They've operated twice but it's not doing any good. He's there again today. We didn't tell him about Ellen. We will if he recovers, but . . .

'He's going to die. Give it a few months and we'll be back here mourning another one.' Her voice was bitter but resigned. 'That's how I'm so calm: I've been preparing for a funeral. He's been very brave. He knows he's dying, but he's trying to make us feel it's no big thing, laughing and cracking jokes. He never laughed so much before.'

'Is, uh, is that why your mum's so . . . ?'

'Mum doesn't know.' Her dread was evident. 'We wanted to keep it from her until we were sure. We've

336

kept it quiet from most of the family. We live outside the city, so we don't see them that much. My husband's side of the family knows. We were going to tell mine soon, after the latest operation, assuming it fails. Now though . . .' She looked over at her weeping mother. 'Excuse me,' she sobbed, voice cracking, and hurried away, frame shaking helplessly.

I sat there, thinking of Ellen, her mother, Donny. Everybody was drifting around like zombies, drinking too much, talking about the past, their jobs, their kids, but very few about Ellen. They didn't want to discuss the dead, not like at other funerals, not with the *grande dame* in hysterics. Ellen's corpse was lying peacefully up on Glade Hill, but might as well have been here, slap in the middle of the room, the way people were acting.

And it was all my fault.

I thought about the coffin being lowered. The words of the priest, trying to comfort the mourners. The sound of the earth as it hit the lid. The vanishing wood. She'd looked so healthy laid out beforehand. The killer hadn't touched her face. She might have been sleeping, except I knew from experience that Ellen slept with her mouth open and was never still: she was forever moving in bed, wriggling her toes, snoring, scrunching up her face. But not any more.

I had to do something. The hunt for the killer would come later, but I couldn't wait that long. Rising slowly, I tracked down Bob and asked if there was a deck of cards somewhere in the house. He looked bemused by the request but fetched one all the same. I located a spare room and asked Bob to guard the door for me.

'What's going on, Al?' he grumbled.

'Trust me,' I said. 'I want to help.'

One of Ellen's aunts was trying to console the weeping mother. I pushed her aside as politely as I could and took the distraught woman by the arm. 'Mrs Fraser? I'm Al Jeery. Remember me?'

'Of course,' she snuffled, not resisting as I led her away.

'I've something to show you. It's something Ellen would have wanted you to see.'

'Ellen?' There was painful hope in her voice, as if she believed I could bring her daughter back from the dead.

'Yes. This way, please. It won't take long.' At the door of the room I told Bob to let no one in and not to interfere until we came out. There was doubt in his eyes but he did as I said, not wishing to create a scene.

I sat Ellen's mother on the bed and turned on the light. Took the cards out of the pack and shuffled. 'I want you to watch the cards, Mrs Fraser,' I said. 'I'm going to show you a trick.'

'A trick?' she echoed uncertainly.

I smiled encouragingly and slapped four cards down, faces up.

'Don't worry. It's a good trick. Now, pick a card, but don't tell me what it is . . .'

Her barrier of grief was hard to pierce but I kept tapping away until cracks appeared and after that things went relatively smoothly. She was eager for consolation and didn't fight as I created a world of colours, followed by the connecting tunnel. There was so much unhappiness inside her, I knew I couldn't relieve her of all her pain, but sometimes a little is enough. Much of her current breakdown was rooted in the way she'd suppressed her feelings when her husband and younger daughter died. By draining her of her old sorrows I made room for the new. I couldn't numb her to the effects of her loss, but by the time I was finished she was in a position to cope with Ellen's demise and (if the worst came to the worst) Donny's.

She wasn't quite so haggard-looking when I led her

from the room, and shortly afterwards she began circulating, thanking people for coming, offering to help make some sandwiches. Bob noted this and must have been bursting with curiosity, but didn't push me for an answer, just slapped me on the back and let his eyes express his thanks.

After that it was back to the fire and thoughts of Ellen. I'd been able to forget her while putting my powers of healing to work on her mother, but now the memories returned with a vengeance and for the longest time I sat there, slumped in the chair, staring at the red-yellow flames, which reminded me of a pantomime backdrop of hell.

The major downside to my curative talent was that no matter how much comfort I was able to bring to others, I was never able to turn my healing power inwards. There was something quietly awful in being able to bring happiness to the lives of others but not myself.

Finally, mercifully, the wake drew to a close and it was safe to depart. I bid Bob and a couple of others farewell, let Ellen's mother hug me to her chest and express sympathy for me, and then I was clear of the mourners, free to shrug off my passive demeanour and get down to the only thing that mattered any more: the business of bloody, final, uncompromising revenge.

22

Bill was sitting out back in his tattered excuse for a rear garden when I returned, sipping from a can of beer, several empties scattered around him. I packed my bag, wandered outside and told him I was leaving, going back to my apartment. He wasn't happy but I said I couldn't stay with him for ever: he'd been great, I couldn't have pulled through without him, but it was time to stand on my own two feet and get on with my life. He told me to take advantage of his hospitality whenever I liked, no matter what the time or circumstances. He didn't wave me off: I think he was afraid I'd see him cry.

Ali spotted me pulling up back home and rushed out to commiserate. I thanked him for his kind words but didn't stay to chat. He told me to call in if there was anything I needed. I said I would, then hurried up the stairs, eager to get inside and make a start.

Somebody had fixed my door while I was away. Probably Bill and his friends. Also, the fridge and freezer were stocked with food, the bed had been made and all the notes that had been strewn around the place were now in boxes, tidied away. I threw my bag down on the floor and started pulling out the notes. I hadn't got through two of the boxes when the door to the bathroom opened and Paucar Wami stepped out.

340

'Al m'boy,' he croaked in his best Uncle Tom voice, 'you've come back to yore dear ole pappy.'

I laid the box down. 'How long have you been in there?' I asked.

'Most of the day,' he answered, flopping into a chair. 'I had a feeling you would return after the funeral. I was expecting you earlier. What delayed you?'

'The wake.'

'You stayed for that? I detest wakes. Everybody speaks so well of the dead. Nobody mentions the infidelities, the scams they pulled, the people they betrayed. Wakes are false. I loathe falseness. One of my greatest worries is that somebody will throw one for me when I pass on.'

'I don't think there's much chance of that,' I replied icily.

'You would be surprised,' he grinned. 'Now: enough beating about the bush. You have had your time of mourning and we have indulged in amiable pleasantries. On to business. Have you learned anything new?'

I thought of the marble and sat down opposite him. 'There's something I have to ask. It may seem improper, but it's in my head and I have to get it out.'

'Oh?' He looked interested.

'Did you kill Ellen?'

He frowned. 'Why do you ask?'

I told him about the marble, black with golden streaks, how I'd discovered it, how it had gone missing and turned up in my locker, how I'd found it on Ellen.

'You think it is a symbol and *I* left it on her?' he asked. 'Signing my name to the murder? Fucking with you from the start?'

'Maybe. I can't think why anyone else would have put it there, or who would have bothered sneaking into my apartment to take it.'

Wami stared at me in cold silence, then slid a dagger out

341

of a trouser pocket. He pressed it into my right hand and placed its blade against his bare, unprotected throat, offering himself to me.

'If you doubt, destroy,' he hissed.

I stared at the blade and the hairless flesh of his throat. I took a deep breath. As agile and powerful as he was, he couldn't stop me if I took it into my mind to kill him. One clean flick of my wrist and he was a dead man.

I started to lower the knife. Wami grabbed my hand and pressed the blade back against his throat. 'Be sure,' he snarled. 'I have never volunteered my life before. I will not do so again. Be sure of me or kill me.'

I withdrew the knife. He didn't stop me this time.

'I had to ask.'

'No,' he disagreed. 'You hadn't. But you did, and it is perhaps just as well. Now we know where we stand.' He took his knife back and pocketed it. 'With the dramatics out of the way, I will ask again: anything new?'

'You first,' I told him. 'What's happened since Ellen was . . . ?' I couldn't say it.

'Nothing much. Nobody knows who killed her. The room at the Skylight was supposed to be empty. The police do not know whether it was a copycat killer or the original.'

'It was the original,' I snapped.

'Of course it was. No luck on the Charlie Grohl front: there are a few out there but none in the city at the time of either murder as far as I can ascertain. I have been following young Master Nicholas, without joy. I tracked down the two leads of Ellen's – I found them while going through your notes – but they knew nothing, either of her or Nicola Hornyak.'

'Did you kill them?' I asked quietly.

'One of them. The other was a crook with political connections: I let him live in case I have use for him in future.'

'You're not entirely merciless,' I remarked snidely.

'I'm all for mercy when there is profit in it.'

'How come you didn't hit on Ziegler?'

'I was saving him for when you returned. We will go after him together, father and son, a team. Now: what news with you?'

For the second time that day I related the story of my underground sojourn. Wami sat through it uncommonly slack-jawed.

'I know of the tunnels and caverns,' he noted at the end. 'I have made use of them. But I never came across anything like that.'

'Can you make sense of what the *villacs* said?'

'No.'

'*Flesh of Dreams* means nothing to you?'

'Should it?'

'It did to the Cardinal.' His eyebrows rose, so I told him about our meeting earlier that afternoon.

'It grows more incredible by the minute,' he sighed happily. 'The Cardinal leaving his fortress to declare his innocence: I never heard the like. It is akin to Hitler nipping out of his bunker at the end of World War Two to apologise to the Allies.'

'The Cardinal knows about these *villacs* and their plans,' I said.

'That does not surprise me: the Cardinal knows something of just about everything.'

'To me their rantings about blood-streams and Dreams were gibberish, but if the Cardinal takes them seriously, so should we.'

'Absolutely,' Wami agreed.

'So find out,' I told him.

'How, precisely, do you suggest I do that?'

'Torture a few blind men. Dig around. Take the Cardinal out back of Party Central and beat the truth out of him. I don't care. That's your concern. My hands will be full with Nick and Ziegler.'

'What is this talk of splitting? Let us pursue Nicholas and Rudi together, then – '

'No,' I cut him short. 'If either was responsible for the murders – or knows who was – he's mine. Same if you find the killer: leave him for me.'

'You have grown greedy, Al m'boy,' Wami murmured. 'You want all the fun for yourself.'

'The hell with fun!' I shouted. 'This isn't a game any more. I *loved* Ellen. Can you understand that, you black-hearted son of a bitch? Do you know what love is?'

'Please,' Wami winced. 'Spare me the pop lyrics.'

'Don't joke about it,' I growled. 'I'm serious.'

'How can you be serious about a little thing like murder?' he protested. 'Your woman was killed: big deal. We all go some time. She is dead: accept it: forget her. It is not like the two of you were still an item. Didn't she dump your sorry black ass?'

'That doesn't matter. I still loved her.'

'*Love*,' he sneered. 'Dogs *love* bones. Monkeys *love* bananas. It is the basest of all human emotions. Love owns those who give themselves over to it; owns and cripples and destroys.'

'You don't know what you're talking about. You've never loved. You can't understand it unless – '

'But I have loved!' he exclaimed. 'I *do* love. I love death.'

'Hardly the same thing as loving a human,' I noted.

'It is better! Death is the only mistress worth our love because it owns us already. Loving one of your own – or money or fame – is a form of voluntary slavery; only by learning to love *death* can one taste freedom. By acknowledging the bonds of death, one is freed to explore the loops that form the chains of life.'

344

'I'm not going to get philosophical with you,' I said. 'Love whatever the hell you want. *I* loved Ellen and I'm gonna find her killer and murder him for her. Alone. If you've got a problem with that . . .' I bunched my fists.

'Al, Al, Al,' he tutted. 'Sons should not pit themselves against their fathers. It runs contrary to the laws of nature.'

'Will you leave the killer to me?'

'If I do not? Would you raise your hand in anger to me?'

'If I have to.'

'And if I raise mine in return?'

I didn't answer. Wami studied me, shook his head and averted his gaze. 'So be it. The killer is yours.'

'Thank you,' I responded coolly.

'You know,' Wami smiled, 'I almost envy you. It's been many years since I took life in anger. Nothing compares with that first drawing of blood, the thrill that accompa – ' He stopped when he saw a shadow pass over my face. 'Did I say something amiss?'

'Just something similar to what the blind priests told me.'

The words of the naked man on the platform surfaced for the first time since I'd regained consciousness: ' . . . you must take blood in anger.' Perhaps it was wrong of me to go this alone. Maybe that was what they wanted, and I was playing into their hands.

'You are having second thoughts,' Wami noted.

'Some,' I admitted.

'You wish to change your mind?'

I considered it thoroughly before replying. 'No. I don't like the idea of flying solo but this is the way it must be.'

'As you wish.' He rose and started for the door. 'If you require assistance, you know how to find me.'

'You'll remember your promise?' I called him back. 'You won't act without contacting me?'

'Unless it is unavoidable.'

'Wait.' I stopped him again as his hand was on the knob. 'You said you only loved death, that nothing else was worth loving.' I looked away. 'Does that mean you don't love me?'

He breathed out through his nostrils. 'You interest me as few other humans do. I have certain fatherly feelings for you.'

'But not love?'

'Perhaps if you were dead,' he chuckled drily and let himself out.

The Red Throat was almost deserted the following morning when I got there, shortly after it had opened for the day. There was no sign of Nick, but I hadn't been expecting him this early. I ordered a mineral water and found a corner where I could sit back and observe.

Nick turned up a couple of hours later. He looked rough, like he hadn't got a lot of sleep the night before, and was dressed plainly in a T-shirt and jeans. He stumbled to the bar, ordered a drink and looked around. Frowned when he saw me, then ambled over.

'My old friend Al,' he commented, running the cool surface of the glass across his forehead as he sat down uninvited. 'More questions?'

'Feel up to them?'

'Not really,' he sighed. 'I went on a bender last night. Still, if you butter me up and ask nicely . . .'

I stood and nodded towards the toilets. 'Want to start the buttering up in there?'

'Don't tell me you've come over queer,' he snorted, suspicion underlacing his humour.

I forced a smile. 'Afraid not. I just want to talk. In private. It won't take long. Will you come?'

He laughed. 'Be careful with your words, Al.' Set off

ahead of me, hips swaying seductively, smirking back over his shoulder. I grinned bleakly in return.

The rest room was brightly lit and empty. 'You know,' he said as I closed the door behind us, 'this isn't the first time I've been in here with a friend, but the management really don't like – '

I was on him before he could say anything else. I jammed his mouth shut, grabbed his left arm and jerked it up behind his back until he screamed soundlessly into my palm. I stopped just short of snapping the bone, rested the arm, then jerked it up again, harder, not releasing until I heard it break. I held him in place, muffling his anguished screams, then swung him around and un-leashed a flurry of punches to the walls of his stomach. As he doubled over, I grabbed the back of his head and slammed him face-first down onto the floor, not hard enough to knock him out, but with force enough to smash a few teeth.

He slumped backwards when I let go, groaning pitifully. I let him get his breath back, then kicked him cruelly, stomach, thighs, the soft parts of the arms. I steered clear of the groin, saving it for later.

When he was whimpering to my satisfaction I took a break. I washed my hands in one of the basins, studying my face in the mirror as I did so, barely recognising the vicious, hate-contorted visage. I'd been a brash, ignorant teenager the last time I beat somebody this badly. I didn't like what I was doing and what I had yet to do, but a quick mental fix on Ellen as she lay in the coffin set me up for round two.

Nick was sobbing, trying to staunch the flow of blood from his mouth with his good hand, building up his breath to scream. I took out my gun and tapped it against the side of the basin. The sobs abated and he breathed out in a fearful sigh. I dried my hands and turned to face him.

'Don't scream,' I said. 'If you scream, I'll have to shoot you.'

'What is this?' he asked through a mouthful of blood and broken teeth. 'Taken up gay-bashing?'

'Gay's got nothing to do with it.'

'Then what?' He spat out a couple of teeth and began crying when he saw them. 'Jesus Christ, Al, what the fuck – '

'I want to know about Ellen.'

He stared, confused. 'Who?'

'Ellen Fraser. My ex-wife.'

'Don't know her.'

'You heard about the copycat killing at the Skylight?'

'Sure. It was on all the – ' He stopped. 'No,' he whispered. 'It wasn't . . . ?'

'I want to know who killed her, Nick.' I pointed the gun at him. 'Tell me.'

His eyes were wide with terror. 'I don't know anything about it.'

'I'll shoot you in the leg first,' I said conversationally. 'Your left, I think. Then the right. People will rush to investigate when I open fire, so I'll have to work quickly. That means moving straight on to your groin. Ever seen someone shot through the groin? Not a pretty sight. Messy as fuck.'

'Al,' he moaned, 'I swear I'd nothing to do with it. On my life, Al, on my goddamn fucking *life*!'

'I don't believe you, Nick,' I said, crouching to give him a closer view of the gun. 'Make me believe. Tell me what you were doing that night in the Skylight. Lie once and I shoot.'

Nick stared at the gun, licked his lips, gathered his wits about him and began. 'It was meant to be a joke. We set it up. We'd done it before.'

'Done what?'

'Swapped partners.' He wiped around his mouth with his hand, eyes glued to the gun. 'Nic arranged the rooms. Both our guys were into bondage. The plan was to get them hot, tie them up, then swap places and . . .' He made a rolling sexual gesture with his fingers.

'You mean you'd screw Nic's guy and she'd get off with yours?' He nodded. 'Seems hers was getting the worse of the bargain.'

He grinned, showing his broken teeth. 'Not really. She'd have been wearing a dildo and my guy likes doing but not being done.'

'Go on.'

'I paid a guard to look the other way when my boy arrived – he doesn't like to be seen in rough company – and we got down to it. I tried stalling him, because I couldn't hear anything in Nic's room, but he was too eager.'

'You didn't see her at the hotel?'

'No. I looked in her room – the door between the rooms was open – about half ten. She wasn't there. I wasn't surprised: she was never the most punctual.

'I kept my guy going, taking it slow. Between eleven and twelve – I can't be more precise – I slipped the mask on him and went to see if Nic had turned up.'

'Why the mask?' I asked.

'We always used masks. We only swapped when we were confident we wouldn't be reported, but you can never say for sure. The masks prevented positive identification.

'I left him tied to the bed, naked and expectant. Left quietly, so he thought I was still in the room. Slipped into 812 and . . .'

I waited for him to continue. He didn't. '*And?*' I hissed.

'I ran,' he answered plainly. 'I saw the state of her back. I saw how still she was. I thought she was dead. So I ran.'

'She was alive between eleven and twelve!' I roared. 'You might have been able to save her!'

'Thanks for reminding me,' he replied bitterly. He was crying, but not from the pain. 'I thought she was *dead*! I should have checked. I should have sought help. But I panicked, fled for the stairs and ran.

'I stopped on the third floor, thinking of the fuss I'd cause if I burst into the lobby half-naked. I ducked into a toilet and cried till I was dry. Then I went back upstairs – the longest fucking climb of my life – and fetched my clothes. That took more guts than I knew I had – the killer could have still been there – but I went back.

'Dressed, I took a lift down and slipped out. Nobody noticed. Went straight home and drank myself dumb. And that was that.' He looked up at me with scared small eyes, awaiting my verdict.

'Who was the man with Nic?' I asked, lowering the barrel of my gun the slightest few degrees.

'I don't know,' he sighed. 'And she didn't know who I'd be with. It was part of the game.'

'Did you see anyone or hear anything?'

'No.'

'Any chance the guy you were with – Charlie Grohl – knows more than you?'

'He was tied up,' Nick said quickly. 'Gagged. Blindfolded.'

'Maybe later, after you left,' I suggested.

'No,' he insisted, but there was something in his denial which interested me: for the first time since he'd started to talk I got the feeling that he wasn't playing straight.

'Nick,' I warned, raising the muzzle of the gun, 'remember what I said I'd do if I caught you lying?'

'I haven't lied!' he yelped, scrabbling backwards.

'Charlie Grohl: did he see something or say something which made you suspicious?'

'No. I swear. He knows no more about it than me.'

'I don't believe you.' I pointed the gun at his groin. 'Three seconds, Nick. Spill the beans or kiss goodbye to your greens.'

'Al, don't do this. You mustn't – '

'One.'

'People will hear. They know your face here. They'll – '

'Two.'

'I swear, I don't know who it was. I haven't – '

'Three.'

'No!' he screamed before I could fire. 'I'll tell you! I'll tell you! There was no Charlie Grohl!'

My eyebrows creased together. 'Come again?'

'It's a name I made up. But I only did it to protect his identity. He said he'd kill me if anyone – '

'It's an alias?' I shouted.

'One of my first lovers was called Charles Grohl. His name sprang into my mind when – '

'Forget that,' I silenced him. 'Who was in the room with you?'

Nick hesitated just the briefest of moments. Then, staring at the floor: 'I was with a cop. His name is Howard Kett.'

I helped Nick clean himself up and rang for an ambulance. He said he wouldn't press charges because he knew how upset I was, but added that he never wanted to see me again, not even if I found out who murdered Nic. I felt ashamed but would do it again if I had to: for Ellen I'd face all the shame in the world. I left Nick cradling his arm and waiting for the medics, then tracked down Howard Kett.

He was on the phone in his office when I walked in, brushing past the startled officers outside, and yanked the cord from the wall, cutting him off mid-sentence.

'What the fuck!' he yelled, stumbling to his feet.

'I know about you and Nick.' I put it to him simply, sitting down.

The rage drained from his face and he fell back into his chair. One of his colleagues came to the door and asked if everything was OK. Kett nodded and asked him to close the door. For a long time after that he sat there, staring at me, then his desk, saying nothing.

Finally: 'We met a couple of years ago. Bill and me busted him one night. I got talking to him. We got along. A few months later we ran into each other and – '

'I'm not interested in ancient history!' I snapped.

'I don't make a habit of it,' he went on, ignoring my outburst. 'Nick was only the third man I've ever – '

'The Skylight, Howie,' I growled.

'My wife has no idea.' He seemed to be in a world of his own. 'A few times she's guessed I'm having an affair, but thinks it's with a woman. You mustn't tell her. My life would be over if she found out.'

'Tell me what happened at the Skylight or I'll get on the phone to her right now,' I threatened, and that brought him out of his daze.

'How much do you know?' he asked.

'I know Nick paid Breton Furst to turn a blind eye so you could slip in unseen. I know he tied you to the bed and masked you. I know Furst freed you later on.'

'I went home after that,' he said. 'I was mad as hell. I rang Nick the next day to chew him out but he couldn't be reached. Spent most of the week trying to contact him.

'A couple of days before I learned about the murder, a photograph turned up on my desk. I don't know how it got there. It was a photo of me and Nick. In the room. Naked. No accompanying note. Just the photo. Christ, it was enough! I stormed over to Nick's, kicked the door down, found him in bed, pissed. Slapped him about – I thought the photo was another of his sick jokes, like chaining me to the bed and vanishing – but he swore blind he knew nothing about it. He told me about his sister, how he'd found her dead.'

'That's when you turned up at the Skylight, looking for her body,' I interjected.

'Was it fuck!' he snorted. 'I kept it to myself. If I started interfering, someone might've found out about me and Nick.

'The next day I got a phone call at home: a man's voice. He didn't give his name but mentioned the photo and asked if my wife would like a blown-up, framed print. I asked what he was after. He told me about Nic – I pretended I didn't know – and how I was to pick up her body after I rang the Cardinal and invented a story about a snitch.'

'What did he tell you to do once you'd recovered the body?'

'Nothing. Keep the news that the corpse was a week old to myself and treat it like any other homicide victim. Which is what I did.

'A few days later, I got another call. This time I was told to go round your place and warn you away from Nick. I didn't want to – it was bound to make you suspicious – but my hands were tied.'

'I wondered what you were up to,' I grunted. 'It made no sense.'

'That's because they were setting us up. I could see that from the start. Broke my fucking melt to play into their hands.'

'And Allegro Jinks: you were told to send Furst to look for him? That story about his mother was a crock of shit?'

Kett nodded. 'It was a printed message that time: I found it in the pocket of my trousers when I was pulling them on one morning. I'd never have approached a Troop for a job like that. You bastards are loyal. I figured Furst had told the Cardinal everything about that night at the Skylight. I thought for a while that he – the Cardinal – was pulling the strings: I couldn't see how anybody could have been wise to me and Nick except through Furst. I still don't.'

It must have been through Nic. Whoever killed her knew about the adjoining rooms. Maybe they also knew Kett's identity in advance, or perhaps they intended to use the poor sap with Nick, no matter who he was.

'Hear anything from them since Furst?' I asked.

Kett shook his head. 'When I got back from holiday and heard about your ex, I thought they'd be in touch, but so far: nothing.'

'If they contact you again, I want to know.'

Kett shrugged. 'I can't make any guarantees.'

'I'll tell your wife about you and Nick if you don't.'

He laughed. 'And they'll tell her about us if I do. Screwed however I turn. Look, Jeery, much as I dislike you, these are scum of a different order. I'll do anything I can to help you knock the shit out of the fuckers if you find them. But don't count on me. I have to blow with the wind, like it or not. If they tell me to squeeze you, I will. I'll have to.'

'You're not much of a man to have in my corner, Howie.'

'Never claimed I was,' he retorted. 'Now, if there's nothing else . . .' He nodded at the door, inviting me to leave.

'One last question. Ellen: any leads?'

His face softened. 'It's not my case.'

'It's your jurisdiction.'

'I cried off: afraid of a conflict of interests. Bill can tell you more about it than me.'

'If you learn anything: will you let me know?'

'If I'm able,' he replied, and I knew that was the most I could expect. Without another word, I took my leave. The last thing I saw as I let myself out was Kett lowering his head into his hands, groaning quietly. Another time and place, I could almost have felt sorry for the bastard.

Rudi Ziegler wasn't surprised to see me. 'Come in,' he said glumly, and took me through to the parlour. He sat at the table and played with his crystal ball in silence, head bowed over it. I gave the room a quick once-over before sitting opposite him, on my guard. I'd made up my mind to start softly – softer than I had on Nick – but if I had to get nasty, I would.

'You know why I'm here?' I asked.

'I heard about Ellen. I'm sorry.'

'Did you know she was my ex when she came to see you?'

'No.' He shook his head resolutely. 'She never mentioned Nicola or you or asked about my other customers. I wouldn't have known the two of you were related if your name hadn't been mentioned in the news.'

'That's *your* story.'

He looked up. 'You think I'm lying?'

'It looks suspicious, wouldn't you agree? Two of your clients go under the knife, exactly the same way, exactly the same place. Coincidence?'

'Maybe,' he muttered.

I placed my gun on the table, barrel aimed discomfortingly at his midriff. 'You're in deep shit, Rudi. Talk.'

He put his face in his hands and breathed deeply through the gap between his palms. His eyes were raw with tears when he looked at me again. 'I never knew it would go this far,' he sobbed.

My fingers slid away from the gun.

'I knew nothing about Ellen, but Nicola . . . It was *her* idea. She involved me. She said it was only meant to be a symbolic sacrifice. There was a ceremony, by the base of the Manco Capac statue, at twilight. It concluded with the symbol of the sun being carved into her back. She was a voluntary victim. There was pain, but she welcomed it, offering it up to the god of the sun. I said rites before, during and after the carving. And that was it. We cleaned up, said our farewells, and I headed home.'

'Nic stayed?'

'At the time I thought she'd left too, but I guess she must have doubled back, or met her killer elsewhere.'

'You didn't kill her?'

'No!' he yelped. 'I worship the sun, life, the positive aspects of the universe. I would never – '

'So who did?' I challenged him.

He bit his lower lip nervously. 'I don't know,' he lied.

'Who arranged this sacrifice of yours?'

'Nicola,' he answered promptly. 'I was in charge of organising the ceremony but she initiated it.'

'She didn't plan on being killed though?'

'Not that I know of.'

'What about the carving? You did the praying. Did you handle the knife as well?'

'Yes,' he said quickly. Too quickly.

'You're lying.'

'No.' Sweating now, flushing around his throat. He was a terrible liar.

'Who was it?' I pressed him. 'You couldn't cut butter. Who did it, Ziegler? Who sliced her?'

'Nobody! We were the only two there, me and – '

His eyes flicked to a spot behind me. It was all the warning I required. Years of training kicked in and I instinctively threw myself to the left, not even pausing to grab for my weapon.

A gun exploded. A bullet screamed through the space I'd evacuated, continued across the table, picking up speed. It hit Ziegler in the chest, propelling him backwards. He went down silently, the arcing mushroom of his breastbone spraying the table and floor. He might not have been dead before hitting the floor, but there couldn't have been much in it.

'Shit!' my would-be assassin cursed. Feet shuffled. A silver pistol barrel glinted in the dim light of the room. I lunged forward as the second shot was fired, feeling it tear through the heel of my shoe, somehow missing my flesh. Then I was on my assailant.

I drove my head into his stomach, my right fist into his face. He grunted, gave a couple of inches, then rooted his feet to the floor and struck at my head with his gun. I took the blow on my shoulder and punched again. This one hurt. He stumbled. Blood was flowing from his nose or mouth. I grabbed his legs and pulled. He fell heavily, the back of his head connecting firmly with the floor.

I scrambled up his body to pound his face. When I got there, I was shocked into brief inactivity. It wasn't a man: it was a large, mean, bull-headed woman. I knew the face, but before I could put a name to it, she went for my eyes with her nails.

I rolled away from her gouging fingers just in time. She scratched my cheeks pretty badly but missed the sensitive globes. With a growl, she was after me, scuttling across the floor in a grotesque arachnid fashion, teeth gnashing at my flesh, hands scrabbling for a hold.

I back-pedalled swiftly, avoiding her lunges, trying to create space for a counter-attack. I made enough room for a kick and struck at her face with both feet. She brought her body up and took the blow on her giant breasts. It slowed her but didn't put her down, and she was on me again moments later, saliva spraying from her lips, teeth seeking my nose.

I hooked my fingers under her gums and pried her away. I tried kneeing her groin but only caught a meaty thigh. She slammed her own knee forward and fared somewhat better, driving much of the wind from my sails.

We thrashed about, grappling at one another, and crashed into the table. Something heavy rolled off and thumped to the floor. My mind registered the noise and put a shape to it. I jerked one hand back and punched the side of her head a few times without any discernible effect. Next, I grabbed an ear and pulled hard. She screamed and drew away, hands loosening round my throat.

I let go of the ear and hit both sides of her neck with the inner edges of my hands. It was one of the first defensive moves you learnt in the Troops. Virtually guaranteed to make an opponent lose interest in a fight every time.

It didn't fail. She screamed breathlessly and sank down heavily, gasping for air. I slid across the floor and grabbed the crystal ball, which was what had toppled moments before. It was cracked but otherwise intact. I came to my knees, raised my hands and slammed the chunky glass globe down over her head with most of my might.

There was no swift recovery from a blow like that, no matter how hard-headed you were. I had plenty of time to truss her up, tend to my injured body and check Ziegler's corpse before she came to.

I spent a few moments studying her as she groaned and returned to life. I had her name now: Valerie Thomas, the maid-with-attitude from the Skylight.

When her eyes opened, she found herself staring down the barrel of my .45. She looked up at my scratched, resolute, forbidding face. And began to laugh.

'Men!' she snorted. 'Always resorting to guns to settle battles.'

'You drew first,' I reminded her.

'That was business,' she disagreed. 'An execution. Once the fight began, I didn't use it, and wouldn't have, no matter what. Only a coward goes for a gun in a fight. A coward, or a man.'

'You killed Ziegler,' I said.

She tried hunching her shoulders dismissively but I had her tied too tight to move. 'So?' she smiled. 'He was a puppet, a silly man who got in over his head. Ziegler was a tepid fool who couldn't tell the difference between fantasy and reality. He dug his own grave.'

'Did you kill Nic too? And Ellen?'

'Your lovely ex-wife,' she cooed.

'You killed her?' My finger tightened on the trigger.

'Eligible Ellen. So sweet. So naive.'

'Did you kill her?' I screamed, jabbing the point of the gun into her mouth, driving it down her throat, giving her a taste of the pain to come if she didn't talk.

She spat the gun out. 'No,' she coughed. 'I didn't kill your precious Ellen. I saw her die though. I watched as her lips widened in a silent scream and her back arched. I saw the terror in her eyes as the blade bit into the soft flesh of her back.'

She laughed again, cruel as an eagle's cry.

'So beautiful,' she sneered. 'So helpless. So terrified. She called out for you. *Al!* she cried. *Al!* After all you'd got her into, she hadn't sense enough to blame you. People like that deserve to die.'

Finally, after so much time, tears came. I cried pitifully, thinking of Ellen in this creature's grasp, crying out for me, dying with my name on her lips. My legs went numb and I collapsed, rolled away from Valerie and wept.

'Poor Al,' she crooned. 'Poor Ellen, poor Nic, poor Rudi. So many victims. So much grief. Have you a hanky? I feel like spilling a few tears myself.'

'Shut up!' I screamed, bringing the gun to bear on her again. 'Who did it?' I hissed through my sobs. 'Who killed them?'

'My lover,' she replied. 'My wily, sensual, murderous lover.'

'The same one Ellen said she was in love with?' I guessed.

'The same. What a fool. It's easy to love one so strong and imaginative, but to miss the heart of that love, the wondrous evil at its core . . . Your wife was blind, Jeery. Blind and dumb and doomed from word go.'

'Tell me his name,' I snarled.

'Love knows no names,' she laughed.

'Tell me the fucking name or I'll kill you!'

'Go ahead. I have no fears. I've witnessed the glorious sexual coupling of the living with death, many times. There is nothing in dying that scares me. Kill me, little man. Send me to my sun god and damn yourself in the process.'

'Sun god,' I repeated. 'Are you in league with the *villacs?*'

'Who are they?' she deadpanned.

'The blind priests.' She smirked knowingly and didn't answer. 'OK. Just tell me who killed Ellen.'

'Still harking on about Ellen?'

'Who killed her?' I roared.

'I told you: my lover.'

'His name, bitch. His name!'

'What's in a name?' she chuckled. Then, seriously: 'No names. Find out yourself. Embrace the sun, accept its god, and you will learn.'

'Don't waste my time with talk of gods,' I warned her. 'Tell me who killed Ellen, or so help me . . .'

'What? You'll torture me? Try, little man. You'll find I'm a hard nut to crack. I'm no weak fool. I *know* pain. Do your worst. I'm up to anything you can throw at me.'

'We'll see about that,' I said grimly, twisted her over onto her stomach and ripped the back of her shirt open.

I'm not sure what I was planning: I'd learnt all sorts of terrible techniques designed to loosen one's tongue during my time with the Troops. I knew the places which hurt most, the everyday instruments I could use to heighten the pain, where to start, where to finish. I'd sworn never to put that knowledge to use, but in that room my resolve crumbled and good intentions went up in waves of bloodstained smoke.

However, upon removal of her shirt, the option disappeared. I discovered a hideous map of pain beneath the cloth. Her flesh was burnt, cut, whipped beyond recognition. Pins were stuck in her, bandages which, when pulled back, revealed deep lacerations and scars. I isolated acid burns, wounds which had salt rubbed into them, fresh sores which were pustular and seeping. She was a walking advert for sick masochism.

I threw the shirt back over her, nauseated. There was nothing I could do to this woman that hadn't already been done.

'You see?' she whispered proudly. 'See the power of the sun? I'm impervious to your slings and arrows. My god fed me pain, so placing me beyond it. He is gracious, generous and wise. If only more knew the beauty of being in service to one as powerful as he, they'd . . .'

I left the woman babbling on about gods and the like. I could listen to no more. I thought about pleading with her or trading her life and freedom for answers, but I knew she'd laugh at such offers. Perhaps I should have interrogated her further and tried to trick the truth out of her but I was in no state to. I was weeping like a baby.

I dialled Bill before leaving. Told him what I'd learned, where to pick up Valerie, what had happened with Ziegler. He told me to stay where I was, but I couldn't. I said I'd be in my flat if he wanted me. He started to say that wasn't good enough and I had to remain at the scene of the crime, but I hung up and walked away, into grief and bitter apathy.

23

Valerie confessed to all three murders: Nic, Ellen and Ziegler. Told the police I'd nothing to do with any of them. Made no mention of an accomplice or lover. I didn't bother contradicting her story. They thought they had their killer; the case was closed; I was a public hero. Why piss on their parade?

An eager reporter uncovered the connections between myself and the two female victims, and for a while I was a marvellous news story: a determined lover who swore to expose the murderer, beat the police to the punch, then did the decent thing and handed her over for trial. I was hounded by journalists and news crews around the city. Bill and Kett kept them off my back: Bill because he cared about me, Kett for fear I'd mention Nick.

Valerie was dead a couple of days after her confession. Hung herself in her cell. Nobody knew how she got the rope. Probably passed on to her by a cop, but the law neither cared nor investigated: they had their signed confession, which was all that mattered. She'd have gone to the chair in any case: this saved the city time and money.

The media went into a feeding frenzy when Valerie killed herself. It was the perfect end to the story and all they needed to cap it was an exclusive interview with yours truly. They pursued me mercilessly till Bill called in some old favours with a few public officials, who pressured the hacks' editors into calling off their hounds.

The next handful of days blurred into one another as I sat in my apartment, staring at the walls, thinking about Nic, Ellen, Valerie. I should have been out chasing the mystery lover, the man who'd lured Nic and Ellen to their deaths and inspired Valerie to lie herself to ruin. But I was too tired. Each time I got up to act, a great depression settled on me and I fell back into my chair, sometimes to curse Valerie and her lover, more often just to weep.

Wami and the Cardinal rang to congratulate me during the course of those dimly realised days. I accepted their praise with barely a murmur, telling neither the truth. I should have informed at least one of them, but again, it seemed like too much trouble: they'd have dragged me out of myself and nagged me back onto the case. I didn't want that. I just wanted to sit in my room and stew in misery.

I let myself go. Ceased washing and shaving. Wore the same clothes day after day after day. Ate rarely and in tiny doses. Lost myself in memories of Ellen. The world around me made no sense any longer. All that seemed real was Ellen.

Bill and Ali tried to guide me out of my slump. They brought fresh food and cleared away the trash. Some mornings I awoke to find one of them had slipped my clothes off while I slept and laundered them. They held one-sided conversations with me, chattering on and on, pretending all was well with the world. I tried responding – I appreciated the effort they were making – but hadn't the strength. I was like a lobotomised halfwit who could only stare, slack-jawed, and nod my head occasionally.

I stayed away from the drink. Even during my lowest moments, I resisted the temptation. I was a pathetic wreck, but part of me knew I could recover. I could haul myself out of this wretched palsy if time and chance conspired in my favour. But if I gave myself over to alcohol there'd be no coming back. If inebriation set in, this mess of a life would be for keeps.

In the midst of my sorrowful broodings, Priscilla Perdue breezed back into my life. She turned up at my door one day, demurely dressed and smiling uncertainly. 'I tried ringing,' she said by way of a hello, 'but you didn't answer. I had to come. I couldn't stay away. I'll leave again if you want me to.'

I said nothing, only ushered her in.

Her nose crinkled when she saw the state of the apartment. Neither Ali nor Bill had been up for a day or two and I'd let things slide. Dirty dinner trays, unwashed clothes, half-eaten meals left to coagulate.

'Is this the cleaner's year off?' she quipped.

'If you don't like it, leave,' I snarled.

That hurt her and she started for the door.

'Wait,' I called her back. 'I'm sorry. Take no notice of me: I'm a zombie. I don't know what I'm saying or thinking half the time. Don't go. Please. Sit.'

She looked around. 'I'd rather stand, if it's all the same.'

I managed a thin smile. 'So,' I said. 'Here you are.'

'Here I am,' she agreed.

There was a long silence.

'Anything in particular you wanted to talk about?' I asked.

'Oh, Al.' She broke down without warning and threw herself into my arms. Her weight knocked me off balance and we toppled backwards onto one of the socks-and-underwear-strewn chairs. 'What that woman did to your wife was awful. I don't know how you didn't rip her throat open. If it was me, I'd have . . . have . . .' She started to cry.

'It's OK,' I said, stroking her hair mechanically, thinking

about Ellen's. 'It's over. She's dead. There's no need for tears.'

She wept a while longer, then looked up at me hopefully. 'It *is* over, isn't it, Al? She *did* kill them?'

'She confessed, didn't she?'

'I know, but . . .' She gulped and sat up straighter on my lap. 'I can't stop thinking about that night I went to the Skylight to meet Nic. It was definitely a man she said she was bringing, even though she didn't tell me his name. I've been reading the papers daily, but there's been no mention of him. According to them, Valerie acted by herself. The reporters say she was mad.'

'They got that much right.'

'And the rest?'

I knew why she was asking: if Valerie had been a lone crazy, and the guy Nic brought to the hotel wasn't involved, it absolved Priscilla. She needn't feel guilty if it had been a random, unavoidable attack rather than a client of Nic's who mightn't have killed her if Priscilla had been there.

I wanted to lie, as I'd lied to the others, so she could sleep easier at night, free of the demonic imps of guilt which plagued my every waking or sleeping moment. But as I stared into her eyes I lost my ability to lie and found myself telling her the worst of all things: the truth. She listened silently, clutching my hands. At the end she said nothing for a long while, then:

'She could have been lying.'

'She wasn't.'

'She was an evil, crazy she-devil. She knew the game was up. This might have been one last sly twist of the knife, to leave you hovering with doubt.'

'No,' I sighed. 'It wasn't a trick. I was face to face with her. I know.'

'But – '

366

'I *know*!' I cut her short.

'Then the killer's still out there,' she whispered, shivering. 'It isn't over.'

'No.'

'I'm scared, Al.'

'I know.'

'I mean *really* scared. Ellen was your wife and Nic was your lover. What if this guy's working his way through every woman you've ever been close to?'

'There're a few old girlfriends whose numbers I wouldn't mind giving him,' I laughed, but she refused to see the funny side.

'I could be next,' she said.

'Why should you be? There's been nothing between us.'

'Not yet.' She leant forward and cautiously kissed me. I pushed her away, harsher than necessary.

'What are you doing?' I snapped. 'You've just got through telling me I'm a walking jinx and now you – '

'That's why I'm so scared,' she interrupted, silencing me with a second kiss. 'If we'd had something in the past, I could run. But what we've got is now and in the future. I can't run from that.' She kissed me again.

'This shouldn't be happening,' I groaned, returning her kisses with interest. I felt one of her hands slide down into my lap. My own fingers were busy, five with her hair, the others with her left breast. 'It's madness.'

'I don't care,' she gasped as I freed the breast and chased it with my lips. 'I need you. I've been so lonely since Nic died, filled with guilt, terrified every time a door swings open unexpectedly. When I read about your wife, do you know what my first reaction was?' I shook my head and fixed on her nipple. 'Thank God it wasn't me.'

She shifted her weight and dragged me to the floor. Undressing and caressing each other, we rolled over, so I was underneath and she was on top.

'You could be signing your death warrant,' I said, mouth dry as sandpaper while she peeled off her underwear.

'At least I won't die alone,' she replied, lowering herself onto me, guiding me in with one hand, passionately digging into the flesh of my neck with the fingernails of the other.

There was no more talking for a long time after that.

She moved into my cramped apartment the next day, uninvited. I wasn't sure I wanted this – there was something inherently unhealthy about a love affair forged courtesy of a brace of murders – but found myself powerless to resist: as much as Priscilla needed me, I needed her ten times more. I'd been going swiftly mad on my own. Without a human companion to cling to, I was most certainly doomed.

Ali found us together that afternoon. He walked in unannounced, as he usually did, and stopped dead when he spotted the beautiful naked woman by my side. He exited rapidly, ears burning, apologising profusely. Just before he left, his head poked round the door for one last sneak look at Priscilla. That produced my first genuine smile in a long, long time, and I squeezed her tightly and cuddled up close, burying my face in her hair, trying not to compare it with Ellen's.

She didn't bring much with her when she moved in – a small bag of clothes, socks, underwear, shoes, cosmetics – but enough to make it clear this was more than a one-night stand. She also brought bottles of spirits and liqueurs. I didn't like having them in the apartment, or the way she left the tops open so they filled the rooms with their sickly-sweet scent, but I didn't say anything: she needed the drink, and I could empathise with that. It wasn't my place to deny her.

368

She slipped out to work every morning while I was asleep and would return as early as she could. We'd make love or talk or simply hold one another. Cook a late dinner, eat slowly, make love again. Most nights we didn't get to bed before two or three.

Bill was delighted to see the two of us together. I hadn't come out of my stupor yet but I could tell he thought Priscilla was having a positive influence on me. He cooked dinner for us on a couple of occasions and we sat around talking about happier times, none of us making mention of Ellen or Nic.

One night, when talk did turn to the murdered women, Priscilla blurted out the truth about Valerie Thomas. I tried silencing her but she burst into tears, sobbed something about not being able to keep it to herself any longer, finished her tale in a rush and fled to the bathroom. A stunned Bill prevented me from going after her and demanded answers. Was it true?

'Yes,' I said, avoiding his eyes.

'Why didn't you tell me?' He sounded more pained than outraged.

'Didn't seem worth it. It would have been my word against her official confession.'

'You know only too damn well which version *I* would have believed,' he growled.

'I know. And I should have told you, even if I kept it quiet from the others. But . . .' I wasn't sure I could explain. 'I want out of this, Bill. I'm sick of it: suspects and clues and twists and death. I want to drop it, the whole sorry sack of shit, and pretend it never happened.'

'Do you think you'll be allowed?' he asked softly. 'Do you think the bastard who killed Nic and Ellen will stop? Whatever his motives, he'll come after you again, you or Priscilla or somebody else you're close to. I wish to God you'd never got involved in this bloody mess, but you're in now. The time to quit elapsed long ago. Drawing in on yourself like this serves no purpose. It only leaves you – and those close to you – open to attack.'

'I don't care.' I locked gazes with him and said it again for added effect. 'I don't care. That's why I didn't tell you about Valerie, why I'm holed up here, letting the case drop. I don't have the energy to worry any more. I can't fight any longer.' Tears were rolling down my cheeks like tap water. 'When they took Ellen, I went ballistic. For a while, I was capable of anything. But then I confronted Valerie and saw the hate in her and . . . something snapped. Until then I was ready to fight to the very end. Now it seems useless. Remember what you told me after my last bout in the ring? "You've got to know when to walk away from it, Al." That's what I'm doing now: walking away.'

'But it's too early,' he insisted. 'This isn't the right time to throw in the towel.'

'I don't care,' I reiterated. 'If they want to kick me while I'm down, let them. I'll let them kick me and beat me, and if they want to kill me, I'll let them do that too.'

'This isn't you, Al,' he said, sadly shaking his head. 'This isn't you speaking. This is someone else.'

'It's me, Bill,' I assured him. 'What's left of me,' I added.

When he departed, it was with a vow to reopen the investigation. He swore he wouldn't rest until the real culprit was brought to justice. He'd even bend the law if he had to. Snap it in two if that was required. It was the first time I'd heard him speak like that. I didn't like it but didn't try talking him out of it either: if he wanted to waste his time chasing ghosts, let him. I was through trying to sort out other people's problems for them.

Priscilla apologised for spilling the beans when she re-emerged. I told her not to worry, took her in my arms and made love to her, and for the first time I realised how dry

370

and mechanical our lovemaking was, and how frightened need far outweighed genuine passion.

I started going out for walks during the day, while Priscilla was at work, not for exercise or relaxation, merely to pass the time. Long, punishing walks, during which I strove to push all thoughts from my mind, concentrating on the muscles in my legs, my lungs, the paths.

Bill rang a couple of times in the afternoons or at night to say he was following leads. I lent him my notes and files when he asked, even material which was strictly confidential, for Troop eyes only. I neither encouraged his investigations nor tried to dissuade him from them. It was his life and he could do what he liked with it.

Frank rang a few times as well, ostensibly to gossip, although we both knew he was in actuality sounding me out (either to satisfy his own curiosity or because the Cardinal had put him up to it). I spoke politely, said I was considering a return to work, but wanted more time to think about it. Never mentioned Valerie or Ellen or any of that, though he tried slipping it into the conversation.

I studied a calendar one Sunday morning and realised it had been almost two months since Nic met with her end at the Skylight, three and a half weeks since Ellen went the same way, and only . . . I had to count three times before I'd believe it . . . ten days since Priscilla moved in. Ten days! It felt like months. I wondered if time was moving as slowly for her as it was for me.

One afternoon, returning from a walk, I discovered Priscilla sitting at the living-room table, looking troubled. She was tapping a small parcel on top of the table, and I immediately sensed danger. I almost turned tail and ran. But I'd nowhere to run.

'Buy something?' I asked, closing the door and facing up

to whatever it was the fates had decided to throw at me now.

'No,' she answered. Then: 'I mean, yes. I had a half-day and I was shopping, which is why I'm home early. But this isn't it. My bags are in the bedroom. I got a . . .' She stopped and pushed the parcel away. 'Nice walk?'

'Lovely,' I replied, sitting down beside her, giving her a quick squeeze, eyes fixed on the box, which was wrapped in plain brown paper, something scrawled across the top.

'I ran into a blind beggar on my way back,' she said, and the ice in my stomach spread. 'He gave me *that*.' She pointed at the box. 'He scurried away after pressing it into my hands. I thought it was a religious book or a bunch of good-luck flowers. I started to tear it open.' There was, indeed, a slight tear in one of the corners. 'Then I saw the name and decided I'd better leave it for you.'

I too could now see the name. Block letters. AL JEERY. No address or note of any other kind. Just my name.

'Do you think it's a bomb?' Priscilla asked.

I smiled. 'I doubt it.'

'But it could be?'

'It could.'

She stiffened. 'Maybe we should call the bomb squad or take it to someone who knows about these things.'

'*I* know about "these things". I learnt everything there is to know about explosives in the Troops.' A barefaced lie – I'd avoided those courses: I never could stand bombs – but it calmed Priscilla down. I picked up the box – praying it *wasn't* wired – and shook it gently, listening intently, as though I could tell from the noise whether it was safe or not.

'It's no bomb,' I told Priscilla, faking confidence.

'Thank God,' she sighed, relaxing. She glanced up at me and licked her lips quickly, nervously. 'Are you going to open it?'

I nodded. 'But you'd better go to the bedroom and lock the door before I do.'

'But you said – '

'I know. But it's as easy to be safe as it is to be sorry.'

She half-rose, hesitated, then sat back down in spite of her fear.

'No,' she said firmly. 'If you stay, I stay too.'

I smiled wistfully, steeled my nerves, then started to unwrap the paper. It peeled away like candy wrapper, revealing an unremarkable white cardboard box. I handed the paper to Priscilla, who crumpled it up and held it in front of her lower face, as if it would protect her from the blast if there was one.

I ran my fingers around the join between the lid and box: no trace of a wire. I thumbed up the section of the lid closest to me, paused, lifted the other end a few centimetres, shifted the entire lid clear of the box and laid it down on the table. Inside was a cloud of pink tissue.

'What is it?' Priscilla asked.

'Tissue,' I told her, rubbing part of it between the thumb and index finger of my right hand.

'Nothing more?' she asked, bewildered.

I studied the rosy stains on the flesh of my thumb and finger, put them to my mouth and tasted blood. 'There's more,' I said quietly.

Parting the folds with patient slowness, I burrowed down through the layers of tissue, noting the way the pink hue darkened the deeper I went. Near the bottom, on a tiny silver tray, I found the source of the blood.

It was a severed human finger.

Priscilla moaned when she saw it, but I was less disturbed: when you've woken up to a severed head in the middle of the night, a lone finger isn't that big a deal.

'Don't touch it,' she pleaded as I leant forward. I ignored her and picked it up by the unharmed tip. It was a white male's, touched by the many wrinkles and blotches of old age. Quite thick, so he must have large hands. Sliced clean through at the base, just above where the first knuckle would have been. Still warm and bleeding, so it was probably amputated some time this morning, maybe early afternoon.

There was a note on the tray, almost unreadable because of all the blood that had soaked into the paper. I had to hold it up and squint to decipher the words, and it fell apart as I was laying it back into the box.

'What did it say?' Priscilla wanted to know.

'It said, "Guess whose, Al m'boy",' I told her, turning the finger around on my palm, closing my own fingers over it and squeezing softly. The sly mother-fuckers. I thought I was out, that nothing could make me care. As Bill had predicted, I was wrong. My tormentors knew exactly which strings to pull to yank me back in.

'Why did it say "Al m'boy"?' Priscilla asked.

I shook my head and lied. 'I don't know.'

'Who do you think it belongs to?' Priscilla asked. When I didn't answer, she pinched me sharply and hissed, '*Who?*'

I looked up, then relaxed my grip and revealed the finger. My hand was stained with blood. In all the red, it could have been anybody's. But I knew whose it was and – once I'd propped the finger up on the table, so it was standing vertically to attention – I informed her in a voice as dead as my hopes:

'It's Bill's.'

part six

'we could all be dead by then'

24

'Guess whose, Al m'boy.'

The killer's depth of knowledge puzzled and worried me. How did he know of my father's ironic term of endearment? Nobody had heard Wami call me that. For the briefest of moments I thought Wami had sent me the finger, that he'd been toying with me all along. Then I recalled the blade at his throat and dismissed such thoughts. Offering himself to me could have been a deadly bluff, but I didn't think so. Wami was many things but he wasn't my enemy, even though my true foe wanted me to think he was.

The killer's identity would come later. Right now there was the finger to ID. I *knew* it was Bill's, but the Troop in me needed convincing. If Allegro Jinks could be passed off as Wami, a detached digit could easily be substituted for one of Bill's. There was no answer when I rang him at home, and nobody at the station had seen him for a couple of days, but that hardly constituted proof.

I could have gone to Party Central with the finger, but I didn't want to involve the Cardinal and his crew. Instead I rang the Fridge and asked for Dr Sines's home address. I wasn't sure if I still had security clearance. By the end of the call, I knew I had.

He was watching TV with his wife and kids when I

arrived. His wife answered the door and sighed resignedly when I asked to see her husband. 'Is this to do with work?' she asked.

'Yes, ma'am,' I replied.

'You guys never give him a break,' she muttered, calling him to the door. He looked even less happy to see me than his wife had been.

'This better be important,' he growled, not inviting me in. 'I put in a full day yesterday. Didn't get home till after midnight.'

'It's personal, Dr Sines,' I said, remembering to address him professionally. 'May I come in?'

'Can't it wait?'

'No, sir.'

He grumbled some curses to himself, then beckoned me in but didn't lead me beyond the front hall. He left the door open a crack as well. 'Make it quick,' he snapped, and I immediately produced the finger, still on its silver tray, though now transferred from the box to a small plastic bag. He studied it in silence, then commented drily, 'If it's my professional opinion you're after: I think it's a finger.'

I chuckled obligingly. When I was through flattering him I said, 'I was hoping you could tell me *whose.*'

'Offhand, I couldn't.' He cracked up with laughter.

'*Offhand,*' I grinned, finding it harder to shape the muscles of my mouth into a smile this time. 'Good one.'

'I'm sorry.' He wiped a few tears of mirth from his eyes. 'Gallows humour. You need it to get by in a job like mine.' He giggled some more, then got serious. 'Any idea who the owner might be?'

'I'd rather not say.'

'It would be quicker if you did.'

'I'd still rather not say.'

'As you wish. Care to tell me why you brought it here, tonight, instead of down to the Fridge tomorrow?'

'I don't want anyone connecting it to me.'

'I smell espionage. May I have the finger?' I handed it over. 'You realise I must make mention of where it came from? I can't waltz in with this and pretend I just found it.'

'Why not?'

'It doesn't work that way. You have gold clearance – congratulations on the promotion – but a report must be filed, even if for the Cardinal's eyes only. It would mean my job if I took your side against the system's and was subsequently discovered.'

I nodded understandingly, then asked if he'd heard about my wife. He said the rumours had reached those at the Fridge and offered his condolences.

'I'd appreciate your assistance more.'

'You don't understand,' he retorted waspishly. 'There are rules and procedures. I can't – '

'You can,' I interrupted. 'You lot are a law unto yourselves at the Fridge, so don't try telling me otherwise. You take bodies as you please and do with them as you wish and everybody turns a blind eye.'

'That's different. Our superiors accept that they have to grant us a certain amount of leeway to get the best out of us. But that leeway doesn't run to bucking the chain of command, to falsifying reports or sneaking bodies – even parts of bodies – in.'

'You could do it if you wanted,' I pressed.

'Probably, but that's not the – '

'You won't get into trouble,' I said quickly. 'All I want you to do is identify who the finger comes from.'

He shook his head. 'I can't. I won't. No offence, but you're not worth risking my career for. I don't know you that well and I certainly don't owe you. Why should I put my neck on the line for you?'

It was a fair question, for which I had no ready answer.

'If *your* wife had been killed – ' I began.

' – I'd be mad as hell, just like you. But my wife's alive and well and in no kind of danger whatsoever. I'd like to keep her that way.'

I thought about threatening him but he'd have gone to the Cardinal if I did. If his aid wasn't voluntary, it was worthless.

'Sorry for disturbing you,' I said, and started for the door.

'That's it?' he asked, startled. 'You're not going to try twisting my arm?'

'No.'

'Wait.' He held out the bagged finger. 'You forgot this.' I reached for the bag but he didn't release it. Instead he turned it upside down and examined the base. 'A clean cut,' he mused. 'Either an extremely sharp blade or an electric implement.'

'Oh?' I'd figured as much myself, but said nothing.

'The smallest finger of the left hand.'

I grunted.

'This ties in with your wife's death?' he asked. I nodded. 'How?'

'I'd rather not say.'

'Fair enough.' He hesitated. I could see fear in his eyes but also professional pride. The human side of him wanted nothing to do with this; his medical half was fascinated. It became a question of which would win out: self-preservation or curiosity.

'Can you tell me anything about where you think it comes from?' he asked. My spirits lifted.

'I think it comes from a cop.'

'Really? That should be simple enough to check. Assuming one was inclined to check . . .' He tossed it about in silence, then said: 'A man in his mid-forties was dropped off with us late last night, unidentified. I could take a print of his little finger, swap it for this one and run the tests. I don't make a habit of turning up for work on my day off but it's not unheard-of.

'OK,' he said, nervous but excited. 'Here's what I'll do. We've got the prints of every police recruit on file. I'll run the print of your finger against them. If I make a match, fine; if I don't, I go no further. Is that acceptable?'

'Great,' I smiled.

'And I'll volunteer no information, but if somebody challenges me, or if a superior asks, I'll 'fess up.'

I frowned: that wasn't so great.

'It's my best offer,' Sines warned before I could object. 'The way I see it, nobody will enquire unless they're already suspicious, so if I have to tell the truth, it'll probably be to someone who's on to you anyway.'

'That's reasonable,' I agreed.

'I'll go now, then,' Sines said, pocketing the finger. 'You know the abandoned car plant three blocks west of the Fridge?' I nodded. 'Wait for me in the showroom there. You can get in by the side door. I shouldn't be more than a couple of hours, unless I get detained. If I'm not there by – ' he checked his watch ' – eleven, go home and I'll be in contact in the morning.'

'I can't tell you how much – ' I started to thank him, but he cut in before I could finish.

'Stow it. I must need my head examining, getting mixed up in something like this. Anything you say now can only convince me I'm being an ass and snap me round to my senses.'

Taking him at his word, I let myself out without a murmur.

I faced a long wait at the car plant. It was nearly ten past eleven when he turned up. I was getting ready to leave.

'Caught you,' he gasped, covering his mouth with a handkerchief to keep out the dust. There was no light inside the room, but it was lit by street lamps from without. Sines pulled a camp bed out from under a shroud of papers and sat down.

'A lot of the guys at work use this place for making out,' he explained when I looked at him curiously. 'I was here a couple of times myself, back in my courting days.'

'You're late,' I noted. 'Any trouble?'

'Not really. Just didn't want to appear anxious to leave.'

'Did you make a match?'

He nodded and came right out with it. 'Bill Casey.' I lowered my head and sighed wearily. 'It's what you expected?'

'Yes.'

'You don't look happy.'

'I hoped I was wrong.'

'Sorry.' He handed the finger back. It was stained with ink.

'You didn't get rid of it?' I asked.

'That wasn't part of our bargain.'

I studied Bill's finger. 'Is it any good now? Could it be sewn back on?'

'No.'

'You're sure?'

He didn't bother to repeat himself. 'I think I got away with it. Nobody asked any questions and it seemed to go without a hitch. But, I warn you, if the Cardinal or one of his men rings tomorrow and starts quizzing me . . .'

'Fine.' I started for the door.

'If it's any consolation,' he called after me, 'he was alive when the finger was amputated.'

I halted in the doorway but didn't look back. 'No,' I said softly. 'That doesn't console me in the slightest.' Not pausing to thank him, I left and went home to tell Priscilla.

We passed most of the night awake in bed. Priscilla

thought Bill was dead and sobbed for him at regular intervals. I, on the other hand, was sure he hadn't been killed: my tormentors hadn't hesitated to mock me with the bodies of my dearly beloved before: why start now? It suited them to keep Bill alive, otherwise they'd have sent more than just his finger.

Perhaps they thought Bill's death would drive me deeper into depression, whereas the possibility of being able to rescue him might draw me back into the game. If that *was* their plan, they knew me at least as well as I knew myself.

At one stage Priscilla pleaded with me to turn the finger over to the police and either place myself in their hands or flee the city with her. She was afraid that if I didn't wind up dead as a result of my investigation, the killers would come after *her*. She clung to me and wept and said I couldn't leave her on her own.

'Do you know how to use a gun?' I asked, as she teetered on the edge of hysteria. She sobered up and quickly nodded. I passed her my .45. 'It's loaded. Stay here when I'm away. Don't go out. If anybody comes to the door, start firing.'

'I've only shot targets before,' she said, handling the gun nervously but capably. 'I don't know if I could shoot a person.'

'Hopefully,' I answered grimly, 'you won't have to.'

In the early hours of the morning, she asked how I was going to set about finding Bill.

'By going after Ellen's killer, like I should have when I was finished with Valerie. When I find that bastard, I'll find Bill.'

'You sound confident,' she remarked.

'That's because whoever it is *wants* me to find him. I guessed as much before: now I'm sure. Bill would have been killed if the plan was just to hurt me. I'm being lured into a trap.'

'Then you can't go after him! You mustn't!' And it was back to calling in the police or getting out of the city, preferably both. I explained why I couldn't: it would mean Bill's death. At least this way he stood a chance. Not much of a one, I had to admit, but it was better than none at all.

When it came time to leave, she begged me to stay. I told her gently but firmly that I couldn't, reminded her not to let anyone in and not to venture out, then left, weaponless – that didn't bother me: I could pick up another gun any time I liked – and low of heart, but no longer immobile or directionless. I won't say it felt *good* to be back on the case, but it beat hanging around my apartment, letting my life go to pieces.

The lover was the link. One person connected Nic, Ziegler, Valerie and Ellen. When I found him, I'd have my killer. That was my goal: to make the connection. I could forget about Jinks, Breton Furst and the rest. All I needed was the lover.

I'd failed in my earlier attempt to get to him through Nic, so it was just as well to let her lie in peace. And I didn't think anything would come of pursuing Valerie or Ziegler's backgrounds: since they'd been in league with the bastard, they'd have covered their tracks, sly snakes that they were.

Ellen was the key. She was the only innocent among the four. She'd been coy when it came to revealing her lover's name, but the chances were that at least one person out there knew who she'd been seeing, or had some idea: a friend she'd spoken to, a colleague who'd overheard her talking on the phone, a shopkeeper who'd seen her with her beau in tow. That person might take some finding, but I had time on my hands and hate in my heart: I'd unearth them.

I began with her family. Rang Bob, Deborah and a few

others. Discussed the funeral and wake, gradually working the conversation round to talk of Ellen's last few weeks. I mentioned to each that I thought she'd been seeing someone, and a couple – Bob included – said that she'd alluded to a new lover, but none knew anything about him. Ellen had been as tight-lipped with her family as she'd been with me. No name, no description, nothing.

I asked Deborah about Donny and her mother. Donny wasn't so good – doctors gave him a month, six weeks top – but the news of her mother was more encouraging: they'd told her about her grandson and she'd been coping with the tragedy far better than they'd dared hope. She was hardly upbeat, but it hadn't destroyed her as they feared it might.

Before moving on to her friends, I rang Party Central and asked if I could meet with the Cardinal. I was thinking that it would be good to utilise his army of informants. Maybe one of them had seen Bill or knew something of his whereabouts; if they didn't, they could be told to keep their eyes and ears open for him. But the Cardinal couldn't be reached. His secretary promised to arrange a meeting as soon as was humanly possible, but it wouldn't be today. Possibly tomorrow. I had no choice but to settle for that.

I rang as many of Ellen's friends as I could think of. Most were no friends of mine (many thought Ellen married beneath herself when she hitched up with me, sentiments which had irked me at the time but which I now found hard to disagree with) and normally wouldn't have passed the time of day with me. But, given the grisly circumstances, they made a once-off exception, put aside their dislikes and spared a few minutes of their time.

As with her family, a few were aware that she'd been seeing someone, but nobody had met him or knew a thing about him. The phone conversations weren't an entire wash-out – her older friends passed on the names of newer acquaintances that I didn't know, and I got the low-down on her romantic associations since the two of us split (it was possible that her new lover had been an old flame) – but no leads of any apparent substance resulted from them.

The last of her friends to see her alive was a woman called Ama Situwa. I'd never met her: she was somebody Ellen had befriended recently and I got her name through one of the others. She sounded nice on the phone. Turned out she was the daughter of the guy who ran Cafran's restaurant, where I'd sweet-talked Ellen onto the path of doom.

Small world.

She'd run into Ellen in the lounge of the Skylight the night before she was murdered. She was there for a birthday party, saw Ellen at the bar with another woman and went over to say hello. Ellen had greeted her warmly and said that they were waiting for dates. Ama had laughed, made a joke about men always being late, and invited them to Cafran's later if they were at a loose end: the birthday gang were moving back there after the Skylight. Ellen said they'd consider dropping by if the men failed to show, and that had been that.

'Any idea who the other lady was?' I asked.

'No. I didn't know many of Ellen's friends.'

I'd have to try and find her companion: she might know the name of the guy Ellen was supposed to meet. 'Can I come round some time and discuss this with you in more detail?' I asked.

'Sure,' she said. 'I'd be happy to help. I think it was terrible, what happened. Ellen was a lovely person.'

'Yes,' I said hollowly. 'She was.'

I dropped by the Skylight and went through the staff one by one, asking if they'd noticed Ellen in the bar that night. Negative answers all round. I paid special attention to the

Troops – since the room hadn't been signed out, it was reasonable to assume that Ellen had been sneaked in, perhaps past a bribed guard – but they swore blind that they knew nothing. Several told me that they'd been more alert since the Nicola Hornyak fuck-up: Frank was coming down hard on shirkers, and a handful of the weaker soldiers had been replaced.

While I was there, I asked after Valerie Thomas, on the off chance that I might stumble across a lead. Nobody knew much about her. She'd been a curt and tetchy lady. Worked at the Skylight a long time, longer than most, but had never once gone out with the girls or attended a staff social event.

'She was creepy,' one workmate opined. 'Like Bette Davis in that movie, the one where she feeds her sister a rat?'

'She worked hard,' an assistant manager assured me. 'She was one of our best workers. I was sorry to see her go. If it had been a minor offence we'd have tried to help her out. She worked hard. Never took anything, not even a sugar cube. Honest, loyal, trustworthy. An ideal employee if you exclude the two dead customers . . .'

'None of us went to her funeral,' a maid said. 'We were told not to, once word of her killings got out, but I doubt if any of us would have gone anyway: she wasn't friendly, never made nice comments or cracked a joke or laughed at someone else's. We sent some flowers and a card, but most of us didn't sign it. I did, but I used real scrawly writing, so it couldn't be read.'

'Boyfriends? None that I knew of.'

'Men in her life? She never mentioned any.'

'Valerie never seemed keen on men. She was forever criticising one guy or another. She hadn't much time for them. Wouldn't surprise me if she'd been a lezbo.'

'*Valerie?* With a *man?* Christ, I don't think so!'

387

It was getting late when I finished at the Skylight. I decided to give Ellen's circle of friends a rest. I still had plenty of names to work through, and more would probably crop up in the course of my enquiries, but they could wait till morning. I rang Priscilla to see if she was all right – as I had several times throughout the day – and told her I'd be a while yet, to go to bed and get some sleep if she could. She agreed, but only if I'd promise to wake her when I got home. It was a promise I was glad to make.

Next I rang Paucar Wami.

My father was surprised to hear from me but agreed to meet, even though I wouldn't tell him over the phone what it was about. He was going to come to my place but I quickly put paid to that suggestion: I didn't want him anywhere near Priscilla. I asked if he could meet me at the site of the Manco Capac statue. That suited him fine, we fixed the hour, I nipped into a burger bar for a bite to eat, then it was rendezvous time.

The site was deserted, apart from a couple of perimeter guards who were childishly easy to dodge. I wandered around, looking for blind men, but none were on parade tonight. I stopped by the foot of the statue and waited for Wami. I was there a few minutes when a small pebble dropped on my head. I scratched my crown and moved aside, but moments later another fell. I glanced up and there was the tattooed face, grinning down.

'You should choose your ground more carefully, Al m'boy. What if I had meant you mischief?'

I hurried up to join him. I looked for the trapdoor as soon as I made the platform but the foundations had been built upon since I was last here and the entrance to the underworld was sealed off.

'The builders have been busy,' Wami noted. He was dressed in black from head to toe and – except for the snakes and green eyes – appeared all but invisible against the dark backdrop of the night sky.

'They're not the only ones,' I said, then told him about Valerie's true confession and what had been happening since. The snakes on his face appeared to flicker angrily when I mentioned the note with the finger, but he said nothing.

'And now they have Bill,' I concluded.

'And are using him as bait,' Wami mused. 'If I ever find the man who has been forging my signature . . .' He scowled. 'Regarding Bill, I think you're right: they have kept him alive to tempt you back into the game. But can you save him or is he doomed whatever you do?'

'Probably the latter,' I sighed, 'but I have to try. I'm dancing to their tune, but what else can I do? If I give up on Bill, he's finished for sure. I'll be getting fingers and toes and other parts in the post from here till doomsday.'

'A despicable ploy,' Wami chuckled. 'I have sent a few men home to their loved ones myself in such a manner: it never fails to elicit bouts of maddened screams and illogical behaviour. If I were you, I would write off Bill Casey.'

'I can't do that,' I said flatly.

'No,' he agreed with a wry smile, 'you cannot. You lack the killer instinct which would make life so much simpler. So: what *can* you do?'

'Go on looking for Ellen's lover. Keep asking questions. Scour the streets. Raid every den in town.'

'You will be an old man by the time you are finished.'

'You know a better way?'

'Go after the blind men,' he suggested. 'Drop your search for your friend and call their bluff. Put out word that if he is not returned intact, immediately, you will quit this city and their game.'

'You think they have him?'

'If not, they can get him.'

I thought about it, then shook my head. 'They wouldn't buy it.'

'They might. They value you highly, judging by your previous encounter. If you threaten to walk, and make it convincing, they might cave in and deliver, if not the answers you seek, at least the friend you wish to save.'

'And if they don't? I up stakes and leave?' He nodded. 'No. I won't gamble with Bill's life.'

'It is your best hope of saving him.'

'I don't agree. I won't do it.'

'Very well. I have proffered my advice. If you choose to ignore it, you must continue as you were, ineffective as your methods have so far proved.'

He slipped towards the ladder, cutting through the cool night wind which was biting this high up.

'I need your help,' I said quietly as he was about to drop out of sight. He stared at me curiously. 'You know more about this city and its underworld than anyone. You can go places no other can go. If I fail to get a fix on Ellen's lover, I'll have to track Bill down the hard way. I'll need you for that.'

'Asking Daddy for help, Al m'boy?' he chortled.

'I need you,' I said again.

'But you do not *want* me.' Then, shrugging: 'Not that it matters. Filial love was never high on my list of priorities.'

'You'll help?'

'I know Bill Casey,' he muttered, almost to himself, and his face creased as though troubled. 'We go back a long way.'

'You do?' I stared uncomprehendingly. 'He never said he knew you.'

'He wouldn't have. He never thought as highly of me as I did of him.' His expression cleared. 'I would save him if I could. Give me a call if all else fails. I will help. In the meantime, I'll keep my ear to the ground and let you know if I hear of anything.'

'Thanks.' I tried to sound grateful.

'I hope you realise my aid does not come free,' he said. 'My time is precious and has grown more so with every passing year. I have gone out of my way to assist you. You owe me. When the day comes for you to repay, I hope you remember.'

'What do you want?' I asked, an icy chill dribbling down my spine.

'I have not decided yet, but it has always been a dream of mine for one of my sons to follow in my footsteps . . .'

'Bullshit,' I laughed. 'You'd have kept in touch with me if that was the case, to mould me into shape. I'm sure you don't give a rat's whiskers what happens to this world once you're dead.'

'What ungrateful creatures the young can be,' he moaned, but the shine of his grinning teeth betrayed him. 'You are right, of course: your actions once I flee this mortal shell matter as much to me as those of a slug. However, it would amuse me while I live to think of you devoting your life to the noble cause espoused by your dedicated demon of a daddy.'

'Forget it,' I snapped. 'I could – *would* – never be like you. I'm not a killer. I've been an executioner, but I've never killed on my own account, and could never kill for kicks or profit.'

'Not even if I made it a condition? Not even to save Bill Casey?'

I shook my head uncertainly. 'I couldn't.'

'You killed for the Cardinal. Why not for Bill?'

'That was different. It was business. I'm not a killer.'

'Perhaps,' Wami smiled. 'Or perhaps you are, but have not realised yet.'

He left me with that unpleasant thought, vanishing

down the ladder like a spider. When, some moments later, I lurched across and scanned the shadows for signs of him, I found nothing below but dark pools of empty, menacing space. To myself I whispered, one last time, 'I'm not a killer.' Then I climbed onto the ladder and started down into the darkness.

I woke Priscilla when I got home, as she'd requested, and told her about my day (omitting the encounter with Wami). I didn't think I'd be able to sleep – on top of my other worries, I now had my debt to Wami to consider: I didn't think he'd ask me to take a life to save Bill's, but it was the sort of warped trick he was capable of pulling – but the exertions of the day and lack of sleep the night before had drained me. I passed out while telling Priscilla about my conversation with Ama Situwa and didn't wake till the sun was high in the sky the next day, Tuesday, at about a quarter to one in the afternoon.

Priscilla cooked a huge breakfast, more than the two of us could finish off, and by the end of it I felt like sitting in a chair all day to vegetate. But there was work to be done, people to be interviewed, and though Priscilla once again pleaded with me not to leave her – less passionately this time – I was shortly out of the apartment and back on the streets.

First, in light of my conversation with Ama, I rang several of those I'd talked to yesterday and asked if they'd been in the Skylight with Ellen the night prior to her murder, or knew who had. Everybody claimed ignorance, though a few had seen her earlier that day. I asked those who didn't sound like they'd had enough of me to make further enquiries, in the hope that one would turn up a name, then started on contacts new.

I concentrated on work colleagues. I didn't know many people from Preston's, the company she worked for, and those I spoke to weren't as forthcoming as her friends had been: some questioned my identity and wanted to know how they could be sure I was who I claimed. I offered to drop by and conduct my enquiries in person but the management personnel I spoke to were against that: yes, Miss Fraser had been a valued employee and they deeply regretted her demise, especially in such lurid circumstances, but life for the insurance firm went on and they didn't appreciate strangers turning up at will, interrupting their routines.

Ellen had always said she worked for the most uptight employers in the city; now I knew she hadn't been kidding. I convinced some of her less icy colleagues to meet me that night for drinks, and a few more said they might fit me into their schedules later in the week, but all claimed to know nothing of Ellen's personal life or the men she'd dated.

During one of the few breaks I allowed myself between calls, my mobile rang. One of the Cardinal's secretaries. The Great One was willing to meet me now, if I got over there in a hurry, but it would have to be brief since he couldn't spare much time.

Party Central was a hive of frenzied activity when I arrived. Teams of Troops were forming in the back-yard, three or four per group, then setting out, armed to the armpits. Frank was coordinating things, clad in full military uniform. During a quiet moment I snuck up and asked what was going on.

'Manhunt,' he snapped, clutching a clipboard as if his life depended on it. 'That bastard Capac Raimi.'

'The Cardinal's golden boy?'

'They got into a fight last night. We could have taken care of him there and then, but the Cardinal – in that glorious, fucked-up way of his – let him go. Vincent Carell and a few others ran into him later: he cut the fuck out of them.'

'Vincent's dead?' The news didn't disturb me – we weren't buddies – but I was startled: close confidants of the Cardinal and his immediate entourage hardly ever met with sticky ends, unless they ran foul of their masters.

'Dead as Disco,' Frank said, and I could hear the grinding of his teeth over the noise of the vehicles pulling out of the back lot: he hated losing any of his men, but always felt doubly sore when it was as a result of one of the Cardinal's twisted fancies.

'On the off chance that I see him, what are the orders? Shoot on sight or bring him in?'

'Officially: bring him in. Off the record: blow the fucker away. There'll be shit to face if you do, but I'll protect you, even if it means my job. Not that you *will* run into him. He's probably out of this city and halfway to Hades by now.'

I proceeded up to the fifteenth floor, checking my shoes and socks in beforehand. The halls up there were buzzing with Troops and other underlings. It took a while to shove through them and make it to the Cardinal's inner sanctuary. His secretary held me up until he was free. About twenty minutes later, a posse of soldiers spilled out of his room, there was a swift check to see if he wanted to receive me, and I was ushered in.

The Cardinal was sitting at his desk, fiddling with a puppet. As I got closer I realised Frank hadn't been kidding when he said the two had been in a fight: I'd thought he meant a verbal disagreement, but it must have been a lot more physical than that, going by the bruised mess of the Cardinal's face.

'You look like hell,' I noted, taking a seat.

He managed a weak smile. 'You should see the other guy,' he chuckled, then grimaced and clutched his sides. 'It hurts when I laugh but that's nothing to what it's like when I piss.'

'I know what you mean,' I sympathised.

'Do you?'

'I was a boxer in my younger days. Took my fair share of beatings. It's not so bad after the first day or two.'

'So my doctors tell me. It's not so much the pain: more the humiliation. Last time I got into a fist fight, Reagan was in office and Space Invaders was at the cutting edge of computer technology.' He sounded so sorry for himself, I had to turn aside to hide my smile.

'I'm getting old, Mr Jeery,' he sighed. 'Time was, I'd have taken a beating like this in my stride. Now I feel like a big lump of shit that's been simmering on low for a couple of hours.' He let the puppet flop to the floor and covered his face with his hands, then ran them through his thinning hair and massaged the back of his neck.

'Enough of my complaints,' he boomed, resorting to form. 'You didn't come here to listen to an old fart moaning on about himself. What can I do for you, Mr Jeery?'

I told him about Bill. I didn't run him through the entire story – time was short – but filled him in on most of the facts.

'It doesn't surprise me,' he grunted when I'd finished. 'About the woman lying to protect another, I mean. I'm always wary of self-indicting confessions. So: what can I do to help?'

'Set your people after him. Maybe one of your informants knows who kidnapped him, or can find out. If they fail, spread the word that you don't want him to be harmed. Demand his safe return.'

'What makes you think his abductors will pay attention to me? They've paid scant regard so far.'

'It's worth a try.'

'Perhaps. But I'm too busy at the moment to deploy my agents in the manner you wish. I'll need a day or two, perhaps the better part of a week. My business with Mr

Raimi – you've heard he was the one I was quarrelling with, I'm sure – should have reached a conclusion one way or the other by then. Once that's done and dusted, I and mine are at your complete disposal.'

'A week's too long. He could be dead by then.'

'We could all be dead by then,' the Cardinal replied blithely. 'My hands are tied. I cannot . . .' He hesitated and ran a speculative eye over me. 'You recall an earlier conversation of ours, when I told you I caved in to the demands of Nicola Hornyak's killer because I was pre-occupied with other affairs?'

'Yes.'

'Capac Raimi was the reason I couldn't risk a run-in with whoever was blackmailing me. You've heard the rumours that I've been grooming him to succeed me when I retire?' I grunted in reply. He leant forward menacingly. 'What I tell you now stays between us. If you mention it to anyone and I hear of it, I'll have you and everyone who ever passed the time of day with you taken out and shot. Understand?'

I nodded wordlessly, wondering what fresh nugget he could be about to impart.

He took a deep breath, then locked gazes with me and said, 'I'm dying. A brain tumour. I learned of it a year ago. By rights I should be dead already, but I fought like a tiger and earned an extra few months. Those months are drawing to a close. I've a few weeks left, the doctors assure me, but any day now I might start to slide. My vision will go. Then I'll have four, maybe five days before my brain shuts down. I'll spend my last week subsisting in a coma.'

He smiled grimly and waited for me to respond. I couldn't. The Cardinal was one of those people I thought would go on for ever. It never occurred to me that he was mortal like the rest of us, subject to the same random laws of life and death.

'Say something,' he snarled. 'Don't sit there gawping.'

'I don't know what to say. I . . . Are you certain?'

'Sure as shit,' he grinned, but there was a sadness in his smile. 'You're the only person who knows, bar my doctors. I've even kept Mr Tasso in the dark. If word had spread, this last year would have been hell. I'd have spent the entire time struggling to hold things together. You know what vultures are like when they scent death.'

'Why are you telling *me?*' I asked, bewildered.

'Because I want you to understand. I've lived a life of sin and corruption, Mr Jeery. I suffer from no illusions: if there's a hell, I'm heading there by express train. I have nothing to look forward to. I never had, not since killing my first man, back when I was a child. All I have is this empire. I've devoted myself to it, and if it dies with me, my entire existence will have been for nothing.

'I've groomed heirs in the past, to no avail. Capac Raimi is my last throw of the dice. If he fails, I've failed. That's why I didn't kill him for doing this to me.' He tapped his face. 'Why I'm still feeding him rope and praying to the gods that he doesn't hang himself with it. Why I'm clasping to hope rather than giving myself over to despair.'

'What does any of this have to do with *me?*'

The Cardinal covered his eyes with the middle three fingers of both hands.

'The blind priests?' I guessed.

'Exactly. If Capac Raimi survives the next seventy-two hours and proves himself worthy of filling my shoes, he's going to need those cursed meddlers. They're more influential than you can imagine, and without their assistance, no man can run this city. That's why I've had to isolate you during your hour of need. Any other time, I would have been there for you, and together we would have found the man who killed your women and put him to the sword. But I'm a servant of fate and there are times when I must bow to forces greater than my own, or be crushed.

'A few days, Mr Jeery, and matters will have been resolved. Capac Raimi will have made his stand or fallen. Either way, I'll be free to act, and then – assuming my tumour doesn't kick in and turn me into a fruitcake – I'll do all I can for you. We'll go after your tormentor, find your friend, and put everything right that *can* be put right. Until then, I must remain neutral.'

I wasn't sure what to make of the Cardinal's extraordinary pledge – there was more to this than I could get my head around – but there was no mistaking his earnestness: if he'd been playing with me before, he wasn't any longer.

'And in the meantime?' I asked quietly.

'Go about your business. I'll make no attempt to stop you. If you find the killer, do with him as you wish. If not, I'll get in touch and we'll make plans.'

His secretary paged him and said Ford Tasso was on his way up. He thanked her and said she should send him straight in when he arrived.

'I'll have to bid you farewell,' he commented. 'Mr Tasso has not taken his son's death well. If I can't calm him down, I'm afraid he might do something silly when and if young Raimi turns up again.'

'His son?' I asked.

'Vincent Carell. Tasso was his father. You didn't know?'

'No,' I gasped.

'Not surprising: Vincent didn't know either. That's why we went out of our way to overlook his deficiencies. In all honesty,' he said in a tone of strictest confidence, 'his death hasn't come as too much of a blow. I'm only surprised the fool survived this long. He won't be missed. Mr Tasso will realise that, once he's had time to think about it. He'd *better*: if Raimi does come through, he'll be the new boss around here. Wouldn't do to have bad blood between them.'

'You really think Tasso would serve under the man who killed his son?' I asked sceptically.

'Mr Tasso was born to serve,' the Cardinal answered, then led me to the door, where he warned me once again not to reveal anything of his imminent demise.

I'd see him once more, two nights later, after he'd plummeted to his death, but that was our last personal encounter. As I made my way downstairs to collect my shoes, I brooded on how healthy he looked for a man on his last legs, and found myself wondering if hell was big enough to accommodate both Ferdinand Dorak and the First of the Fallen, and if it wasn't, which of the two would be forced to go. Old Nick was a mighty foe, but I couldn't see the Cardinal playing second fiddle to anyone, no matter whose joint it was. The Devil might be about to get his ass kicked. I almost wished I could be there to see it.

25

More blind alleys Tuesday night and Wednesday morning. Ellen's workmates proved as clueless as I'd suspected. None knew anything of her love life. I showed them photographs of Valerie and Ziegler and Nick, along with snaps of everyone else associated with the case, on the off chance that one would jog somebody's memory, but although several recognised the infamous Miss Thomas, nobody could connect any of the suspects to Ellen.

Late Wednesday afternoon, following an uninformative interview with one of Ellen's friends – a pianist – I realised I was close to Cafran's and called in to have a few words with Ama Situwa, to see if she could tell me anything about Ellen's dinner companion. I guessed it had been Valerie in the Skylight bar with Ellen, but if luck was with me, I'd be proved wrong.

It was quiet when I arrived and a bored-looking waiter pointed Ama out. She was laying cutlery on one of the tables. The silverware jangled loudly in her hands, which shook as though she was nervous. This impression was reinforced when I tapped her on the shoulder and she jumped into the air.

'Easy,' I said quickly as she turned, fire in her eyes, brandishing one of the knives. 'I come in peace.'

'Then why are you sneaking up on people?' she snapped.

'Sorry. Didn't mean to.' I stuck out a hand. 'My name's Al Jeery. I rang about Ellen and said I might come round?'

'Oh.' Her face relaxed into a warm grin. 'Mr Jeery. I wasn't expecting you. Sorry for biting.'

'No need to apologise.'

She laid the cutlery down in a bundle and signalled one of the waiters to carry on where she'd left off. 'Shall we go through to the kitchen? We can talk in private back there.'

'That'd be great,' I said and followed her into the back. It was small, hot, shiny white and clean as a whistle. The chefs and waiters were orderly and at ease.

Ama found a quiet spot and pulled up a couple of stools. She asked if I'd like anything to eat. I said I didn't want to impose.

'So,' she smiled. 'What would you like to know?'

'You saw Ellen in the Skylight the night before her murder?'

'Yes.'

'Any idea of the time?'

'After nine, maybe a quarter past or thereabouts.'

'She was with another woman?'

'Yes. They were waiting for dates.'

'Do you know if they were going on together with the dates or if they were going to separate?'

'I've no idea. It was a brief conversation. The bar was noisy, I'd had a few drinks. We didn't say much.'

'The other woman: could you describe her?'

'White. Pretty. Well dressed.' She shrugged. 'I wasn't paying attention. I might recognise her if I saw her again, but . . .'

'No problem.' I forced the professional smile I'd been making a lot of use of lately. 'You've been most helpful. If you can spare the time, I'd like you to look at some photos.'

'Sure.'

I took out the envelope with the photos, shook a few loose onto the table and sifted through the pile, searching for a good picture of Valerie.

'You can look through the lot,' I said, locating the snap and slipping it aside to lay on her at the end. 'I doubt if you'll – '

She wasn't listening. Her eyes had focused on a photo and her lips were pursed. She leant her head sideways, reached down, stopped. 'May I?' she asked.

'By all means,' I told her, heart starting to pound.

I watched like a hawk as she picked the photo up and studied it. She sorted through the rest of the pile until she found another which she could compare the first to.

'This woman,' she said after some deliberation. 'I can't say for sure – it was dark and I didn't get that good a look – but I *think* this is the woman I saw with Ellen.'

'It can't be,' I said shakily. 'You must be mistaken. That can't be her.'

'Maybe not,' she admitted, 'but she sure looks like the woman I saw. I'm not certain, but . . .' She shrugged and smiled prettily, having contributed as much as she felt she had a right to.

I looked down at the photos in her hand and suddenly, terribly, it made sense.

'Thank you,' I muttered, sliding off the stool, almost stumbling to the floor as my limbs turned to lead.

'Are you all right?' she asked, reaching out to steady me.

'I'll be fine. Thanks. I . . . I have to leave now. Thank you. I have to go. You're been very helpful. Thank – '

I started for the door.

'Mr Jeery: your photographs!'

'Keep them. I don't . . . No good any more. Thank you. Goodbye.'

I rushed out of the restaurant and fell to the pavement,

panting for breath, forcing back the bile which was rising in waves. I raised a hand and watched it shake like crazy. Gradually, as the minutes passed, the shaking subsided and I began to breathe normally. When I felt up to it, I stood, fetched my bike, didn't hop on, but walked along beside it for a while, collecting my thoughts.

I knew who the link was. The lover. The pieces fell into place easily in retrospect. Ellen saying she might surprise me. The porter in the Skylight who said Valerie Thomas could well be a lezbo. Priscilla and Nic, tricking together, closer than ordinary friends. Ellen laughing: a wedding wouldn't be appropriate.

So obvious. Hard to believe it had taken me this long to figure it out. I didn't know the motive, but that would come. One short ride and all the answers would be at my fingertips, there for the taking. I wouldn't even have to search for the villain: I knew exactly where to find the monster.

I climbed up on the saddle and started pedalling, slowly at first, then, as my rage surged to the surface, faster, faster still, till I was flying, a hurricane on two wheels, destination: home.

Ali was bagging bagels as I started up the stairs. I slowed to a stop and retraced my steps. He burst into a huge smile when he saw me entering. 'Hello, my friend!' he greeted me, emerging from behind the counter to pump my hand. 'Back on your feet and hungry again? I bet I can guess what you are after: salmon and cream-cheese, yes?'

'No,' I said softly.

'The new lady in your life is changing you,' he chuckled. 'An occupational hazard of love.'

'Ali . . .' I cleared my throat. 'I think you should shut up shop for a while.'

He frowned uncertainly. 'Is this a joke, my friend?'

I shook my head. 'Shut up shop and leave. Go for a walk or to see some friends and don't come back for a couple of hours, OK?'

Ali stared at me curiously. 'You know I cannot do that. I cannot desert my post.'

'You're not a soldier, Ali.'

'Still . . .'

'Trust me.' I grasped his shoulder and squeezed softly. 'You don't want to be here. You don't want to get involved.'

His eyes slowly swivelled upwards, as though he could see through the ceiling. When he looked back at me, he wasn't any the wiser, but he was resigned. He didn't know what I was going to do, but he knew I wouldn't ask him to leave unless it was something bad.

'I will go for a walk,' he decided. 'A long one. I could do with the exercise, yes?'

'Good man.' I clapped his back and helped him lock up the store.

'I will be seeing you soon?' he asked as I resumed my climb.

'Maybe,' I lied.

'I hope so,' he said, though I think he sensed this was our final rendezvous.

As I turned the key, I remembered I'd left my gun with Priscilla and hadn't picked up a new one. I glanced down at my feet, took a deep breath, collected my wits, opened the door and entered. 'I'm back!' I called out brightly.

'You're home early,' she welcomed me, stepping through from the kitchen. She stood on her tiptoes for a kiss. I took her in my arms and obliged. She stared at me, puzzled, when I let go abruptly.

'You're looking very enigmatic,' she remarked. 'What's up?'

'Nothing. Just . . . I've got a lead.' I gazed around the

apartment, searching for the gun. 'I have to go out again. There's a rough spot up-city I'm heading for. Can I have the gun back? I might need it.'

'Sure. No prob. It's in the kitchen.' She trotted off like a frisky lamb. Good enough to eat. She came back moments later and slapped the pistol into my hand.

'Thanks,' I said, holding it by the barrel.

'So, where are you – ' she began.

I slammed the butt of the gun into her face, smashing her nose, cutting her short. She reeled away, stunned. The action sickened me, but I induced emotional numbness and followed after her. Clubbed the back of her head and she fell to the floor, where I pinned her and handcuffed her wrists behind her waist. Then I turned her over.

I'd been expecting a torrent of abuse but she only laughed at me, spitting blood out of the side of her mouth.

'You found out!' she howled gleefully.

'Bitch!' I slapped her face with the gun. 'Murdering whore!' Drove my fist into her stomach. Grabbed her hair and yanked her head forward, ramming the gun up under her chin. '*Why?*' I hissed.

'Why not?' she giggled, then added, as I started to shake: 'Get a grip, Al. You'll topple over dead from a heart attack if you carry on like this. Deep breaths, lover.'

I sat back and regarded her contemptuously. 'You killed them both? Nic and Ellen?'

'Guilty,' she admitted. 'Valerie finished off Nic, but I did most of the damage. I handled Ellen on my own. She was easier. Weaker.'

'You were their lover. Valerie, Nic, Ellen. You fucked them and killed them.'

'It wasn't hard. Even Ellen: she'd never been with a woman before, but once I set my tongue in action, she lapped it up.' A sick chuckle. 'So to speak.'

I grinned in spite of myself, the grin of a lion with its

keeper trapped in its cage. 'You played me for a fool,' I whispered. 'I was suspicious of you at the start, but you convinced me of your innocence. I cut you out of the investigation. Took you into my life, my bed, my apartment, and never guessed, not once. It never even crossed my mind.'

She laughed. 'Don't be hard on yourself. I did a bit of acting in my earlier days. I was quite the little actress. Could have gone into the movies if Mumsy and Dadsy hadn't been dead set against it. Never gave a performance this good though. This has been my *pièce de résistance*.'

'Why waste it on me?' I asked.

'Why not?' she replied again.

'It's as simple as that? You picked my name out of a book?'

'Not quite. I was following orders.'

'Whose?'

'The sun god's,' she smirked.

I cocked the hammer of the gun. 'Don't fuck with me,' I growled.

'I'm through fucking, Al,' she said, ignoring the gun. 'Nic was a sacrifice, a boon to ensure prosperous construction on the Manco Capac statue. She knew what was up. She didn't know *she* was to be the sacrifice, but once things got under way she realised the position she was in and played along, making the most of a bad lot. She always was a good sport.'

'Ziegler said he didn't know she was going to be killed.'

'He didn't. We brought Rudi along to read the necessary passages from an ancient scroll. When he went home, Jinks and I carved her up and carted her over to the Skylight. I thought she was dead, but she was still alive when Valerie checked later on. Not for long though.' She sung out the last line.

'You killed Nic to appease a fucking sun god,' I

muttered, thinking quickly. 'But why leave the body at the Skylight?'

'Orders.'

'The sun god's?'

'Yes.'

'Did he tell you to fuck up my life as well?'

'Sure did.'

'You've got a direct line to him?' I sneered.

'He spoke to me through his earthly agent. Told me to spin a web and draw you in. I don't know why he wanted to bother with a sap like you, but you don't question the god of the sun. You obey his word or burn with his next.'

'Did he tell you to kill Ellen?'

'Yes. But through his priests this time. I ran into Ellen a couple of days after our encounter in Cafran's. An impartial observer might say it was coincidence, but I'm sure it was destiny. We got chatting. I saw she was attracted to me and lured her on. Told my agent and suggested killing her: he vetoed the idea. I'd have dropped it, but the blind priests got in touch and said to proceed. I'm not sure how they knew about us or what I was planning, but I was glad they did. I got a real buzz out of killing her.'

Then the *villacs* had told the truth: they hadn't murdered Ellen, not as such. But they'd sanctioned the murder. I'd make the bastards pay if I could.

'Why did you want to kill Ellen?' I asked.

'To destroy you. The sun god said it was very important to destroy you. I don't know why, and I never asked. I just followed orders and used my initiative when the opportunity arose.' She started humming.

'You're crazy as a coyote,' I muttered softly.

'Says you!' she laughed. 'Who are you to judge? What do you think you look like to the god of the sun? Have you any idea how insignificant you are? How tiny? How – '

407

I gagged her. I'd heard all I wanted. I had my confession. The full story. There was still Bill to ask about but that could come later, when I'd loosened her lips some. Right now I wanted to focus on the payback. I thought of all the tools in the apartment that I could use. I had a small Bunsen burner somewhere which would come in handy. A hacksaw. Strong pliers. A hammer and nails. A drill. All manner of knives.

I was well equipped.

Once I'd gathered my implements of torture, I laid them on the floor where she could see. There was fear in her eyes, which excited me. Unlike Valerie, she hadn't immunised herself against pain. She could be hurt. I could do untold things to her beautiful body and have her writhing in agony.

I took the smallest finger of her left hand – the same digit she'd cut off Bill – and wedged it between the heads of the pliers. I gave a gentle squeeze and her body stiffened as she yelped into the gag. I stood there a moment and thought about what I was doing. Could I justify this? Revenge murder was one thing. But torture? Did I have that in me? Could I inflict deliberate pain on a woman I'd thought I might be in love with less than an hour ago?

I thought about Paucar Wami and the dark blood running through my veins. Ellen in the Skylight, back cut to ribbons, short life cruelly ended, hair plastered across the pillows.

My hands tightened on the pliers as the muscles in my arms bulged. I saw her caught flesh whiten. A thin stream of blood trickled from the first cut. She was made of weak stuff. One good wrench and the finger would be off. One sudden burst of energy and . . .

I relaxed my grip. Let the pliers drop to the floor. Seconds later dropped beside them myself. Tears rolled down my cheeks and my chest heaved with sobs.

I couldn't do it. I had reason to, and I had it in me to – I was the son of Paucar Wami: I could have done worse if I'd wished – but something was holding me back. I'd killed, yes, but never crossed the threshold between violence and evil. Now that I'd come to it and was desperate to make the leap, some traitorous, decent part of me stood firm and wouldn't let me take that last damning step.

I removed the gag from Priscilla's mouth.

'Coward,' she laughed.

'Yes,' I agreed sadly. 'I am.'

'I thought you meant business. I should have known better. You're a waste of human flesh. What sort of man are you, that you can't take it upon yourself to avenge the poor, murdered love of your life?'

'Who said I won't avenge her?' I tapped the barrel of the gun on the floor. 'I mightn't be able to torture, but I can kill.'

'Who cares about killing? Any fool can kill. You might as well leave me for the chair if that's all you're going to do. Why couldn't you be a man, just once in your life? I didn't hesitate when it came time to torture Ellen. You should have seen the way she jerked and – '

'Shut up. I don't want to hear it. I took the gag off so you could make your peace with this sun god of yours. I don't know what sort of afterlife awaits, if you believe in one or not – '

'I do,' she assured me. 'I do.'

' – but,' I continued, 'if you want to depart this world with as clear a conscience as possible, you'll tell me what happened to Bill, where I can find him, and who your sun god's *agent* is.'

'Al, Al, Al, Al, Al,' she tutted. 'Don't you see? Can't you guess? You don't go looking for one with the power of the god of the sun: *he* finds *you* whenever it is his wish.'

'Even so, I'd like to know his name. For reference's sake.'

'You won't like it, Al,' she mocked. 'Ignorance is bliss. You'll hate yourself if you make me tell.'

'Leave me to worry about that. Who is he?'

She let out an exaggerated sigh, then said, 'Lean close and I'll whisper his name in your ear.'

I expected her to spit on me or bite my lobe, something petty like that, but she had something far more effective in mind: the truth.

'Here's a clue,' she said, her words faint but unmistakable. 'I'll leave you to guess the rest. My sun god's agent's first name rhymes with . . . *kill*.' Then she kissed the side of my face, threw her head back and laughed.

I finished the job without any fuss. A sole bullet through the middle of her eyes. As she'd said, so simple, a fool could do it. I thought I'd feel bad but I was too numb to be fully aware of the consequences of my actions. She deserved to die and I'd killed her. For the time being, that was the end of the story. Later there'd be nightmares and self-recriminations; right now I was as unemotional as an android.

I left the gun by the corpse's side and went to the bathroom to wash. The water was cold and fast and fresh. I ducked my head under the tap and wet my neck and head. I needed the cold shock to the system. Things had been hot in that room. Hot as hell.

(Rhymes with *kill*)

My body was better for the rinsing, but my mind was stuck in low gear, reeling from her final blow. Maybe it had been a vicious tease, intended solely to torment me. I knew it wasn't, but I prayed to whatever gods there might be that it was.

(Rhymes with *kill*)

I saw a couple of Priscilla's vodka bottles lying around. I picked one up and sniffed from its open top. I could have done with a drink. More than ever before. Just one. One for the road. One to gear me up for the confrontation still to come. One wouldn't hurt. I could handle it. In my present state, I could handle a crate. But one would do. One . . .

I put it down, unsupped.

Not yet. Not until this was over and there was nothing left but the drink and the grave. When the last hand was played, I'd toast my damnation and let the alcohol have its wicked way. Not while there was still a round to go.

(Rhymes with *kill*)

Leaving the bathroom, I changed clothes, grabbed the few articles I needed, stepped over the dead body and exited. There were facts to be checked. Deductions to be drawn. I knew what rhymed with *kill* but I didn't know how he tied in with Priscilla and Nic and the rest. I wouldn't confront him till I was sure, till I'd pieced at least part of the jigsaw together.

One of the blind *villacs* was outside, hovering by my bike. His white eyes were fixed to my window and he was chanting in the strange foreign language of theirs, his face a picture of rapture. I didn't stop to question him: *villacs* and Incas and sun gods didn't matter any more. I got on my bike, turned a blind eye to the blind priest, and left without a second's thought for why he was here and what he was doing.

I headed straight for Party Central. It was quieter than it had been the day before. From what I gathered, the search for Capac Raimi had been called off, though nobody knew whether this was because he'd been found or because the Cardinal had given up on him. Either way, I wasn't particularly bothered.

With the aid of several obliging secretaries, I took to the floors above the fifteenth – I had the clearance – and set about wading through the masses of paperwork never before available to one of my standing. I was there the whole night – the secretaries called for replacements when it became too much for them – and well into the next day, forgoing sleep, becoming one with the records, painfully picking apart the woven webs of deceit, layer by heart-rending layer.

I started with Howard Kett because he was the easiest to connect to Bill. The pair had been colleagues for fifteen years. Though they were never close, it would have been a simple matter for Bill to keep tabs on his superior. Kett himself had told me Bill had been with him when he first busted Nick. Maybe Bill realised at the time how Howie swung, or maybe he learned of their affair later. However he became aware, he must have known about them before he moved on Nicola; known of the brother and sister's penchant for playing tricks on their men; told Nick to get Kett into the room and set him up, so he could be used to lead me on.

I tried finding further sinister links between Bill and Nick, couldn't, so moved on to Nic. There was no hard evidence that they'd ever met, but in this instance I didn't need any: I could connect the dots using a little imagination. For starters there was the lie she'd spun about her reasons for joining AA. Said her brother forced her to seek help. I'd thought nothing of the lie when it surfaced but now I reconsidered. If she'd set out – or been set up – to ensnare me, she must have known I was a member. I'd kept my membership secret from everyone except Ellen and Bill. Someone else could have found out and put her up to it, but I saw no reason to ignore the obvious: Bill had sent her.

Allegro Jinks had been arrested several times, as I knew, but it was only now that I checked his files more thoroughly that I noted the name of one of his arresting officers on his final arrest sheet: the good Bill Casey. Jinks had been a perpetual offender, as much at home in jail as out, yet his record since being paroled (he got out early, on the recommendation of the aforesaid arresting officer) was spotless. Had he seen the light and mended his ways?

Had he fuck! According to the files he'd been as active these last few years as ever, only recently he'd had a guardian angel looking out for him, somebody with connections who'd persuaded cops to change statements and drop charges, convinced informers to forget the name of Allegro Jinks, kept things quiet when it would have been far easier to let the shit hit the fan. The records didn't state the name of this solid, upright citizen, but I had no difficulty supplying it, even if the Cardinal's stoolies couldn't.

Valerie Thomas: *there* was a tricky customer. Not much on her that I could find. Nobody knew where she came from or what sort of a past she'd led, even how old she was or if Valerie Thomas was her real name. She'd never been arrested and had no apparent connection to Bill or anyone else involved with the case. However, on the copy of the application form she'd filled out years earlier, when arriving at the Skylight, the two referees she listed were a certain Rudi Ziegler and (wait for it) Bill Casey. There were no copies of the references the men had submitted, but I'm sure they'd nothing but praise for the hard-working, honest, devoted Miss Thomas.

Apart from their names appearing together on Valerie's form, it took me a long time to find anything linking Ziegler to Bill. There was nothing in their immediate files to connect them, and it was only when I asked the secretaries to check for mentions of anything Incan that results rose like dead fish after an underwater explosion.

There had been many meetings for those interested in Incan history and artefacts down through the years, and the names of Bill and Rudi cropped up regularly, usually as audience members, though in a couple of instances Rudi had given lectures. There was no proof that the two had met at these meetings, but I took it for granted that they had.

My enquiries were exhaustive. I even managed to link Bill to Ho Yun Fen, the unfortunate tattooist who created Allegro Jinks's serpent look, only to run foul of the original lord of the snakes. He used to return home to mainland China every few years and had brought back small parcels of valuable fireworks on a couple of occasions, for the use of a friend of his: Bill (you guessed it) Casey.

Pinning down evidence of a conspiratorial partnership between Bill and Priscilla proved damn near impossible but I was determined to do so, not wanting to believe the very worst of my oldest friend until my nose was rubbed in it. Priscilla was the key link in the abominable chain. She had introduced Nic to Ziegler and dragged her into the world of sun gods and human sacrifices; manipulated Valerie and Rudi, acting as the main line of communication between Bill and his team of puppets. I refused to leave the safety of Party Central till I'd tied her to him.

It took laborious hours and countless blind alleys, but eventually I found it. A photograph in Bill's file which I'd previously passed over, an innocuous group photo taken at one of his fireworks displays several years earlier. He was pictured with a group of grinning girls in pirate costumes, young actresses who'd performed a short play as part of the show. He had his arm around one of the fresh-faced beauties, a cute, innocent waif of a girl, recognisable on closer scrutiny as a younger version of the viperous Priscilla Perdue.

Tucking the photograph away, I took a short break, shovelled some food down and ducked in for a shower. While drying myself, I wondered how I was going to track Bill down and if he was aware that I knew about him. I was sure he did and, after more thought, figured I knew where I'd be able to find him.

Returning to the upper floors of Party Central, I set about cross-referencing the players, connecting Priscilla to Jinks, Nic to Valerie, and so on, just for the hell of it. I'd barely made a start when my mobile rang. I would have ignored it but thought it might be Bill.

It wasn't. It was Paucar Wami.

'Events are coming to a head,' he told me, voice hushed, sounding unusually agitated. 'The secrets of the Ayuamarca file are about to be revealed, and you, lucky boy, are invited to the grand unveiling.'

'What are you talking about?'

'The Cardinal is laying his cards on the table and I have a fly on the wall. It promises to be an invigorating experience.'

'I don't have time for this,' I sighed, then said: 'I know who set us up.'

I was expecting a huge gasp of surprise and a hundred questions, one after the other, but all he said was: 'You found out?'

'Yes.'

'Bully for you. Now get your black ass over here, promptly.'

'Don't you want to know who it is?' I asked, taken aback by his lack of interest.

'Tell me later. This is far more important.'

'Not to me it isn't.'

'Oh, but it is,' he disagreed. 'I was *told* to invite you to the grand unravelling. Can you guess by whom?'

'The *villacs*?'

'Ten out of ten. Interested now?'

I didn't want to get sidetracked, not at this stage of the game, but glancing down at the reams of paperwork, I found myself unwilling to return to them, and hadn't yet worked up the courage to face Bill. I asked Wami where he was and learned he was holed up in an empty office on the sixth floor of Party Central. I said I'd be with him presently, asked the secretaries to tidy away the files, checked to make sure I was leaving nothing of any importance behind, and headed down for what would prove to be the most surreal few hours of my already complex, confusing puzzle-box of a life.

The room stood next to a doorway by the unpoliced stairs. Wami was within, perched on a bare desk, half a headset plugged into one ear, listening intently. I started to speak, only to be shushed, directed to a chair and offered the second earpiece. Fitting it into my left ear I found myself eavesdropping on a conversation between the Cardinal and a younger man whose voice I didn't recognise. I listened while he regaled the Cardinal with the story of a strange trip he'd taken and a woman he'd met who claimed to be his wife and told him he was dead.

'What's going on?' I whispered to Wami. 'Who is this?'

'Capac Raimi,' he answered. 'He is one of the Ayuamar-cans. He fled the city when the Cardinal put a death warrant out on him and retreated to the town he originally seems to have come from. I will tell you more later. For now: listen.'

And I did, as Raimi spun a grave-robbing yarn of sneaking into a cemetery late at night with his 'wife' and digging up the coffin in which he had allegedly been laid to rest. Inside he found a corpse, which the woman identified as her late husband. The two got into an argument – she wasn't too keen on a gangster masquerading in her dead husband's body – which ended with him caving her head in with a shovel and burying her along with the corpse.

'Nice fellow,' I muttered drily. 'Any relation?'

'Shhh!' Wami snapped, in no mood for levity.

It was the Cardinal's turn next, and his tale made Raimi's sound like a kindergarten story. He started with his past – a fascinating history of a grubby street urchin who by reluctant chance mutated into the being known as the Cardinal – which was lurid but credible. Then he went off at a fantastical tangent and made far-fetched claims which would have landed any other man an instant spot in the nearest lunatic asylum.

According to him, he had the ability to make people. Not as in 'make or break': he believed he could *create* human beings. He described a vision he'd had as a teenager, in which he'd imagined the face of Leonora Shankar and thought how wonderful it would be if she was a real person who would take it upon herself to educate and direct him. The next day he wandered into a puppet shop and met a couple of blind priests (I paid special attention to this part) who ran him through a bizarre ceremony which involved taking blood from his hands, daubing a puppet with it and chanting. The day after, a real-life Leonora Shankar turned up and took him under her wing, as he'd wished.

It didn't stop there: years later, he created another person, some guy called Victor Chag, realised what he was capable of and began to experiment. He found he could keep eight or nine of his Ayuamarcans – the name he'd coined for his created humans – on the go at the same time: any more and they 'came apart'. His bent little finger was a result of his fiddling with the laws of reality: every time he made somebody new, it bent a little more. To 'unmake' someone, he pierced the heart of their puppet (each had a lookalike puppet, which explained the marionettes of the fifteenth floor) and the blind priests summoned a magical fog – our famous green fog – which spread through the city and cleansed people's memories of the discarded Ayuamarcans.

Raimi didn't believe him (I found myself liking the young pretender to the throne: he could smell bullshit and wasn't afraid to say so) and asked where these blind priests were. The Cardinal told him they were down in the basement of Party Central and the two descended in the lift for a powwow. Something odd happened – I couldn't tell for sure by the sounds, but Raimi seemed to have been touched by the priests and subjected to some form of vision – at the end of which the young would-be successor stood as a convert, now a firm believer in every crazy lie the madman had fed him.

The pair headed for the roof (while my admiration for Raimi headed for the door), where the Cardinal talked about 'one-week pockets' – Ayuamarcans were tied to the city and couldn't survive more than a week away from it – and Paucar Wami: he told Raimi that the killer was an exception to the rules, who could not only make it on his own in the big bad world, but was fertile to boot: the others, he insisted, were sterile.

'Hear that?' I remarked, nudging my father in the ribs. 'You're a one of a kind.'

He shushed me again, his face a mask of frowning creases: he was taking this shit seriously. I thought better of irritating him and tuned back into the weirdest conversation of the decade, if not the century.

The Cardinal next spoke of his inability to create a worthy successor. He told Raimi – as he'd told me a couple of days before – that his empire meant everything to him, and though he was resigned to death (he didn't mention his illness here, as I was expecting him to) he wanted his legacy to survive. No human could extend and maintain his empire indefinitely, so he'd set about making a leader of his own, capable of overcoming the sturdiest of obstacles, even death itself. He'd made Raimi resistant to physical damage – if injured, his body would heal quickly and painlessly – and, in the event of death, he would be reincarnated and could return and continue from where he'd left off. In a nutshell, he was immortal.

A lengthy silence followed – a good hour's worth – in which the only things to be heard were the howls of the wind which blew over the roof of Party Central and the beating of Capac Raimi's understandably agitated heart.

'You don't believe any of this, do you?' I asked after several minutes of no exchange.

'Every word,' Wami responded quietly.

'But it's madness!'

'Yes,' he agreed, 'but that which is mad can also be true. Roughly fifty-five million people died during the six-year jamboree that was World War Two. Madness? Certainly. True?'

'Hardly the same thing,' I noted stiffly.

'Hitler tried to create a master race. The Cardinal set out to create a single superman. Which sounds more plausible?'

'Don't throw first-grade intellectual arguments like that at me,' I retorted. 'The Cardinal's a grade A loon, end of story. Anyone who believes that bullshit yarn of his is crazy too.'

Wami nodded slowly. 'Were I in any other's shoes, I would be inclined to agree. But I have spent the better part of my life trying to unravel a mystery which defies the laws of logic. I have observed people come into existence and pop out of it as quickly as they appeared, all traces of their lives vanishing with their bodies, failing to register even in the memory banks of those who knew them. One of the axioms I live by is: only the incredible can explain away the impossible.' He paused. 'If that's not original, I probably stole it from Arthur Conan Doyle.'

'You're as crazy as they are,' I sighed. 'You, the Cardinal, Capac Raimi: nuts, the lot of you.'

'And you are the only sane person in the building,' Wami smirked. 'How fortunate you are.'

'Look,' I started, 'you can't really believe – '

'Flesh of Dreams,' he interrupted softly.

'Pardon?'

'The *villacs* called you Flesh of Dreams.'

'So?'

'You can be incredibly dense when you wish,' he chided me. 'Think, boy. If what the Cardinal says is true, we Ayuamarcans are creatures of the dreamworld. Dreams Made Flesh, if you will. And you are the son of a dream person, who happens to be the only one capable of reproducing. You are human, because your mother was human, but you are also ethereal. One could say you are of Flesh *and* of Dreams. Plain "Flesh of Dreams" if you want something that rolls off the tongue.'

'So the priests are crazy too,' I muttered, though with less conviction this time.

'So many crazies,' Wami noted wryly. 'Are you sure that all of us are in the wrong, while you alone are right?'

I decided not to argue. Partly because you can't argue with a madman, partly because a small section of me believed this tissue of lunatic lies. The more we discussed it, the more I seemed to be sucked into the madly intricate mire. It would be simpler to let it go and cling to sanity while it was still viable.

'How did you get here?' I asked instead, returning to more practical matters.

'The *villacs* contacted me through one of their messengers last Monday night, not long after you and I had parted,' Wami explained. 'They knew the Cardinal had put out word for Capac Raimi's execution and they knew where the fugitive was heading. They said, if I helped him escape, it would lead to the solving of the mystery. So I did.

'They sent another messenger two days later. This one

bid me make haste to the train station, which Raimi would sooner or later be returning by. He told me to plant a bug on the young man, to give you a call as soon as they were in conference, and for both of us to listen in on his conversation with the Cardinal.'

'They told you to include me?' He nodded. 'Any idea why?'

'Obviously, this ties in with the murders of your two bedmates, but I cannot see how. Perhaps we will learn more when the pair on the roof resume their talks: I have a feeling there are a few twists left to the tale.'

He got *that* right.

Capac Raimi started things up again. 'It's a trap,' he muttered, and the two discussed the downside of immortality and the Cardinal's insane plan. Raimi didn't believe the Ayuamarcans could survive their creator's demise and asked what made the Cardinal think his successor wouldn't pop out of existence along with the rest of the gang. The Cardinal admitted he couldn't guarantee Raimi's survival but had made provisions which would hopefully ensure it. Raimi mulled this over, then delivered the bombshell which changed the course of the evening entirely. He told the Cardinal he'd play along and replace him as the head of the empire, run it from here to doomsday, *but* . . .

(The *but* was the killer; he couldn't have played it better if it had been scripted.)

. . . he wanted an immediate shift of power. He wasn't prepared to sit around, waiting for the Cardinal to die, worrying about what was going to happen. Either all would be handed over now, or the Cardinal could go screw himself and cast his nets again.

I knew that wasn't an option – the Cardinal was dying; Capac Raimi was his final chance to spit in the face of mortality – and expected the Cardinal to accept the condition with unbounded joy, but instead he acted cautiously, advising against premature decisions. He encouraged Raimi to make use of his creator's years of experience, to keep him around and exploit him. But Raimi was having none of it. In tones of imperious scorn, he told the Cardinal to go take a jump. Literally. Off the roof of Party Central.

Wami stiffened when he heard that and the tattooed snakes on his cheeks seemed to shimmer nervously.

'What's wrong?' I asked.

'He cannot jump,' Wami replied, uneasily. 'He mustn't.'

'Do you like the old bastard so much?'

'I care nothing for him. But if what he says is true – if I am one of his creations, dependent on his survival for my very existence – then his death means my own.'

'Oh, come on,' I groaned incredulously, 'don't tell me you buy into any of that sh – '

'Quiet!' he hissed, concentrating on the dialogue taking place several storeys above us.

The Cardinal was in the process of throwing Raimi a curved ball. Ford Tasso was on the roof with them – he'd been hiding since the start of the conversation – and now emerged, a bound woman in tow, a certain Ama Situwa (the same one who'd set me on to Priscilla: and if *that* was coincidence, I was the proverbial monkey's uncle), who, going by the talk which followed, was the love of Raimi's life. Once again, the Cardinal acted as if he had years left and tried talking his successor out of calling for his instant death, urging him to keep his old master around for Ama's sake (she also was an Ayuamarcan, but hadn't been granted special powers).

Raimi hesitated at condemning his lover to execution by proxy. He asked the Cardinal if he could remake her, this time granting her the ability to transcend her maker's death and live for ever. The Cardinal said he couldn't and started to explain why, which was when Wami tore the headphone from his ear and leapt off the table.

'What are you doing?' I asked as he launched for the door.

'The fucker's going to make him jump!' he shouted. 'I have to stop him. I won't die, not now, not like this.'

'You can't stop him.'

'I can try,' he growled.

'But he's going to die anyway. He's – ' I started to tell him about the Cardinal's brain tumour and imminent death, but he was gone, up the stairs like a squirrel, acting rashly for what I'm sure was the first and only time of his otherwise lethally precise clockwork life.

Picking up his discarded earpiece, I tuned back into the rooftop soap opera, now with the benefit of stereo, and placed bets with myself on how it would end.

Raimi gave up on Ama Situwa and told the Cardinal to jump. I heard the sound of the old goat's footsteps as he walked towards the edge of the roof, his voice coming faintly now over the airwaves. He was preparing for his final leap when Wami burst onto the roof, roaring at him to stop. 'He knows?' I heard the Cardinal ask, surprised, and Raimi explained about the bug.

I felt sorry for my father, listening to him issue threats which were worthless. As a merchant of death, he had power only over those who wished to cling to life. A man who'd surrendered himself to the fates as the Cardinal had was beyond the killer's murderous reach.

The Cardinal cut Wami down with a few withering words. Wami vowed to kill Capac Raimi if he survived the kingpin's death. Then the Cardinal made his final-ever speech, wrapped matters up with a hearty 'Farewell!'

And jumped.

Tearing out the headphones, I rushed to the window but wasn't in time to catch the downfall of the city's legendary leader. However, I was in a good position to study his corpse, smashed to pieces on the hard concrete at the base of the building, arms stretched out as if he'd attempted to spread them in the manner of wings and fly. A crowd of startled Troops was forming around the crumpled mess and within a matter of minutes the place would be black with those wishing to associate themselves with this moment of bloody history.

I wanted to return to the headphones and listen for signs of life on the roof but two thoughts stopped me. One was practical: when word of the Cardinal's death spread, a cordon would be thrown around Party Central, through which passage would be impossible, setting my date with Bill back by anything from a number of hours to days. The second consideration was mystically rooted: though I didn't believe the Cardinal's outlandish story, part of me couldn't help speculating on what it would mean if it *was* true. If it wasn't a load of bull, then a green fog would soon be spreading and minds would be washed clean. People would forget about Ama Situwa, Paucar Wami and Leonora Shankar; the remaining Ayuamarcans would become ghost figures, like those in my father's file.

What if *Bill* was one of them?

A crazy notion, but the fear of losing him to the realm of dreams, forgetting about him and the evil he'd done, would have been enough to galvanise me into action even if the reality of the cordon hadn't already set me running for the stairs.

I raced down to ground level and rushed out into the rear yard, not pausing to collect my socks or shoes. I grabbed my bike and was wheeling it clear of the building when I glanced up and noticed – to my disbelieving horror – banks of thick green fog billowing down from the roof like a giant's clammy fingers.

For a handful of seconds I stared up at the fog, thinking

everything the Cardinal had said was true, rooted to the spot with superstitious fear. Then I snapped out of it, decided to give the fog a run for its money, and struck for the gate as fast as I could.

The Troops on guard were already beginning to restrict access in and out of the yard. If not for my gold clearance, I'd have been turned back like several others who were attempting to leave. As it was, they let me through without an argument, though I'm sure they'd have been stricter had I been five or ten minutes later. When word had come down from Tasso or Frank not to let anybody out.

As I took a right turn away from Party Central I noted a familiar-looking motorbike: Wami's. I braked, jumped off my bike and ran over to check for keys. Wami wasn't a man to leave his keys in the open, but this had been a special occasion and in his rush to learn the truth about the Ayuamarcans he might have acted uncommonly. To my delight, I found he had: the keys were in the ignition, the fob – a tiny shrunken head – dangling gently from them in the brisk night wind.

I jumped on, started her up, and tore off ahead of the banks of creeping fog, thinking how awfully fitting it was for the son to be following in the saddle of his father.

26

It had been a long couple of days and I was all but dead on my feet. If Bill wasn't waiting for me at home, I wouldn't know where to turn. Thankfully the light out front was on when I pulled up outside, as was the light in the living room. I rapped loudly on the window as I passed and he was at the door when I got there. He nodded sombrely and ushered me in without saying a word. I sat in the guest chair in the living room, the huge window to my rear, Bill directly opposite. Our usual positions.

'I've been waiting for you.' He sounded tired.

'How did you know I was coming?'

'I know everything you say and do. I had your apartment bugged before you moved in. I recommended it to you and introduced you to Ali, remember?'

Then he'd been eavesdropping on me for years!

'Did Ali have anything to do with this?' I asked.

'No,' he answered, to my relief.

'You heard me kill Priscilla?'

A heavy sigh. 'Yes. That's when I returned, to wait. I was expecting you last night. Where'd you get to?'

'Party Central. I wanted to make sure.'

'You didn't believe her?'

'I didn't want to.'

He smiled sadly, then said very softly, 'The house is

wired. The explosives in the cellar are linked and ready to blow.' He showed me a tiny detonator in his left hand (which was wrapped in bandages and short a finger). 'When we're done talking, I'll push this button and it's all over.'

'We're dead men?'

'Yes.'

'So we can speak the truth?'

'That's the idea. No more lies. Only truth.'

I took a deep breath and said the words which tore my heart apart. 'Why did you kill Ellen?'

'That was Priscilla's doing,' he answered immediately. 'Priscilla belonged to the blind priests. I recruited her when she was a child, and I was her superior in this matter, but her first loyalty was to the *villacs*. When she suggested killing Ellen, I refused. That should have been the end of it. But the priests contacted her unknown to me. I wasn't told about it. I'd have stopped them if I knew. I never meant to involve Ellen. I loved her like a daughter.'

'I don't believe you,' I sneered.

'It's true,' he insisted. 'I loved Ellen. I love *you*.'

'Then why destroy my life?' I screamed.

'The usual motive,' he said, fake-casually. 'Revenge.'

'*Revenge?* What the fuck did I ever do to you?'

'I've been planning this longer than you dare imagine,' he said by way of reply. 'I've had my sights set on you since you were a snotty-nosed kid given to chasing girls around the schoolyard and pulling their knickers down. Remember that? You were a real mini-monster.'

I ignored his attempt to lighten the atmosphere. 'What have I done to you, Bill? What did I do that made you hate me?'

'I don't hate you.'

'So why fuck with me like this?'

'I didn't want to take it this far. I only wanted to enrage

you. It was the *villacs*. They were determined to ruin you. I had to go along with them. They wouldn't have played ball otherwise.'

'I don't understand,' I moaned. 'Just tell me, Bill. Why did you do it?'

'Revenge,' he repeated, then added: 'Not revenge for anything *you* did. I was after . . .' He reached into a pocket with his right hand, pulled something out, leant down and rolled it across the floor to me. My fingers snatched reflexively for it. A black marble with golden squiggles down the sides.

'Wami!' I gasped, and the fury drained out of me. I stared at him, horrified. He looked so small, so timid, so harmless. He wasn't enjoying this as a true villain would. He wasn't gloating or full of self-satisfaction.

'Wami,' I said again, blinking. Now I knew how the marble had got into the trout's mouth.

'I've known you were his son, practically all your life. I've been shadowing you since you were a kid, observing you, looking out for you, plotting around you. That's how I teamed up with the priests: they were also interested in you, and feared I meant you harm. They wormed my scheme out of me, then struck a deal, whereby I'd help them and they'd help me. I'd give them you and they'd give me Wami. It was a lousy deal, but if I'd turned them down, they'd have killed me.'

'Wami,' I said again. He'd told me he knew Bill. I tried recalling exactly what it was he had said, but couldn't.

'The *villacs* have plans for you,' Bill went on. 'I don't know what they are, but I've gathered that this has been to prepare you for the future. They've destroyed your old life in order to build a new one. I helped. As your closest friend, I showed them how to hurt you. I didn't want to – if only you knew how awful this has been – but if I hadn't, they'd have eliminated me and Wami would have waltzed. I couldn't let that happen.'

'Wami,' I said for the fourth time, then leant forward and hissed, 'Tell me about Wami.'

'He did something terrible to me a long time ago.'

'What?' I asked.

Bill shook his head. 'I can't tell you. I can't speak of it.'

'He killed someone close to you? Your mother? A brother? A lover?'

'Don't ask, Al. Don't push me there. My hand might slip if you do, and you'll die in ignorance.'

I didn't like it, but I was in no position to argue. 'OK,' I growled. 'He did something terrible to you. *And?*'

'And I've spent my entire life plotting to get even.' Bill's eyes were dark. 'At first I meant to kill him. Plain, simple, uncomplicated revenge. Track him down, put a gun to his head, blow the fucker's brains out the back of his skull.'

'Why didn't you?'

He shrugged. 'It wouldn't have been enough. I wanted . . .' His Adam's apple bobbed up and down as he gulped. 'I guess you could say "poetic justice", though that doesn't really explain the way I feel or why I did it. I wanted *you* to kill him, you or one of his other sons. I didn't want him looking into my eyes when he died. That would have been too easy. I wanted him to stare into the eyes of one he gave life to, one he brought into the world. I don't expect you to understand, but there it is. That's my motive. That was my plan.'

'You're crazy,' I whispered.

'No!' he snapped. 'I knew what I was doing and why I was doing it. I spent years preparing for this. I used Nicola and Jinks to throw the two of you together. I thought you'd hate him when you found out he was your father, that he'd murdered Nic and the Fursts. I was sure you'd kill him.

429

'When I learned of Ellen's murder ahead of anyone else, I put my horror on hold, rushed round to your apartment, found the marble and planted it. I was sure you'd go for him then.

'And when I sent you my finger, I thought, "This time. This time he'll react and strike the monster down." I never dreamt the two of you would unite, that you'd side with him and take him at his word when he denied involvement with the murders.'

He was crying now, hoarsely.

'Why did you trust him, Al?' he croaked. 'Why didn't you kill the black-hearted bastard when you had the chance?'

'He was my father,' I answered.

'All the more reason!' Bill yelled. 'If *I* was related to a monster like that, I'd move as swiftly as I could to put an end to him. You should have killed him. Ellen would be alive today if you'd done the proper thing and – '

'Don't!' I snarled. 'Don't pass the buck, you hypocritical son of a bitch. Ellen's dead because of *you*. Not Wami, not me, not the blind fucking priests. *You*. You could have warned me, told me they were after me. You were my friend, Bill. I trusted you, loved you, took you into my confidence, made you part of my life, and you fucked me over. This is your fault. I don't care what Wami did to you. Hurting me to get back at him is the act of a sick, unholy fucker.'

'Maybe you're right.' He grinned through his tears. 'But it wasn't just Wami I was after. There were the priests and the Cardinal. They could have stopped him. All those years ago, they knew what he was up to. They could have stepped in and shielded me. But they sat back and let him destroy me. I wanted to stick it to those demons as well.

'The *villacs* would have destroyed your life anyway. You don't know how powerful they are. I couldn't have

430

protected you from them, even if I'd tried. They'd have swatted me aside and spun their own devious webs. I could have used one of Wami's other children – I've discovered several – but, by using you, I could hit the *villacs* and the Cardinal too. Ruin their futures like they ruined mine.

'So I worked with them. I betrayed you. I handed your head to them on a plate. And you know something, Al? It would have been worth it.' He nodded viciously. 'Your life, Ellen's, Nicola's, my own. If you'd killed Wami, I could have gone to my grave a happy man. I'd have sacrificed this whole stinking city if I had to.'

I shook my head slowly, uncomprehendingly. 'You were like a father to me,' I muttered. 'What you were doing to me never bothered you?'

'Why should it?' he replied weakly. 'I was willing to give up my own life and sell my soul in return for a slice of revenge. A man who surrenders himself to a bloody-minded quest will hesitate at nothing. I'm not saying it was easy – my love for you was true; I've grown to look on you as a son – but if I had to do it over again, and even if you *were* my son, I wouldn't do any different.'

He tapped his chest, where his heart lay. 'I'm empty here, Al. Wami tore my heart out and devoured it. I'd have killed myself years ago, but hatred kept me alive. I couldn't die before I'd finished with him.'

I felt we were going in self-pitying circles, telling each other how upset we were. It was time to pin him down to facts.

'Tell me more about your *plan*,' I encouraged him, wiping the tears from my cheeks. 'You set me up with Nic to start me off, then used Jinks to pit me against Wami?'

'Yes.' A slight hint of pride invaded his tone. 'I noticed Allegro's resemblance to Wami when I busted him and had been keeping him in reserve. Nicola wasn't part of the *villac* organisation – she was one of Priscilla's puppets – but she knew a bit about them and was a willing accessory.'

'OK,' I moved on. 'Manipulating Nick, the Fursts, Kett and the rest: I can follow most of that. What about Ellen and Priscilla? Did you plan to thrust them together?'

'I already told you I didn't. Priscilla didn't know about Ellen until she ran into her in Cafran's. The plan had been for you to fall in love with Priscilla, then for *her* to be killed. You'd have found evidence linking her murder to Wami, and that should have been enough to prompt you into action.' He paused. 'Priscilla wasn't aware of that particular element of the plan. She thought *you* were being set up for a fall. The *villacs* had told her you were to be sacrificed to the god of the sun.'

'What did you plan to do if I didn't kill Wami?' I asked, breathing heavily to control my temper.

Bill frowned. 'I hadn't considered it. I was so sure you'd . . .' He petered out. 'Of course, after Ellen, it would have been redundant to kill Priscilla: since Ellen's death had failed to draw a reaction, it was unlikely that Priscilla's would. Instead I faked my kidnapping, hoping my disappearance might push you over the edge.'

'You didn't arrange for Ama Situwa to see Priscilla and Ellen together?'

'No. That was either a stroke of misfortune or set up by the *villacs*. You found out the truth far swifter than I imagined. I was working on ways to convince you that Wami had kidnapped me. Now . . .' He sighed miserably.

I leant back in the chair and thought over what I'd learned. There was much I couldn't get my head around. Bill's decision to use me to kill Wami wouldn't make sense if he was sane, but I think Bill had left sanity behind many years before, and there was a certain warped logic to his calculated evil plan.

'What I don't understand,' I said softly, 'is why you assumed I'd be able to kill Wami. He's an assassin elite. What made you think I stood a chance?'

'You're his son,' Bill said.

I raised a spurious eyebrow. 'You thought paternal instinct would stay his hand?'

Bill nodded.

'That's ridiculous!' I snorted.

'I know Wami better than you do,' he disagreed. 'He appears emotionally lacking, but he isn't, not completely. I wouldn't say he's capable of love, pity or fondness, but he can feel vague attachment. His children mean something to him and he's never harmed any of them. I'd no guarantee that he *wouldn't* deal harshly with you when you came into conflict with him, but if anyone was capable of piercing his armour and getting close enough to him to strike, it was you or one of your siblings.'

While I considered that, my mind strayed back to Party Central and Wami's possible demise following the death of the Cardinal. I thought about asking Bill if he knew about the Ayuamarca file but that might have side-tracked the conversation. This was Bill's hour of accountability. I didn't want to waste time talking about the Cardinal.

'What about Valerie at Ziegler's?' I resumed the questioning. 'She came within a hair's breadth of killing me. What would have become of your plans then?'

'They'd have evaporated.' He shrugged. 'But I trusted you to deal with her. I know what you're capable of.'

'Your finger. Who chopped it off?'

'I did it myself,' he said, caressing the bandaged stub at the end of his left hand. 'Hurts like the devil. It would have been simpler to send hair samples or toenail clippings, but I wanted to be dramatic.'

Bill reached behind his chair, produced a bottle of vodka

and tossed it over. I caught it mid-air. 'A toast to our success?' he suggested.

'No thanks,' I responded. 'Later, when we're through.' I put it aside. 'How many people have you killed over the years?'

'Do numbers matter?' he retorted. 'One or one hundred: would it make a difference? Would murdering one person make me less evil than if I confessed to the slaughter of a thousand?'

'You admit you're evil?'

'If murder is evil, regardless of motive, yes.' He grinned blackly. 'But by that standard, so are you.'

'Tell me what Wami did to you, Bill.' It seemed a good time to ask again, but he shook his head mutely.

'Have a drink,' he said instead. 'We'll get roaring drunk together and maybe I'll tell you then.'

It sounded like a good idea. I'd be dead soon: why not enjoy one last tipple? The bottle had slipped down the side of the chair. I retrieved it and unscrewed the top. The fumes were intoxicating. I pressed the tip to my mouth and my arm began to rise.

I stopped before the liquid flowed. Lowered my arm and fixed the top back in place.

'Why do you keep pressing alcohol on me?' I asked.

Bill frowned. 'What?'

'This isn't the first time you've invited me to drown my sorrows. Why are you so anxious to wean me back onto the bottle?'

Bill stared at me in silence, then at the vodka. 'Do you know,' he mumbled, 'I wasn't aware I was doing it. But you're right. I brought you the bottle after Ellen's death. I told Priscilla to stock up with plenty of liquor when she moved in. And now here I am, trying to . . .'

He began to smile. Then he laughed outright. 'Jesus Christ!' he chortled. 'You know what I was up to?'

I shook my head. 'Tell me.'

'I was trying to save you!' His face had lit up. 'All those years of planning, manipulating people like puppets, working hand in glove with the priests, secretly plotting against them and the Cardinal and Wami. And here I am, closing in on the end, and I've been trying to screw myself over.'

'I don't follow.'

'The drink!' he shouted. 'If I'd driven you back to the drink, you wouldn't have been of any use to me. That's why I was so furious when I found you pissing your life away: I was afraid you'd wreck my plans. It would have been a waste sending a drunken sot up against Paucar Wami. Part of me must have wanted to rescue you from the trap I'd set. If you'd hit the bottle again, I'd have had to shelve my plans and turn to one of his other sons.'

'You were subconsciously offering me a helping hand?' I asked dubiously.

Bill nodded. 'Must have been. Crazy, I know, but there you have it. I guess I wasn't as entirely hell-bent on exploiting you as I believed.' He was delighted by this admission of self-deception. 'Not as big a bastard as I thought I was,' he giggled, winking at me as if it was one big joke. I couldn't help smiling in response, though I saw nothing humorous in it.

The sound of the front door opening wiped the smile from Bill's face. He sat up straighter and buried the detonator down between his thigh and the arm of his chair.

'More company,' he noted. 'How delightful.' He was trying to make light of it, but there was a strain to his voice, and I sensed the tension mounting within him.

Moments later a robed *villac* – the old priest with the mole, who'd been seated on the mysterious underground platform – and the translator, clad in a rough brown cape, entered with exaggerated dignity. They kept to Bill's rear but he could see their reflections in the dark glass of the huge front window.

'Gentlemen,' he greeted them. 'You're late.'

'You were supposed to bring him to us, Bill Casey.' The translator spoke harshly. 'We have been waiting.'

'Change of plan,' Bill said easily. 'It's a cold night. I have a weak chest. I decided to stay in. You don't mind, do you?'

The young man grunted. 'It makes no difference. As long as he is safe, we are content.'

'Oh he's perfectly safe. Aren't you, Al?'

'Perfectly,' I echoed quietly. Then, to Bill: 'You were supposed to take me to them?'

'Learning the truth about me was supposed to be the end of your hardships. They wanted to reel you in when Priscilla broke the news. I told them to leave you to me: I said I'd be able to calm you down.'

'They went along with that?'

He smiled. 'I'm the Al Jeery expert. They bow to my knowledge of you.'

'Where do they want to take me?' I asked.

'Underground, I'd imagine.'

My eyes narrowed. 'Do they know about . . . ?' My gaze flicked to the concealed detonator.

Bill's spreading smile was answer enough.

I looked up at the two modern-day Incas and gloated inside as I realised I was a step ahead of them for once. They'd been pulling the strings from the start – mine, Wami's and the Cardinal's, to name but three – but it seemed Bill had turned the tables on them and was playing a game of his own, whose rules they weren't privy to. Life was about to get very interesting.

'Good to see you, boys,' I said smugly, buoyed by the dark sword of Damocles dangling over their accursed heads.

'It is good to see you also, Flesh of Dreams,' the translator replied stiffly.

'You know what happened with Priscilla?' I asked.

'We do.'

'And at Party Central? The Cardinal and – '

'We are fully aware,' he interrupted.

'What's this about the Cardinal?' Bill asked.

'Tell you later,' I teased, then focused on the genial monsters. 'Bill's been telling me his side of things. Time for *your* story.'

The younger man looked for guidance to the blind *villac*, who shook his head slightly. 'This is not the place, Flesh of Dreams. Our brothers are preparing for your arrival. Come with us, assume your rightful position, and soon all will be revealed.'

'My "rightful position"? Where might that be?'

'On the *inti watana*. The platform of thrones,' he added, when I looked blank. 'It is the hitching post of the sun, the source of our power, our link to the gods. When the bloodlines merge and flow as one, we shall raise the giant stone from where it lies and the city shall be ours.'

'That's my "rightful position"?'

'It is the heart of the city,' he said earnestly, 'where all blood mingles. The three thrones you saw are thrones of power, thrones of blood. One is yours, Flesh of Dreams, by right of birth, by right of will, by right of blood.'

'Hear that, Bill? They've a throne for me.'

'Very nice,' he chuckled. 'Is there a crown as well?'

'*Is* there a crown?' I asked politely.

'This is not a joking matter,' the translator growled.

'Murder never is.'

'Forget the murder,' he snapped. 'That was necessary but is now in the past. We need dwell on it no longer.'

'Oh, I think we should,' I disagreed. 'In fact I insist on it. I'm going nowhere till you tell me what it was all about.'

The young man looked again to his mentor. The blind priest thought on it a moment, contemplatively stroking the mole on his chin, then gave the shortest of nods. The translator began to talk.

'You had to come to us cleansed. To grasp your future, you had first to abandon your past. That meant severing all ties to the life you'd misconstrued as your own. It was harsh of us to strip you bare of all you cherished, but we had to push you to the point where you had nothing but us, no family but us, no friends but us, nothing to come between you and your destiny, your blood and ours.

'You must join with us, Flesh of Dreams, because only we remain. Without us you are nothing, nobody, a shell of a man doomed to lonely suffering and death. Those you loved have died or betrayed you. There is no returning to the life you once enjoyed. None but us of the sun will love or accept you. Embrace your fate and we'll make a king of you, a leader of men. This city shall be yours and your sons will rule from here till the death of the sun.'

'You had Bill destroy me so you could give me a leg-up?' I asked incredulously. The translator nodded. '*Why?* Of all the people in the city, why pick on me?'

'Because you are the son of Dreams Made Flesh. You are the union of the physical and mental, the progeny of – '

' – an Ayuamarcan and a human,' I finished for him, shaking my head with disgust. 'You believe that shit of the Cardinal's?'

'*We* empowered him. *We* provided the means for him to take control of this city for the duration of his short, mortal life. He was a street urchin when we found him. We granted him the powers of a full *watana*.'

'A *watana*?' Bill asked politely.

'The hitching post of our community. As our sacred stone is to the sun, so stands our *watana* in relation to our people. Our *watanas* have the power to seize the fabric of

438

dreams and mould it into flesh. They create the transubstantial beings which the Cardinal called Ayuamarcans, beings capable of responding to the community's most earnest needs and desires.

'That is why you were invited to Party Central,' he went on. 'We knew this was the day of the Cardinal's fall and wanted you there to hear the truth from his own lips, to make it easier for you to understand and accept.'

'You're saying he told the truth?'

'As much of it as he knew.'

'Capac Raimi's immortal?'

'Yes.'

'Who's immortal?' Bill asked, perplexed, but I ignored him.

'In that case, what do you want *me* for? From what I gathered, the Cardinal's left Raimi to run things himself: a successor who can live for ever and rule the world alone.'

'No man can rule alone,' the translator said pompously, 'not even one as powerful and enduring as Capac Raimi. He will need assistance. We will be there, of course, but he might be wary of us: though he may live to control the world itself, *we* will always control *him*. We believe he will be more amenable to one of his own kind. Thus, a son of Paucar Wami must serve as our go-between.

'Also, three bloodlines are ideal. The *inti watana* has been fashioned with three thrones to reflect this. One for Capac Raimi, whose blood is the blood of Dreams: he shall occupy the right-hand throne. We, the *villacs*, provide the blood of Flesh: one of our number shall lie for ever to the left. And you, Al Jeery, the blood of the union, son of Flesh and Dreams, shall take the centre seat, to mediate between the two.

'Our three blood-streams, thus united, shall ensure the longevity and well-being of our city. Inti – the god of the sun – shall look upon our trinity and bless us. As long as the sun burns bright in the sky, our city shall prosper on the ground. Though all else crumbles, we shall endure.'

'You're loco,' I said softly. 'I've met some crazies in my time, but you loons . . .'

The translator smiled and pointed to the window behind me. Looking over my shoulder, I noticed clouds of green fog rolling by the panes of glass, which glistened in their wake.

'That's supposed to convince me?' I scoffed, as though the fog and their ability to summon it didn't perturb me in the slightest.

'We do not expect you to believe at the beginning,' the translator said. 'In time, you will learn to accept the truth. Under the folds of this earth you'll see wonders that will convince you. For now, believe only this: however crazy we appear, however little faith you place in our spiritual power, our earthly power is undeniably real. We control this city. The Cardinal was our puppet. Capac Raimi will bow to our will also. Nothing happens here which we do not control. Is this not true, Bill Casey?'

'True as mutton,' Bill said. They were still to his rear and he hadn't turned once to look at them. His eyes were trained on mine. 'I don't know shit about gods or bloodlines, but the rest is genuine.'

'We offer a third of all we rule,' the translator said, his voice hushed and reverential. 'If you join with us, a third of this city is yours. Money and women will surround you. Politicians will obey you. Businessmen will follow your lead.

'This city can be your playground. You need not believe in our gods, but believe this: we can make *you* a god. We can fill your remaining time with every imaginable luxury and pleasure.'

'And all you ask in return is my soul,' I said quietly, bitterly.

'No. There is no price on a soul the like of yours. We ask nothing of you, only that you accept us as allies, assume your rightful place at the centre of the *inti watana*, and act as our link to Capac Raimi. Later, you may nominate one of your line to take your place – your children, when they come, will be as revered as yourself – and free yourself of all responsibility, if you so desire.'

'A tempting offer,' I mused aloud. And it was. It's not every day somebody offers you a third of a city. It was a big step up, but who was to say I didn't deserve it? My life had been no bed of roses. Maybe this was the reason. Perhaps the setbacks were destiny's way of evening out the scales. Thirty-odd years of lousiness against however many might be left of abundant privilege and wealth.

'A man could do a lot of good with that kind of power,' Bill remarked. 'Build hospitals. House the homeless.' He winked: 'Rehabilitate the addicted.'

'That's true,' I agreed.

'Of course, they do say power corrupts.'

'You think it might turn my head?'

He shrugged. 'I've never heard of a tyrant ruling with a kind hand and a smile. You need a heart of stone to run a city. I can't see you operating on a par with the Cardinal or his successor. You're too human.'

'Would *you* take it?' I asked.

'Not for anything,' he answered bluntly. 'I've only ruined a handful of lives, yet the guilt is almost unbearable. I'd be lost within a week if I controlled the destinies of millions.'

'Of course, it doesn't matter what I decide, does it? With things poised the way they are – ' I nodded at his closed hand ' – it's purely academic.'

'Not so,' he disagreed. 'If you choose to go with them, you can. I won't stop you.'

'You mean that?'

441

He nodded. 'I wasn't in this to destroy you. It was always and only Wami. I like the idea of hitting the heavens with you. It would be nice, in spite of all I've done, if you made up your mind to die here with me, together, as friends. But, if you want to go with them, I won't stand in your way.'

'Maybe we could both stick around. I could give Wami to you.'

He smiled sadly. 'I wouldn't want him if he was brought to me in chains and cowed. I meant to defeat him on his own turf, through his own flesh and blood. That's the only way it would matter.'

'Seems a shame to fall at the last hurdle,' I noted. 'It looks to me like Wami's going to come out of this considerably better off. An enemy dead, his son in control of a third of the city. He'll laugh at you, Bill.'

Bill's face twitched. 'He won't be laughing long,' he muttered, then forced a chuckle. 'Death can't keep a good man down. Maybe I'll rise from the dead and get even with him yet.'

I faced the translator. 'What if I reject you?' I asked.

'We will turn to one of Paucar Wami's other sons if we must,' he sighed. 'We hope to avoid such complications. You are the first-born, and have been blessed by Inti: your healing powers are a boon of the sun god's, and may prove useful when dealing with Capac Raimi. But we cannot force you. Alternative measures exist should we have need of them.'

'Why do you say you can't force me? Isn't that what you've been doing these last few months?'

'No. We have been cleansing you of your past, leading you to a point where you have to choose. But your cooperation must be volunteered, not commandeered. That is not to say we'll accept a refusal: we will keep after you if you turn us down, harrying you, destroying those who come close to you, interfering in your affairs, depriving you of any sort of satisfying future. We shall not shy away from the use of strong-arm tactics, but we will not – cannot – openly force you to pledge yourself to our cause.'

'Thank heavens for small mercies,' I commented drily, then fell to thinking what it would be like to have the *villacs* on my back for the rest of my life. Suddenly my choice was clear. Welcome, even, since I had nothing to lose and no life to go back to. If they'd come to me a year ago, before Priscilla and Nicola, before killing Ellen, I might have accepted the offered third of the city. But by pushing so hard, they'd rendered me immune to temptation. They'd misjudged me entirely, or had been *led* to misjudge me by Bill. They thought they had me in the palms of their hands, but Bill was calling the shots here, and had a card up his sleeve which would wipe the smiles clean off their faces and place me beyond their reach for ever.

I sat back and gripped the arms of the chair. 'It would've been an interesting life,' I remarked to Bill.

'It sure would,' he agreed, reading my intentions and tensing the muscles of his left hand.

'Do you think I'd have made a good god?'

'No,' he laughed.

'Don't make any hasty decisions,' the translator warned, sensing something rotten in the air. 'It does not pay to – '

But I wasn't interested in his words any longer and cut him short with a curt command: 'Let's blow this joint.'

Bill's fist unclenched. There was a tiny click. The face of the *villac* – composed until now – creased with uncertainty and he started talking rapidly, words of gibberish, blind eyes filling with doubt. The translator craned forward, alarmed, looking for the concealed object in Bill's palm. He opened his mouth to ask a question. Before he could say anything, the world exploded. There was a roar of undiluted rage. Bill, the *villac* and his translator were lost to jagged shards of red and white. I flew into black.

epilogue

_____

'to catch the dead'

27

I awoke in hospital, suffering from pain the like of which I'd never dreamt of. I was on a drip for weeks, bedridden much longer. It was almost three months before I was fit to release myself, and even then it was against the advice of the doctors.

I caught the force of the explosion straight-on, but rather than obliterate me, it sent me flying, chair and all, crashing through the huge front window. The neighbours found me spreadeagled on the lawn, a burnt chunk of flesh, barely alive.

Later, the investigators found three corpses amongst the ashes and debris, too charred for definite identification, teeth melted, flesh burnt away to nothing, bones shattered and scattered. When I was able to respond to their questions, I told them about Bill and the Incan descendants, and that cleared up the mystery of the bodies.

Bill left a note for Kett, clearing my name and confessing to his part in the murders of Nic Hornyak, Ellen Fraser and Valerie Thomas, to whom he'd slipped the rope she'd hung herself with. He even took credit for Priscilla's death, swearing blind that *he'd* shot her. Kett knew better – he'd been round to my apartment while I was recovering in hospital and found the gun with my prints all over it – but went along with the lie and 'lost' the evidence.

If I wished to be ungracious, I could say it was because he feared my dragging him into the public mire if I was put on trial. But I believe that'd be doing him a disservice. I think he did it because he felt sorry for me and reckoned I'd been through enough. He called in to see me when I was feeling up to it. Told me he was quitting his job and the city. Warned me to keep my trap shut about his relationship with Nick, then wished me well.

While I recuperated, strapped to a hospital bed, paranoid voices mocked me. 'Bill isn't dead,' they whispered. 'He could have got his hands on a corpse as easily as a bottle of milk. He was an explosives expert who could have arranged it so you'd go out the window and the Incas to hell, while he walked away untouched.' And so on, day and night, almost without pause.

I didn't believe the voices, but nor could I rid myself of them. I knew I was only torturing myself, that I'd grown accustomed to betrayal and was now seeing it where it didn't exist, but part of me was convinced that Bill was out there, waiting to finish me off, and I often woke screaming from nightmares of him.

When I could think straight, I spent uncountable hours wondering about Bill and my father. What did Wami *do* to him? What could drive a man to seek revenge on his tormentor through his own loved ones? Wami must have killed somebody close to Bill, but that only accounted for Bill's motive. It didn't shed light on why he had been so intent on working through *me*, why he'd devoted his life to manipulating mine. No matter how I looked at it, it didn't make sense. I had a horrible feeling it never would.

As for the *villacs*, my father and his fellow Ayuamarcans . . .

They'd disappeared. The priests, I presumed, were merely keeping their heads down, but the Ayuamarcans had vanished from the face of the earth and history, as prophesied by the Cardinal. Nobody – my good self excluded – recognised Leonora Shankar's name any longer, or Ama Situwa's, or any of the others on the list. They'd been erased from records and the minds of the city's citizens. Nobody remembered them, not even Ama's supposed father, Cafran Reed, who swore on his soul when I interrogated him that he had no daughter of that name or description.

There was one exception: Paucar Wami. *His* name lived on. People's memories of him were sketchy – when I questioned Fabio, he remembered a rumour about a killer by that name, but could recall no more – but some small part of his evil legend had survived.

Was it that true evil could never be eradicated, that horror lived on in the collective consciousness? Or had the *villacs* just failed to deal adequately with those who'd known of Wami? I still wasn't convinced they were as powerful as they – and the Cardinal – claimed. The green fog which had covered the city for ten days following the Cardinal's demise had gone a long way to backing their extraordinary claims, but the ability to summon a fog doesn't mean one is able to create human life at will. The Ayuamarcans could have been ordinary people under the control of the *villacs*. Having served their purpose, they were then exterminated, and those who'd known them were subjected to vigorous hypnotic brainwashing – not entirely successful in the case of Paucar Wami – which accounted for the lost memories.

Far-fetched? Absolutely. But my interpretation of the events made more sense to me than the *villacs'* and the Cardinal's.

Of course, if the Ayuamarcans *were* ethereal creations – and I was only saying *if* – Wami had been unique, according to the Cardinal. The rest were sterile and city-bound, but the master assassin was capable of reproducing and exploring the outside world. Had *this* something to do with his lingering presence? Via myself and his other children, he had a toehold in reality. Were *we* sustaining his legend, by our very real existence keeping his memory alive? And was my relationship to him the reason why I alone could remember the other Ayuamarcans?

I thought of confronting the Cardinal's successor, Capac Raimi: as the man I'd been 'destined' to share the city with, perhaps he too remembered the Ayuamarcans. It would have been interesting to discuss the situation with him and hear his take on it. But that would have been playing into the hands of the *villacs* – the translator had said they wanted the two of us to team up – and I'd no intention of doing anything that might favour those meddling bastards.

I kept expecting the blind priests to turn up, but they appeared to have been put off by the deaths of their two envoys. There were no late-night visits, no sign that they were following me, no threats or evidence that they were conspiring against me. They might have given up on me and gone after one of Wami's other sons, or they could be biding their time, letting me recover and build a new life, so they could step back in and wreck it all over again.

Tough luck if that was their game. I was through building. It was solitary misery for me from now on. I would never leave myself open to personal annihilation again.

I drove out to the Manco Capac statue one afternoon, drawn to it as I had been before. The statue was coming along nicely. It was a long way from completion, but the skeleton of the upper body had been manoeuvred into place. It was a pity Ziegler hadn't lived to see it: he'd have appreciated it more than I could.

While there, I thought about the decision I'd made back at Bill's. I'd never been a dreamer. My feet had always been rooted firmly in the real. I believed I'd been born to a life of drudgery and had brushed aside any nobler aspirations as idle fantasies. But in light of the *villacs'* offer . . .

A third of the city. Was I crazy to turn it down? Maybe. I didn't regret my choice – Bill was right: I'd have made a lousy god – but I couldn't help thinking what life might have been like if I'd accepted. Al Jeery: lord of the city.

Heh.

I never returned to my apartment. I couldn't face it after what I had done there. I steered clear of Ali and the few other well-wishers who tried bringing some light into my dark hell of a life: I couldn't risk getting close to anyone, involving them in my affairs, making them a target. I had to be by myself from here on in. No lovers, no friends, no associates: nothing. I rented a tiny apartment in a cheap sector of the city, in which I pretty much cemented myself, cutting out the external world.

After a while I bought a bottle of vile vodka and laid it reverently over the foot of my bed. I'd lie back for hours on end. Studying it, gazing into its depths, seeing hell, and Bill reaching out towards me from its fiery pits. I often reached back and, though we never quite touched, our palms were getting closer every day. It was only a matter of time before I surrendered to its charms and sought the sanctuary of drunken oblivion.

While waiting for my resolve to crumble and the vodka to take me, I walked over to Bill's house during one of my few outdoor sojourns, to face the ghosts of my recent past. Nobody had cleared the debris away and the rain had turned the mess to ashy mud. It was filthy, stinking, offensive. I walked among the ruins, gingerly stepping over broken bricks, scorched scraps of wood, bits of vases and even a few old soggy fireworks.

I didn't notice the discrepancy until I was about to leave,

451

though it was in the back of my mind the whole time. I think that's why I went there: part of me had suspected all along.

When I realised what had been bothering me, I retraced my steps and checked the rubble again, this time with purpose.

They weren't there. Not a trace of one.

I went home, washed and shaved for the first time since getting out of hospital, then popped across to Bill's old station. His ex-colleagues were sympathetic and let me study the photographs of the site which had been taken following the blast, when the ashes were smouldering and everything was fresh.

The photos covered every conceivable angle, ground-level and overhead, admirably precise. I went through each with a magnifying glass. It took hours but I was patient. Eventually, the file exhausted, I returned the photos, said nothing of what I'd discovered, thanked the curious officers for their assistance, and left.

There were no books.

Amidst the rubble, the bits and pieces from Bill's past, ragged strips of clothes and blankets, splinters of porcelain and wood, there wasn't a single page from any of his books. Bill's thousands of precious books, which he'd cherished, loved and adored. He'd spent so much time and money on them, but wasn't concerned about their long-term prospects. How often had he said they could rot with him when he died, that he didn't care what happened to them once he was dead?

Bill's first-edition books – which only mattered to him as long as he was *alive* – had been removed. He'd known what was coming. He knew things were reaching a head, and – even with so much else to do, the *villacs* to cross, bombs to wire, his speech to compose – he'd taken the time to spirit the books away.

Why? Because he wanted them to survive his passing, so some other bibliophile could profit from his years of collecting? Nuh-uh. I didn't buy it. Bill shifted those books for one reason, and one reason only: he wanted to take them with him.

I stayed locked away in my poky flat for months on end once I'd come to the realisation that the voices had been right and Bill was still alive, out there somewhere, waiting, planning. I lay back on my bed and stared at the vodka and reviewed my ruined life. I thought about Nic, Ellen, Wami, the Incas, and marvelled at how much I'd lost. Mostly, I'd think of the bottle and its demons, and how easy it would be to let them have me, to forget everything and place myself beyond Bill's reach and the *villacs'* and anyone else who might have a vested interest in me.

Each day I grew closer to the bottle, until it reached the stage where I took it in my hands and clutched it to my chest, slept with it, lived with it, unscrewed the top a thousand times a day, never sure if I'd re-cap it or down the liquid damnation. I was nearing my limit and couldn't have lasted much longer: a week, maybe two, and I'd have succumbed to the first drink. The second would have followed swiftly, and I've have soon lost all control, direction and purpose. I'd have been free.

But things have changed. A thought sneaked through the barriers of pain and grief a few days ago and altered everything. I was recalling Bill and our conversation, as I'd been doing every day, when suddenly I flashed on his expression near the end, when I'd referred to Wami's triumph. I said the killer would come out of this laughing. Bill had sneered and said he wouldn't laugh very long, then muttered something about rising from the dead and getting even with him.

'Rise from the dead' be fucked! Bill's not dead and Bill's

not finished. He plans coming back, but not from the grave. He's out there, alive, scheming. I wasn't Paucar Wami's only son, and I'm sure Bill's sights are now fixed on one of my half-brothers, intent on using him as he'd used me. I was a fool to think he'd give up so easily, that he'd stop with me. There are others to do his dirty work for him. His hatred for Wami is so strong, and his thirst for 'poetic justice' so overwhelming, that he won't be able to rest – never mind die – till one of Wami's children lays low their father.

But Wami doesn't exist any more! He's fled these waters for oceans new, seas beyond the confines of reality. Whether he snapped out of existence when the Cardinal jumped to his doom, or was disposed of more traditionally by the *villacs*, he's dead. There's no one for Bill to destroy, no one for him to set his hounds after.

I was willing to forgive Bill when I thought he was dead. Someone who'd blow themselves up like that was to be pitied, not hated. But the thought of him faking his death, continuing the game, putting one of my half-brothers through the crazed hell he inflicted on me . . .

That pisses me off. It's aroused an anger inside which is stronger by far than the self-pity and determination to fade away anonymously. I won't let the bastard get away with it. For what he did, death's the least he deserves. And I'm going to make sure the son of a bitch gets it.

But how to track him down? With no Paucar Wami to strike against, there's no reason for Bill to show his face, nothing to tempt him out of hiding. He went to a lot of trouble to make people think he was dead. He's unlikely to show his face and risk blowing his cover, not without good reason, not without Wami to tempt him. How does one set about finding a dead man?

The answer struck me in the middle of a long dark night, as I lay staring at the bottle of vodka: send the dead to catch the dead! Paucar Wami must return to haunt the streets of the city. If the killer can be brought back to life, I'm sure Bill will be attracted and seek him out like a knight of King Arthur upon hearing a rumour of the Holy Grail. (Bill won't have forgotten Wami. His hatred will have kept his memories of the killer alive. I hope.) I can't resurrect Wami, not physically, but his *spirit* can be rekindled . . .

There's not much of a view from this flat. A filthy avenue and the backs of a couple of other buildings. But it's great for studying the sky come evening. I sit by the window and watch the sun fade on the horizon. I let my eyes linger on its jagged shadows, stretched out like so many bloodstained fingers across the sky. I stare into the red flames of horizoned hell, and empathise with the tortured edge of the earth's rim.

When the sun drops out of sight and the glass turns reflective, I fall to studying my image. I shaved my head two nights ago, with an electric razor. It was hard to adapt to – bareheaded, I realised how closely I resembled my father, though my skin's a few shades lighter – but I'm getting used to it. I no longer jump nervously when I spot my reflection.

The left side of my face is its same old self but when I rotate my neck the rough shape of a twisting snake comes into view on my right. The tattooing will take longer than I thought: the sort of serpentine design I asked for is tricky to create, and will require time and patience to get right. But I can wait. A week or two won't matter. When it's finished, I'll have the tattoos and the smooth skull, as well as the motorbike. The clothes and green eyes will be easy to replicate. Then I'll take his name, hit the streets and spread the word: *Wami's back!*

That should draw Bill out. He'll have to come investigate. Even if he senses a trap, he won't be able to stay away. His hatred will drag him out of his pit and back into the playpen of this city, I'm sure of it. When it does, and he shows himself, and I capture him – I'm certain I'll capture him: I know more than he does now: I'm the one with the upper hand – I'll put a sharp knife to his throat, kiss him once on the forehead, then make a swift end of him. Mere murder wasn't revenge enough for Bill Casey, but it will be for me.

And if he doesn't show? If the charade isn't enough to lure him out of hiding?

I spin away from the window and study the photograph hanging next to the bottle of vodka, the snapshot of Bill and a young Priscilla, the only photograph of my past that I've kept. My eyes turn to the trinket hanging from a chain around my neck: Bill's little finger, varnished so it will last. I stroke it from tip to base, for luck, as I have many times since I conceived the ruse to tempt Bill out into the open and back into my life.

The look might not be enough. Bill's no fool. Maybe he won't fall for the trick. I may have to do more than recreate my father's image if I'm to tweak Bill's curiosity and trick him into showing his face. Wami's body of work might also have to be duplicated.

I think I'll have to kill.